I Sing the Body Electric!

And Other Stories

Books by Ray Bradbury

DANDELION WINE
DARK CARNIVAL
DEATH IS A LONELY BUSINESS
DRIVING BLIND
FAHRENHEIT 451
THE GOLDEN APPLES OF THE SUN
A GRAVEYARD FOR LUNATICS
GREEN SHADOWS, WHITE WHALE
THE HALLOWEEN TREE
I SING THE BODY ELECTRIC!
THE ILLUSTRATED MAN
JOURNEY TO FAR METAPHOR
KALEIDOSCOPE
LONG AFTER MIDNIGHT
THE MARTIAN CHRONICLES
THE MACHINERIES OF JOY
THE OCTOBER COUNTRY
ONE TIMELESS SPRING
QUICKER THAN THE EYE
R IS FOR ROCKET
SOMETHING WICKED THIS WAY COMES
THE STORIES OF RAY BRADBURY
S IS FOR SPACE
THE TOYNBEE CONVECTOR
WHEN ELEPHANTS LAST IN THE DOORYARD BLOOMED
YESTERMORROW
ZEN IN THE ART OF WRITING

I Sing the Body Electric!
And Other Stories

Ray Bradbury

WILLIAM MORROW

An Imprint of HarperCollins*Publishers*

"Any Friend of Nicholas Nickleby's Is a Friend of Mine" (originally titled "Charlie Is My Darling") and "I Sing the Body Electric!" (originally titled "The Beautiful One Is Here") first appeared in *McCall's* magazine. "The Cold Wind and the Warm" was originally published in *Harper's* magazine. "The Women" was originally published in *Famous Fantastic Mysteries*. "The Tombling Day" was originally published in *Shenandoah*. "Heavy-Set," "The Man in the Rorschach Suit," "Lost City of Mars," and "Downwind from Gettysburg" were originally published in *Playboy* magazine. "The Kilimanjaro Device" (originally titled "The Kilimanjaro Machine") first appeared in *Life* magazine. "Henry IX" (originally titled "A Final Sceptre, a Lasting Crown") first appeared in *Fantasy & Science Fiction*. "The Blue Bottle" Copyright 1950 by Love Romances Publishing Inc. "Punishment Without Crime" Copyright 1950 by *Other Worlds*. "One Timeless Spring" first appeared in *Collier's*. "A Piece of Wood" first appeared in *Esquire*. "The Utterly Perfect Murder" (originally titled "My Perfect Murder") and "The Parrot Who Met Papa" first appeared in *Playboy* magazine. "Drink Entire: Against the Madness of Crowds" first appeared in *Gallery*..

HarperCollins books may be purchased for educational, business, or sales promotional use. For information, please e-mail the Special Markets Department at SPsales@ harpercollins.com.

First Avon Books edition published 1998.

Reprinted in Perennial 2001.

Library of Congress Cataloging-in-Publication Data is available.

ISBN 0-380-78962-0

23 24 25 26 27 LBC 20 19 18 17 16

This book, a bit late in the
day, but with admiration, affection,
and friendship, is for
NORMAN CORWIN.

I sing the Body Electric;
The armies of those I love engirth me,
    and I engirth them;
They will not let me off till I go with them,
    respond to them,
And discorrupt them,
And charge them full with the charge of the Soul.

WALT WHITMAN

contents

I Sing the Body Electric!

And Other Stories

I arrived in the truck very early in the morning. I had been driving all night, for I hadn't been able to sleep at the motel so I thought I might as well drive and I arrived among the mountains and hills near Ketchum and Sun Valley just as the sun came up and I was glad I had kept busy with driving.

I drove into the town itself without looking up at that one hill. I was afraid if I looked at it, I would make a mistake. It was very important not to look at the grave. At least that is how I felt. And I had to go on my hunch.

I parked the truck in front of an old saloon and walked around the town and talked to a few people and breathed the air and it was sweet and clear. I found a young hunter, but he was wrong; I knew that after talking to him for a few minutes. I found a very old man, but he was no better. Then I found me a hunter about fifty, and he was just right. He knew, or sensed, everything I was looking for.

I bought him a beer and we talked about a lot of things, and then I bought him another beer and led the conversation around to what I was doing here and why I wanted to talk to him. We were silent for a while and I waited, not showing my impatience, for the hunter, on his own, to bring up the past, to speak of other days three years ago, and of driving toward Sun Valley at this time or that and what he saw and knew about a man who had once sat in this bar and drunk beer and talked about hunting or gone hunting out beyond.

And at last, looking off at the wall as if it were the highway and the mountains, the hunter gathered up his quiet voice and was ready to speak.

"That old man," he said. "Oh, that old man on the road. Oh, that poor old man."

I waited.

"I just can't get over that old man on the road," he said, looking down now into his drink.

I drank some more of my beer, not feeling well, feeling very old myself and tired.

When the silence prolonged itself, I got out a local map and laid it on the wooden table. The bar was quiet. It was midmorning and we were completely alone there.

"This is where you saw him most often?" I asked.

The hunter touched the map three times. "I used to see him walking here. And along there. Then he'd cut across the land here. That poor old man. I wanted to tell him to keep off the road. I didn't want to hurt or insult him. You don't tell a man like that about roads or that maybe he'll be hit. If he's going to be hit, well that's it. You figure it's his business, and you go on. Oh, but he was old there at the last."

"He was," I said, and folded the map and put it in my pocket.

"You another of those reporters?" said the hunter.

"Not quite *those*," I said.

"Didn't mean to lump you in with them," he said.

"No apology needed," I said. "Let's just say I was one of his readers."

"Oh, he had readers all right, all kinds of readers. Even me. I don't touch books from one autumn to the next. But I touched his. I think I liked the Michigan stories best. About the fishing. I think the stories about the fishing are good. I don't think anybody ever wrote about fishing that way and maybe won't ever again. Of course, the bullfight stuff is good, too. But that's a little far off. Some of the cowpokes like them; they been around the animals all their life. A bull here or a bull there, I guess it's the same. I know one cowpoke has read just the bull stuff in the Spanish stories of the old man's forty times. He could go over there and fight, I swear."

"I think all of us felt," I said, "at least once in our lives, when we were young, we could go over there, after reading the bull stuff in the Spanish stories, that we could go over there and fight. Or at least jog ahead of the running of the bulls, in the early morning, with a good drink waiting at the other end of the run, and your best girl with you there for the long weekend."

I stopped. I laughed quietly. For my voice had, without knowing, fallen into the rhythm of his way of saying, either out of his mouth, or from his hand. I shook my head and was silent.

"You been up to the grave yet?" asked the hunter, as if he knew I would answer yes.

"No," I said.

That really surprised him. He tried not to show it.

"They all go up to the grave," he said.

"Not this one."

He explored around in his mind for a polite way of asking. "I mean . . ." he said. "Why *not?*"

"Because it's the wrong grave," I said.

"All graves are wrong graves when you come down to it," he said.

"No," I said. "There are right graves and wrong ones, just as there are good times to die and bad times."

He nodded at this. I had come back to something he knew, or at least smelled was right.

"Sure, I knew men," he said, "died just perfect. You always felt, yes, that was good. One man I knew, sitting at the table waiting for supper, his wife in the kitchen, when she came in with a big bowl of soup there he was sitting dead and neat at the table. Bad for her, but, I mean, wasn't that a good way for him? No sickness. No nothing but sitting there waiting for supper to come and never knowing if it came or not. Like another friend. Had an old dog. Fourteen years old. Dog was going blind and tired. Decided at last to take the dog to the pound and have him put to sleep. Loaded the old blind tired dog on the front seat of his car. The dog licked his hand, once. The man felt awful. He drove toward the pound. On the way there, with not one sound, the dog passed away, died on the front seat, as if he knew and, knowing, picked the better way, just handed over his ghost, and there you are. That's what you're talking about, right?"

I nodded.

"So you think that grave up on the hill is a wrong grave for a right man, do you?"

"That's about it," I said.

"You think there are all kinds of graves along the road for all of us?"

"Could be," I said.

"And if we could see all our life one way or another, we'd choose better? At the end, looking back," said the hunter, "we'd say, hell, *that* was the year and the place, not the *other* year and the other place, but that one year, that one place. Would we say that?"

"Since we have to choose or be pushed finally," I said, "yes."

"That's a nice idea," said the hunter. "But how many of us have that much sense? Most of us don't have brains enough to leave a party when the gin runs out. We hang around."

"We hang around," I said, "and what a shame."

We ordered some more beer.

The hunter drank half the glass and wiped his mouth.

"So what can you do about wrong graves?" he said.

"Treat them as if they didn't exist," I said. "And maybe they'll go away, like a bad dream."

The hunter laughed once, a kind of forlorn cry. "God, you're crazy. But I like listening to crazy people. Blow some more."

"That's all," I said.

"Are you the Resurrection and the Life?" said the hunter.

"No."

"You going to say Lazarus come forth?"

"No."

"What then?"

"I just want, very late in the day," I said, "to choose right places, right times, right graves."

"Drink that drink," said the hunter. "You need it. Who in hell sent you?"

"Me," I said. "I did. And some friends. We all chipped in and picked one out of ten. We bought that truck out on the street and I drove it across country. On the way I did a lot of hunting and fishing to put myself in the right frame. I was in Cuba last year. Spain the summer before. Africa the summer before that. I got a lot to think about. That's why they picked me."

"To do *what,* to do *what,* goddammit?" said the hunter urgently, half wildly, shaking his head. "You can't do anything. It's all over."

"Most of it," I said. "Come on."

I walked to the door. The hunter sat there. At last, examining the fires lit in my face by my talking, he grunted, got up, walked over, and came outside with me.

I pointed at the curb. We looked together at the truck parked there.

"I've seen those before," he said. "A truck like that, in a movie. Don't they hunt rhino from a truck like that? And lions and things like that? Or at least travel in them around Africa?"

"You remember right."

"No lions around here," he said. "No rhino, no water buffalo, nothing."

"No?" I asked.

He didn't answer that.

I walked over and touched the open truck.

"You know what this is?"

"I'm playing dumb from here on," said the hunter. "What is it?"

I stroked the fender for a long moment.

"A Time Machine," I said.

His eyes widened and then narrowed and he sipped the beer he was carrying in one large hand. He nodded me on.

"A Time Machine," I repeated.

"I heard you," he said.

He walked out around the safari truck and stood in the street looking at it. He wouldn't look at me. He circled the truck one entire round and stood back on the curb and looked at the cap on the gas tank.

"What kind of mileage you get?" he said.

"I don't know yet."

"You don't know anything," he said.

"This is the first trip," I said. "I won't know until it's over."

"What do you fuel a thing like that with?" he said.

I was silent.

"What kind of stuff you put *in*?" he asked.

I could have said: Reading late at night, reading many nights over the years until almost morning, reading up in the mountains in the snow or reading at noon in Pamplona, or reading by the streams or out in a boat somewhere along the Florida coast. Or I could have said: All of us put our hands on this Machine, all of us thought about it and bought it and touched it and put our love in it and our remembering what his words did to us twenty years or twenty-five or thirty years ago. There's a lot of life and remembering and love put by here, and that's the gas and the fuel and the stuff or whatever you want to call it; the rain in Paris, the sun in Madrid, the snow in the high Alps, the smoke off the guns in the Tyrol, the shine of light off the Gulf Stream, the explosion of bombs or explosions of leapt fish, that's the gas and the fuel and the stuff here; I should have said that, I thought it, but I let it stay unsaid.

The hunter must have smelled my thought, for his eyes squinted up and, telepath that he was from long years in the forest, chewed over my thinking.

Then he walked over and did an unexpected thing. He reached out and . . . *touched* . . . my Machine.

He laid his hand on it and left it there, as if feeling for the life, and approving what he sensed beneath his hand. He stood that way for a long time.

Then he turned without a word, not looking at me, and went back into the bar and sat drinking alone, his back turned toward the door.

I didn't want to break the silence. It seemed a good time to go, to try.

I got in the truck and started the motor.

What kind of mileage? What kind of fuel? I thought. And drove away.

I kept on the road and didn't look right or left and I drove for what must have been an hour, first this direction and then that, part of the time my eyes shut for full seconds, taking a chance I might go off and get hurt or killed.

And then, just before noon, with the clouds over the sun, suddenly I knew it was all right.

I looked up at the hill and I almost yelled.

The grave was gone.

I drove down into a little hollow just then and on the road ahead, wandering along by himself, was an old man in a heavy sweater.

I idled the safari truck along until I was pacing him as he walked. I saw he was wearing steel-rimmed glasses and for a long moment we moved together, each ignoring the other until I called his name.

He hesitated, and then walked on.

I caught up with him in the truck and said again, "Papa."

He stopped and waited.

I braked the car and sat there in the front seat.

"Papa," I said.

He came over and stood near the door.

"Do I know you?"

"No. But I know you."

He looked me in the eyes and studied my face and mouth. "Yes. I think you do."

"I saw you on the road. I think I'm going your way. Want a lift?"

"It's good walking this time of day," he said. "Thanks."

"Let me tell you where I'm going," I said.

He had started off but now stopped and, without looking at me, said, "Where?"

"A long way," I said.

"It sounds long, the way you tell it. Can't you make it shorter?"

"No. A long way," I said. "About two thousand six hundred days, give or take some days, and half an afternoon."

He came back and looked into the car.

"Is that how far you're going?"

"That's how far."

"In which direction? Ahead?"

"Don't you want to go ahead?"

He looked at the sky. "I don't know. I'm not sure."

"It's not ahead," I said. "It's back."

His eyes took on a different color. It was a subtle shift, a flex, like a man stepping out from the shade of a tree into sunlight on a cloudy day.

"Back."

"Somewhere between two thousand and three thousand days, split half a day, give or take an hour, borrow or loan a minute, haggle over a second," I said.

"You really talk," he said.

"Compulsive," I said.

"You'd make a lousy writer," he said. "I never knew a writer yet was a good talker."

"That's my albatross," I said.

"Back?" He weighed the word.

"I'm turning the car around," I said. "And I'm going back down the road."

"Not miles but days?"

"Not miles but days."

"Is it that kind of car?"

"That's how it's built."

"You're an inventor then?"

"A reader who happens to invent."

"If the car works, that's some car you got there."

"At your service," I said.

"And when you get where you're going," said the old man, putting his hand on the door and leaning and then, seeing what he had done, taking his hand away and standing taller to speak to me, "where will you be?"

"January 10, 1954."

"That's quite a date," he said.

"It is, it was. It can be more of a date."

Without moving, his eyes took another step out into fuller light.

"And where will you be on that day?"

"Africa," I said.

He was silent. His mouth did not work. His eyes did not shift.

"Not far from Nairobi," I said.

He nodded, once, slowly.

"Africa, not far from Nairobi."

I waited.

"And when we get there, if we go?" he said.

"I leave you there."

"And then?"

"You stay there."

"And then?"

"That's all."

"That's all?"

"Forever," I said.

The old man breathed out and in, and ran his hand over the edge of the doorsill.

"This car," he said, "somewhere along the way does it turn into a plane?"

"I don't know," I said.

"Somewhere along the way do you turn into my pilot?"

"It could be. I've never done this before."

"But you're willing to try?"

I nodded.

"Why?" he said, and leaned in and stared me directly in the face with a terrible, quietly wild intensity. *"Why?"*

Old man, I thought, I can't tell you why. Don't ask me.

He withdrew, sensing he had gone too far.

"I didn't say that," he said.

"You didn't say it," I said.

"And when you bring the plane in for a forced landing," he said, "will you land a little differently this time?"

"Different, yes."

"A little harder?"

"I'll see what can be done."

"And will I be thrown out but the rest of you okay?"

"The odds are in favor."

He looked up at the hill where there was no grave. I looked at the same hill. And maybe he guessed the digging of it there.

He gazed back down the road at the mountains and the sea that could not be seen beyond the mountains and a continent beyond the sea.

"That's a good day you're talking about."

"The best."

"And a good hour and a good second."

"Really, nothing better."

"Worth thinking about."

His hand lay on the doorsill, not leaning, but testing, feeling, touching, tremulous, undecided. But his eyes came full into the light of African noon.

"Yes."

"Yes?" I said.

"I think," he said, "I'll grab a lift with you."

I waited one heartbeat, then reached over and opened the door.

Silently he got in the front seat and sat there and quietly shut the door without slamming it. He sat there, very old and very tired. I waited.

"Start her up," he said.

I started the engine and gentled it.

"Turn her around," he said.

I turned the car so it was going back on the road.

"Is this really," he said, "that kind of car?"

"Really, that kind of car."

He looked out at the land and the mountains and the distant house.

I waited, idling the motor.

"When we get there," he said, "will you remember something . . .?"

"I'll try."

"There's a mountain," he said, and stopped and sat there, his mouth quiet, and he didn't go on.

But I went on for him. There is a mountain in Africa named Kiliman-jaro, I thought. And on the western slope of that mountain was once found the dried and frozen carcass of a leopard. No one has ever explained what the leopard was seeking at that altitude.

We will put you up on that same slope, I thought, on Kilimanjaro, near the leopard, and write your name and under it say nobody knew what he was doing here so high, but here he is. And write the date born and died, and go away down toward the hot summer grass and let mainly dark warriors and white hunters and swift okapis know the grave.

The old man shaded his eyes, looking at the road winding away over the hills. He nodded.

"Let's go," he said.

"Yes, Papa," I said.

And we motored away, myself at the wheel, going slow, and the old man beside me, and as we went down the first hill and topped the next, the sun came out full and the wind smelled of fire. We ran like a lion in the long grass. Rivers and streams flashed by. I wished we might stop for one hour and wade and fish and lie by the stream frying the fish and talking or not talking. But if we stopped we might never go on again. I gunned the engine. It made a great fierce wondrous animal's roar. The old man grinned.

"It's going to be a great day!" he shouted.

"A great day."

Back on the road, I thought, How must it be now, and now, us disappearing? And now, us gone? And now, the road empty. Sun Valley quiet in the sun. What must it be, having us gone?

I had the car up to ninety.

We both yelled like boys.

After that I didn't know anything.

"By God," said the old man, toward the end. "You know? I think we're . . . flying?"

The Terrible Conflagration Up at the Place

T he men had been hiding down by the gatekeeper's lodge for half an hour or so, passing a bottle of the best between, and then, the gatekeeper having been carried off to bed, they dodged up the path at six in the evening and looked at the great house with the warm lights lit in each window.

"That's the place," said Riordan.

"Hell, what do you mean, 'that's the place'?" cried Casey, then softly added, "We seen it all our lives."

"Sure," said Kelly, "but with the Troubles over and around us, sudden-like a place looks *different*. It's quite a toy, lying there in the snow."

And that's what it seemed to the fourteen of them, a grand playhouse laid out in the softly falling feathers of a spring night.

"Did you bring the matches?" asked Kelly.

"Did I bring the—what do you think I *am!*"

"Well, *did* you, is all I ask."

Casey searched himself. When his pockets hung from his suit he swore and said, "I did not."

"Ah, what the hell," said Nolan. "They'll have matches inside. We'll borrow a few. Come on."

Going up the road, Timulty tripped and fell.

"For God's sake, Timulty," said Nolan, "where's your sense of romance? In the midst of a big Easter Rebellion we want to do everything just so. Years from now we want to go into a pub and tell about the Terrible Conflagration up at the Place, do we not? If it's all mucked up with the sight of you landing on your ass in the snow, that makes no fit picture of the Rebellion we are now in, does it?"

Timulty, rising, focused the picture and nodded. "I'll mind me manners."

"Hist! Here we are!" cried Riordan.

"Jesus, stop saying things like 'that's the place' and 'here we are,' "
said Casey. "We see the damned house. Now what do we do next?"

"Destroy it?" suggested Murphy tentatively.

"Gah, you're so dumb you're hideous," said Casey. "Of course we
destroy it, but first . . . blueprints and plans."

"It seemed simple enough back at Hickey's Pub," said Murphy. "We
would just come tear the damn place down. Seeing as how my wife
outweighs me, I need to tear *something* down."

"It seems to me," said Timulty, drinking from the bottle, "we go rap
on the door and ask permission."

"Permission!" said Murphy. "I'd hate to have you running hell, the
lost souls would never get fried! We—"

But the front door swung wide suddenly, cutting him off.

A man peered out into the night.

"I say," said a gentle and reasonable voice, "would you mind keeping
your voices down. The lady of the house is sleeping before we drive to
Dublin for the evening, and—"

The men, revealed in the hearth-light glow of the door, blinked and
stood back, lifting their caps.

"Is that you, Lord Kilgotten?"

"It is," said the man in the door.

"We will keep our voices down," said Timulty, smiling, all amiability.

"Beg pardon, your Lordship," said Casey.

"Kind of you," said his Lordship. And the door closed gently.

All the men gasped.

" 'Beg pardon, your Lordship,' 'We'll keep our voices down, your
Lordship.' " Casey slapped his head. "What were we saying? Why
didn't someone catch the door while he was still there?"

"We was dumfounded, that's why; he took us by surprise, just like
them damned high and mighties. I mean, we weren't *doing* anything out
here, were we?"

"Our voices *were* a bit high," admitted Timulty.

"Voices, hell," said Casey. "The damn Lord's come and gone from
our fell clutches!"

"*Shh,* not so loud," said Timulty.

Casey lowered his voice. "So, let us sneak up on the door, and—"

"That strikes me as unnecessary," said Nolan. "He *knows* we're
here now."

"Sneak up on the door," repeated Casey, grinding his teeth, "and
batter it down—"

The door opened again.

The Lord, a shadow, peered out at them and the soft, patient, frail old
voice inquired, "I say, what *are* you doing out there?"

"Well, it's this way, your Lordship—" began Casey, and stopped, paling.

"We come," blurted Murphy, "we come . . . to *burn* the Place!"

His Lordship stood for a moment looking out at the men, watching the snow, his hand on the doorknob. He shut his eyes for a moment, thought, conquered a tic in both eyelids after a silent struggle, and then said, "Hmm, well in that case, you had best come in."

The men said that was fine, great, good enough, and started off when Casey cried, "Wait!" Then to the old man in the doorway, "We'll come in, when we are good and ready."

"Very well," said the old man. "I shall leave the door ajar and when you have decided the time, enter. I shall be in the library."

Leaving the door a half inch open, the old man started away when Timulty cried out, "When we are *ready?* Jesus, God, when will we ever be readier? Out of the way, Casey!"

And they all ran up on the porch.

Hearing this, his Lordship turned to look at them with his bland and not-unfriendly face, the face of an old hound who has seen many foxes killed and just as many escape, who has run well, and now in late years, paced himself down to a soft, shuffling walk.

"Scrape your feet, please, gentlemen."

"Scraped they are." And everyone carefully got the snow and mud off his shoes.

"This way," said his Lordship, going off, his clear, pale eyes set in lines and bags and creases from too many years of drinking brandy, his cheeks bright as cherry wine. "I will get you all a drink, and we shall see what we can do about your . . . how did you put it . . . burning the Place?"

"You're Sweet Reason itself," admitted Timulty, following as Lord Kilgotten led them into the library, where he poured whisky all around.

"Gentlemen." He let his bones sink into a wing-backed chair. "Drink."

"We decline," said Casey.

"Decline?" gasped everyone, the drinks almost in their hands.

"This is a sober thing we are doing and we must be sober for it," said Casey, flinching from their gaze.

"Who do we listen to?" asked Riordan. "His Lordship or Casey?"

For answer all the men downed their drinks and fell to coughing and gasping. Courage showed immediately in a red color through their faces, which they turned so that Casey could see the difference. Casey drank his, to catch up.

Meanwhile, the old man sipped his whisky, and something about his calm and easy way of drinking put them far out in Dublin Bay and sank them again. Until Casey said, "Your Honor, you've heard of the Troubles? I mean not just the Kaiser's war going on across the sea, but our own very great Troubles and the Rebellion that has reached even this far, to our town, our pub, and now, your Place?"

"An alarming amount of evidence convinces me this is an unhappy time," said his Lordship. "I suppose what must be must be. I know you all. You have worked for me. I think I have paid you rather well on occasion."

"There's no doubt of that, your Lordship." Casey took a step forward. "It's just, 'the old order changeth,' and we have heard of the great houses out near Tara and the great manors beyond Killashandra going up in flames to celebrate freedom and—"

"Whose freedom?" asked the old man, mildly. "Mine? From the burden of caring for this house which my wife and I rattle around in like dice in a cup or—well, get on. *When* would you like to burn the Place?"

"If it isn't too much trouble, sir," said Timulty, "now."

The old man seemed to sink deeper into his chair.

"Oh, dear," he said.

"Of course," said Nolan quickly, "if it's inconvenient, we could come back later—"

"Later! What kind of talk is *that?*" asked Casey.

"I'm terribly sorry," said the old man. "Please allow me to explain. Lady Kilgotten is asleep now, we have guests coming to take us into Dublin for the opening of a play by Synge—"

"That's a damn fine writer," said Riordan.

"Saw one of his plays a year ago," said Nolan, "and—"

"Stand off!" said Casey.

The men stood back. His Lordship went on with his frail moth voice, "We have a dinner planned back here at midnight for ten people. I don't suppose—you could give us until tomorrow night to get ready?"

"No," said Casey.

"Hold on," said everyone else.

"Burning," said Timulty, "is one thing, but tickets is another. I mean, the theater is *there,* and a dire waste not to see the play, and all that food set up, it might as well be eaten. And all the guests coming. It would be hard to notify them ahead."

"Exactly what *I* was thinking," said his Lordship.

"Yes, I know!" shouted Casey, shutting his eyes, running his hands over his cheeks and jaw and mouth and clenching his fists and turning around in frustration. "But you *don't* put off burnings, you *don't* reschedule them like tea parties, dammit, you *do* them!"

"You do if you remember to bring the matches," said Riordan under his breath.

Casey whirled and looked as if he might hit Riordan, but the impact of the truth slowed him down.

"On top of which," said Nolan, "the Missus above is a fine lady and needs a last night of entertainment and rest."

"Very kind of you." His Lordship refilled the man's glass.

"Let's take a vote," said Nolan.

"Hell." Casey scowled around. "I see the vote counted already. Tomorrow night will do, dammit."

"Bless you," said old Lord Kilgotten. "There will be cold cuts laid out in the kitchen, you might check in there first, you shall probably be hungry, for it will be heavy work. Shall we say eight o'clock tomorrow night? By then I shall have Lady Kilgotten safely to a hotel in Dublin. I should not want her knowing until later that her home no longer exists."

"God, you're a Christian," muttered Riordan.

"Well, let us not brood on it," said the old man. "I consider it past already, and I never think of the past. Gentlemen."

He arose. And, like a blind old sheepherder-saint, he wandered out into the hall with the flock straying and ambling and softly colliding after.

Half down the hall, almost to the door, Lord Kilgotten saw something from the corner of his blear eye and stopped. He turned back and stood brooding before a large portrait of an Italian nobleman.

The more he looked the more his eyes began to tic and his mouth to work over a nameless thing.

Finally Nolan said, "Your Lordship, what is it?"

"I was just thinking," said the Lord, at last, "you love Ireland, do you not?"

My God, yes! said everyone. Need he ask?

"Even as do I," said the old man gently. "And do you love all that is in it, in the land, in her heritage?"

That too, said all, went without saying!

"I worry then," said the Lord, "about things like this. This portrait is by Van Dyck. It is very old and very fine and very important and very expensive. It is, gentlemen, a National Art Treasure."

"Is *that* what it is!" said everyone, more or less, and crowded around for a sight.

"Ah, God, it's fine work," said Timulty.

"The flesh itself," said Nolan.

"Notice," said Riordan, "the way his little eyes seem to follow you?" Uncanny, everyone said.

And were about to move on, when his Lordship said, "Do you realize this Treasure, which does not truly belong to me, nor you, but to all the people as precious heritage, this picture will be lost forever tomorrow night?"

Everyone gasped. They had *not* realized.

"God save us," said Timulty, "we can't have that!"

"We'll move it out of the house, first," said Riordan.

"Hold on!" cried Casey.

"Thank you," said his Lordship, "but where would you put it? Out in the weather it would soon be torn to shreds by wind, dampened by rain, flaked by hail; no, no, perhaps it is best it burns quickly—"

"None of that!" said Timulty. "I'll take it home myself."

"And when the great strife is over," said his Lordship, "you will then deliver into the hands of the new government this precious gift of Art and Beauty from the past?"

"Er . . . every single one of those things, I'll do," said Timulty.

But Casey was eyeing the immense canvas, and said, "How much does the monster weigh?"

"I would imagine," said the old man, faintly, "seventy to one hundred pounds, within that range."

"Then how in hell do we get it to Timulty's house?" asked Casey.

"Me and Brannahan will carry the damn treasure," said Timulty, "and if need be, Nolan, *you* lend a hand."

"Posterity will thank you," said his Lordship.

They moved on along the hall, and again his Lordship stopped, before yet two more paintings.

"These are two nudes—"

They *are* that! said everyone.

"By Renoir," finished the old man.

"That's the French gent who made them?" asked Rooney. "If you'll excuse the expression?"

It looks French all right, said everyone.

And a lot of ribs received a lot of knocking elbows.

"These are worth several thousand pounds," said the old man.

"You'll get no argument from me," said Nolan, putting out his finger, which was slapped down by Casey.

"I—" said Blinky Watts, whose fish eyes swam about continuously in tears behind his thick glasses, "I would like to volunteer a home for the two French ladies. I thought I might tuck those two Art Treasures one under each arm and hoist them to the wee cot."

"Accepted," said the Lord with gratitude.

Along the hall they came to another, vaster landscape with all sorts of monster beast-men cavorting about treading fruit and squeezing summer-melon women. Everyone craned forward to read the brass plate under it: *Twilight of the Gods.*

"Twilight, hell," said Rooney, "it looks more like the start of a great afternoon!"

"I believe," said the gentle old man, "there is irony intended both in title and subject. Note the glowering sky, the hideous figures hidden in the clouds. The gods are unaware, in the midst of their bacchanal, that Doom is about to descend."

"I do not see," said Blinky Watts, "the Church or any of her girly priests up in them clouds."

"It was a different kind of Doom in them days," said Nolan. "Everyone knows *that.*"

"Me and Tuohy," said Flannery, "will carry the demon gods to my place. Right, Tuohy?"

"Right!"

And so it went now, along the hall, the squad pausing here or there as on a grand tour of a museum, and each in turn volunteering to scurry home through the snowfall night with a Degas or a Rembrandt sketch or a large oil by one of the Dutch masters, until they came to a rather grisly oil of a man, hung in a dim alcove.

"Portrait of myself," muttered the old man, "done by her Ladyship. Leave it there, please."

"You mean," gasped Nolan, "you want it to go up in the Conflagration?"

"Now, this next picture—" said the old man, moving on.

And finally the tour was at an end.

"Of course," said his Lordship, "if you really want to be saving, there are a dozen exquisite Ming vases in the house—"

"As good as collected," said Nolan.

"A Persian carpet on the landing—"

"We will roll it and deliver it to the Dublin Museum."

"And that exquisite chandelier in the main dining room."

"It shall be hidden away until the Troubles are over," sighed Casey, tired already.

"Well, then," said the old man, shaking each hand as he passed. "Perhaps you might start now, don't you imagine? I mean, you do indeed have a largish job preserving the National Treasures. Think I shall nap five minutes now before dressing."

And the old man wandered off upstairs.

Leaving the men stunned and isolated in a mob in the hall below, watching him go away out of sight.

"Casey," said Blinky Watts, "has it crossed your small mind, if you'd remembered to bring the matches there would be no such long night of work as this ahead?"

"Jesus, where's your taste for the ass-thetics?" cried Riordan.

"Shut up!" said Casey. "Okay, Flannery, you on one end of the

Twilight of the Gods, you, Tuohy, on the far end where the maid is being given what's good for her. Ha! *Lift!*''

And the gods, soaring crazily, took to the air.

By seven o'clock most of the paintings were out of the house and racked against each other in the snow, waiting to be taken off in various directions toward various huts. At seven fifteen, Lord and Lady Kilgotten came out and drove away, and Casey quickly formed the mob in front of the stacked paintings so the nice old lady wouldn't see what they were up to. The boys cheered as the car went down the drive. Lady Kilgotten waved fraily back.

From seven thirty until ten the rest of the paintings walked out in one's and two's.

When all the pictures were gone save one, Kelly stood in the dim alcove worrying over Lady Kilgotten's Sunday painting of the old Lord. He shuddered, decided on a supreme humanitarianism, and carried the portrait safely out into the night.

At midnight, Lord and Lady Kilgotten, returning with guests, found only great shuffling tracks in the snow where Flannery and Tuohy had set off one way with the dear bacchanal; where Casey, grumbling, had led a parade of Van Dycks, Rembrandts, Bouchers, and Piranesis another; and, where last of all, Blinky Watts, kicking his heels, had trotted happily into the woods with his nude Renoirs.

The dinner party was over by two. Lady Kilgotten went to bed satisfied that all the paintings had been sent out, en masse, to be cleaned.

At three in the morning, Lord Kilgotten still sat sleepless in his library, alone among empty walls, before a fireless hearth, a muffler about his thin neck, a glass of brandy in his faintly trembling hand.

About three fifteen there was a stealthy creaking of parquetry, a shift of shadows, and, after a time, cap in hand, there stood Casey at the library door.

"Hist!" he called softly.

The Lord, who had dozed somewhat, blinked his eyes wide. "Oh dear me," he said, "is it time for us to go?"

"That's tomorrow night," said Casey. "And anyways, it's not you that's going, it's Them is coming back."

"Them? Your friends?"

"No, *yours.*" And Casey beckoned.

The old man let himself be led through the hall to look out the front door into a deep well of night.

There, like Napoleon's numbed dog-army of foot-weary, undecided, and demoralized men, stood the shadowy but familiar mob, their hands full of pictures—pictures leaned against their legs, pictures on their backs, pictures stood upright and held by trembling, panic-whitened hands in the drifted snow. A terrible silence lay over and among the men. They seemed stranded, as if one enemy had gone off to fight far better wars while yet another enemy, as yet unnamed, nipped silent and trackless at their behinds. They kept glancing over their shoulders at the hills and the town as if at any moment Chaos herself might unleash her dogs from there. They alone, in the infiltering night, heard the far-off baying of dismays and despairs that cast a spell.

"Is that *you,* Riordan?" called Casey, nervously.

"Ah, who the hell *would* it be!" cried a voice out beyond.

"What do they *want?*" asked the old party.

"It's not so much what *we* want as what *you* might now want from *us,*" called a voice.

"You see," said another, advancing until all could see it was Hannahan in the light, "considered in all its aspects, your Honor, we've decided, you're such a fine gent, we—"

"We will *not* burn your house!" cried Blinky Watts.

"Shut up and let the man talk!" said several voices.

Hannahan nodded. "That's it. We will *not* burn your house."

"But see here," said the Lord, "I'm quite prepared. Everything can easily be moved out."

"You're taking the whole thing too lightly, begging your pardon, your Honor," said Kelly. "Easy for you is not easy for us."

"I see," said the old man, not seeing at all.

"It seems," said Tuohy, "we have all of us, in just the last few hours, developed problems. Some to do with the home and some to do with transport and cartage, if you get my drift. Who'll explain first? Kelly? No? Casey? Riordan?"

Nobody spoke.

At last, with a sigh, Flannery edged forward. "It's this way—" he said.

"Yes?" said the old man, gently.

"Well," said Flannery, "me and Tuohy here got half through the woods, like damn fools, and was across two thirds of the bog with the large picture of the *Twilight of the Gods* when we began to sink."

"Your strength failed?" inquired the Lord kindly.

"Sink, your Honor, just plain sink, into the *ground,*" Tuohy put in.

"Dear me," said the Lord.

"You can say that again, your Lordship," said Tuohy. "Why together, me and Flannery and the demon gods must have weighed close on to six hundred pounds, and that bog out there is infirm if it's anything, and the more we walk the deeper we sink, and a cry strangled in me throat, for I'm thinking of those scenes in the old story where the Hound of the Baskervilles or some such fiend chases the heroine out in the moor and down she goes, in a watery pit, wishing she had kept at that diet, but it's too late, and bubbles rise to pop on the surface. All of this a-throttling in me mind, your Honor."

"And so?" the Lord put in, seeing he was expected to ask.

"And so," said Flannery, "we just walked off and left the damn gods there in their twilight."

"In the middle of the *bog?*" asked the elderly man, just a trifle upset.

"Ah, we covered them up, I mean we put our mufflers over the scene. The gods will not die twice, your Honor. Say, did you hear *that,* boys? The gods—"

"Ah, shut up," cried Kelly. "Ya dimwits. Why didn't you bring the damn portrait in off the bog?"

"We thought we would come get two more boys to help—"

"Two more!" cried Nolan. "That's four men, plus a parcel of gods, you'd all sink *twice* as fast, and the bubbles rising, ya nitwit!"

"Ah! said Tuohy. "I never thought of that."

"It has been thought of now," said the old man. "And perhaps several of you will form a rescue team—"

"It's done, your Honor," said Casey. "Bob, you and Tim dash off and save the pagan deities."

"You won't tell Father Leary?"

"Father Leary my behind. Get!" And Tim and Bob panted off.

His Lordship turned now to Nolan and Kelly.

"I see that you, too, have brought your rather large picture back."

"At least we made it within a hundred yards of the door, sir," said Kelly. "I suppose you're wondering *why* we have returned it, your Honor?"

"With the gathering in of coincidence upon coincidence," said the old man, going back in to get his overcoat and putting on his tweed cap so he could stand out in the cold and finish what looked to be a long converse, "yes, I was given to speculate."

"It's me back," said Kelley. "It gave out not five hundred yards down the main road. The back has been springing out and in for five years now, and me suffering the agonies of Christ. I sneeze and fall to my knees, your Honor."

"I have suffered the self-same delinquency," said the old man. "It is as if someone had driven a spike into one's spine." The old man touched his back, carefully, remembering, which brought a gasp from all, nodding.

"The agonies of Christ, as I said," said Kelly.

"Most understandable then that you could not finish your journey with that heavy frame," said the old man, "and most commendable that you were able to struggle back this far with the dreadful weight."

Kelly stood taller immediately, as he heard his plight described. He beamed. "It was nothing. And I'd do it again, save for the string of bones above me ass. Begging pardon, your Honor."

But already his Lordship had passed his kind if tremulous gray-blue, unfocused gaze toward Blinky Watts who had, under either arm, like a dartful prancer, the two Renoir peach ladies.

"Ah, God, there was no trouble with sinking into bogs or knocking my spine out of shape," said Watts, treading the earth to demonstrate his passage home. "I made it back to the house in ten minutes flat, dashed into the wee cot, and began hanging the pictures on the wall, when my wife came up behind me. Have ya ever had your wife come up behind ya, your Honor, and just stand there mum's the word?"

"I seem to recall a similar circumstance," said the old man, trying to remember if he did, then nodding as indeed several memories flashed over his fitful baby mind.

"Well, your Lordship, there is no silence like a woman's silence, do you agree? And no standing there like a woman's standing there like a monument out of Stonehenge. The mean temperature dropped in the room so quick I suffered from the polar concussions, as we call it in our house. I did not dare turn to confront the Beast, or the daughter of the Beast, as I call her in deference to her mom. But finally I heard her suck in a great breath and let it out very cool and calm like a Prussian general. 'That woman is naked as a jay bird,' and 'That other woman is raw as the inside of a clam at low tide.'

" 'But,' said I, 'these are studies of natural physique by a famous French artist.'

" 'Jesus-come-after-me-French,' she cried; 'the-skirts-half-up-to-your-bum-French. The-dress-half-down-to-your-navel-French. And the gulping and smothering they do with their mouths in their dirty novels French, and now you come home and nail 'French' on the walls, why don't you while you're at it, pull the crucifix down and nail one fat naked lady *there?*'

"Well, your Honor, I just shut up my eyes and wished my ears would fall off. 'Is *this* what you want our boys to look at last thing at night as they go to sleep?' she says. Next thing I know, I'm on the path and here I am and here's the raw-oyster nudes, your Honor, beg your pardon, thanks, and much obliged."

"They *do* seem to be unclothed," said the old man, looking at the two pictures, one in either hand, as if he wished to find all that this man's wife said was in them. "I had always thought of summer, looking at them."

"From your seventieth birthday on, your Lordship, perhaps. But *before* that?"

"Uh, yes, yes," said the old man, watching a speck of half-remembered lechery drift across one eye.

When his eye stopped drifting it found Bannock and Toolery on the edge of the far rim of the uneasy sheepfold crowd. Behind each, dwarfing them, stood a giant painting.

Bannock had got his picture home only to find he could not get the damn thing through the door, nor any window.

Toolery had actually got his picture *in* the door when his wife said what a laughingstock they'd be, the only family in the village with a Rubens worth half a million pounds and not even a cow to milk!

So that was the sum, total, and substance of this long night. Each man had a similar chill, dread, and awful tale to tell, and all were told at last, and as they finished a cold snow began to fall among these brave members of the local, hard-fighting I.R.A.

The old man said nothing, for there was nothing really to say that wouldn't be obvious as their pale breaths ghosting the wind. Then, very quietly, the old man opened wide the front door and had the decency not even to nod or point.

Slowly and silently they began to file by, as past a familiar teacher in an old school, and then faster they moved. So in flowed the river returned, the Ark emptied out before, not after, the Flood, and the tide of animals and angels, nudes that flamed and smoked in the hands, and noble gods that pranced on wings and hoofs, went by, and the old man's eyes shifted gently, and his mouth silently named each, the Renoirs, the Van Dycks, the Lautrec, and so on until Kelly, in passing, felt a touch at his arm.

Surprised, Kelly looked over.

And saw that the old man was staring at the small painting beneath his arm.

"My wife's portrait of me?"

"None other," said Kelly.

The old man stared at Kelly and at the painting beneath his arm and then out toward the snowing night.

Kelly smiled softly.

Walking soft as a burglar, he vanished out into the wilderness, carrying the picture. A moment later, you heard him laughing as he ran back, hands empty.

The old man shook his hand, once, tremblingly, and shut the door.

Then he turned away as if the event was already lost to his wandering child mind and toddled down the hall with his scarf like a gentle weariness over his thin shoulders, and the mob followed him in where they found drinks in their great paws and saw that Lord Kilgotten was blinking at the picture over the fireplace as if trying to remember, was the Sack of Rome there in the years past? or was it the Fall of Troy? Then he felt their gaze and looked full on the encircled army and said:

"Well now, what shall we *drink* to?"

The men shuffled their feet.

Then Flannery cried, "Why, to his Lordship, of course!"

"His Lordship!" cried all, eagerly, and drank, and coughed and choked and sneezed, while the old man felt a peculiar glistering about his eyes, and did not drink at all till the commotion stilled, and then said, "To Our Ireland," and drank, and all said Ah God and Amen to that, and the old man looked at the picture over the hearth and then at last shyly observed, "I do hate to mention it—that picture—"

"Sir?"

"It seems to me," said the old man, apologetically, "to be a trifle off-centered, on the tilt. I wonder if you might—"

"*Mightn't* we, boys!" cried Casey.

And fourteen men rushed to put it right.

He did not want to be the father of a small blue pyramid. Peter Horn hadn't planned it that way at all. Neither he nor his wife imagined that such a thing could happen to them. They had talked quietly for days about the birth of their coming child, they had eaten normal foods, slept a great deal, taken in a few shows, and, when it was time for her to fly in the helicopter to the hospital, her husband held her and kissed her.

"Honey, you'll be home in six hours," he said. "These new birth-mechanisms do everything but father the child for you."

She remembered an old-time song. "No, no, they can't take that away from me!" and sang it, and they laughed as the helicopter lifted them over the green way from country to city.

The doctor, a quiet gentlemen named Wolcott, was very confident. Polly Ann, the wife, was made ready for the task ahead and the father was put, as usual, out in the waiting room where he could suck on cigarettes or take highballs from a convenient mixer. He was feeling pretty good. This was the first baby, but there was not a thing to worry about. Polly Ann was in good hands.

Dr. Wolcott came into the waiting room an hour later. He looked like a man who has seen death. Peter Horn, on his third highball, did not move. His hand tightened on the glass and he whispered:

"She's dead."

"No," said Wolcott, quietly. "No, no, she's fine. It's the baby."

"The baby's dead, then."

"The baby's alive, too, but—drink the rest of that drink and come along after me. Something's happened."

Yes, indeed, something had happened. The "something" that had happened had brought the entire hospital out into the corridors. People were going and coming from one room to another. As Peter Horn was led through a hallway where attendants in white uniforms were standing around peering into each other's faces and whispering, he became quite ill.

"Hey, looky looky! The child of Peter Horn! Incredible!"

They entered a small clean room. There was a crowd in the room, looking down at a low table. There was something on the table.

A small blue pyramid.

"Why've you brought me here?" said Horn, turning to the doctor.

The small blue pyramid moved. It began to cry.

Peter Horn pushed forward and looked down wildly. He was very white and he was breathing rapidly. "You don't mean that's it?"

The doctor named Wolcott nodded.

The blue pyramid had six blue snakelike appendages and three eyes that blinked from the tips of projecting structures.

Horn didn't move.

"It weighs seven pounds, eight ounces," someone said.

Horn thought to himself, they're kidding me. This is some joke. Charlie Ruscoll is behind all this. He'll pop in a door any moment and cry "April Fool!" and everybody'll laugh. That's not my child. Oh, horrible! They're kidding me.

Horn stood there, and the sweat rolled down his face.

"Get me away from here." Horn turned and his hands were opening and closing without purpose, his eyes were flickering.

Wolcott held his elbow, talking calmly. "This is your child. Understand that, Mr. Horn."

"No. No, it's not." His mind wouldn't touch the thing. "It's a nightmare. Destroy *it!*"

"You can't kill a human being."

"Human?" Horn blinked tears. "That's not human! That's a crime against God!"

The doctor went on, quickly. "We've examined this—child—and we've decided that it is not a mutant, a result of gene destruction or rearrangement. It's not a freak. Nor is it sick. Please listen to everything I say to you."

Horn stared at the wall, his eyes wide and sick. He swayed. The doctor talked distantly, with assurance.

"The child was somehow affected by the birth pressure. There was a dimensional distructure caused by the simultaneous short-circuitings and malfunctionings of the new birth and hypnosis machines. Well, anyway," the doctor ended lamely, "your baby was born into—another dimension."

Horn did not even nod. He stood there, waiting.

Dr. Wolcott made it emphatic. "Your child is alive, well, and happy. It is lying there, on the table. But because it was born into another dimension it has a shape alien to us. Our eyes, adjusted to a three-dimensional concept, cannot recognize it as a baby. But it *is*. Underneath that camouflage, the strange pyramidal shape and appendages, it is *your* child.''

Horn closed his mouth and shut his eyes. ''Can I have a drink?''

''Certainly.'' A drink was thrust into Horn's hands.

''Now, let me just sit down, sit down somewhere a moment.'' Horn sank wearily into a chair. It was coming clear. Everything shifted slowly into place. It was his child, no matter what. He shuddered. No matter how horrible it looked, it was his first child.

At last he looked up and tried to see the doctor. ''What'll we tell Polly?'' His voice was hardly a whisper.

''We'll work that out this morning, as soon as you feel up to it.''

''What happens after that? Is there any way to—change it back?''

''We'll try. That is, if you give us permission to try. After all, it's your child. You can do anything with him you want to do.''

''Him?'' Horn laughed ironically, shutting his eyes. ''How do you know it's a him?'' He sank down into darkness. His ears roared.

Wolcott was visibly upset. ''Why, we—that is—well, we don't know, for sure.''

Horn drank more of his drink. ''What if you *can't* change him back?''

''I realize what a shock it is to you, Mr. Horn. If you can't bear to look upon the child, we'll be glad to raise him here, at the Institute, for you.''

Horn thought it over. ''Thanks. But he still belongs to me and Polly. I'll give him a home. Raise him like I'd raise any kid. Give him a normal home life. Try to learn to love him. Treat him right.'' His lips were numb, he couldn't think.

''You realize what a job you're taking on, Mr. Horn? This child can't be allowed to have normal playmates; why, they'd pester it to death in no time. You know how children are. If you decide to raise the child at home, his life will be strictly regimented, he must *never* be seen by anyone. Is that clear?''

''Yes. Yes, it's clear. Doc. Doc, is he all right mentally?''

''Yes. We've tested his reactions. He's a fine healthy child as far as nervous response and such things go.''

''I just wanted to be sure. Now, the only problem is Polly.''

Wolcott frowned. ''I confess that one has me stumped. You know it is pretty hard on a woman to hear that her child has been born dead. But *this,* telling a woman she's given birth to something not recognizable as human. It's not as clean as death. There's too much chance for shock. And yet I must tell her the truth. A doctor gets nowhere by lying to his patient.''

Horn put his glass down. "I don't want to lose Polly, too. I'd be prepared now, if you destroyed the child, to take it. But I don't want Polly killed by the shock of this whole thing."

"I think we may be able to change the child back. That's the point which makes me hesitate. If I thought the case was hopeless I'd make out a certificate of euthanasia immediately. But it's at least worth a chance."

Horn was very tired. He was shivering quietly, deeply. "All right, doctor. It needs food, milk, and love until you can fix it up. It's had a raw deal so far, no reason for it to go on getting a raw deal. When will we tell Polly?"

"Tomorrow afternoon, when she wakes up."

Horn got up and walked to the table which was warmed by a soft illumination from overhead. The blue pyramid sat upon the table as Horn held out his hand.

"Hello, Baby," said Horn.

The blue pyramid looked up at Horn with three bright blue eyes. It shifted a tiny blue tendril, touching Horn's fingers with it.

Horn shivered.

"Hello, Baby."

The doctor produced a special feeding bottle.

"This is woman's milk. Here we go."

Baby looked upward through clearing mists. Baby saw the shapes moving over him and knew them to be friendly. Baby was newborn, but already alert, strangely alert. Baby was aware.

There were moving objects above and around Baby. Six cubes of a gray-white color, bending down. Six cubes with hexagonal appendages and three eyes to each cube. Then there were two other cubes coming from a distance over a crystalline plateau. One of the cubes was white. It had three eyes, too. There was something about this White Cube that Baby liked. There was an attraction. Some relation. There was an odor to the White Cube that reminded Baby of itself.

Shrill sounds came from the six bending-down gray-white cubes. Sounds of curiosity and wonder. It was like a kind of piccolo music, all playing at once.

Now the two newly arrived cubes, the White Cube and the Gray Cube, were whistling. After a while the White Cube extended one of its hexagonal appendages to touch Baby. Baby responded by putting out one of its tendrils from its pyramidal body. Baby liked the White Cube. Baby liked. Baby was hungry. Baby liked. Maybe the White Cube would give it food . . .

The Gray Cube produced a pink globe for Baby. Baby was now to be fed. Good. Good. Baby accepted food eagerly.

Food was good. All the gray-white cubes drifted away, leaving only the nice White Cube standing over Baby looking down and whistling over and over. Over and over.

They told Polly the next day. Not everything. Just enough. Just a hint. They told her the baby was not well, in a certain way. They talked slowly, and in ever-tightening circles, in upon Polly. Then Dr. Wolcott gave a long lecture on the birth-mechanisms, how they helped a woman in her labor, and how, this time, they short-circuited. There was another man of scientific means present and he gave her a dry little talk on dimensions, holding up his fingers, so! one, two, three, and four. Still another man talked of energy and matter. Another spoke of underprivileged children.

Polly finally sat up in bed and said, "What's all the talk for? What's wrong with my baby that you should all be talking so long?"

Wolcott told her.

"Of course, you can wait a week and see it," he said. "Or you can sign over guardianship of the child to the Institute."

"There's only one thing I want to know," said Polly.

Dr. Wolcott raised his brows.

"Did I *make* the child that way?" asked Polly.

"You most certainly did *not!*"

"The child isn't a monster, genetically?" asked Polly.

"The child was thrust into another continuum. Otherwise, it is perfectly normal."

Polly's tight, lined mouth relaxed. She said, simply, "Then, bring me my baby. I want to see him. Please. Now."

They brought the "child."

The Horns left the hospital the next day. Polly walked out on her own two good legs, with Peter Horn following her, looking at her in quiet amazement.

They did not have the baby with them. That would come later. Horn helped his wife into their helicopter and sat beside her. He lifted the ship, whirring, into the warm air.

"You're a wonder," he said.

"Am I?" she said, lighting a cigarette.

"You are. You didn't cry. You didn't do anything."

"He's not so bad, you know," she said. "Once you get to know him. I can even—hold him in my arms. He's warm and he cries and he even needs his triangular diapers." Here she laughed. He noticed a nervous tremor in the laugh, however. "No, I didn't cry, Pete, because that's my baby. Or he will be. He isn't dead, I thank God for that. He's—I don't know how to explain—still unborn. I like to think he hasn't been born yet. We're waiting for him to show up. I have confidence in Dr. Wolcott. Haven't you?''

"You're right. You're right." He reached over and held her hand. "You know something? You're a peach."

"I can hold on," she said, sitting there looking ahead as the green country swung under them. "As long as I know something good will happen, I won't let it hurt or shock me. I'll wait six months, and then maybe I'll kill myself."

"Polly!"

She looked at him as if he'd just come in. "Pete, I'm sorry. But this sort of thing doesn't happen. Once it's over and the baby is finally 'born' I'll forget it so quick it'll never have occurred. But if the doctor can't help us, then a mind can't take it, a mind can only tell the body to climb out on a roof and jump."

"Things'll be all right," he said, holding to the guide-wheel. "They have to be."

She said nothing, but let the cigarette smoke blow out of her mouth in the pounding concussion of the helicopter fan.

Three weeks passed. Every day they flew in to the Institute to visit "Py." For that was the quiet calm name that Polly Horn gave to the blue pyramid that lay on the warm sleeping-table and blinked up at them. Dr. Wolcott was careful to point out that the habits of the "child" were as normal as any others; so many hours sleep, so many awake, so much attentiveness, so much boredom, so much food, so much elimination. Polly Horn listened, and her face softened and her eyes warmed.

At the end of the third week, Dr. Wolcott said, "Feel up to taking him home now? You live in the country, don't you? All right, you have an enclosed patio, he can be out there in the sunlight, on occasion. He needs a mother's love. That's trite, but nevertheless true. He should be suckled. We have an arrangement where he's been fed by the new feed-mech; cooing voice, warmth, hands, and all." Dr. Wolcott's voice was dry. "But still I feel you are familiar enough with him now to know he's a pretty healthy child. Are you game, Mrs. Horn?"

"Yes, I'm game."

"Good. Bring him in every third day for a checkup. Here's his formula. We're working on several solutions now, Mrs. Horn. We should have some results for you by the end of the year. I don't want to say anything definite, but I have reason to believe we'll pull that boy right out of the fourth dimension, like a rabbit out of a hat."

The doctor was mildly surprised and pleased when Polly Horn kissed him, then and there.

*   *   *

Pete Horn took the copter home over the smooth rolling greens of Griffith. From time to time he looked at the pyramid lying in Polly's arms. She was making cooing noises at it, it was replying in approximately the same way.

"I wonder," said Polly.

"What?"

"How do *we* look to it?" asked his wife.

"I asked Wolcott about that. He said we probably look funny to him, also. He's in one dimension, we're in another."

"You mean we don't look like men and women to him?"

"If we could see ourselves, no. But remember, the baby knows nothing of men or women. To the baby whatever shape we're in, we are natural. It's accustomed to seeing us shaped like cubes or squares or pyramids, as it sees us from its separate dimension. The baby's had no other experience, no other norm with which to compare what it sees. We *are* its norm. On the other hand, the baby seems weird to us because we compare it to our accustomed shapes and sizes."

"Yes, I see. I see."

Baby was conscious of movement. One White Cube held him in warm appendages. Another White Cube sat further over, within an oblong of purple. The oblong moved in the air over a vast bright plain of pyramids, hexagons, oblongs, pillars, bubbles, and multi-colored cubes.

One White Cube made a whistling noise. The other White Cube replied with a whistling. The White Cube that held him shifted about. Baby watched the two White Cubes, and watched the fleeing world outside the traveling bubble.

Baby felt—sleepy. Baby closed his eyes, settled his pyramidal youngness upon the lap of the White Cube, and made faint little noises . . .

"He's asleep," said Polly Horn.

Summer came, Peter Horn himself was busy with his export-import business. But he made certain he was home every night. Polly was all right during the day, but, at night, when she had to be alone with the child, she got to smoking too much, and one night he found her passed out on the davenport, an empty sherry bottle on the table beside her. From then on, he took care of the child himself nights. When it cried it made a weird whistling noise, like some jungle animal lost and wailing. It wasn't the sound of a child.

Peter Horn had the nursery soundproofed.

"So your wife won't hear your baby crying?" asked the workman.

"Yes," said Pete Horn. "So she won't hear."

They had few visitors. They were afraid that someone might stumble on Py, dear sweet pyramid little Py.

"What's that noise?" asked a visitor one evening, over his cocktail.
"Sounds like some sort of bird. You didn't tell me you had an aviary,
Peter?"

"Oh, yes," said Horn, closing the nursery door. "Have another drink.
Let's drink, everyone."

It was like having a dog or a cat in the house. At least that's how
Polly looked upon it. Peter Horn watched her and observed exactly how
she talked and petted the small Py. It was Py this and Py that, but
somehow with some reserve, and sometimes she would look around the
room and touch herself, and her hands would clench, and she would look
lost and afraid, as if she were waiting for someone to arrive.

In September, Polly reported to her husband: "He can say Father. Yes
he can. Come on, Py. Say, Father!"

She held the blue warm pyramid up.

"Wheely," whistled the little warm blue pyramid.

"Again," repeated Polly.

"Wheely!" whistled the pyramid.

"For God's sake, stop!" said Pete Horn. He took the child from her
and put it in the nursery where it whistled over and over that name, that
name, that name. Horn came out and poured himself a stiff drink. Polly
was laughing quietly.

"Isn't that terrific?" she said. "Even his *voice* is in the fourth dimension. Won't it be nice when he learns to talk later? We'll give him
Hamlet's soliloquy to memorize and he'll say it but it'll come out like
something from James Joyce! Aren't we lucky? Give me a drink."

"You've had enough," he said.

"Thanks, I'll help myself," she said and did.

October, and then November. Py was learning to talk now. He whistled
and squealed and made a bell-like tone when he was hungry. Dr. Wolcott
visited. "When his color is a constant bright blue," said the doctor,
"that means he's healthy. When the color fades, dull—the child is feeling
poorly. Remember that."

"Oh, yes, I will, I will," said Polly. "Robin's-egg blue for health,
dull cobalt for illness."

"Young lady," said Wolcott. "You'd better take a couple of these
pills and come see me tomorrow for a little chat. I don't like the way
you're talking. Stick out your tongue. Ah-hmm. You been drinking?
Look at the stains on your fingers. Cut the cigarettes in half. See you
tomorrow."

"You don't give me much to go on," said Polly. "It's been almost
a year now."

"My dear Mrs. Horn, I don't want to excite you continually. When
we have our mechs ready we'll let you know. We're working every day.

There'll be an experiment soon. Take those pills now and shut that nice mouth." He chucked Py under the "chin." "Good healthy baby, by God! Twenty pounds if he's an *ounce!*"

Baby was conscious of the goings and comings of the two nice White Cubes who were with him during all of his waking hours. There was another cube, a gray one, who visited on certain days. But mostly it was the two White Cubes who cared for and loved him. He looked up at the one warm, rounder, softer White Cube and made the low warbling soft sound of contentment. The White Cube fed him. He was content. He grew. All was familiar and good.

The New Year, the year 1989, arrived.

Rocket ships flashed on the sky, and helicopters whirred and flourished the warm California winds.

Peter Horn carted home large plates of specially poured blue and gray polarized glass, secretly. Through these, he peered at his "child." Nothing. The pyramid remained a pyramid, no matter if he viewed it through X-ray or yellow cellophane. The barrier was unbreakable. Horn returned quietly to his drinking.

The big thing happened early in February. Horn, arriving home in his helicopter, was appalled to see a crowd of neighbors gathered on the lawn of his home. Some of them were sitting, others were standing, still others were moving away, with frightened expressions on their faces.

Polly was walking the "child" in the yard.

Polly was quite drunk. She held the small blue pyramid by the hand and walked him up and down. She did not see the helicopter land, nor did she pay much attention as Horn came running up.

One of the neighbors turned. "Oh, Mr. Horn, it's the cutest thing. Where'd you *find* it?"

One of the others cried, "Hey, you're quite the traveler, Horn. Pick it up in South America?"

Polly held the pyramid up. "Say Father!" she cried, trying to focus on her husband.

"Wheel!" cried the pyramid.

"Polly!" Peter Horn said.

"He's friendly as a dog or a cat," said Polly moving the child with her. "Oh, no, he's not dangerous. He's friendly as a baby. My husband brought him from Afghanistan."

The neighbors began to move off.

"Come back!" Polly waved at them. "Don't you want to see my baby? Isn't he simply beautiful!"

He slapped her face.

"My baby," she said, brokenly.

He slapped her again and again until she quit saying it and collapsed.

He picked her up and took her into the house. Then he came out and took Py in and then he sat down and phoned the Institute.

"Dr. Wolcott, this is Horn. You'd better have your stuff ready. It's tonight or not at all."

There was a hesitation. Finally Wolcott sighed. "All right. Bring your wife and the child. We'll try to have things in shape."

They hung up.

Horn sat there studying the pyramid.

"The neighbors thought he was grand," said his wife, lying on the couch, her eyes shut, her lips trembling . . .

The Institute hall smelled clean, neat, sterile. Dr. Wolcott walked along it, followed by Peter Horn and his wife Polly, who was holding Py in her arms. They turned in at a doorway and stood in a large room. In the center of the room were two tables with large black hoods suspended over them.

Behind the tables were a number of machines with dials and levers on them. There was the faintest perceptible hum in the room. Pete Horn looked at Polly for a moment.

Wolcott gave her a glass of liquid. "Drink this." She drank it. "Now. Sit down." They both sat. The doctor put his hands together and looked at them for a moment.

"I want to tell you what I've been doing in the last few months," he said. "I've tried to bring the baby out of whatever hell dimension, fourth, fifth, or sixth, that it is in. Each time you left the baby for a checkup we worked on the problem. Now, we have a solution, but it has nothing to do with bringing the baby out of the dimension in which *it* exists."

Polly sank back. Horn simply watched the doctor carefully for anything he might say. Wolcott leaned forward.

"I can't bring Py out, but I can put you people *in*. That's it." He spread his hands.

Horn looked at the machine in the corner. "You mean you can send *us* into Py's dimension?"

"If you want to go badly enough."

Polly said nothing. She held Py quietly and looked at him.

Dr. Wolcott explained. "We know what series of malfunctions, mechanical and electrical, forced Py into his present state. We can reproduce those accidents and stresses. But bringing him *back* is something else. It might take a million trials and failures before we got the combination. The combination that jammed him into another space was an accident, but luckily we saw, observed, and recorded it. There are no records for bringing one back. We have to work in the dark. Therefore, it will be easier to put *you* in the fourth dimension than to bring Py into ours."

Polly asked, simply and earnestly, "Will I see my baby as he really is, if I go into his dimension?"

Wolcott nodded.

Polly said, "Then, I want to go."

"Hold on," said Peter Horn. "We've only been in this office five minutes and already you're promising away the rest of your life."

"I'll be with my real baby. I won't care."

"Dr. Wolcott, what will it be like, in that dimension on the other side?"

"There will be no change that *you* will notice. You will both seem the same size and shape to one another. The pyramid will become a baby, however. You will have added an extra sense, you will be able to interpret what you see differently."

"But won't we turn into oblongs or pyramids ourselves? And won't you, doctor, look like some geometrical form instead of a human?"

"Does a blind man who sees for the first time give up his ability to hear or taste?"

"No."

"All right, then. Stop thinking in terms of subtraction. Think in terms of addition. You're gaining something. You lose nothing. You know what a human looks like, which is an advantage Py doesn't have, looking out from his dimension. When you arrive 'over there' you can see Dr. Wolcott as *both* things, a geometrical abstract or a human, as you choose. It will probably make quite a philosopher out of you. There's one other thing, however."

"And that?"

"To everyone else in the world you, your wife and the child will look like abstract forms. The baby a triangle. Your wife an oblong perhaps. Yourself a hexagonal solid. The world will be shocked, not you."

"We'll be freaks."

"You'll be freaks. But you won't know it. You'll have to lead a secluded life."

"Until you find a way to bring all three of us out together."

"That's right. It may be ten years, twenty. I won't recommend it to you, you may both go quite mad as a result of feeling apart, different. If there's a grain of paranoia in you, it'll come out. It's up to you, naturally."

Peter Horn looked at his wife, she looked back gravely.

"We'll go," said Peter Horn.

"Into Py's dimension?" said Wolcott.

"Into Py's dimension."

They stood up from their chairs. "We'll lose no other sense, you're

certain, doctor? Will you be able to understand us when we talk to you?
Py's talk is incomprehensible.''

"Py talks that way because that's what he thinks we sound like when
our talk comes through the dimensions to him. He imitates the sound.
When you are over there and talk to me, you'll be talking perfect English,
because you know *how*. Dimensions have to do with senses and time
and knowledge.''

"And what about Py? When we come into his strata of existence.
Will he see us as humans, immediately, and won't that be a shock to
him? Won't it be dangerous?''

"He's awfully young. Things haven't got too set for him. There'll be
a slight shock, but your odors will be the same, and your voices will
have the same timber and pitch and you'll be just as warm and loving,
which is most important of all. You'll get on with him well.''

Horn scratched his head slowly. "This seems such a long way around
to where we want to go.'' He sighed. "I wish we could have another
kid and forget all about this one.''

"This baby is the one that counts. I dare say Polly here wouldn't want
any other, would you, Polly?''

"This baby, *this* baby,'' said Polly.

Wolcott gave Peter Horn a meaningful look. Horn interpreted it cor-
rectly. This baby or no more Polly ever again. This baby or Polly would
be in a quiet room somewhere staring into space for the rest of her life.

They moved toward the machine together. "I guess I can stand it, if
she can,'' said Horn, taking her hand. "I've worked hard for a good
many years now, it might be fun retiring and being an abstract for
a change.''

"I envy you the journey, to be honest with you,'' said Wolcott, making
adjustments on the large dark machine. "I don't mind telling you that
as a result of your being 'over there' you may very well write a volume
of philosophy that will set Dewey, Bergson, Hegel, or any of the others
on their ears. I might 'come over' to visit you one day.''

"You'll be welcome. What do we need for the trip?''

"Nothing. Just lie on these tables and be still.''

A humming filled the room. A sound of power and energy and warmth.

They lay on the tables, holding hands, Polly and Peter Horn. A double
black hood came down over them. They were both in darkness. From
somewhere far off in the hospital, a voice-clock sang, "Tick tock, seven
o'clock. Tick tock, seven o'clock . . .'' fading away in a little soft gong.

The low humming grew louder. The machine glittered with hidden,
shifting, compressed power.

"Is there any danger?'' cried Peter Horn.

"None!''

The power screamed. The very atoms of the room divided against each other, into alien and enemy camps. The two sides fought for supremacy. Horn gaped his mouth to shout. His insides became pyramidal, oblong with terrific electric seizures. He felt a pulling, sucking, demanding power claw at his body. The power yearned and nuzzled and pressed through the room. The dimensions of the black hood over his torso were stretched, pulled into wild planes of incomprehension. Sweat, pouring down his face, was not sweat, but a pure dimensional essence! His limbs were wrenched, flung, jabbed, suddenly caught. He began to melt like running wax.

A clicking sliding noise.

Horn thought swiftly, but calmly. How will it be in the future with Polly and me and Py at home and people coming over for a cocktail party? How will it be?

Suddenly he knew how it would be and the thought of it filled him with a great awe and a sense of credulous faith and time. They would live in the same white house on the same quiet, green hill, with a high fence around it to keep out the merely curious. And Dr. Wolcott would come to visit, park his beetle in the yard below, come up the steps and at the door would be a tall slim White Rectangle to meet him with a dry martini in its snakelike hand.

And in an easy chair across the room would sit a Salt White Oblong with a copy of Nietzsche open, reading, smoking a pipe. And on the floor would be Py, running about. And there would be talk and more friends would come in and the White Oblong and the White Rectangle would laugh and joke and offer little finger sandwiches and more drinks and it would be a good evening of talk and laughter.

That's how it would be.

Click.

The humming noise stopped.

The hood lifted from Horn.

It was all over.

They were in another dimension.

He heard Polly cry out. There was much light. Then he slipped from the table, stood blinking. Polly was running. She stooped and picked up something from the floor.

It was Peter Horn's son. A living, pink-faced, blue-eyed boy, lying in her arms, gasping and blinking and crying.

The pyramidal shape was gone. Polly was crying with happiness.

Peter Horn walked across the room, trembling, trying to smile himself, to hold on to Polly and the child, both at the same time, and weep with them.

"Well!" said Wolcott, standing back. He did not move for a long

while. He only watched the White Oblong and the slim White Rectangle
holding the Blue Pyramid on the opposite side of the room. An assistant
came in the door.

"Shhh," said Wolcott, hand to his lips. "They'll want to be alone
awhile. Come along." He took the assistant by the arm and tiptoed across
the room. The White Rectangle and the White Oblong didn't even look
up when the door closed.

It was as if a light came on in a green room.

The ocean burned. A white phosphorescence stirred like a breath of steam through the autumn morning sea, rising. Bubbles rose from the throat of some hidden sea ravine.

Like lightning in the reversed green sky of the sea it was aware. It was old and beautiful. Out of the deeps it came, indolently. A shell, a wisp, a bubble, a weed, a glitter, a whisper, a gill. Suspended in its depths were brainlike trees of frosted coral, eyelike pips of yellow kelp, hairlike fluids of weed. Growing with the tides, growing with the ages, collecting and hoarding and saving unto itself identities and ancient dusts, octopus-inks and all the trivia of the sea.

Until now—it was aware.

It was a shining green intelligence, breathing in the autumn sea. Eyeless but seeing, earless but hearing, bodyless but feeling. It was of the sea. And being of the sea it was—feminine.

It in no way resembled man or woman. But it had a woman's ways, the silken, sly, and hidden ways. It moved with a woman's grace. It was all the evil things of vain women.

Dark waters flowed through and by and mingled with strange memory on its way to the gulf streams. In the water were carnival caps, horns, serpentine, confetti. They passed through this blossoming mass of long green hair like wind through an ancient tree. Orange peels, napkins, papers, eggshells, and burnt kindling from night fires on the beaches; all the flotsam of the gaunt high people who stalked on the lone sands of the continental islands, people from brick cities, people who shrieked in metal demons down concrete highways, gone.

It rose softly, shimmering, foaming, into cool morning airs.

The green hair rose softly, shimmering, foaming, into cool morning airs. It lay in the swell after the long time of forming through darkness.

It perceived the shore.

The man was there.

He was a sun-darkened man with strong legs and a cow body.

Each day he should have come down to the water, to bathe, to swim. But he had never moved. There was a woman on the sand with him, a woman in a black bathing suit who lay next to him talking quietly, laughing. Sometimes they held hands, sometimes they listened to a little sounding machine that they dialed and out of which music came.

The phosphorescence hung quietly in the waves. It was the end of the season. September. Things were shutting down.

Any day now he might go away and never return.

Today he must come in the water.

They lay on the sand with the heat in them. The radio played softly and the woman in the black bathing suit stirred fitfully, eyes closed.

The man did not lift his head from where he cushioned it on his muscled left arm. He drank the sun with his face, his open mouth, his nostrils. "What's wrong?" he asked.

"A bad dream," said the woman in the black suit.

"Dreams in the daytime?"

"Don't *you* ever dream in the afternoon?"

"I *never* dream. I've never had a dream in my life."

She lay there, fingers twitching. "God, I had a horrible dream."

"What about?"

"I don't know," she said, as if she really didn't. It was so bad she had forgotten. Now, eyes shut, she tried to remember.

"It was about me," he said, lazily, stretching.

"No," she said.

"Yes," he said, smiling to himself. "I was off with another woman, that's what."

"No."

"I insist," he said. "There I was, off with another woman, and you discovered us, and somehow, in all the mix-up, I got shot or something."

She winced involuntarily. "Don't talk that way."

"Let's see now," he said. "What sort of woman was I with? Gentlemen prefer blondes, don't they?"

"Please don't joke," she said. "I don't feel well."

He opened his eyes. "Did it affect you that much?"

She nodded. "Whenever I dream in the daytime this way, it depresses me something terrible."

"I'm sorry." He took her hand. "Anything I can get you?"

"No."

"Ice-cream cone? Eskimo pie? A Coke?"

"You're a dear, but no. I'll be all right. It's just that, the last four days haven't been right. This isn't like it used to be early in the summer. Something's happened.''

''Not between us,'' he said.

''Oh, no, of course not,'' she said quickly. ''But don't you feel that sometimes *places* change? Even a thing like a pier changes, and the merry-go-rounds, and all that. Even the hot dogs taste different this week.''

''How do you mean?''

''They taste old. It's hard to explain, but I've lost my appetite, and I wish this vacation were over. Really, what I want to do most of all is go home.''

''Tomorrow's our last day. You know how much this extra week means to me.''

''I'll try,'' she said. ''If only this place didn't feel so funny and changed. I don't know. But all of a sudden I just had a feeling I wanted to get up and run.''

''Because of your dream? Me and my blonde and me dead all of a sudden.''

''Don't,'' she said. ''Don't talk about dying that way!''

She lay there very close to him. ''If I only knew what it was.''

''There.'' He stroked her. ''I'll protect you.''

''It's not me, it's you,'' her breath whispered in his ear. ''I had the feeling that you were tired of me and went away.''

''I wouldn't do that; I love you.''

''I'm silly.'' She forced a laugh. ''God, what a silly thing I am.''

They lay quietly, the sun and sky over them like a lid.

''You know,'' he said, thoughtfully, ''I get a little of that feeling you're talking about. This place has changed. There *is* something different.''

''I'm glad you feel it, too.''

He shook his head, drowsily, smiling softly, shutting his eyes, drinking the sun. ''Both crazy. Both crazy.'' Murmuring. ''Both.''

The sea came in on the shore three times, softly.

The afternoon came on. The sun struck the skies a grazing blow. The yachts bobbed hot and shining white in the harbor swells. The smells of fried meat and burnt onion filled the wind. The sand whispered and stirred like an image in a vast, melting mirror.

The radio at their elbow murmured discreetly. They lay like dark arrows on the white sand. They did not move. Only their eyelids flickered with awareness, only their ears were alert. Now and again their tongues might slide along their baking lips. Sly prickles of moisture appeared on their brows to be burned away by the sun.

He lifted his head, blindly, listening to the heat.

The radio sighed.

He put his head down for a minute.

She felt him lift himself again. She opened one eye and he rested on one elbow looking around, at the pier, at the sky, at the water, at the sand.

"What's wrong?" she asked.

"Nothing," he said, lying down again.

"Something," she said.

"I thought I heard something."

"The radio."

"No, not the radio. Something else."

"Somebody *else's* radio."

He didn't answer. She felt his arm tense and relax, tense and relax.

"Dammit," he said. "There it is, again."

They both lay listening.

"I don't hear anything—"

"Shh!" he cried. "For God's sake—"

The waves broke on the shore, silent mirrors, heaps of melting, whispering glass.

"Somebody singing."

"What?"

"I'd swear it was someone singing."

"Nonsense."

"No, listen."

They did that for a while.

"I don't hear a thing," she said, turning very cold.

He was on his feet. There was nothing in the sky, nothing on the pier, nothing on the sand, nothing in the hot-dog stands. There was a staring silence, the wind blowing over his ears, the wind preening along the light, blowing hairs of his arms and legs.

He took a step toward the sea.

"Don't!" she said.

He looked down at her, oddly, as if she were not there. He was still listening.

She turned the portable radio up full, loud. It exploded words and rhythm and melody:

"—I found a million-dollar baby—"

He made a wry face, raising his open palm violently. "Turn it off."

"No, I like it!" She turned it louder. She snapped her fingers, rocking her body vaguely, trying to smile.

It was two o'clock.

The sun steamed the waters. The ancient pier expanded with a loud groan in the heat. The birds were held in the hot sky, unable to move. The sun struck through the green liquors that poured about the pier;

struck, caught and burnished an idle whiteness that drifted in the off-
shore ripples.

The white foam, the frosted coral brain, the kelp pip, the tide dust lay
in the water, spreading.

The dark man still lay on the sand, the woman in the black suit
beside him.

Music drifted up like mist from the water. It was a whispering music
of deep tides and passed years, of salt and travel, of accepted and familiar
strangenesses. The music sounded not unlike water on the shore, rain
falling, the turn of soft limbs in the depths. It was a singing of a time-
lost voice in a caverned seashell. The hissing and sighing of tides in
deserted holds of treasure ships. The sound the wind makes in an empty
skull thrown out on the baked sand.

But the radio on the blanket on the beach played louder.

The phosphorescence, light as a woman, sank down, tired, from sight.
Only a few more hours. They might leave at any time. If only he would
come in, for an instant, just an instant. The mists stirred silently, aware
of his face and his body in the water, deep under. Aware of him caught,
held, as they sank ten fathoms down, on a sluice that bore them twisting
and turning in frantic gesticulations, to the depths of a hidden gulf in
the sea.

The heat of his body, the water taking fire from his warmth, and the
frosted coral brain, the jeweled dusts, the salted mists feeding on his hot
breath from his open lips.

The waves moved the soft and changing thoughts into the shallows
which were tepid as bath waters from the two o'clock sun.

He mustn't go away. If he goes now, he'll not return.

Now. The cold coral brain drifted, drifted. *Now.* Calling across the hot
spaces of windless air in the early afternoon. *Come down to the water.*
Now, said the music. *Now.*

The woman in the black bathing suit twisted the radio dial.

"Attention!" cried the radio. "Now, today, you can buy a new car
at—"

"Jesus!" The man reached over and tuned the scream down. "Must
you have it so loud!"

"I like it loud," said the woman in the black bathing suit, looking
over her shoulder at the sea.

It was three o'clock. The sky was all sun.

Sweating, he stood up. "I'm going in," he said.

"Get me a hot dog first?" she said.

"Can't you wait until I come out?"

"Please." She pouted. "*Now.*"

"Everything on it?"

"Yes, and bring *three* of them."

"Three? God, what an appetite!" He ran off to the small café.

She waited until he was gone. Then she turned the radio off. She lay listening a long time. She heard nothing. She looked at the water until the glints and shatters of sun stabbed through her eyes like needles.

The sea had quieted. There was only a faint, far and fine net of ripples giving off sunlight in infinite repetition. She squinted again and again at the water, scowling.

He bounded back. "Damn, but the sand's hot; burns my feet off!" He flung himself on the blanket. "Eat 'em up!"

She took the three hot dogs and fed quietly on one of them. When she finished it, she handed him the remaining two. "Here, you finish them. My eyes are bigger than my stomach."

He swallowed the hot dogs in silence. "Next time," he said, finishing, "don't order more than you can use. Helluva waste."

"Here," she said, unscrewing a thermos, "you must be thirsty. Finish our lemonade."

"Thanks." He drank. Then he slapped his hands together and said, "Well, I'll go jump in the water now." He looked anxiously at the bright sea.

"Just one more thing," she said, just remembering it. "Will you buy me a bottle of suntan oil? I'm all out."

"Haven't you some in your purse?"

"I used it all."

"I wish you'd told me when I was up there buying the hot dogs," he said. "But, okay." He ran back, loping steadily.

When he was gone, she took the suntan bottle from her purse, half full, unscrewed the cap, and poured the liquid into the sand, covering it over surreptitiously, looking out at the sea, and smiling. She rose then and went down to the edge of the sea and looked out, searching the innumerable small and insignificant waves.

You can't have him, she thought. Whoever or whatever you are, he's mine, and you can't have him. I don't know what's going on; I don't know anything, really. All I know is we're going on a train tonight at seven. And we won't be here tomorrow. So you can just stay here and wait, ocean, sea, or whatever it is that's wrong here today.

Do your damnedest; you're no match for me, she thought. She picked up a stone and threw it at the sea.

"There!" she cried. "You."

He was standing beside her.

"Oh?" She jumped back.

"Hey, what gives? You standing here, muttering?"

"Was I?" She was surprised at herself. "Where's the suntan oil? Will you put it on my back?"

He poured a yellow twine of oil and massaged it onto her golden back. She looked out at the water from time to time, eyes sly, nodding at the water as if to say, "Look! You see? Ah-ha!" She purred like a kitten.

"There." He gave her the bottle.

He was half into the water before she yelled.

"Where are you going! Come here!"

He turned as if she were someone he didn't know. "For God's sake, what's wrong?"

"Why, you just finished your hot dogs and lemonade—you can't go in the water now and get cramps!"

He scoffed. "Old wives' tales."

"Just the same, you come back up on the sand and wait an hour before you go in, do you hear? I won't have you getting a cramp and drowning."

"Ah," he said, disgusted.

"Come along." She turned, and he followed, looking back at the sea.

Three o'clock. Four.

The change came at four ten. Lying on the sand, the woman in the black suit saw it coming and relaxed. The clouds had been forming since three. Now, with a sudden rush, the fog came in from off the bay. Where it had been warm, now it was cold. A wind blew up out of nothing. Darker clouds moved in.

"It's going to rain," she said.

"You sound absolutely pleased," he observed, sitting with arms folded. "Maybe our last day, and you sound pleased because it's clouding up."

"The weatherman," she confided, "said there'd be thunder showers all tonight and tomorrow. It might be a good idea to leave tonight."

"We'll stay, just in case it clears. I want to get one more day of swimming in, anyway," he said. "I haven't been in the water yet today."

"We've had so much fun talking and eating, time passes."

"Yeah," he said, looking at his hands.

The fog flailed across the sand in soft strips.

"There," she said. "That was a raindrop on my nose!" She laughed ridiculously at it. Her eyes were bright and young again. She was almost triumphant. "Good old rain."

"Why are you so pleased? You're an odd duck."

"Come on, rain!" she said. "Well, help me with these blankets. We'd better run!"

He picked up the blankets slowly, preoccupied. "Not even one last swim, dammit. I've a mind to take just one dive." He smiled at her. "Only a minute!"

"No." Her face paled. "You'll catch cold, and I'll have to nurse you!"

"Okay, okay." He turned away from the sea. Gentle rain began to fall.

Marching ahead of him, she headed for the hotel. She was singing softly to herself.

"Hold on!" he said.

She halted. She did not turn. She only listened to his voice far away.

"There's someone out in the water!" he cried. "Drowning!"

She couldn't move. She heard his feet running.

"Wait here!" he shouted. "I'll be right back! There's someone there! A woman, I think!"

"Let the lifeguards get her!"

"Aren't any! Off duty; late!" He ran down to the shore, the sea, the waves.

"Come back!" she screamed. "There's no one out there! Don't, oh, don't!"

"Don't worry, I'll be right back!" he called. "She's drowning out there, see?"

The fog came in, the rain pattered down, a white flashing light raised in the waves. He ran, and the woman in the black suit ran after him, scattering beach implements behind her, crying, tears rushing from her eyes. "Don't!" She put out her hands.

He leaped into an onrushing dark wave.

The woman in the black bathing suit waited in the rain.

At six o'clock the sun set somewhere behind black clouds. The rain rattled softly on the water, a distant drum snare.

Under the sea, a move of illuminant white.

The soft shape, the foam, the weed, the long strands of strange green hair lay in the shallows. Among the stirring glitter, deep under, was the man.

Fragile. The foam bubbled and broke. The frosted coral brain rang against a pebble with thought, as quickly lost as found. Men. Fragile. Like dolls, they break. Nothing, nothing to them. A minute under water and they're sick and pay no attention and they vomit out and kick and then, suddenly, just lie there, doing nothing. Doing nothing at all. Strange. Disappointing, after all the days of waiting.

What to do with him now? His head loils, his mouth opens, his eyelids loosen, his eyes stare, his skin pales. Silly man, wake up! Wake up!

The water surged about him.

The man hung limply, loosely, mouth agape.

The phosphorescence, the green hair weed withdrew.

He was released. A wave carried him back to the silent shore. Back to his wife, who was waiting for him there in the cold rain.

The rain poured over the black waters.

Distantly, under the leaden skies, from the twilight shore, a woman screamed.

Ah—the ancient dusts stirred sluggishly in the water—isn't that *like* a woman? Now, *she* doesn't want him, either!

At seven o'clock the rain fell thick. It was night and very cold and the hotels all along the sea had to turn on the heat.

It was in the Depression, deep down in the empty soul of the Depression in 1932, when we were heading west by 1928 Buick, that my mother, father, my brother Skip, and I came upon what we ever after called the Inspired Chicken Motel.

It was, my father said, a motel straight out of Revelations. And the one strange chicken at that motel could no more help making said Revelations, writ on eggs, than a holy roller can help going wild with utterances of God, Time, and Eternity writhing along his limbs, seeking passage out the mouth.

Some creatures are given to talents inclined one way, some another. But chickens are the greatest dumb brute mystery of them all. Especially hens who think or intuit messages calcium-scrawled forth in a nice neat hand upon the shells wherein their offspring twitch asleep.

Little did we know that long autumn of 1932, as we blew tires and flung fan belts like lost garters down Highway 66, that somewhere ahead that motel, and that most peculiar chicken, were waiting.

Along the way, our family was a wonderful nest of amiable contempt. Holding the maps, my brother and I knew we were a helluva lot smarter than Dad, Dad knew he was smarter than Mom, and Mom knew she could brain the whole bunch, any time.

That makes for perfection.

I mean, any family that has a proper disrespect, each for the other, can stay together. As long as there is something to fight about, people will come to meals. Lose that and the family disintegrates.

So we leaped out of bed each day hardly able to wait to hear what dumb thing someone might say over the hard-fried bacon and the under-fried scrambleds. The toast was too dark or too light. There was jam for only one person. Or it was a flavor that two out of four hated. Hand us a set of bells and we could ring all the wrong changes. If Dad claimed he was still growing, Skip and I ran the tape measure out to prove he'd shrunk during the night. That's humanity. That's nature. That's family.

But like I said, there we were grousing down Illinois, quarreling through the leaf change in the Ozarks autumn where we stopped sniping all of ten minutes to see the fiery colors. Then, pot-shotting and sniveling across Kansas and Oklahoma we plowed into a fine deep-red muck and slid off the road on a detour where each of us could bless himself and blame others for the excavations, the badly painted signs, and the lack of brakeage in our old Buick. Out of the ditch, we unloaded ourselves into a great Buck-a-Night Bungalow Court in a murderers' ambush behind a woods and on the rim of a deep rock-quarry where our bodies might be found years later at the bottom of a lost and sourceless lake, and spent the night counting the rain that leaked in through the shingle-sieve roof and fighting over who had the most covers on the wrong side of the bed.

The next day was even better. We steamed out of the rain into 100-degree heat that took the sap and spunk out of us, save for a few ricochet slaps Dad threw at Skip but landed on me. By noon we were sweated fresh out of contempt, and were settling into a rather refined if exhausted period of familiar insult, when we drove up by this chicken farm outside Amarillo, Texas.

We sat up, instantly.

Why?

Because we found that chickens are kicked the same as families kick each other, to get them out of the way.

We saw an old man boot a rooster and smile as he came toward the auto gate. We all beamed. He leaned in to say he rented rooms for fifty cents a night, the price being low because the smell was high.

The starch being out of Dad, and him sunk in a despond of good will, and this looking like another dandy place to raise grouse, he turned in his chauffeur's cap and shelled out fifty cents in nickels and pennies.

Our great expectations were not punctured. The flimsy room we moved into was a beaut. Not only did all the springs give injections wherever you put flesh down, but the entire bungalow suffered from an oft-rehearsed palsy. Its foundations were still in shock from the thousand mean invaders who had cried "Timber!" and fallen upon the impaling beds.

By its smell, some wild parties had died here. There was an odor of false sincerity and lust masquerading as love. A wind blew up between the floorboards redolent of chickens under the bungalow who spent nights running crazy from diarrhea induced by pecking the bathtub liquor that seeped down through the fake Oriental linoleum.

Anyway, once we had hunched in out of the sun and slunk through a cold pork-and-beans-on-bread lunch, with white oleomargarine greasing it down the ways, my brother and I found a desert creek nearby and heaved rocks at each other to cool off. That night we went into town and found a greasy spoon and read the flyspecks and fought off the crickets that came into the café to skinnydip in the soup. We saw a ten-cent James Cagney gangster movie and came out heading back to the chicken ranch delighted with all the mayhem, the Great Depression gone and forgotten.

At eleven that hot night everyone in Texas was awake because of the heat. The landlady, a frail woman whose picture I had seen in every newsphoto of Dust Bowl country, eroded down to the bones but with a fragile sort of candlelight hollowed in her eyes, came to sit and chat with us about the eighteen million unemployed and what might happen next and where we were going and what would next year bring.

Which was the first cool respite of the day. A cold wind blew out of tomorrow. We grew restive. I looked at my brother, he looked at Mom, Mom looked at Dad, and we were a family, no matter what, and we were together tonight, going somewhere.

"Well . . ." Dad took out a road map and unfolded it and showed the lady where he had marked in red ink as if it was a chart of our four lives' territory, just how we would live in the days ahead, just how survive, just how make do, sleep just so, eat how much, and sleep with no dreams guaranteed. "Tomorrow"—he touched the roads with one nicotine-stained finger—"we'll be in Tombstone. Day after that Tucson. Stay in Tucson looking for work. We got enough cash for two weeks there if we cut it close. No jobs there, we move on to San Diego. Got a cousin there in Customs Inspection on the docks. We figure one week in San Diego, three weeks in Los Angeles. Then we've just enough money to head home to Illinois, where we can put in on relief or, who knows, maybe get our job back at the Power and Light Company that laid me off six months ago."

"I see," said the landlady.

And she did see. For all eighteen million people had come along this road and stopped here going somewhere anywhere nowhere and then going back to the nowhere somewhere anywhere they had got lost from in the first place and, not needed, gone wandering away.

"What kind of job are you looking for?" asked the landlady.

And it was a joke. She knew it as soon as she said it. Dad thought about it and laughed. Mother laughed. My brother and I laughed. We all laughed together.

For of course no one asked what *kind* of job, there were just jobs to be found, jobs without names, jobs to buy gas and feed faces and maybe, on occasion, buy ice-cream cones. Movies? They were something to be seen once a month, perhaps. Beyond that, my brother and I snuck in around back theaters or in side doors or down through basements up through orchestra pits or up fire escapes and down into balconies. Nothing could keep us from Saturday matinees except Adolph Menjou.

We all stopped laughing. Sensing that a proper time had come for a particular act, the landlady excused herself, went out, and in a few minutes returned. She brought with her two small gray cardboard boxes. The way she carried them at first it almost seemed she was bearing the family heirlooms or the ashes of a beloved uncle. She sat and held the two small boxes on her aproned lap for a long moment, shielding them quietly. She waited with the inherent sense of drama most people learn when small quick events must be slowed and made to seem large.

And strangely, we were moved by the hush of the woman herself, by the lostness of her face. For it was a face in which a whole lifetime of lostness showed. It was a face in which children, never born, gave cry. Or it was a face in which children, born, had passed to be buried not in the earth but in her flesh. Or it was a face in which children, born, raised, had gone off over the world never to write. It was a face in which her life and the life of her husband and the ranch they lived on struggled to survive and somehow managed. God's breath threatened to blow out her wits, but somehow, with awe at her own survival, her soul stayed lit.

Any face like that, with so much loss in it, when it finds something to hold and look at, how can you help but pay attention?

For now our landlady was holding out the boxes and opening the small lid of the first.

And inside the first box . . .

"Why," said Skip, "it's just an egg . . ."

"Look close," she said.

And we all looked close at the fresh white egg lying on a small bed of aspirin-bottle cotton.

"Hey," said Skip.

"Oh, yeah," I whispered. "Hey."

For there in the center of the egg, as if cracked, bumped and formed by mysterious nature, was the skull and horns of a longhorn steer.

It was as fine and beautiful as if a jewelsmith had worked the egg some magic way to raise the calcium in obedient ridges to shape that skull and those prodigious horns. It was, therefore, an egg any boy would have proudly worn on a string about his neck or carried to school for friends to gasp over and appraise.

"This egg," said our landlady, "was laid, with this design on it, exactly three days ago."

Our hearts beat once or twice. We opened our mouths to speak. "It—"

She shut the box. Which shut our mouths. She took a deep breath, half closed her eyes, then opened the lid of the second box.

Skip cried, "I bet I know what's—"

His guess would have been right.

In the second box, revealed, lay a second fat white egg on cotton.

"There," said the lady who owned the motel and the chicken ranch way out in the middle of the land under a sky that went forever and fell over the horizon into more land that went on forever and more sky over that.

We all bent forward, squinting.

For there were words written on this egg in white calcium outline, as if the nervous system of the chicken, moved by strange night talks that only it could hear, had lettered the shell in painful half-neat inscriptions.

And the words we saw upon the egg were these:

REST IN PEACE. PROSPERITY IS NEAR.

And suddenly it was very quiet.

We had begun to ask questions about that first egg. Our mouths had jumped wide to ask: How could a chicken, in its small insides, make marks on shells? Was the hen's wristwatch machinery tampered with by outside influences? Had God used that small and simple beast as a Ouija board on which to spell out shapes, forms, remonstrances, unveilings?

But now, with the second egg before us, our mouths stayed numbly shut.

REST IN PEACE. PROSPERITY IS NEAR.

Dad could not take his eyes from that egg.

Nor could any of us.

Our lips moved at last, saying the words soundlessly.

Dad looked up, once, at our landlady. She gazed back at him with a gaze that was as calm, steady, and honest as the plains were long, hot, empty, and dry. The light of fifty years withered and bloomed there. She neither complained nor explained. She had found an egg beneath a hen. Here the egg was. Look at it, her face said. Read the words. Then . . . please . . . read them again.

We inhaled and exhaled.

Dad turned slowly at last and walked away. At the screen door he looked back and his eyes were blinking rapidly. He did not put his hand up to his eyes, but they were wet and bright and nervous. Then he went out the door and down the steps and between the old bungalows, his hands deep in his pockets.

My brother and I were still staring at that egg, when the landlady closed the lid, carefully, rose, and went to the door. We followed, silent.

Outside, we found Dad standing in the last of the sun and the first of the moon by the wire fence. We all looked over at ten thousand chickens veering this way and that in tides, suddenly panicked by wind or startled by cloud shadows or dogs barking off on the prairie, or a lone car moving on the hot-tar road.

"There," said our landlady. "There she is."

She pointed at the sea of rambling fowl.

We saw thousands of chickens hustling, heard thousands of bird voices suddenly raised, suddenly dying away.

"There's my pet, there's my precious. See?"

She held her hand steady, moving it slowly to point to one particular hen among the ten thousand. And somewhere in all the flurry . . .

"Isn't she *grand?*" said our landlady.

I looked, I stood on tiptoe, I squinted. I stared wildly.

"There! I think—!" cried my brother.

"The white one," supplied our landlady, "with ginger flecks."

I looked at her. Her face was very serene. She knew her hen. She knew the look of her love. Even if we could not find and see, the hen was there, like the world and the sky, a small fact in much that was large.

"There," said my brother, and stopped, confused. "No, there. No, wait . . . over *there!*"

"Yeah," I said. "I see him!"

"Her, you dimwit!"

"Her!" I said.

And for a brief moment I thought I *did* see one chicken among many, one grand bird whiter than the rest, plumper than the rest, happier than the rest, faster, more frolicsome and somehow strutting proud. It was as if the sea of creatures parted before our Bible gaze to show us, alone among island shadows of moon on warm grass, a single bird transfixed for an instant before a final dog bark and a rifle shot from a passing car exhaust panicked and scattered the fowls. The hen was gone.

"You *saw?*" asked the landlady, holding to the wire fence, searching for her love lost in the rivering hens.

"Yes." I could not see my father's face, whether it was serious or if he gave a dry smile to himself. "I saw."

He and mother walked back to our bungalow.

But the landlady and Skip and I stayed on at the fence not saying anything, not even pointing anymore, for at least another ten minutes.

Then it was time for bed.

I lay there wide awake with Skip. For I remembered all the other nights when Dad and Mom talked and we liked to listen to them talk about grown-up things and grown-up places, Mother asking concerned and Dad answering final and very sure and calm and quiet. Pot of Gold, End of Rainbow. I didn't believe in that. Land of Milk and Honey. I didn't believe in that. We had traveled far and seen too much for me to believe . . . but . . .

Someday My Ship Will Come in . . .

I believed that.

Whenever I heard Dad say it, tears welled in my eyes. I had seen such ships on Lake Michigan summer morns coming in from festivals across the water full of merry people, confetti on the air, horns blowing, and in my private dream, projected on my bedroom wall through countless nights, there we stood on the dock, Mom, Dad, Skip, and I! and the ship huge, snow-white, coming in with millionaires on her upper decks tossing not confetti but greenbacks and gold coins down in a clattering rain all around, so we danced to catch and dodge and cry Ouch! when hit about the ears by especially fierce coins or laughed when licked by a snow flurry of cash . . .

Mom asked about it. Dad answered. And in the night, Skip and I went down in the same dream to wait on a dock.

And this night here, lying in bed, after a long while I said, "Dad? What does it mean?"

"What does *what* mean?" said Dad, way over there in the dark with Mom.

"The message on the egg. Does it mean the Ship? It'll come in soon?"

There was a long silence.

"Yes," said Dad. "That's what it means. Go to sleep, Doug."

"Yes, sir."

And, weeping tears, I turned away.

We drove out of Amarillo at six the next morning in order to beat the heat, and for the first hour out we didn't say anything because we weren't awake, and for the second hour we said nothing because we were thinking about the night before. And then at last Dad's coffee started perking in him and he said:

"Ten thousand."

We waited for him to go on and he did, shaking his head slowly:

"Ten thousand dumb chickens. And *one* of them, out of nowhere, takes it to mind to scribble us a note."

"Dad," said Mom.

And her voice by its inflection said, You don't really *believe?*

"Yeah, Dad," said my brother in the same voice, with the same faint criticism.

"It's something to think about," said Dad, his eyes just on the road, riding easy, his hands on the wheel not gripping tight, steering our small raft over the desert. Just beyond the hill was another hill and beyond that another hill, but just beyond *that* . . .?

Mother looked over at Dad's face and hadn't the heart to say his name in just that way right now. She looked back at the road and said so we could barely hear it:

"How did it go again?"

Dad took us around a long turn in the desert highway toward White Sands, and then he cleared his throat and cleared a space on the sky ahead as he drove and said, remembering:

"Rest in Peace. Prosperity Is Near."

I let another mile go by before I said, "How much . . . unh. How much . . . an egg like that worth, Dad?"

"There's no putting a human price on a thing like that," he said, not looking back, just driving for the horizon, just going on. "Boy, you can't set a price on an egg like that, laid by an inspired chicken at the Inspired Chicken Motel. Years from now, that's what we'll call it. The Inspired Chicken Motel."

We drove on at an even forty miles an hour into the heat and dust of day-after-tomorrow.

My brother didn't hit me, I didn't hit my brother, carefully, secretly, until just before noon when we got out to water the flowers by the side of the road.

At eight thirty that night he heard the sharp crack from the theater down the hall.

Backfire, he thought. No. Gun.

A moment later he heard the great lift and drop of voices like an ocean surprised by a landfall which stopped it dead. A door banged. Feet ran.

An usher burst through his office door, glanced swiftly about as if blind, his face pale, his mouth trying words that would not come.

"Lincoln . . . Lincoln . . ."

Bayes glanced up from his desk.

"What about Lincoln?"

"He . . . he's been *shot.*"

"Good joke. Now—"

"Shot. Don't you understand? Shot. Really shot. For the second time, shot!"

The usher wandered out, holding to the wall.

Bayes felt himself rise. "Oh, for Christ—"

And he was running and passed the usher who, feeling him pass, began to run with him.

"No, no," said Bayes. "It didn't happen. It didn't. It couldn't. It didn't, couldn't . . ."

"Shot," said the usher.

As they made the corridor turn, the theater doors exploded wide and a crowd that had turned mob shouted or yelled or screamed or stunned simply said, "Where is he?" "There!" "Is that him?" "Where?" "Who did it?" "He did? *Him?*" "Hold him!" "Watch out!" "Stop!"

Two security guards stumbled to view, pushed, pulled, twisted now this way and that, and between them a man who struggled to heave back from the bodies, the grasping hands and now the upflung and downfell fists. People snatched, pecked, pummeled, beat at him with packages or frail sun parasols which splintered like kites in a great storm. Women turned in dazed circles seeking lost friends, whimpering. Men, crying out, shoved them aside to squirm through to the center of the push and thrust and backward-pumping guards and the assaulted man who now masked his cut face with splayed fingers.

"Oh God, God." Bayes froze, beginning to believe. He stared upon the scene. Then he sprang forward. "This way! Back inside! Clear off! Here! Here!"

And somehow the mob was breached, a door cracked wide to shove flesh through, then slammed.

Outside, the mob hammered, threatening damnations and scourges unheard of by living men. The whole theatre structure quaked with their muted wails, cries and estimates of doom.

Bayes stared a long moment at the shaken and twisted door-knobs, the chattering locks, then over to the guards and the man slumped between them.

Bayes leaped back suddenly, as if an even fresher truth had exploded there in the aisle.

Dimly, he felt his left shoe kick something which spun skittering like a rat chasing its tail along the carpeting under the seats. He bent to let his blind hand search, grope, find the still-half-warm pistol which, looked at but disbelieved, he shoved in his coat pocket as he backed down the aisle. It was a full half minute before he forced himself to turn and face the inevitable stage and that figure in the center of the stage.

Abraham Lincoln sat in his carved highback chair, his head bent forward at an unfamiliar angle. Eyes flexed wide, he gazed upon nothing. His large hands rested gently on the chair arms, as if he might momentarily shift weight, rise, and declare this sad emergency at an end.

Moving as under a tide of cold water, Bayes mounted the steps.

"Lights, dammit! Give us more lights!"

Somewhere, an unseen technician remembered what switches were for. A kind of dawn grew in the dim place.

Bayes, on the platform, circled the occupant of the chair, and stopped.

Yes. There it was. A neat bullet hole at the base of the skull, behind the left ear.

"*Sic semper tyrannis,*" a voice murmured somewhere.

Bayes jerked his head up.

The assassin, seated now in the last row of the theatre, face down but sensing Bayes' preoccupation with Lincoln, spoke to the floor, to himself:

"*Sic—*"

He stopped. For there was an outraged stir above him. One security guard's fist flew up, as if the man had nothing to do with it. The fist, urgent to itself, was on its way down to silence the killer when—

"Stop!" said Bayes.

The fist paused halfway, then withdrew to be nursed by the guard with mixtures of anger and frustration.

None, thought Bayes, I believe none of it. Not that man, not the guards and not . . . he turned to again see the bullet hole in the skull of the slain leader.

From the hole a slow trickle of machinery oil dripped.

From Mr. Lincoln's mouth, a similar slow exudation of liquid moved down over the chin and whiskers to rain drop by drop upon his tie and shirt.

Bayes knelt and put his ear to the figure's chest.

Faintly within there was the whine and hum of wheels, cogs, and circuitries still intact but malfunctioning.

For some reason this sound reared him to his feet in alarm.

"Phipps . . .!?"

The guards blinked with incomprehension.

Bayes snapped his fingers. "Is Phipps coming in tonight? Oh God, he mustn't see this! Head him off! Tell him there's an emergency, yes, emergency at the machine plant in Glendale! Move!"

One of the guards hurried out the door.

And watching him run, Bayes thought, please, God, keep Phipps *home*, keep him off . . .

Strange, at such a time, not your own life but the lives of others flashed by.

Remember . . . that day five years past when Phipps first slung his blueprints, his paintings, his watercolors out on a table and announced his Grand Plan? And how they had all stared at the plans and then up at him and gasped:

Lincoln?

Yes! Phipps had laughed like a father just come from a church where some sweet high vision in some strange Annunciation has promised him a most peculiar son.

Lincoln. That was the idea. Lincoln born again.

And Phipps? He would both engender and nurture this fabulous ever-ready giant robot child.

Wouldn't it be fine . . . if they could stand in the meadow fields of Gettysburg, listen, learn, see, hone the edge of their razor souls, and *live?*

Bayes circled the slumped figure in the chair and, circling, numbered the days and remembered years.

Phipps, holding up a cocktail glass one night, like a lens that simultaneously proportions out the light of the past and the illumination of the future:

"I have always wanted to do a film on Gettysburg and the vast crowd there and far away out at the edge of that sun-drowsed impatient lost thick crowd, a farmer and his son trying so hard to hear, not hearing, trying to catch the wind-blown words from the tall speaker there on the distant stand, that gaunt man in the stovepipe hat who now takes off his hat, looks in it as to his soul rummaged there on scribbled letterbacks and begins to speak.

"And this farmer, in order to get his son up out of the crush, why, he hefts the boy up to sit upon his shoulders. There the boy, nine years old, a frail encumbrance, becomes ears to the man, for the man indeed cannot hear nor see but only guess what the President is speaking far across a sea of people there at Gettysburg and the President's voice is high and drifts now clear, now gone, seized and dispersed by contesting breeze and wind. And there have been too many speakers before him and the crowd all crumpled wool and sweat, all mindless stockyard squirm and jostled elbow, and the farmer talks up to his son on his shoulders in a yearning whisper: What? What's he *say?* And the boy, tilting his head, leaning his peach-fuzz ear to the wind, replies:

" 'Fourscore and seven years . . .' "

"Yes?"

" '. . . ago, our fathers brought forth . . .' "

"Yes, yes!?"

" '. . . on this continent . . .' "

"Eh?"

"Continent! 'A new nation, conceived in liberty, and dedicated to the proposition that all men are . . .'

"And so it goes, the wind leaning against the frail words, the far man uttering, the farmer never tiring of his sweet burden of son and the son obedient cupping and catching and telling it all down in a fierce good whisper and the father hearing the broken bits and some parts missing and some whole but all fine somehow to the end . . .

" '. . . of the people, by the people, for the people, shall not perish from the earth.'

"The boy stops whispering.

"It is done.

"And the crowd disperses to the four directions. And Gettysburg is history.

"And for a long time the father cannot bring himself to ease his translator of the wind down to set him on the earth, but the boy, changed, comes down at last . . ."

Bayes sat looking at Phipps.

Phipps slugged down his drink, suddenly chagrined at his own expansiveness, then snorted:

"I'll never make that film. But I will make *this!*"

And that was the moment he pulled forth and unfolded the blueprints of the Phipps Eveready Salem, Illinois, and Springfield Ghost Machine, the Lincoln mechanical, the electro-oil-lubricated plastic India-rubber perfect-motioned and outspoken dream.

Phipps and his born-full-tall-at-birth Lincoln. Lincoln. Summoned live from the grave of technology, fathered by a romantic, drawn by need, slapped to life by small lightnings, given voice by an unknown actor, to be placed there to live forever in this far southwest corner of old-new America! Phipps and Lincoln.

And that was the day, yes, of the first wild bursts of laughter which Phipps ignored by simply saying, "We must, oh we must, stand all of us, downwind from Gettysburg. It's the only hearing place."

And he shared out his pride amongst them. This man he gave armatures, to that the splendid skull, another must trap the Ouija-spirit voice and sounding word, yet others must grow the precious skin, hair, and fingerprints. Yes, even Lincoln's *touch* must be borrowed, copied, the same!

Derision then was their style of life.

Abe would never really speak, they all knew that, nor move. It would all be summed and written off with taxes as a loss.

But as the months lengthened into years, their outcries of hilarity turned to accepting smiles and stunned wild grins. They were a gang of boys caught up in some furtive but irritably joyous mortuary society who met midnights in marble vaults to disperse through graveyards at dawn.

The Lincoln Resurrection Brigade yeasted full and prospered. Instead of one mad fool, a dozen maniacs fell to rifling old mummy-dust newsfiles, begging and then pilfering death masks, burying and then digging up new plastic bones.

Some toured the Civil War battlefields in hopes that history, borne on some morning wind, might whip their coats like flags. Some prowled the October fields of Salem, starched brown with farewell summer, sniffing airs, pricking ears, alert for some lank lawyer's unrecorded voice, anxious for echoes, pleading their case.

And none more anxious nor paternal-proud worrying than Phipps until the month when the robot was spread out on delivery tables, there to be ball and socketed, voice box locked in, rubber eyelids peeled back to sink therein the deep sad eyes which, gazing out, had seen too much. The generous ears were appended that might hear only time lost. The large-knuckled hands were hung like pendulums to guess that time. And then upon the tall man's nakedness they shucked on suiting, buttoned buttons, fixed his tie, a gathering of tailors, no, Disciples now on a bright and glorious Easter morn and them on Jerusalem's hills ready to roll aside the rock and stand Him forth at their cry.

And in the last hour of the last day Phipps had locked them all out as he finished the final touches on the recumbent flesh and spirit and at last opened the door and, not literally, no, but in some metaphoric sense, asked them to hoist him on their shoulders a last time.

And in silence watched as Phipps called across the old battlefield and beyond, saying the tomb was *not* his place; arise.

And Lincoln, deep in his cool Springfield marbled keep, turned in his slumbers and dreamed himself awake.

And rose up.

And spoke.

A phone rang.

Bayes jerked.

The memories fell away.

The theater phone on one far stage wall buzzed.

Oh, God, he thought, and ran to lift the phone.

"Bayes? This is Phipps. Buck just called and told me to get over there! Said something about Lincoln—"

"No," said Bayes. "You know Buck. Must have called from the nearest bar. I'm here in the theater. Everything's fine. One of the generator's acted up. We just finished repairs—"

"*He's* all right, then?"

"He's great." He could not take his eyes off the slumped body. Oh Christ. Oh God. Absurd.

"I—I'm coming over."

"No, don't!"

"Jesus, why are you *shouting?*"

Bayes bit his tongue, took a deep breath, shut his eyes so he could not see the thing in the chair and said, slowly:

"Phipps, I'm not shouting. There. The lights just came back on. I can't keep the crowd waiting. I swear to you—"

"You're lying."

"Phipps!"

But Phipps had hung up.

Ten minutes, thought Bayes wildly, oh God, he'll be here in ten minutes. Ten minutes before the man who brought Lincoln out of the grave meets the man who put him back in it . . .

He moved. A mad impulse made him wish to run backstage, start the tapes, see how much of the fallen creature would motivate, which limbs jerk, which lie numb—more madness. Time for that tomorrow.

There was only time now for the mystery.

And the mystery was enclosed in the man who sat in the third seat over in the last row back from the stage.

The assassin—he was an assassin, wasn't he? The assassin, what did he look like?

He had seen his face, some few moments ago, hadn't he? And wasn't it a face from an old, a familiar, a faded and put-away daguerreotype? Was there a full mustache? Were there dark and arrogant eyes?

Slowly Bayes stepped down from the stage. Slowly he moved up the aisle and stopped, looking in at that man with his head bent into clutching fingers.

Bayes inhaled then slowly exhaled a question in two words:

"Mr. . . . *Booth?*"

The strange faraway man stiffened, then shuddered and let forth a terrible whisper:

"Yes . . ."

Bayes waited. Then he dared ask:

"Mr. . . . John *Wilkes* Booth?"

To this the assassin laughed quietly. The laugh faded into a kind of dry croak.

"Norman Llewellyn Booth. Only the last name is . . . the same."

Thank God, thought Bayes. I couldn't have stood the other.

Bayes spun and paced up the aisle, stopped, and fixed his eyes to his watch. No time. Phipps was on the freeway now. Any moment, he'd be hammering at the door. Bayes spoke rigidly to the theater wall directly in front of him:

"Why?"

And it was an echo of the affrighted cry of three hundred people who had sat here not ten minutes ago and jumped to terror at the shot.

"Why!?"

"I don't know!" cried Booth.

"Liar!" cried Bayes, in the same breath and instant.

"Too good a chance to miss."

"What?" Bayes whirled.

". . . nothing."

"You don't dare say that again!"

"Because," said Booth, head down, half hid, now light, now dark, jerking into and out of emotions he only sensed as they came, went, rose, faded with barks of laughter and then silence. "Because . . . it's the truth." In awe, he whispered, stroking his cheeks. "I did it. I actually *did* it."

"Bastard!"

Bayes had to keep walking up, around, down the aisles, circling, afraid to stop, afraid he might rush and strike and keep on striking this stupid genius, this bright killer—

Booth saw this and said:

"What are you waiting for? Get it over."

"I will not—!" Bayes forced his yell down to a steady calmness. "I will not be tried for murder because I killed a man who killed another man who wasn't really a man at all, but a machine. It's enough to shoot a thing that seems alive. I won't have some judge or jury trying to figure a law for a man who kills because a humanoid computer was shot. I won't repeat your stupidity."

"Pity," mourned the man named Booth, and saying it, the light went out of his face.

"Talk," said Bayes, gazing through the wall, imagining the night roads, Phipps in his car, and time running out. "You've got five minutes, maybe more, maybe less. Why did you do it, why? Start somewhere. Start with the fact you're a coward."

He waited. The security guard waited behind Booth, creaking uneasily in his shoes.

"Coward, yes," said Booth. "How did you know?"

"I know."

"Coward," said Booth. "That's me. Always afraid. You name it. Things. People. Places. Afraid. People I wanted to hit, but never hit. Things I always wanted, never had. Places I wanted to go, never went. Always wanted to be big, famous, why not? That didn't work either. So, I thought, if you can't find something to be glad about, find something to be sad. Lots of ways to enjoy being sad. Why? Who knows? I just had to find something awful to do and then cry about what I had done. That way you felt you had accomplished something. So, I set out to do something bad."

"You've succeeded."

Booth gazed down at his hands hung between his knees as if they held an old but suddenly remembered and simple weapon.

"Did you ever kill a turtle?"

"What?"

"When I was ten I found out about death. I found out that the turtle, that big dumb rocklike thing, was going to live long after I was dead. I figured if I had to go, the turtle went first. So I took a brick and hit him on the back until I broke his shell and he died . . ."

Bayes slowed in his constant pacing and said, "For the same reason, I once let a butterfly live."

"No," said Booth, quickly, then added, "no, not for the same reason. A butterfly lit on my hand once. The butterfly opened and shut its wings, just resting there. I knew I could crush it. But I didn't because I knew that in ten minutes or an hour some bird would eat it. So I let it just fly away. But turtles?! They lie around backyards and live forever. So I

went and got a brick and I was sorry for months after. Maybe I still
am. Look . . .''

His hands trembled before him.

"And what," said Bayes, "has all this to do with your being here
tonight?"

"Do? What!" cried Booth, looking at Bayes as if *he* were mad.
"Haven't you been *listening?* Great God, I'm jealous! Jealous of anything that works right, anything that's perfect, anything that's beautiful
all to itself, anything that lasts I don't care what it is! Jealous!"

"You can't be jealous of machines."

"Why not, dammit?" Booth clutched the back of the seat in front of
him and slowly pulled himself forward staring at the slumped figure in
that highback chair in the center of the stage. "Aren't machines more
perfect, ninety-nine times out of a hundred than most people you've ever
known? I mean *really?* Don't they do things right? How many people
can you name do things right one third, one half the time? That damned
thing up there, that machine, not only looks perfection, but speaks and
acts perfection. More, if you keep it oiled and wound and fixed it'll be
looking, speaking, acting right and grand and beautiful a hundred, two
hundred years after I'm in the earth! Jealous? Damn right I am!"

"But a machine doesn't *know* what it is."

"I know, *I* feel!" said Booth. "I'm outside it looking in. I'm always
outside things like that. I've never been in. The machine has it. I don't.
It was built to do one or two things exactly on the nose. No matter how
much I learned or knew or tried the rest of my life, no matter what I
did, I could never be as perfect, as fine, as maddening, as deserving of
destruction as that thing up there, that man, that thing, that creature,
that president . . .''

He was on his feet now, shouting at the stage eighty feet away.

Lincoln said nothing. Machinery oil gathered glistening on the floor
under the chair.

"That president—" murmured Booth, as if he had come upon the real
truth at last. "That president. Yes. Lincoln. Don't you see? He died a
long time ago. He can't be alive. He just can't be. It's not right. A
hundred years ago and yet here he is. He was shot once, buried once,
yet here he is going on and on and on. Tomorrow and the day after that
and all the days. So his name being Lincoln and mine Booth . . . I just
had to come . . .''

His voice faded. His eyes had glazed over.

"Sit down," said Bayes, quietly.

Booth sat, and Bayes nodded to the remaining security guard. "Wait
outside, please."

When the guard was gone and there was only Booth and himself and

the quiet thing waiting up there in the chair, Bayes turned slowly at last
and looked at the assassin. He weighed his words carefully and said:
"Good but not good enough."
"What?"
"You haven't given all the reasons why you came here tonight."
"I have!"
"You just think you have. You're kidding yourself. All Romantics do.
One way or the other. Phipps when he invented this machine. You when
you destroyed it. But it all comes down to this . . . very plain and very
simple, you'd love to have your picture in the papers, wouldn't you?"
Booth did not answer, but his shoulder straightened, imperceptibly.
"Like to be seen coast-to-coast on magazine covers?"
"No."
"Get free time on TV?"
"No."
"Be interviewed on radio?"
"No!"
"Like to have trials and lawyers arguing whether a man can be tried
for proxy-murder . . ."
"No!"
". . . that is, attacking, shooting a humanoid machine . . ."
"No!"
Booth was breathing fast now, his eyes moving wildly in his face.
Bayes let more out:
"Great to have two hundred million people talking about you tomor-
row morning, next week, next month, next year!"
Silence.
But a smile appeared, like the faintest drip of saliva, at the corner of
Booth's mouth. He must have felt it. He raised a hand to touch it away.
"Fine to sell your personal true real story to the international syndi-
cates for a fine chunk?"
Sweat moved down Booth's face and itched in his palms.
"Shall I give you the answer to all, all the questions I have just asked?
Eh? Eh? Well," said Bayes, "the answer is—"
Someone rapped on a far theater door.
Bayes jumped. Booth turned to stare.
The knock came, louder.
"Bayes, let me in, this is Phipps," a voice cried outside in the night.
Hammering, pounding, then silence. In the silence, Booth and Bayes
looked at each other like conspirators.
"Let me in, oh Christ, let me in!"
More hammering, then a pause and again the insistent onslaught, a

crazy drum and tattoo, then silence again, the man outside panting, circling perhaps to find another door.

"Where was I?" said Bayes. "No. Yes. The answer to all those questions? Do you get worldwide TV radio film magazine newspaper gossip broadcast publicity . . .?"

A pause.

"No."

Booth's mouth jerked but he stayed silent.

"N," Bayes spelled it, "O."

He reached in, found Booth's wallet, snapped out all the identity cards, pocketed them, and handed the empty wallet back to the assassin.

"No?" said Booth, stunned.

"No, Mr. Booth. No pictures. No coast-to-coast TV. No magazines. No columns. No papers. No advertisement. No glory. No fame. No fun. No self-pity. No resignation. No immortality. No nonsense about triumphing over the dehumanization of man by machines. No martyrdom. No respite from your own mediocrity. No splendid suffering. No maudlin tears. No renunciation of possible futures. No trial. No lawyers. No analysts speeding you up this month, this year, thirty years, sixty years, ninety years after, no stories with double spreads, no money, no."

Booth rose up as if a rope had hauled him tall and stretched him gaunt and washed him pale.

"I don't understand. I—"

"You went to all this trouble? Yes. And I'm ruining the game. For when all is said and done, Mr. Booth, all the reasons listed and all the sums summed, you're a has-been that never was. And you're going to stay that way, spoiled and narcissistic and small and mean and rotten. You're a short man and I intend to squash and squeeze and press and batter you an inch shorter instead of force-growing you, helping you gloat nine feet tall."

"You can't!" cried Booth.

"Oh, Mr. Booth," said Bayes, on the instant, almost happy, "I *can*. I can do anything with this case I wish, and I wish not to press charges. More than that, Mr. Booth, it *never happened*."

The hammering came again, this time on a locked door up on the stage.

"Bayes, for God's sake, let me in! This is Phipps! Bayes! Bayes!"

Booth stared at the trembling, the thundershaken, the rattling door, even while Bayes called very calmly and with an ease that was beautiful:

"Just a moment."

He knew that in a few minutes this calm would pass, something would break, but for now there was this splendidly serene thing he was doing; he must play it out. With fine round tones he addressed the assassin and watched him dwindle and spoke further and watched him shrink.

"It never happened, Mr. Booth. Tell your story, but we'll deny it. You were never here, no gun, no shot, no computerized data-processed assassination, no outrage, no shock, no panic, no mob. Why now, look at your face. Why are you falling back? Why are you sitting down? Why do you shake? Is it the disappointment? Have I turned your fun the wrong way? Good.'' He nodded at the aisle. "And now, Mr. Booth, get out.''

"You can't make—''

"Sorry you said that, Mr. Booth.'' Bayes took a soft step in, reached down, took hold of the man's tie and slowly pulled him to his feet so he was breathing full in his face.

"If you ever tell your wife, any friend, employer, child, man, woman, stranger, uncle, aunt, cousin, if you ever tell even yourself out loud going to sleep some night about this thing you did, do you know what I am going to do to you, Mr. Booth? If I hear one whisper, one word, one breath, I shall stalk you, I shall follow you for a dozen or a hundred or two hundred days, you'll never know what day, what night, what noon, where, when or how but suddenly I'll be there when you least expect and then do you know what I am going to do to you, Mr. Booth? I won't say, Mr. Booth, I can't tell. But it will be awful and it will be terrible and you'll wish you had never been born, that's how awful and terrible it will be.''

Booth's pale face shook, his head bobbed, his eyes peeled wide, his mouth open like one who walks in a heavy rain.

"What did I just say, Mr. Booth? Tell me!''

"You'll kill me?''

"Say it again!''

He shook Booth until the words fell out of his chattered teeth:

"Kill me!''

He held tight, shaking and shaking the man firmly and steadily, holding and massaging the shirt and the flesh beneath the shirt, stirring up the panic beneath the cloth.

So long, Mr. Nobody, and no magazine stories and no fun and no TV, no celebrity, an unmarked grave and you not in the history books, no, now get out of here, get out, run, run before I kill you.

He shoved Booth. Booth ran, fell, picked himself up, and lunged toward a theater door which, on the instant, from outside, was shaken, pounded, riven.

Phipps was there, calling in the darkness.

"The other door,'' said Bayes.

He pointed and Booth wheeled to stumble in a new direction to stand swaying by yet another door, putting one hand out—

"Wait,'' said Bayes.

He walked across the theater and when he reached Booth raised his flat hand up and hit Booth once, hard, a slapping strike across the face. Sweat flew in a rain upon the air.

"I," said Bayes, "I just had to do that. Just once."

He looked at his hand, then turned to open the door.

They both looked out into a world of night and cool stars and no mob.

Booth pulled back, his great dark liquid eyes the eyes of an eternally wounded and surprised child, with the look of the self-shot deer that would go on wounding, being shot by itself forever.

"Get," said Bayes.

Booth darted. The door slammed shut. Bayes fell against it, breathing hard.

Far across the arena at another locked door, the hammering, pounding, the crying out began again. Bayes stared at that shuddering but remote door. Phipps. But Phipps would have to wait. Now . . .

The theater was as vast and empty as Gettysburg in the late day with the crowd gone home and the sun set. Where the crowd had been and was no more, where the Father had lifted the Boy high on his shoulders and where the Boy had spoken and said the words, but the words now, also, gone . . .

On the stage, after a long moment, he reached out. His fingers brushed Lincoln's shoulder.

Fool, he thought standing there in the dusk. Don't. Now, don't. Stop it. Why are you doing this? Silly. Stop. Stop.

And what he had come to find he found. What he needed to do he did. For tears were running down his face.

He wept. Sobs choked his mouth. He could not stop them. They would not cease.

Mr. Lincoln was dead. Mr. Lincoln was *dead!*

And *he* had let his murderer go.

At one minute to nine he should have rolled the wooden Indian back into warm tobacco darkness and turned the key in the lock. But somehow he waited because there were so many lost men walking by in no special direction for no special reason. A few of them wandered in to drift their gaze over the tribal cigars laid out in their neat brown boxes, then glanced up suddenly surprised to find where they were and said, evasively, "Evening, Charlie."

"So it is," said Charlie Moore.

Some of the men wandered off empty-handed, others moved on with a nickel cigar unlit in their mouths.

So it was nine thirty of a Thursday night before Charlie Moore finally touched the wooden Indian's elbow as if disturbing a friend and hating to bother. Gently he maneuvered the savage to where he became watchman of the night. In the shadows, the carved face stared raw and blind through the door.

"Well, Chief, what do you see?"

Charlie followed that silent gaze beyond to the highway that cut through the very center of their lives.

In locust hordes, cars roared up from Los Angeles. With irritation they slowed to thirty miles per hour here. They crept between some three dozen shops, stores, and old livery stables become gas stations, to the north rim of town. There the cars exploded back to eighty, racing like Furies on San Francisco, to teach it violence.

Charlie snorted softly.

A man passed, saw him standing with his silent wooden friend, said, "Last night, eh?" and was gone.

Last night.

There. Someone had dared use the words.

Charlie wheeled to switch off the lights, lock the door and, on the sidewalk, eyes down, freeze.

As if hypnotized, he felt his gaze rise again to the old highway which swept by with winds that smelled a billion years ago. Great bursts of headlight arrived, then cut away in departures of red taillight, like schools of small bright fish darting in the wake of sharks and blind-traveling whales. The lights sank away and were lost in the black hills.

Charlie broke his stare. He walked slowly on through his town as the clock over the Oddfellows Lodge struck the quarter hour and moved on toward ten and still he walked and was amazed and then not amazed anymore to see how every shop was still open long after hours and in every door stood a man or woman transfixed even as he and his Indian brave had been transfixed by a talked-about and dreadful future suddenly become Here Now Tonight.

Fred Ferguson, the taxidermist, kin to the family of wild owls and panicked deer which stayed on forever in his window, spoke to the night air as Charlie passed:

"Hard to believe, ain't it?"

He wished no answer, for he went on, immediately:

"Keep thinking: just can't be. Tomorrow, the highway dead and us dead with it."

"Oh, it won't be that bad," said Charlie.

Ferguson gave him a shocked look. "Wait. Ain't you the one hollered two years ago, wanted to bomb the legislature, shoot the road contractors, steal the concrete mixers and earth-movers when they started the new highway three hundred yards west of here? What you mean, it won't be bad? It will, and you know it!"

"I know," said Charlie Moore, at last.

Ferguson brooded on the near distance.

"Three hundred little bitty yards. Not much, eh? But seeing as how our town is only a hundred yards wide, that puts us, give or take, about two hundred yards from the new superroad. Two hundred yards from people who need nuts, bolts, or house-paint. Two hundred from jokers who barrel down from the mountains with deer or fresh shot alley-cats of all sorts and need the services of the only A-1 taxidermist on the Coast. Two hundred yards from ladies who need aspirin—" He eyed the drugstore. "Haircuts." He watched the red-striped pole spin in its glass case down the street. "Strawberry sodas." He nodded at the malt shop. "You name it."

They named it all in silence, sliding their gaze along the stores, the shops, the arcades.

"Maybe it's not too late."

"Late, Charlie? Hell. Cement's mixed and poured and set. Come dawn they yank the roadblocks both ends of the new road. Governor might cut a ribbon from the first car. Then . . . people might remember Oak

Lane the first week, sure. The second week not so much. A month from now? We'll be a smear of old paint on their right running north, on their left running south, burning rubber. There's Oak Lane! Remember? Ghost town. Oops! It's gone."

Charlie let his heart beat two or three times.

"Fred . . . what you going to do?"

"Stay on awhile. Stuff a few birds the local boys bring in. Then crank the old Tin Lizzie and drive that new superfreeway myself going no-where, anywhere, and so long to you, Charlie Moore."

"Night, Fred. Hope you sleep."

"What, and miss welcoming in the New Year, middle of July . . .?"

Charlie walked and that voice faded behind and he came to the barber-shop where three men, laid out, were being strenuously barbered behind plate glass. The highway traffic slid over them in bright reflections. They looked like they were drowning under a stream of huge fireflies.

Charlie stepped in. Everyone glanced up.

"Anyone got any ideas?"

"Progress, Charlie," said Frank Mariano, combing and cutting, "is an idea can't be stopped with no other idea. Let's yank up the whole damn town, lock, stock, and tar barrel, carry it over, nail it down by that new road."

"We figured the cost last year. Four dozen stores at three thousand dollars average to haul them just three hundred yards west."

"So ends that master plan," muttered someone under a hot-steam towel, buried in inescapable fact.

"One good hurricane would do the job, carriage-free."

They all laughed quietly.

"We should all celebrate tonight," said the man under the hot towel. He sat up, revealing himself as Hank Summers, the groceryman. "Snort a few stiff drinks and wonder where the hell we'll all be this time next year."

"We didn't fight hard enough," said Charlie. "When it started, we didn't pitch in."

"Hell." Frank snipped a hair out of the inside of a fairly large ear. "When times move, not a day passes someone's not hurt. This month, this year, it's our turn. Next time *we* want something, someone else gets stepped on, all in the name of Get Up and Go. Look, Charlie, go form a vigilantes. Mine that new road. But watch out. Just crossing the lanes to place the bomb, you're sure to be run down by a manure truck bound for Salinas."

More laughter, which faded quickly.

"Look," said Hank Summers, and everybody looked. He spoke to his own fly-specked image in the ancient mirror as if trying to sell his twin

on a shared logic. "We lived here thirty years now, you, me, all of us.
Won't kill us to move on. Good God, we're all root and a yard wide.
Graduation. School of hard knocks is throwing us out the door with no
never-mind's and no thank-you's. I'm ready. Charlie, are *you?*"

"Me, now," said Frank Mariano. "Monday morning six a.m. I load
my barbership in a trailer and shoot off after those customers, ninety
miles an hour!"

There was a laugh sounded like the very last one of the day, so Charlie
turned with one superb and mindless drift and was back on the street.

And still the shops stayed open, the lights stayed on, the doors stood
wide, as if each owner was reluctant to go home, so long as that river
out there was flowing and there was the great motion and glint and sound
of people and metal and light in a tide they had grown so accustomed
to it was hard to believe the river bottom would ever know a dry season.

Charlie lingered on, straying from shop to shop, sipping a chocolate
Coke at the malted-milk counter, buying some stationery he couldn't use
from the drugstore under the soft fluttering wood fan that whispered to
itself in the ceiling. He loitered like a common criminal, thieving sights.
He paused in alleys where, Saturday afternoons, gypsy tie salesmen or
kitchenware spielers laid out their suitcase worlds to con the pedestrians.
Then, at last he reached the gas station where Pete Britz, deep in the oil
pit, was mending the dumb brute underside of a dead and uncomplaining
1947 Ford.

At ten o'clock, as if by some secret but mutual consent, all the shops
went dark, all the people walked home, Charlie Moore among them.

He caught up with Hank Summers, whose face was still shining pink
from the shave he hadn't needed. They ambled in silence for a time past
houses where it seemed the whole population was sitting out smoking
or knitting, rocking in chairs or fanning themselves against a nonexistent
hot spell.

Hank laughed suddenly at some private thought. A few paces on, he
decided to make it public:

> *"Yes, we'll gather at the River.*
> *River, River.*
> *Yes, we'll gather at the River*
> *That flows by the Throne of God."*

He half-sang it and Charlie nodded.

"First Baptist Church, when I was twelve."

"The Lord giveth and the Highway Commissioner taketh away," said
Hank, drily. "Funny. Never thought how much a town is people. Doing
things, that is. Under the hot towel back there, thought: what's this place

to me? Shaved, I had the answer. Russ Newell banging a carburetor at the Night Owl Garage? Yep. Allie Mae Simpson . . ."

He swallowed his voice in embarrassment.

Allie Mae Simpson . . . Charlie took up the count in his own mind . . . Allie Mae fixing wet curlicues in old ladies' hair in the bay window of her Vogue Salon . . . Doc Knight stacking pill bottles in the drug emporium cases . . . hardware store laid out in the hot noon sun, Clint Simpson middle of it all, running his hands over, sorting out the million blinks and shines of brass and silver and gold, all the nails, hinges, knobs, all the saws, hammers, and snaked up copper wire and stacks of aluminum foil like the junk shaken free of a thousand boys' pockets in a thousand summers past . . . and then . . .

. . . then there was his own place, warm dark, brown, comfortable, musky as the den of a tobacco smoking bear . . . thick with the humidor smells of whole families of odd-sized cigars, imported cigarettes, snuffs just waiting to be exploded on the air . . .

Take all that away, thought Charlie, you got nothing. Buildings, sure. Anyone can raise a frame, paint a sign to say what might go on inside. But it was people that made the damn thing *get*.

Hank surfaced in his own long thoughts.

"Guess right now I'm sad. Want to send everyone back to open their shops so I can see what they were up to. Why wasn't I looking closer, all these years? Hell, hell. What's got into you, Hank Summers. There's another Oak Lane on up the line or down the line and people there busy as they are here. Wherever I land, next time I'll look close, swear to God. Good-bye, Charlie."

"To hell with good-bye."

"All right, then, good night."

And Hank was gone and Charlie was home and Clara was waiting at the screen door with a glass of ice water.

"Sit out awhile?"

"Like everyone else? Why not?"

They sat in the dark on the porch in the chain-hung wooden swing and watched the highway flush and drain, flush and drain with arrivals of headlight and departures of angry red fire like the coals from an immense brazier scattered to the fields.

Charlie drank the water slowly and, drinking, thought: In the old days you couldn't see the roads die. You felt them gradually fade, yes, lying in bed nights, maybe your mind got hold of some hint, some nudge or commotion that warned you it was sinking away. But it took years and years for any one road to give up its dusty ghost and another to stir alive. That's how things were, slow arriving and slow passing away. That's how things had always been.

But no more. Now, in a matter of hours.

He paused.

He touched in upon himself to find a new thing.

"I'm not mad anymore."

"Good," said his wife.

They rocked awhile, two halves of a similar content.

"My God, I was stirred up there for awhile."

"I remember," she said.

"But now I figure, well . . ." he drifted his voice, mostly to himself. "Millions of cars come through every year. Like it or not, the road's just not big enough, we're holding up the world, that old road there and this old town. The world says it's got to move. So now, on that new road, not one but two million will pass just a shotgun blast away, going where they got to go to get things done they say are important, doesn't matter if they're important or not, folks *think* they are, and thinking makes the game. If we'd really seen it coming, thought in on it from every side, we'd have taken a steam-driven sledge and just mashed the town flat and said, 'Drive through!' instead of making them lay the damn road over in that next clover patch. This way, the town dies hard, strangled on a piece of butcher string instead of being dropped off a cliff. Well, well." He lit his pipe and blew great clouds of smoke in which to poke for past mistakes and present revelations. "Us being human, I guess we couldn't have done but as we did . . ."

They heard the drugstore clock strike eleven and the Oddfellows Hall clock chime eleven thirty, and at twelve they lay in bed in the dark, each with a ceilingful of thoughts above them.

"Graduation."

"What?"

"Frank the barber said it and had it right. This whole week feels like the last days of school, years ago. I remember how I felt, how I was afraid, ready to cry, and how I promised myself to live every last moment right up to the time the diploma was in my hand, for God only knew what tomorrow might bring. Unemployment. Depression. War. And then the day arrived, tomorrow did get around to finally coming, and I found myself still alive, by God, and I was still all in one piece and things were starting over, more of the same, and hell, everything turned out okay. So this is another graduation all right. Frank said, and I'm the last to doubt."

"Listen," said his wife much later. "Listen."

In the night, the river came through the town, the river of metal quiet now but still coming and going with its ancient smells of tidelands and dark seas of oil. Its glimmer, on the ceiling above their graveyard bed, had the shine of small craft gliding upstream and down as their eyelids slowly, slowly shut and their breathing took on the regular sound of the motion of those tides . . . and then they slept.

In the first light of dawn, half the bed lay empty.

Clara sat up, almost afraid.

It was not like Charlie to be gone so early.

Then, another thing frightened her. She sat listening, not certain what had suddenly made her tremble, but before she had a chance to find out why, she heard footsteps.

They came from a long distance away and it was quite awhile before they came up the walk and up the steps and into the house. Then, silence. She heard Charlie just standing there in the parlor for a long moment, so she called out:

"Charlie? Where you been?"

He came into the room in the faint light of dawn and sat on the bed beside her, thinking about where he had been and what he had done.

"Walked a mile up the coast and back. All the way to those wood barricades where the new highway starts. Figured it was the least I could do, be part of the whole darn thing."

"The new road's open . . . ?"

"Open and doing business. Can't you tell?"

"Yes." She rose slowly up in bed, tilting her head, closing her eyes for a moment, listening. "So that's it? That's what bothered me. The old road. It's *really* dead."

They listened to the silence outside the house, the old road gone empty and dry and hollow as a river bottom in a strange season of summers that would never stop, that would go on forever. The stream had indeed moved and changed its course, its banks, its bed, during the night. Now all you could hear were the trees in the blowing wind outside the house and the birds beginning to sing their arousal choirs in the time just before the sun really made it over the hills.

"Be real quiet."

They listened again.

And there, far away, some two hundred fifty or three hundred yards off across a meadow field, nearer the sea, they heard the old, the familiar, but the diminished sound of their river taking its new course, moving and flowing—it would never cease—through lengths of sprawling land away north and then on south through the hushed light. And beyond it, the sound of real water, the sea which might almost have drawn the river to come down along the shore . . .

Charlie Moore and his wife sat not moving for a moment longer, with that dim sound of the river across the fields moving and moving on.

"Fred Ferguson was there before dawn," said Charlie in a voice that already remembered the Past. "Crowd of people. Highway officials and all. Everyone pitched in. Fred, why he just walked over and grabbed hold of one end. I took the other. We moved one of those wood barricades, together. Then we stood back . . . and let the cars through."

Good God in heaven, what's that?"

"What's what?"

"Are you blind, man, look!"

And Garrity, elevator operator, looked out to see what the hall porter was staring at.

And in out of the Dublin morn, sweeping through the front doors of the Royal Hibernian Hotel, along the entryway and to the registry was a tall willowy man of some forty years followed by five short willowy youths of some twenty years, a burst of bird song, their hands flapping all about on the air as they passed, their eyes squinching, batting, and flickering, their mouths pursed, their brows enlightened and then dark, their color flushed and then pale, or was it both?, their voices now flawless piccolo, now flute, now melodious oboe but always tuneful. Carrying six monologues, all sprayed forth upon each other at once, in a veritable cloud of self-commiseration, peeping and twitting the discouragements of travel and the ardors of weather, the *corps de ballet* as it were flew, cascaded, flowed eloquently in a greater bloom of cologne by astonished hall porter and transfixed elevator man. They collided deliciously to a halt at the desk where the manager glanced up to be swarmed over by their music. His eyes made nice round o's with no centers in them.

"What," whispered Garrity, "was that?"

"You may well ask," said the porter.

At which point the elevator lights flashed and the buzzer buzzed. Garrity had to tear his eyes off the summery crowd and heft himself skyward.

"We," said the tall slender man with a touch of gray at the temples, "should like a room, please."

The manager remembered where he was and heard himself say, "Do you have reservations, sir?"

"Dear me, no," said the older man as the others giggled. "We flew in unexpectedly from Taormina," the tall man with the chiseled features and the moist flower mouth continued. "We were getting so awfully bored, after a long summer, and someone said, Let's have a complete change, let's do something wild. What? I said. Well, where's the most improbable place in the world? Let's name it and go there. Somebody said the North Pole, but that was silly. Then I cried, Ireland! Everyone fell down. When the pandemonium ceased we just scrambled for the airport. Now sunshine and Sicilian shorelines are like yesterday's lime sherbet to us, all melted to nothing. And here we are to do . . . something *mysterious!*"

"Mysterious?" asked the manager.

"We don't know what it is," said the tall man. "But we shall know it when we see it, or it happens, or perhaps we shall have to make it happen, right, cohorts?"

The cohorts responded with something vaguely like tee-hee.

"Perhaps," said the manager, with good grace, "if you gave me some idea what you're looking for in Ireland, I could point out—"

"Goodness, no," said the tall man. "We shall just plummet forth with our intuitions scarved about our necks, taking the wind as 'twere and see what we shall tune in on. When we solve the mystery and find what we came to find, you will know of our discovery by the ululations and cries of awe and wonder emanating from our small tourist group."

"You can say *that* again," said the hall porter, under his breath.

"Well, comrades, let us sign in."

The leader of the encampment reached for a scratchy hotel pen, found it filthy, and flourished forth his own absolutely pure 14-carat solid gold pen with which in an obscure but rather pretty cerise calligraphy he inscribed the name DAVID followed by SNELL followed by dash and ending with ORKNEY. Beneath, he added "and friends."

The manager watched the pen, fascinated, and once more recalled his position in all this. "But, sir, I haven't said if we have space—"

"Oh, surely you must, for six miserable wanderers in sore need of respite from overfriendly airline stewardesses—one room would do it!"

"One?" said the manager, aghast.

"We wouldn't mind the crowd, would we, chums?" asked the older man, not looking at his friends.

No, they wouldn't mind.

"Well," said the manager, uneasily fumbling at the registry. "We just happen to have two adjoining—"

"*Perfecto!*" cried David Snell-Orkney.

And the registration finished, the manager behind the desk and the visitors from a far place stood regarding each other in a prolonged silence. At last the manager blurted, "Porter! Front! Take these gentlemen's luggage—"

But just then the hall porter ran over to look at the floor.

Where there was no luggage.

"No, no, none." David Snell-Orkney airily waved his hand. "We travel light. We're here only for twenty-four hours, or perhaps only twelve, with a change of underwear stuffed in our overcoats. Then back to Sicily and warm twilights. If you want me to pay in advance—"

"That won't be necessary," said the manager, handing the keys to the hall porter. "Forty-six and forty-seven, please."

"It's done," said the porter.

And like a collie dog silently nipping the hooves of some woolly longhaired, bleating, dumbly smiling sheep, he herded the lovely bunch toward the elevator which wafted down just at that precise moment.

At the desk, the manager's wife came up, steel-eyed behind him. "Are you mad?" she whispered, wildly. "Why? Why?"

"All my life," said the manager, half to himself, "I have wished to see not one Communist but ten close by, not two Nigerians but twenty in their skins, not three cowboy Americans but a gross fresh from the saddle. So when six hothouse roses come in a bouquet, I could not resist potting them. The Dublin winter is long, Meg; this may be the only lit fuse in the whole year. Stand by for the lovely concussion."

"Fool," she said.

As they watched, the elevator, freighted with hardly more than the fluff from a blown dandelion, whisked up the shaft, away.

It was exactly at high noon that a series of coincidences occurred that tottered and swerved toward the miraculous.

Now the Royal Hibernian Hotel lies half between Trinity College, if you'll excuse the mention, and St. Stephen's Green, which is more like it, and around behind is Grafton Street, where you can buy silver, glass, and linen, or pink hacking coats, boots, and caps to ride off to the goddamned hounds, or better still duck in to Heeber Finn's pub for a proper proportion of drink and talk—an hour of drink to two hours of talk is about the best prescription.

Now the boys most often seen in Finn's are these: Nolan, you know Nolan; Timulty, who could forget Timulty; Mike MaGuire, surely *everyone's* friend; then there's Hannahan, Flaherty, Kilpatrick, and, on occasion, when God seems a bit untidy and Job comes to mind, Father Liam Leary himself, who strides in like Justice and glides forth like Mercy.

Well, that's the lot, and it's high noon, and out of the Hibernian

Hotel front who should come now but Snell-Orkney and his canary five.

Which resulted in the first of a dumfounding series of confrontations.

For passing below, sore torn between the sweet shops and Heeber Finn's, was *Timulty* himself.

Timulty, as you recall, when Blight, Famine, Starvation, and other mean Horsemen drive him, works a day here or there at the post office. Now, idling along between dread employments, he smelled a smell as if the gates of Eden had swung wide again and him invited back in after a hundred million years. So Timulty looked up to see what made the wind blow out of the Garden.

And the wind, of course, was in tumult about Snell-Orkney and his uncaged pets.

"I tell you," said Timulty, years later, "I felt my eyes start as if I'd been given a good bash on the skull. A new part ran down the center of my hair."

Timulty, frozen to the spot, watched the Snell-Orkney delegation flow down the steps and around the corner. At which point he decided on sweeter things than candy and rushed the long way to Finn's.

At that instant, rounding the corner, Mr. David Snell-Orkney-plus-five passed a begger-lady playing a harp in the street. And there, with nothing else to do but dance the time away, was Mike MaGuire himself, flinging his feet about in a self-involved rigadoon to "Lightly o'er the Lea." Dancing, Mike MaGuire heard a sound that was like the passing by of warm weather from the Hebrides. It was not quite a twittering nor a whirr, and it was not unlike a pet shop when the bell tinkles as you step in and a chorus of parakeets and doves start up in coos and light shrieks. But hear he did, above the sound of his own shoes and the pringle of harp. He froze in mid-jig.

As David Snell-Orkney-plus-five swept by all tropic smiled and gave him a wave.

Before he knew what he was doing, Mike waved back, then stopped and seized his wounded hand to his breast. "What the hell am I waving for?" he cried to no one. "I don't know them, *do* I?"

"Ask God for strength!" said the harpist to her harp and flung her fingers down the strings.

Drawn as by some strange new vacuum cleaner that swept all before it, Mike followed the Team down the street.

Which takes care of two senses now, the sense of smell and the use of the ears.

It was at the *next* corner that Nolan, leaving Finn's pub because of an argument with Finn himself, came around the bend fast and ran bang into David Snell-Orkney. Both swayed and grabbed each other for support.

"Top of the afternoon!" said David Snell-Orkney.

"The Back Side of Something!" replied Nolan, and fell away, gaping to let the circus by. He had a terrible urge to rush back to Finn's. His fight with the owner of the pub was obliterated. He wished now to report upon this fell encounter with a feather duster, a Siamese cat, a spoiled Pekingese, and three others gone ghastly frail from undereating and overwashing.

The six stopped outside the pub looking up at the sign.

Ah, God, thought Nolan. They're going in. What will *come* of it? Who do I warn first? Them? Or Finn?

Then, the door opened. Finn himself looked out. Damn, thought Nolan, that spoils it! Now we won't be allowed to describe this adventure. It will be Finn this, Finn that, and shut up to us all! There was a long moment when Snell-Orkney and his cohorts looked at Finn. Finn's eyes did not fasten on them. He looked above. He looked over. He looked beyond.

But he *had* seen them, this Nolan knew. For now a lovely thing happened.

All the color went out of Finn's face.

Then an even lovelier thing happened.

All the color rushed back into Finn's face.

Why, cried Nolan to himself, he's . . . *blushing!*

But still Finn refused to look anywhere save the sky, the lamps, the street, until Snell-Orkney trilled, "Sir, which way to St. Stephen's Green?"

"Jesus," said Finn and turned away. "Who knows *where* they put it, *this* week!" and slammed the door.

The six went on up the street, all smiles and delight, and Nolan was all for heaving himself through the door when a worse thing happened.

Garrity, the elevator operator from the Royal Hibernian Hotel, whipped across the sidewalk from nowhere. His face ablaze with excitement, he ran first into Finn's to spread the word.

By the time Nolan was inside, and Timulty rushing in next, Garrity was all up and down the length of the bar while Finn stood behind it suffering concussions from which he had not as yet recovered.

"It's a shame you missed it!" cried Garrity to all. "I mean it was the next thing to one of them fiction-and-science fillums they show at the Gayety Cinema!"

"How do you mean?" asked Finn, shaken out of his trance.

"*Nothing* they weigh!" Garrity told them. "Lifting them in the elevator was throwing a handful of chaff up a chimney! And you should have *heard.* They're here in Ireland for . . ." He lowered his voice and squinched his eyes. ". . . for *mysterious reasons!*"

"Mysterious!" Everyone leaned in at him.

"They'll put no name to it, but, mark my declaration, they're up to no good! Have you ever seen the like?"

"Not since the great fire at the convent," said Finn. "I—"

But the word "convent" seemed one more magic touch. The doors sprang wide at this. Father Leary entered in reverse. That is to say he backed into the pub one hand to his cheek as if the Fates had dealt him a proper blow unbewares.

Reading the look of his spine, the men shoved their noses in their drinks until such time as the father had put a bit of the brew into himself, still staring as if the door were the gates of Hell ajar.

"Beyond," said the father, at last, "not two minutes gone, I saw a sight as would be hard to credit. In all the days of her collecting up the grievances of the world, has Ireland indeed gone mad?"

Finn refilled the priest's glass. "Was you standing in the blast of *The Invaders from the Planet Venus,* Father?"

"Have you seen them, then, Finn?" the father said.

"Yes, and do you guess them bad, your Holiness?"

"It's not so much bad or good as strange and *outré,* Finn, and words like rococo, I should guess, and baroque if you go with my drift?"

"I lie easy in the tide, sir."

"When last seen, where heading?" asked Timulty.

"On the edge of the Green," said the priest. "You don't imagine there'll be a bacchanal in the park now?"

"The weather won't allow, beg your pardon, Father," said Nolan, "but it strikes me, instead of standing with the gab in our mouth we should be out on the spy—"

"You move against my ethics," said the priest.

"A drowning man clutches at anything," said Nolan, "and ethics may drown with him if *that's* what he grabs instead of a lifebelt."

"Off the Mount, Nolan," said the priest, "and enough of the Sermon. What's your point?"

"The point is, Father, we have had no such influx of honorary Sicilians since the mind boggles to remember. For all we know, at this moment, they may be reading aloud to Mrs. Murphy, Miss Clancy, or Mrs. O'Hanlan in the midst of the park. And reading aloud from *what,* I ask you?"

"*The Ballad of Reading Gaol?*" asked Finn.

"You have rammed the target and sunk the ship," said Nolan, mildly irritated the point had been plucked from him. "How do we know these imps out of bottles are not selling real-estate tracts in a place called Fire Island? Have you *heard* of it, Father?"

"The American gazettes come often to my table, man."

"Well, do you remember the great hurricane of nineteen-and-fifty-six when the waves washed over Fire Island there in New York? An uncle of mine, God save his sanity and sight, was with the Coast Guard there which evacuated the entirety of the population of Fire Island. It was worse than the twice-a-year showing at Fennelly's dressworks, he said. It was more terrible than a Baptist Convention. Ten thousand men came rushing down to the stormy shore carrying bolts of drape material, cages full of parakeets, tomato-and-tangerine-colored sport coats, and lime-colored shoes. It was the most tumultuous scene since Hieronymus Bosch laid down his palette after he painted Hell for all generations to come. You do not easily evacuate ten thousand Venetian-glass boyos with their great blinky cow-eyes and their phonograph symphonic records in their hands and their rings in their ears, without tearing down the middle. My uncle, soon after, took to the heavy drink."

"Tell us *more* about that night," said Kilpatrick, entranced.

"More, hell," said the priest. "Out, I say. Surround the park. Keep your eyes peeled. And meet me back here in an hour."

"That's more like it," cried Kelly. "Let's *really* see what dread thing they're up to!"

The doors banged wide.

On the sidewalk, the priest gave directions. "Kelly, Murphy, you around the north side of the park. Timulty, you to the south. Nolan and Garrity, the east; Moran, MaGuire, and Kilpatrick, the west. Git!"

But somehow or other in all the ruction, Kelly and Murphy wound up at the Four Shamrocks pub halfway to the Green and fortified themselves for the chase, and Nolan and Moran each met their wives on the street and had to run the other way, and MaGuire and Kilpatrick, passing the Elite Cinema and hearing Lawrence Tibbett singing inside, cadged their way in for a few half-used cigarettes.

So it wound up with just two, Garrity on the east and Timulty on the south side of the park, looking in at the visitors from another world.

After half an hour of freezing weather, Garrity stomped up to Timulty and said, "What's *wrong* with the fiends? They're just *standing* there in the midst of the park. They haven't moved half the afternoon. And it's cut to the bone is my toes. I'll nip around to the hotel, warm up, and rush back to stand guard with you, Tim."

"Take your time," called Timulty in a strange sad wandering, philosophical voice as the other charged away.

Left alone, Timulty walked in and sat for a full hour watching the six men who, as before, did not move. You might almost have thought to see Timulty there, with his eyes brooding, and, his mouth gone into a tragic crease, that he was some Irish neighbor of Kant or Schopenhauer, or had just read something by a poet or thought of a song that declined his spirits. And when at last the hour was up and he had gathered his thoughts like a handful of cold pebbles, he turned and made his way out of the park. Garrity was there, pounding his feet and swinging his hands but before he could explode with questions, Timulty pointed in and said, "Go sit. Look. Think. Then *you* tell *me.*"

Everyone at Finn's looked up sheepishly when Timulty made his entrance. The priest was still off on errands around the city, and after a few walks about the Green to assuage their consciences, all had returned, nonplussed, to intelligence headquarters.

"Timulty!" they cried. "Tell us! What? What?"

Timulty took his time walking to the bar and sipping his drink. Silently, he observed his own image remotely buried beneath the lunar ice of the barroom mirror. He turned the subject this way. He twisted it inside out. He put it back wrong-side-to. Then he shut his eyes and said:

"It strikes me as how—"

Yes, said all silently, about him.

"From a lifetime of travel and thought, it comes to the top of my mind," Timulty went on, "there is a strange resemblance between the likes of them and the likes of us."

There was such a gasp as changed the scintillation, the goings and comings of light in the prisms of the little chandeliers over the bar. When the schools of fish-light had stopped swarming at this exhalation, Nolan cried, "Do you mind putting your hat on so I can knock it off!?"

"Consider," Timulty calmly said. "Are we or are we not great ones for the poem and the song?"

Another kind of gasp went through the crowd. There was a warm burst of approval. "Oh, sure, we're *that!*" "My God, is *that* all you're up to?" "We were afraid—"

"Hold it!" Timulty raised a hand, eyes still closed.

And all shut up.

"If we're not singing the songs, we're writing them, and if not writing, dancing them, and aren't *they* fond admirers of the song and the writing of same and the dancing out the whole? Well, just now, I heard them at a distance reciting poems and singing, to themselves, in the Green."

Timulty had something there. Everyone had to paw everybody and admit it.

"Do you find any *other* resemblances?" asked Finn, heavily, glowering.

"I do," said Timulty, with a judge's manner.

There was a still more fascinated indraw of breath and the crowd drew nearer.

"They do not mind a drink now and then," said Timulty.

"By God, he's right!" cried Murphy.

"Also," intoned Timulty, "they do not marry until very late, if ever at all! And—"

But here the tumult was such he had to wait for it to subside before he could finish:

"And they—ah—have very little to do with women."

After that there was a great clamor, a yelling and shoving about and ordering of drinks and someone invited Timulty outside. But Timulty wouldn't even lift one eyelid, and the brawler was held off and when everyone had a new drink in them and the near-fistfights had drained away, one loud clear voice, Finn's, declared:

"Now would you mind explaining the criminal comparison you have just made in the clean air of my honorable pub?"

Timulty sipped his drink slowly and then at last opened his eyes and looked at Finn steadily, and said, with a clear bell-trumpet tone and wondrous enunciation:

"Where in all of Ireland can a man lie down with a woman?"

He let that sink in.

"Three hundred twenty-nine days a damn year it rains. The rest it's so wet there's no dry piece, no bit of land you would dare trip a woman out flat on for fear of her taking root and coming up in leaves, do you deny that?"

The silence did not deny.

"So when it comes to places to do sinful evils and perform outrageous acts of the flesh, it's to Arabia the poor damn fool Irishman must take himself. It's Arabian dreams we have, of warm nights, dry land, and a decent place not just to sit down but to lie down on, and not just lie down on but to roister joyfully about on in clinches and clenches of outrageous delight."

"Ah, Jaisus," said Flynn, "you can say *that* again."

"Ah, Jaisus," said everyone, nodding.

"That's number one." Timulty ticked it off on his fingers. "Place is lacking. Then, second, time and circumstances. For say you should sweet talk a fair girl into the field, eh? in her rainboots and slicker and her shawl over her head and her umbrella over that and you making noises like a stuck pig half over the sty gate, which means you've got one hand in her bosom and the other wrestling with her boots, which is as far as you'll damn well get, for who's standing there behind you, and you feel his sweet spearmint breath on your neck?''

"The father from the local parish?'' offered Garrity.

"The father from the local parish,'' said everyone, in despair.

"There's nails number two and three in the cross on which all Ireland's males hang crucified,'' said Timulty.

"Go on, Timulty, go on.''

"Those fellows visiting here from Sicily run in teams. *We* run in teams. Here we are, the gang, in Finn's, are we *not?*''

"Be damned and we are!''

"*They* look sad and are melancholy half the time and then spitting like happy demons the rest, either up or down, never in between, and who does *that* remind you of?''

Everyone looked in the mirror and nodded.

"If we had the choice,'' said Timulty, "to go home to the dire wife and the dread mother-in-law and the old-maid sister all sour sweats and terrors, or stay here in Finn's for one more song or one more drink or one more story, *which* would all of us men choose?''

Silence.

"Think on that,'' said Timulty. "Answer the truth. Resemblances. Similarities. The long list of them runs off one hand and up the other arm. And well worth the mulling over before we leap about crying Jaisus and Mary and summoning the Guard.''

Silence.

"I,'' said someone, after a long while, strangely, curiously, "would like . . . to see them closer.''

"I think you'll get your wish. Hist!''

All froze in a tableau.

And far off they heard a faint and fragile sound. It was like the wondrous morning you wake and lie in bed and know by a special feel that the first fall of snow is in the air, on its way down, tickling the sky, making the silence to stir aside and fall back in on nothing.

"Ah, God,'' said Finn, at last, "it's the first day of spring . . .''

And it was that, too. First the dainty snowfall of feet drifting on the cobbles, and then a choir of bird song.

And along the sidewalk and down the street and outside the pub came the sounds that were winter *and* spring. The doors sprang wide. The men reeled back from the impact of the meeting to come. They steeled their nerves. They balled their fists. They geared their teeth in their anxious mouths, and into the pub like children come into a Christmas place and everything a bauble or a toy, a special gift or color, there stood the tall thin older man who looked young and the small thin younger men who had old things in their eyes. The sound of snowfall stopped. The sound of spring birds ceased.

The strange children herded by the strange shepherd found themselves suddenly stranded as if they sensed a pulling away of a tide of people, even though the men at the bar had flinched but the merest hair.

The children of a warm isle regarded the short child-sized and runty full-grown men of this cold land and the full-grown men looked back in mutual assize.

Timulty and the men at the bar breathed long and slow. You could smell the terrible clean smell of the children way over here. There was too much spring in it.

Snell-Orkney and his young-old boy-men breathed swiftly as the heart-beats of birds trapped in a cruel pair of fists. You could smell the dusty, impacted, prolonged, and dark-clothed smell of the little men way over here. There was too much winter in it.

Each might have commented upon the other's choice of scent, but—

At this moment the double doors at the side banged wide and Garrity charged in full-blown, crying the alarm:

"Jesus, I've seen everything! Do you know where they are *now,* and what *doing?*"

Every hand at the bar flew up to shush him.

By the startled look in their eyes, the intruders knew they were being shouted about.

"They're still at St. Stephen's Green!" Garrity, on the move, saw naught that was before him. "I stopped by the hotel to spread the news. Now it's your turn. Those fellows—"

"Those fellows," said David Snell-Orkney, "are here in—"He hesitated.

"Heeber Finn's pub," said Heeber Finn, looking at his shoes.

"Heeber Finn's," said the tall man, nodding his thanks.

"Where," said Garrity, gone miserable, "we will all be having a drink instantly."

He flung himself at the bar.

But the six intruders were moving, also. They made a small parade to either side of Garrity and just by being amiably there made him hunch three inches smaller.

"Good afternoon," said Snell-Orkney.

"It is and it isn't," said Finn, carefully, waiting.

"It seems," said the tall man surrounded by the little boy-men, "there is much talk about what we are doing in Ireland."

"That would be putting the mildest interpretation on it," said Finn.

"Allow me to explain," said the stranger.

"Have you ever," continued Mr. David Snell-Orkney, "heard of the Snow Queen and the Summer King?"

Several jaws trapped wide down.

Someone gasped as if booted in the stomach.

Finn, after a moment in which he considered just where a blow might have landed upon him, poured himself a long slow drink with scowling precision. He took a stiff snort of the stuff and with the fire in his mouth, replied, carefully, letting the warm breath out over his tongue:

"Ah . . . *what* Queen is that again, *and* the King?"

"Well," said the tall pale man, "there was this Queen who lived in Iceland who had never seen summer, and this King who lived in the Isles of Sun who had never seen winter. The people under the King almost died of heat in the summers, and the people under the Snow Queen almost died of ice in the winters. But the people of both countries were saved from their terrible weathers. The Snow Queen and the Sun King met and fell in love and every summer when the sun killed people in the islands they moved North to the lands of ice and lived temperately. And every winter when the snow killed people in the North, all of the Snow Queen's people moved South and lived in the mild island sun. So there were no longer two nations, two peoples, but *one* race which commuted from land to land with the strange weathers and wild seasons. *The end.*"

There was a round of applause, not from the canary boys, but from the men lined up at the bar who had been spelled. Finn saw his own hands out clapping on the air, and put them down. The others saw their own hands and dropped them.

But Timulty summed it up, "God, if you only had a brogue! What a teller of tales you would make."

"Many thanks, many thanks," said David Snell-Orkney.

"All of which brings us around to the point of the story," Finn said. "I mean, well, about that Queen and the King and all."

"The point is," said Snell-Orkney, "that we have not seen a leaf fall in five years. We hardly know a cloud when we see it. We have not felt snow in ten years, or hardly a drop of rain. Our story is the reverse. We must have rain or we'll perish, right, chums?"

"Oh, yes, right," said all five, in a sweet chirruping.

"We have followed summer around the world for six or seven years. We have lived in Jamaica and Nassau and Port-au-Prince and Calcutta, and Madagascar and Bali and Taormina but finally just today we said we must go north, we must have cold again. We didn't quite know what we were looking for, but we found it in St. Stephen's Green."

"The *mysterious* thing?" Nolan burst out. "I mean—"

"Your friend here will tell you," said the tall man.

"*Our* friend? You mean—Garrity?"

Everyone looked at Garrity.

"As I was going to say," said Garrity, "when I came in the door. They was in the park standing there . . . *watching the leaves turn colors.*"

"Is that *all?*" said Nolan, dismayed.

"It seemed sufficient unto the moment," said Snell Orkney.

"Are the leaves changing color up at St. Stephen's?" asked Kilpatrick.

"Do you know," said Timulty numbly, "it's been twenty years since I *looked.*"

"The most beautiful sight in all the world," said David Snell-Orkney, "lies up in the midst of St. Stephen's this very hour."

"He speaks deep," murmured Nolan.

"The drinks are on me," said David Snell-Orkney.

"He's touched *bottom,*" said MaGuire.

"Champagne all around!"

"Don't mind if I do!" said everyone.

And not ten minutes later they were all up at the park, together.

And well now, as Timulty said years after, did you ever see as many damned leaves on a tree as there was on the first tree just inside the gate at St. Stephen's Green? No! cried all. And what, though, about the *second* tree? Well, that had a *billion* leaves on it. And the more they looked the more they saw it was a wonder. And Nolan went around craning his neck so hard he fell over on his back and had to be helped up by two or three others, and there were general exhalations of awe and proclamations of devout inspiration as to the fact that as far as they could remember there had never *been* any goddamn leaves on the trees to begin with, but now they were there! Or if they had been there they had *never* had any color, or if they *had* had color, well, it was so long ago . . . Ah, what the hell, shut up, said everyone, and look!

Which is exactly what Nolan and Timulty and Kelly and Kilpatrick and Garrity and Snell-Orkney and his friends did for the rest of the declining afternoon. For a fact, autumn had taken the country, and the bright flags were out by the millions through the park.

Which is exactly where Father Leary found them.

But before he could say anything, three out of the six summer invaders asked him if he would hear their confessions.

And next thing you know with a look of great pain and alarm the father was taking Snell-Orkney & Co. back to see the stained glass at the church and the way the apse was put together by a master architect, and they liked his church so much and said so out loud again and again that he cut way down on their Hail Marys and the rigamaroles that went with.

But the top of the entire day was when one of the young-old boy-men back at the pub asked what would it be? Should he sing "Mother Machree" or "My Buddy"?

Arguments followed, and with polls taken and results announced, he sang *both*.

He had a dear voice, all said, eyes melting bright. A sweet high clear voice.

And as Nolan put it, "He wouldn't make much of a son. But there's a great daughter there somewhere!"

And all said "aye" to that.

And suddenly it was time to leave.

"But great God!" said Finn, "you just arrived!"

"We found what we came for, there's no need to stay," announced the tall sad happy old young man. "It's back to the hothouse with the flowers . . . or they wilt overnight. We never stay. We are always flying and jumping and running. We are always on the move."

The airport being fogged-in, there was nothing for it but the birds cage themselves on the Dun Laoghaire boat bound for England, and there was nothing for it but the inhabitants of Finn's should be down at the dock to watch them pull away in the middle of the evening. There they stood, all six, on the top deck, waving their thin hands down, and there stood Timulty and Nolan and Garrity and the rest waving their thick hands up. And as the boat hooted and pulled away the keeper-of-the-birds nodded once, and winged his right hand on the air and all sang forth: "*As I was walking through Dublin City, about the hour of twelve at night, I saw a maid, so fair was she . . . combing her hair by candelight.*"

"Jesus," said Timulty, "do you *hear*?"

"Sopranos, every *one* of them!" cried Nolan.

"Not Irish sopranos, but real *real* sopranos," said Kelly. "Damn, why didn't they *say*? If we'd known, we'd have had a good hour of *that* out of them before the boat."

Timulty nodded and added, listening to the music float over the waters. "Strange. Strange. I hate to see them go. Think. Think. For a hundred years or more people have said we had none. But now they have returned, if but for a little time."

"We had none of *what*?" asked Garrity. "And *what* returned?"

"Why," said Timulty, "the fairies, of course, the fairies that once lived in Ireland, and live here no more, but who came this day and changed our weather, and there they go again, who once stayed all the while."

"Ah, shut up!" cried Kilpatrick. "And listen!"

And listen they did, nine men on the end of a dock as the boat sailed out and the voices sang and the fog came in and they did not move for a long time until the boat was far gone and the voices faded like a scent of papaya on the mist.

By the time they walked back to Finn's it had begun to rain.

What made the old poem run in his mind he could not guess, but run it did:

> *Suppose and then suppose and then suppose*
> *That wires on the far-slung telephone black poles*
> *Sopped up the billion-flooded words they heard*
> *Each night all night and saved the sense*
> *And meaning of it all.*

He stopped. What next? Ah, yes . . .

> *Then, jigsaw in the night,*
> *Put all together and*
> *In philosophic phase*
> *Tried words like moron child.*

Again he paused. How did the thing end? Wait—

> *Thus mindless beast*
> *All treasuring of vowels and consonants*
> *Saves up a miracle of bad advice*
> *And lets it filter whisper, heartbeat out*
> *One lisping murmur at a time.*
> *So one night soon someone sits up*
> *Hear sharp bell ring, lifts phone*
> *And hears a Voice like Holy Ghost*
> *Gone far in nebulae*
> *That Beast upon the wire,*
> *Which with sibilance and savorings*
> *Down continental madnesses of time*

Says Hell and O
And then Hell-o.

He took a breath and finished:

To such Creation
Such dumb brute lost Electric Beast,
What is your wise reply?

He sat silently.

He sat, a man eighty years old. He sat in an empty room in an empty house on an empty street in an empty town on the empty planet Mars.

He sat as he had sat now for fifty years, waiting.

On the table in front of him lay a telephone that had not rung for a long, long time.

It trembled now with some secret preparation. Perhaps that trembling had summoned forth the poem . . .

His nostrils twitched. His eyes flared wide.

The phone shivered ever so softly.

He leaned forward, staring at it.

The phone . . . *rang.*

He leapt up and back, the chair fell to the floor. He cried out: cried out: "No!"

The phone rang again.

"No!"

He wanted to reach out, he did reach out and knock the thing off the table. It fell out of the cradle at the exact moment of its third ring.

"No . . . oh, no, no," he said softly, hands covering his chest, head wagging, the telephone at his feet. "It can't be . . . can't be . . ."

For after all, he was alone in a room in an empty house in an empty town on the planet Mars where no one was alive, only he lived, he was King of the Barren Hill . . .

And yet . . .

". . . Barton . . ."

Someone called his name.

No. Some thing buzzed and made a noise of crickets and cicadas in far desertlands.

Barton? he thought. Why . . . why that's *me!*

He hadn't heard anyone say his name in so long he had quite forgot. He was not one for ambling about calling himself by name. He had never—

"Barton," said the phone. "Barton. Barton. Barton."

"Shut up!!" he cried.

And kicked the receiver and bent sweating, panting, to put the phone back on its cradle.

No sooner did he do this than the damned thing rang again.

This time he made a fist around it, squeezed it, as if to throttle the sound, but at last, seeing his knuckles burn color away to whiteness, let go and picked up the receiver.

"Barton," said a far voice, a billion miles away.

He waited until his heart had beat another three times and then said: "Barton here," he said.

"Well, well," said the voice, only a million miles away now. "Do you know who this is?"

"Christ," said the old man. "The first call I've had in half a lifetime, and we play games."

"Sorry. How stupid of me. Of course you wouldn't recognize your own voice on the telephone. No one ever does. We are accustomed, all of us, to hearing our voice conducted through the bones of our head. Barton, this is Barton."

"What?"

"Who did you think it was?" said the voice. "A rocket captain? Did you think someone had come to rescue you?"

"No."

"What's the date?"

"July 20, 2097."

"Good Lord. Fifty years! Have you been sitting there *that* long waiting for a rocket to come from Earth?"

The old man nodded.

"Now, old man, do you know who I am?"

"Yes." He trembled. "I remember. We are one. I am Emil Barton and you are Emil Barton."

"With one difference. You're eighty, I'm only twenty. All of life before me!"

The old man began to laugh and then to cry. He sat holding the phone like a lost and silly child in his fingers. The conversation was impossible, and should not be continued, yet he went on with it. When he got hold of himself he held the phone close and said, "You there! Listen, oh God, if I could warn you! How can I? You're only a voice. If I could show you how lonely the years are. End it, kill yourself! Don't wait! If you knew what it is to change from the thing you are to the thing that is me, today, here, now, at *this* end."

"Impossible!" The voice of the young Barton laughed, far away. "I've no way to tell if you ever get this call. This is all mechanical. You're talking to a transcription, no more. This is 2037. Sixty years in

your past. Today, the atom war started on Earth. All colonials were
called home from Mars, by rocket. I got left behind!''

"I remember," whispered the old man.

"Alone on Mars," laughed the young voice. "A month, a year, who
cares? There are foods and books. In my spare time I've made transcription
libraries of ten thousand words, responses, my voice, connected to
phone relays. In later months I'll call, have someone to talk with."

"Yes."

"Sixty years from now my own tapes will ring me up. I don't really
think I'll be here on Mars that long, it's just a beautifully ironic idea of
mine, something to pass the time. Is that really you, Barton? Is that
really *me?*"

Tears fell from the old man's eyes. "Yes."

"I've made a thousand Bartons, tapes, sensitive to all questions, in
one thousand Martian towns. An army of Bartons over Mars, while I
wait for the rockets to return."

"Fool." The old man shook his head, wearily. "You waited sixty
years. You grew old waiting, always alone. And now you've become me
and you're still alone in the empty cities."

"Don't expect my sympathy. You're like a stranger, off in another
country. I can't be sad. I'm alive when I make these tapes. And you're
alive when you hear them. Both of us, to the other, incomprehensible.
Neither can warn the other, even though both respond, one to the other,
one automatically, the other warmly and humanly. I'm human now.
You're human later. It's insane. I can't cry, because not knowing the
future I can only be optimistic. These hidden tapes can only react to a
certain number of stimuli from you. Can you ask a dead man to weep?"

"Stop it!" cried the old man. He felt the familiar seizures of pain.
Nausea moved through him, and blackness. "Oh God, but you were
heartless. Go away!''

"Were, old man? I *am.* As long as the tapes glide on, as long as
spindles and hidden electronic eyes read and select and convert words
to send to you, I'll be young and cruel. I'll go on being young and cruel
long after you're dead. Good-bye."

"Wait!" cried the old man.

Click.

Barton sat holding the silent phone a long time. His heart gave him
intense pain.

What insanity it had been. In his youth how silly, how inspired, those
first secluded years, fixing the telephonic brains, the tapes, the circuits,
scheduling calls on time relays:

The phone bell.

"Morning, Barton. This is Barton. Seven o'clock. Rise and shine!"
Again!

"Barton? Barton calling. You're to go to Mars Town at noon. Install a telephonic brain. Thought I'd remind you."

"Thanks."

The bell!

"Barton? Barton. Have lunch with me? The Rocket Inn?"

"Right."

"See you. So long!"

Brrrrinnnnng!

"That you, B.? Thought I'd cheer you. Firm chin, and all that. The rescue rocket might come tomorrow, to save us."

"Yes, tomorrow, tomorrow, tomorrow, tomorrow."

Click.

But the years had burned into smoke. Barton had muted the insidious phones and their clever, clever repartee. They were to call him only after he was eighty, if he still lived. And now today, the phone ringing, the past breathing in his ear, whispering, remembering.

The phone!

He let it ring.

I don't have to answer it, he thought.

The bell!

There's no one there at all, he thought.

The ringing!

It's like talking to yourself, he thought. But different. Oh God, how different.

He felt his hands lift the phone.

"Hello, old Barton, this is young Barton. I'm twenty-one today! In the last year I've put voice-brains in two hundred more towns. I've populated Mars with Bartons!"

"Yes." The old man remembered those nights six decades ago, rushing over blue hills and into iron valleys, with a truckful of machinery, whistling, happy. Another telephone, another relay. Something to do. Something clever and wonderful and sad. Hidden voices. Hidden, hidden. In those young days when death was not death, time was not time, old age a faint echo from the long cavern of years ahead. That young idiot, that sadistic fool, never thinking someday he might reap this harvest.

"Last night," said Barton, aged twenty-one, "I sat alone in a movie theater in an empty town. I played an old Laurel and Hardy. God, how I laughed."

"Yes."

"I got an idea. I recorded my voice one thousand times on one tape. Broadcast from the town, it sounds like a thousand people. A comforting noise, the noise of a crowd. I fixed it so doors slam in town, children sing, music boxes play, all by clockworks. If I don't look out the window, if I just listen, it's all right. But if I look, it spoils the illusion. I guess I'm getting lonely.''

The old man said, "That was your first sign.''

"What?''

"The first time you admitted you were lonely.''

"I've experimented with smells. As I walk the empty streets, the smell of bacon, eggs, ham, fillets, come from the houses. All done with hidden machines.''

"Madness.''

"Self-protection!''

"I'm tired.'' Abruptly, the old man hung up. It was too much. The past drowning him . . .

Swaying, he moved down the tower stairs to the streets of the town.

The town was dark. No longer did red neons burn, music play, or cooking smells linger. Long ago he had abandoned the fantasy of the mechanical lie. Listen! Are those footsteps? Smell! Isn't that strawberry pie! He had stopped it all.

He moved to the canal where the stars shone in the quivering waters.

Underwater, in row after fishlike row, rusting, were the robot population of Mars he had constructed over the years, and, in a wild realization of his own insane inadequacy, had commanded to march, one two three four! into the canal deeps, plunging, bubbling like sunken bottles. He had killed them and shown no remorse.

Faintly a phone rang in a lightless cottage.

He walked on. The phone ceased.

Another cottage ahead rang its bell as if it knew of his passing. He began to run. The ringing stayed behind. Only to be taken up by a ringing from now this house—now that, now here, there! He darted on. Another phone!

"All right!'' he shrieked, exhausted. "I'm coming!''

"Hello, Barton.''

"What do you want!''

"I'm lonely. I only live when I speak. So I must speak. You can't shut me up forever.''

"Leave me alone!'' said the old man, in horror. "Oh, my heart!''

"This is Barton, age twenty-four. Another couple of years gone. Waiting. A little lonelier. I've read *War and Peace,* drunk sherry, run restaurants with myself as waiter, cook, entertainer. Tonight, I star in a film at the Tivoli—Emil Barton in *Love's Labor Lost,* playing all the parts, some with wigs!''

"Stop calling me—or I'll kill you!"

"You can't kill me. You'll have to find me, first!"

"I'll find you!"

"You've forgotten where you hid me. I'm everywhere, in boxes, houses, cables, towers, underground! Go ahead, try! What'll you call it? Telecide? Suicide? Jealous, are you? Jealous of me here, only twenty-four, bright-eyed, strong, young. All right, old man, it's war! Between us. Between me! A whole regiment of us, all ages from against you, the real one. Go ahead, declare war!"

"I'll kill you!"

Click. Silence.

He threw the phone out the window.

In the midnight cold, the automobile moved in deep valleys. Under Barton's feet on the floorboard were revolvers, rifles, dynamite. The roar of the car was in his thin, tired bones.

I'll find them, he thought, and destroy all of them. Oh, God, how can he do this to me?

He stopped the car. A strange town lay under the late moons. There was no wind.

He held the rifle in his cold hands. He peered at the poles, the towers, the boxes. Where was this town's voice hidden? That tower? Or that one there! So many years ago. He turned his head now this way, now that, wildly.

He raised the rifle.

The tower fell with the first bullet.

All of them, he thought. All of the towers in this town will have to be cut apart. I've forgotten. Too long.

The car moved along the silent street.

A phone rang.

He looked at the deserted drugstore.

A phone.

Pistol in hand, he shot the lock off the door, and entered.

Click.

"Hello, Barton? Just a warning. Don't try to rip down all the towers, blow things up. Cut your own throat that way. Think it over . . ."

Click.

He stepped out of the phone booth slowly and moved into the street and listened to the telephone towers humming high in the air, still alive, still untouched. He looked at them and then he understood.

He could not destroy the towers. Suppose a rocket came from Earth, impossible idea, but suppose it came tonight, tomorrow, next week? And landed on the other side of the planet, and used the phones to try to call Barton, only to find the circuits dead?

Barton dropped his gun.

"A rocket won't come," he argued, softly with himself, "I'm old. It's too late."

But suppose it came, and you never knew, he thought. No, you've got to keep the lines open.

Again, a phone ringing.

He turned dully. He shuffled back into the drugstore and fumbled with the receiver.

"Hello?" A strange voice.

"Please," said the old man, "don't bother me."

"Who's this, who's there? Who is it? Where are you?" cried the voice, surprised.

"Wait a minute." The old man staggered. "This is Emil Barton, who's that?"

"This is Captain Rockwell, Apollo Rocket 48. Just arrived from Earth."

"No, no, no."

"Are you there, Mr. Barton?"

"No, no, it can't be."

"Where are you?"

"You're lying!" The old man had to lean against the booth. His eyes were cold blind. "It's you, Barton, making fun of me, lying again!"

"This is Captain Rockwell. Just landed. In New Chicago. Where are you?"

"In Green Villa," he gasped. "That's six hundred miles from you."

"Look, Barton, can you come here?"

"What?"

"We've repairs on our rocket. Exhausted from the flight. Can you come help?"

"Yes, yes."

"We're at the field outside town. Can you come by tomorrow?"

"Yes, but—"

"Well?"

The old man petted the phone. "How's Earth? How's New York? Is the war over? Who's President now? What happened?"

"Plenty of time for gossip when you arrive."

"Is everything fine?"

"Fine."

"Thank God." The old man listened to the far voice. "Are you sure you're Captain Rockwell?"

"Dammit, man!"

"I'm sorry!"

He hung up and ran.

They were here, after many years, unbelievable, his own people who would take him back to Earth's seas and skies and mountains.

He started the car. He would drive all night. It would be worth a risk, to see people, to shake hands, to hear them again.

The car thundered in the hills.

That voice. Captain Rockwell. It couldn't be himself, forty years ago. He had never made a recording like that. Or had he? In one of his depressive fits, in a spell of drunken cynicism, hadn't he once made a false tape of a false landing on Mars with a synthetic captain, an imaginary crew? He jerked his head, savagely. No. He was a suspicious fool. Now was no time to doubt. He must run with the moons of Mars, all night. What a party they would have!

The sun rose. He was immensely tired, full of thorns and brambles, his heart plunging, his fingers fumbling the wheel, but the thing that pleased him most was the thought of one last phone call: Hello, *young* Barton, this is *old* Barton. I'm leaving for Earth today! Rescued! He smiled weakly.

He drove into the shadowy limits of New Chicago at sundown. Stepping from his car he stood staring at the rocket tarmac, rubbing his reddened eyes.

The rocket field was empty. No one ran to meet him. No one shook his hand, shouted, or laughed.

He felt his heart roar. He knew blackness and a sensation of falling through the open sky. He stumbled toward an office.

Inside, six phones sat in a neat row.

He waited, gasping.

Finally: the bell.

He lifted the heavy receiver.

A voice said, "I was wondering if you'd get there alive."

The old man did not speak but stood with the phone in his hands.

The voice continued, "Captain Rockwell reporting for duty. Your orders, sir?"

"You," groaned the old man.

"How's your heart, old man?"

"No!"

"Had to eliminate you some way, so I could live, if you call a transcription living."

"I'm going out now," replied the old man. "I don't care. I'll blow up everything until you're all dead!"

"You haven't the strength. Why do you think I had you travel so far, so fast? This is your last trip!"

The old man felt his heart falter. He would never make the other towns. The war was lost. He slid into a chair and made low, mournful noises with his mouth. He glared at the five other phones. As if at a signal, they burst into chorus! A nest of ugly birds screaming!

Automatic receivers popped up.

The office whirled. "Barton, Barton, Barton!"

He throttled a phone in his hands. He choked it and still it laughed at him. He beat it. He kicked it. He furled the hot wire like serpentine in his fingers, ripped it. It fell about his stumbling feet.

He destroyed three other phones. There was a sudden silence.

And as if his body now discovered a thing which it had long kept secret, it seemed to sink upon his tired bones. The flesh of his eyelids fell away like petals. His mouth withered. The lobes of his ears were melting wax. He pushed his chest with his hands and fell face down. He lay still. His breathing stopped. His heart stopped.

After a long spell, the remaining two phones rang.

A relay snapped somewhere. The two phone voices were connected, one to the other.

"Hello, Barton?"

"Yes, Barton?"

"Aged twenty-four."

"I'm twenty-six. We're both young. What's happened?"

"I don't know. Listen."

The silent room. The old man did not stir on the floor. The wind blew in the broken window. The air was cool.

"Congratulate me, Barton, this is my twenty-sixth birthday!"

"Congratulations!"

The voices sang together, about birthdays, and the singing blew out the window, faintly, faintly, into the dead city.

I hadn't been in Dublin for years. I'd been round the world—everywhere but Ireland—but now within the hour of my arrival the Royal Hibernian Hotel phone rang and on the phone: Nora herself, God Bless!

"Charles? Charlie? Chuck? Are you rich at last? And do rich writers buy fabulous estates?"

"Nora!" I laughed. "Don't you ever say hello?"

"Life's too short for hellos, and now there's no time for decent good-byes. *Could* you buy Grynwood?"

"Nora, Nora, your family house, two hundred rich years old? What would happen to wild Irish social life, the parties, drinks, gossip? You can't throw it all away!"

"Can and shall. Oh, I've trunks of money waiting out in the rain this moment. But, Charlie, Charles, I'm *alone* in the house. The servants have fled to help the Aga. Now on this final night, Chuck, I need a writer-man to see the Ghost. Does your skin prickle? Come. I've mysteries and a home to give away. Charlie, oh, Chuck, oh, Charles."

Click. Silence.

Ten minutes later I roared round the snake-road through the green hills toward the blue lake and the lush grass meadows of the hidden and fabulous house called Grynwood.

I laughed again. Dear Nora! For all her gab, a party was probably on the tracks this moment, lurched toward wondrous destruction. Bertie might fly from London, Nick from Paris, Alicia would surely motor up from Galway. Some film director, cabled within the hour, would para-chute or helicopter down, a rather seedy manna in dark glasses. Marion would show with his Pekingese dog troupe, which always got drunker, and sicker, than he.

I gunned my hilarity as I gunned the motor.

You'll be beautifully mellow by eight o'clock, I thought, stunned to sleep by concussions of bodies before midnight, drowse till noon, then even more nicely potted by Sunday high tea. And somewhere in between, the rare game of musical beds with Irish and French contesses, ladies, and plain field-beast art majors crated in from the Sorbonne, some with chewable mustaches, some not, and Monday ten million years off. Tuesday, I would motor oh so carefully back to Dublin, nursing my body like a great impacted wisdom tooth, gone much too wise with women, pain-flashing with memory.

Trembling, I remembered the first time I had drummed out to Nora's, when I was twenty-one.

A mad old Duchess with flour-talcummed cheeks, and the teeth of a barracuda had wrestled me and a sports car down this road fifteen years ago, braying into the fast weather:

"You shall love Nora's menagerie zoo and horticultural garden! Her friends are beasts and keepers, tigers and pussies, rhododendrons and flytraps. Her streams run cold fish, hot trout. Hers is a great greenhouse where brutes grow outsize, force-fed by unnatural airs, enter Nora's on Friday with clean linen, sog out with the wet-wash-soiled bedclothes Monday, feeling as if you had meantime inspired, painted, and lived through all Bosch's Temptations, Hells, Judgments, and Dooms! Live at Nora's and you reside in a great warm giant's cheek, deliciously gummed and morseled hourly. You will pass, like victuals, through her mansion. When it has crushed forth your last sweet-sour sauce and dismarrowed your youth-candied bones, you will be discarded in a cold iron-country train station lonely with rain."

"I'm coated with enzymes?" I cried above the engine roar. "No house can break down my elements, or take nourishment from my Original Sin."

"Fool!" laughed the Duchess. "We shall see most of your skeleton by sunrise Sunday!"

I came out of memory as I came out of the woods at a fine popping glide and slowed because the very friction of beauty stayed the heart, the mind, the blood, and therefore the foot upon the throttle.

There under a blue-lake sky by a blue-sky lake lay Nora's own dear place, the grand house called Grynwood. It nestled in the roundest hills by the tallest trees in the deepest forest in all Eire. It had towers built a thousand years ago by unremembered peoples and unsung architects for reasons never to be guessed. Its gardens had first flowered five hundred years back and there were outbuildings scattered from a creative explosion two hundred years gone amongst old tomb yards and crypts. Here was a convent hall become a horse barn of the landed gentry, there were new wings built on ninety years ago. Out around the lake was a hunting-lodge ruin where wild horses might plunge through minted shadow to sink away in green-water grasses by yet further cold ponds and single graves of daughters whose sins were so rank they were driven forth even in death to the wilderness, sunk traceless in the gloom.

As if in bright welcome, the sun flashed vast tintinnabulations from scores of house windows. Blinded, I clenched the car to a halt. Eyes shut, I licked my lips.

I remembered my first night at Grynwood.

Nora herself opening the front door. Standing stark naked, she announced:

"You're too late. It's all over!"

"Nonsense. Hold this, boy, and this."

Whereupon the Duchess, in three nimble moves, peeled herself raw as a blanched oyster in the wintry doorway.

I stood aghast, gripping her clothes.

"Come in, boy, you'll catch your death." And the bare Duchess walked serenely away among the well-dressed people.

"Beaten at my own game," cried Nora. "Now, to compete, I must put my clothes back on. And I was so hoping to shock you."

"Never fear," I said. "You have."

"Come help me dress."

In the alcove, we waded among her clothes, which lay in misshapen pools of musky scent upon a parqueted floor.

"Hold the panties while I slip into them. You're Charles, aren't you?"

"How do you do." I flushed, then burst into an uncontrollable fit of laughter. "Forgive me," I said at last, snapping her bra in back, "it's just here it is early evening, and I'm putting you *into* your clothes. I—"

A door slammed somewhere. I glanced around for the Duchess.

"Gone," I murmured. "The house has devoured her, already."

True. I didn't see the Duchess again until the rainy Tuesday morn she had predicted. By then she had forgotten my name, my face, and the soul behind my face.

"My God," I said, "what's that, and *that?*"

Still dressing Nora, we had arrived at the library door. Inside, like a bright mirror-maze, the weekend guests turned.

"That," Nora pointed, "is the Manhattan Civic Ballet flown over on ice by jet stream. To the left, the Hamburg Dancers, flown the opposite way. Divine casting. Enemy ballet mobs unable, because of language, to express their scorn and vitriol. They must pantomime their cat-fight. Stand aside, Charlie. What was Valkyrie must become Rhine Maiden. And those boys *are* Rhine Maidens. Guard your flank!"

Nora was right.

The battle was joined.

The tiger lilies leapt at each other, jabbering in tongues. Then, frustrated, they fell away, flushed. With a bombardment of slammed doors, the enemies plunged off to scores of rooms. What was horror became horrible friendship and what was friendship became steamroom oven-bastings of unabashed and, thank God, hidden affection.

After that it was one grand crystal-chandelier avalanche of writer-artist-choreographer-poets down the swift-sloped weekend.

Somewhere I was caught and swept in the heaped pummel of flesh headed straight for a collision with the maiden-aunt reality of Monday noon.

Now, many lost parties, many lost years later, here I stood.

And there stood Grynwood manse, very still.

No music played. No cars arrived.

Hello, I thought. A new statue seated by the shore. Hello again. Not a statue . . .

But Nora herself seated alone, legs drawn under her dress, face pale, staring at Grynwood as if I had not arrived, was nowhere in sight.

"Nora . . .?" But her gaze was so steadily fixed to the house wings, its mossy roofs and windows full of empty sky, I turned to stare at it myself.

Something *was* wrong. Had the house sunk two feet into the earth? Or had the earth sunk all about, leaving it stranded forlorn in the high chill air?

Had earthquakes shaken the windows atilt so they mirrored intruders with distorted gleams and glares?

The front door of Grynwood stood wide open. From this door, the house breathed out upon me.

Subtle. Like waking by night to feel the push of warm air from your wife's nostrils, but suddenly terrified, for the scent of her breath has changed, she smells of someone else! You want to seize her awake, cry her name. Who *is* she, how, what? But heart thudding, you lie sleepless by some stranger in bed.

I walked. I sensed my image caught in a thousand windows moving across the grass to stand over a silent Nora.

A thousand of me sat quietly down.

Nora, I thought. Oh dear God, here we are again.

That first visit to Grynwood . . .

And then here and there through the years we had met like people brushing in a crowd, like lovers across the aisle and strangers on a train, and with the whistle crying the quick next stop touched hands or allowed our bodies to be bruised together by the crowd cramming out as the doors flung wide, then, impelled, no more touch, no word, nothing for years.

Or, it was as if at high noon midsummer every year or so we ran off up the vital strand away, never dreaming we might come back and collide in mutual need. And then somehow another summer ended, a sun went down, and there came Nora dragging her empty sandpail and here came I with scabs on my knees, and the beach empty and a strange season gone, and just us left to say hello Nora, hello Charles as the wind rose and the sea darkened as if a great herd of octopi suddenly swam by with their inks.

I often wondered if a day might come when we circled the long way round and stayed. Somewhere back perhaps twelve years ago there had been one moment, balanced like a feather upon fingertip when our breaths from either side had held our love warmly and perfectly in poise.

But that was because I had bumped into Nora in Venice, with her roots packed, far from home, away from Grynwood, where she might truly belong to someone else, perhaps even to me.

But somehow our mouths had been too busy with each other to ask permanence. Next day, healing our lips, puffed from mutual assaults, we had not the strength to say forever-as-of-now, more tomorrows this way, an apartment, a house anywhere, not Grynwood, not Grynwood ever again, stay! Perhaps the light of noon was cruel, perhaps it showed too many pores in people. Or perhaps, more accurately, the nasty children were bored again. Or terrified of a prison of two! Whatever the reason, the feather, once briefly lofted on champagne breath, toppled. Neither knew which ceased breathing upon it first. Nora pretended an urgent telegram and fled off to Grynwood.

Contact was broken. The spoiled children never wrote. I did not know what sand castles she had smashed. She did not know what Indian Madras had bled color from passion's sweat on my back. I married. I divorced. I traveled.

And now here we were again come from opposite directions late on a strange day by a familiar lake, calling to each other without calling, running to each other without moving, as if we had not been years apart.

"Nora." I took her hand. It was cold. "What's happened?"

"Happened!?" She laughed, grew silent, staring away. Suddenly she laughed again, that difficult laughter that might instantly flush with tears. "Oh, my dear Charlie, think wild, think all, jump hoops and come round to maniac dreams. Happened, Charlie, happened?!"

She grew frightfully still.

"Where are the servants, the guests—?"

"The party," she said,"was last night."

"Impossible! You've never had just a Friday-night bash. Sundays have always seen your lawn littered with demon wretches strewn and bandaged with bedclothes. Why—?"

"Why did I invite you out today, you want to ask, Charles?" Nora still looked only at the house. "To give you Grynwood. A gift, Charlie, if you can force it to let you stay, if it will put up with you—"

"I don't want the house!" I burst in.

"Oh, it's not if you want *it*, but if it wants *you*. It threw us all out, Charlie."

"Last night . . .?"

"Last night the last great party at Grynwood didn't come off. Mag flew from Paris. The Aga sent a fabulous girl from Nice. Roger, Percy, Evelyn, Vivian, Jon were here. That bullfighter who almost killed the playwright over the ballerina was here. The Irish dramatist who falls off stages drunk was here. Ninety-seven guests teemed in that door between five and seven last night. By midnight they were gone."

I walked across the lawn.

Yes, still fresh in the grass: the tire marks of three dozen cars.

"It wouldn't let us have the party, Charles," Nora called, faintly.

I turned blankly. "It? The house?"

"Oh, the music was splendid but went hollow upstairs. We heard our laughter ghost back from the topmost halls. The party clogged. The *petits fours* were clods in our throats. The wine ran over our chins. No one got to bed for even three minutes. Doesn't it sound a lie? But, Limp Meringue Awards were given to all and they went away and I slept bereft on the lawn all night. Guess why? Go look, Charlie."

We walked up to the open front door of Grynwood.

"What shall I look for?"

"Everything. All the rooms. The house itself. The mystery. Guess. And when you've guessed a thousand times I'll tell you why I can never live here again, must leave, why Grynwood is yours if you wish. Go in, alone."

And in I went, slowly, one step at a time.

I moved quietly on the lovely lion-yellow hardwood parquetry of the great hall. I gazed at the Aubusson wall tapestry. I examined the ancient white marble Greek medallions displayed on green velvet in a crystal case.

"Nothing," I called back to Nora out there in the late cooling day.

"No. Everything," she called. "Go on."

The library was a deep warm sea of leather smell where five thousand books gleamed their colors of hand-rubbed cherry, lime, and lemon bindings. Their gold eyes, bright titles, glittered. Above the fireplace which could have kenneled two firedogs and ten great hounds hung the exquisite Gainsborough *Maidens and Flowers* that had warmed the family for generations. It was a portal overlooking summer weather. One wanted to lean through and sniff wild seas of flowers, touch harvest of peach maiden girls, hear the machinery of bees bright-stitching up the glamorous airs.

"Well?" called a far voice.

"Nora!" I cried. "Come here. There's nothing to fear! It's still daylight!"

"No," said the far voice sadly. "The sun is going down. What do you see, Charlie?"

"Out in the hall again, the spiral stairs. The parlor. Not a dust speck on the air. I'm opening the cellar door. A million barrels and bottles. Now the kitchen. Nora, this is lunatic!"

"Yes, isn't it?" wailed the far voice. "Go back to the library. Stand in the middle of the room. See the Gainsborough *Maidens and Flowers* you always loved?"

"It's there."

"It's not. See the silver Florentine humidor?"

"I see it."

"You don't. See the great maroon leather chair where you drank sherry with Father?"

"Yes."

"No," sighed the voice.

"Yes, no? Do, don't? Nora, enough!"

"More than enough, Charlie. Can't you guess? Don't you *feel* what happened to Grynwood?"

I ached, turning. I sniffed the strange air.

"Charlie," said Nora, far out by the open front door, ". . . four years ago," she said faintly. "Four years ago . . . Grynwood burned completely to the ground."

I ran.

I found Nora pale at the door.

"It *what!?*" I shouted.

"Burned to the ground," she said. "Utterly. Four years ago."

I took three long steps outside and looked up at the walls and windows.

"Nora, it's standing, it's all here!"

"No, it isn't, Charlie. That's not Grynwood."

I touched the gray stone, the red brick, the green ivy. I ran my hand over the carved Spanish front door. I exhaled in awe. "It can't be."

"It is," said Nora. "All new. Everything from the cellar stones up. New, Charles. New, Charlie. New."

"This *door?*"

"Sent up from Madrid, last year."

"This pavement?"

"Quarried near Dublin two years ago. The windows from Waterford this spring."

I stepped through the front door.

"The parqueting?"

"Finished in France and shipped over autumn last."

"But, but, that *tapestry!?*"

"Woven near Paris, hung in April."

"But it's all the *same,* Nora!"

"Yes, isn't it? I traveled to Greece to duplicate the marble relics. The crystal case I had made, too, in Rheims."

"The library!"

"Every book, all bound the same way, stamped in similar gold, put back on similar shelves. The library alone cost one hundred thousand pounds to reproduce."

"The same, the same, Nora," I cried, in wonder, "oh God, the same," and we were in the library and I pointed at the silver Florentine humidor. "That, of course, was saved out of the fire?"

"No, no, I'm an artist. I remembered. I sketched, I took the drawings to Florence. They finished the fraudulent fake in July."

"The Gainsborough *Maidens and Flowers!?*"

"Look close! That's Fritzi's work. Fritzi, that horrible drip-dry beatnik painter in Montmartre? Who threw paint on canvas and flew them as kites over Paris so the wind and rain patterned beauty for him, which he sold for exorbitant prices? Well, Fritzi, it turns out, is a secret Gainsborough fanatic. He'd kill me if he knew I told. He painted this *Maidens* from memory, isn't it *fine?*"

"Fine, fine, oh God, Nora, are you telling the truth?"

"I wish I weren't. Do you think I've been mentally ill, Charles? Naturally you might think. Do you believe in good and evil, Charlie? I didn't used. But now, quite suddenly, I have turned old and rain-dowdy. I have hit forty, forty has hit me, like a locomotive. Do you know what I think? . . . the house destroyed *itself.*"

"It *what?*"

She went to peer into the halls where shadows gathered now, coming in from the late day.

"When I first came into my money, at eighteen, when people said Guilt I said Bosh. They cried Conscience. I cried Crappulous Nonsense! But in those days the rain barrel was empty. A lot of strange rain has fallen since and gathered in me, and to my cold surprise I find me to the brim with old sin and know there *is* conscience and guilt.

"There are a thousand young men in me, Charles.

"They thrust and buried themselves there. When they withdrew, Charles, I thought they withdrew. But no, no, now I'm sure there is not a single one whose barb, whose lovely poisoned thorn is not caught in my flesh, one place or another. God, God, how I loved their barbs, their thorns. God how I loved to be pinned and bruised. I thought the medicines of time and travel might heal the grip marks. But now I know I am all fingerprints. There lives no inch of my flesh, Chuck, is not FBI file systems of palm print and Egyptian whorl of finger stigmata. I have been stabbed by a thousand lovely boys and thought I did not bleed but God I do bleed now. I have bled all over this house. And my friends who denied guilt and conscience, in a great subway heave of flesh have trammeled through here and jounced and mouthed each other and sweat upon floors and buckshot the walls with their agonies and descents, each from the other's crosses. The house has been stormed by assassins, Charlie, each seeking to kill the other's loneliness with their short swords, no one finding surcease, only a momentary groaning out of relaxation.

"I don't think there has ever been a happy person in this house, Charles, I see that now.

"Oh, it all *looked* happy. When you hear so much laughter and see so much drink and find human sandwiches in every bed, pink and white morsels to munch upon, you think: what joy! How happy-fine!

"But it is a lie, Charlie, you and I know that, and the house drank the lie in my generation and Father's before me and Grandfather beyond. It was always a happy house, which means a dreadful estate. The assassins have wounded each other here for long over two hundred years. The walls dripped. The door-knobs were gummy. Summer turned old in the Gainsborough frame. So the assassins came and went, Charlie, and left sins and memories of sins which the house kept.

"And when you have caught up just so much darkness, Charles, you must vomit, mustn't you?

"My life is my emetic. I choke on my own past.

"So did this house.

"And finally, guilt ridden, terribly sad, one night I heard the friction of old sins rubbing together in attic beds. And with this spontaneous combustion the house smouldered ablaze. I heard the fire first as it sat in the library, devouring books. Then I heard it in the cellar drinking wine. By that time I was out the window and down the ivy and on the lawn with the servants. We picnicked on the lake shore at four in the morning with champagne and biscuits from the gatekeeper's lodge. The fire brigade arrived from town at five to see the roofs collapse and vast fire founts of spark fly over the clouds and the sinking moon. We gave them champagne also and watched Grynwood die finally, at last, so at dawn there was nothing.

"It had to destroy itself, didn't it, Charlie, it was so evil from all my people and from me?"

We stood in the cold hall. At last I stirred myself and said, "I guess so, Nora."

We walked into the library where Nora drew forth blueprints and a score of notebooks.

"It was then, Charlie, I got my inspiration. Build Grynwood again. A gray jigsaw puzzle put back together! Phoenix reborn from the sootbin. So no one would know of its death through sickness. Not you, Charlie, or any friends off in the world; let all remain ignorant. My guilt over its destruction was immense. How fortunate to be rich. You can buy a fire brigade with champagne and the village newspapers with four cases of gin. The news never got a mile out that Grynwood was strewn sackcloth and ashes. Time later to tell the world. Now! to work! And off I raced to my Dublin solicitor's where my father had filed architectural plans and interior details. I sat for months with a secretary, word-associating to summon up Grecian lamps, Roman tiles. I shut my eyes to recall every hairy inch of carpeting, every fringe, every rococo ceiling odament, all, all brasswork decor, firedog, switchplates, log-bucket, and doorknob. And when the list of thirty thousand items was compounded, I flew in carpenters from Edinburgh, tile setters from Sienna, stone-cutters from Perugia, and they hammered, nailed, thrived, carved, and set for four years, Charlie, and I loitered at the factory outside Paris to watch spiders weave my tapestry and floor the rugs. I rode to hounds at Waterford while watching them blow my glass.

"Oh, Charles, I don't think it has ever happened, has it in history, that anyone ever put a destroyed thing back the way it was? Forget the past, let the bones cease! Well, not for me, I thought, no: Grynwood shall rise and be as ever it was. But, while looking like the old Grynwood, it would have the advantage of being really new. A fresh start, I thought, and while building it I led such a *quiet* life, Charles. The work was adventure enough.

"As I did the house over, I thought I did myself over. While I favored it with rebirth, I favored myself with joy. At long last, I thought, a happy person comes and goes at Grynwood.

"And it was finished and done, the last stone cut, the last tile placed, two weeks ago.

"And I sent invitations across the world, Charlie, and last night they all arrived, a pride of lion-men from New York, smelling of St. John's breadfruit, the staff of life. A team of lightfoot Athens boys. A Negro *corps de ballet* from Johannesburg. Three Sicilian bandits, or were they actors? Seventeen lady violinists who might be ravished as they laid down their violins and picked up their skirts. Four champion polo players. One tennis pro to restring my guts. A darling French poet. Oh God, Charles, it was to be a swell grand fine re-opening of the Phoenix Estates, Nora Gryndon, proprietress. How did I know, or guess, the house would not want us here?"

"Can a house want or not want?"

"Yes, when it is very new and everyone else, no matter what age, is very old. It was freshly born. We were stale and dying. It was good. We were evil. It wished to stay innocent. So it turned us out.''

"How?"

"Why, just by being itself. It made the air so quiet, Charlie, you wouldn't believe. We all felt someone had died.

"After awhile, with no one saying but everyone feeling it, people just got in their cars and drove away. The orchestra shut up its music and sped off in ten limousines. There went the entire party, around the lake drive, as if heading for a midnight outdoor picnic, but no, just going to the airport or the boats, or Galway, everyone cold, no one speaking, and the house empty, and the servants themselves pumping away on their bikes, and me alone in the house, the last party over, the party that never happened, that never could begin. As I said, I slept on the lawn all night, alone with my old thoughts and I knew this was the end of all the years, for I was ashes, and ashes cannot build. It was the new grand lovely fine bird lying in the dark, to itself. It hated my breath in the dooryard. I was over. It had begun. There.''

Nora was finished with her story.

We sat silently for a long while in the very late afternoon as dusk gathered to fill the rooms, and put out the eyes of the windows. A wind rippled the lake.

I said,"It can't all be true. Surely you *can* stay here."

"A final test, so you'll not argue with me again. We shall try to spend the night here."

"Try?"

"We won't make it through till dawn. Let's fry a few eggs, drink some wine, go to bed early. But lie on top your covers with your clothes on. You shall want your clothes, swiftly, I imagine."

We ate almost in silence. We drank wine. We listened to the new hours striking from the new brass clocks everywhere in the new house.

At ten, Nora sent me up to my room.

"Don't be afraid," she called to me on the landing. "The house means us no harm. It simply fears *we* may hurt *it*. I shall read in the library. When you are ready to leave, no matter what hour, come for me."

"I shall sleep snug as a bug," I said.

"*Shall* you?" said Nora.

And I went up to my new bed and lay in the dark smoking, feeling neither afraid nor smug, calmly waiting for any sort of happening at all.

I did not sleep at midnight.

I was awake at one.

At three, my eyes were still wide.

The house did not creak, sigh, or murmur. It waited, as I waited, timing its breath to mine.

At three thirty in the morning the door to my room slowly opened.
There was simply a motion of dark upon dark. I felt the wind draught
over my hands and face.

I sat up slowly in the dark.

Five minutes passed. My heart slowed its beating.

And then far away below, I heard the front door open.

Again, not a creak or whisper. Just the click and the shadowing change
of wind motioning the corridors.

I got up and went out into the hall.

From the top of the stairwell I saw what I expected: the front door
open. Moonlight flooded the new parqueting and shone upon the new
grandfather's clock which ticked with a fresh oiled bright sound.

I went down and out the front door.

"*There* you are," said Nora, standing down by my car in the drive.

I went to her.

"You didn't hear a thing," she said, "and yet you heard something,
right?"

"Right."

"Are you ready to leave now, Charles?"

I looked up at the house. "Almost."

"You know now, don't you, it is all over? You feel it, surely, that it
is the dawn come up on a new morning? And, feel my heart, my soul
beating pale and mossy within my heart, my blood so black, Charlie,
you have felt it often beating under your own body, you know how old
I am. You know how full of dungeons and racks and late afternoons and
blue hours of French twilight I am. Well . . .''

Nora looked at the house.

"Last night, as I lay in bed at two in the morning, I heard the front
door drift open. I knew that the whole house had simply leant itself ajar
to let the latch free and glide the door wide. I went to the top of the
stairs. And, looking down, I saw the creek of moonlight laid out fresh
in the hall. And the house so much as said, here is the way you go,
tread the cream, walk the milky new path out of this and away, go, old
one, go with your darkness. You are with child. The sour-gum ghost is
in your stomach. It will never be born. And because you cannot drop it,
one day it will be your death. What are you waiting for?

"Well, Charles, I was afraid to go down and shut that door. And I
knew it was true, I would never sleep again. So, I went down and out.

"I have a dark old sinful place in Geneva. I'll go there to live. But
you are younger and fresher, Charlie, so I want this place to be yours."

"Not so young."

"Younger than I."

"Not so fresh. It wants me to go, too, Nora. The door to *my* room just now. It opened, too."

"Oh, Charlie," breathed Nora, and touched my cheek. "Oh, Charles," and then, softly, "I'm sorry."

"Don't be. We'll go together."

Nora opened the car door.

"Let me drive. I must drive now, very fast, all the way to Dublin. Do you mind?"

"No. But what about your luggage?"

"What's in there, the house can have. Where are you going?"

I stopped walking. "I must shut the front door."

"No," said Nora. "Leave it open."

"But . . . people will come in."

Nora laughed quietly. "Yes. But only good people. So that's all right, isn't it?"

I finally nodded. "Yes. That's all right."

I came back to stand by my car, reluctant to leave. Clouds were gathering. It was beginning to snow. Great gentle white leaflets fell down out of the moonlit sky as harmlessly soft as the gossip of angels.

We got in and slammed the car doors. Nora gunned the motor.

"Ready?" she said.

"Ready."

"Charlie?" said Nora. "When we get to Dublin, will you sleep with me, I mean *sleep,* the next few days. I shall need someone the next few days. Will you?"

"Of course."

"I wish," she said. And tears filled her eyes. "Oh God, how I wish I could burn myself down and start over. Burn myself down so I could go up to the house now and go in and live forever like a dairy maid full of berries and cream. Oh but hell. What's the use of talk like that?"

"Drive, Nora," I said, gently.

And she drummed the motor and we ran out of the valley, along the lake, with gravel buckshotting out behind, and up the hills and through the deep snow forest, and by the time we reached the last rise, Nora's tears were shaken away, she did not look back, and we drove at seventy through the dense falling and thicker night toward a darker horizon and a cold stone city, and all the way, never once letting go, in silence I held one of her hands.

Grandma!

I remember her birth.

Wait, you say, *no* man remembers his own grandma's birth.

But, yes, *we* remember the day that she was born.

For we, her grandchildren, slapped her to life. Timothy, Agatha, and I, Tom, raised up our hands and brought them down in a huge crack! We shook together the bits and pieces, parts and samples, textures and tastes, humors and distillations that would move her compass needle north to cool us, south to warm and comfort us, east and west to travel round the endless world, glide her eyes to know us, mouth to sing us asleep by night, hands to touch us awake at dawn.

Grandma, O dear and wondrous electric dream . . .

When storm lightnings rove the sky making circuitries amidst the clouds, her name flashes on my inner lid. Sometimes still I hear her ticking, humming above our beds in the gentle dark. She passes like a clock-ghost in the long halls of memory, like a hive of intellectual bees swarming after the Spirit of Summers Lost. Sometimes still I feel the smile I learned from her, printed on my cheek at three in the deep morn . . .

All right, all right! you cry, what was it like the day your damned and wondrous-dreadful-loving Grandma was born?

It was the week the world ended . . .

Our mother was dead.

One late afternoon a black car left Father and the three of us stranded on our own front drive staring at the grass, thinking:

That's not our grass. There are the croquet mallets, balls, hoops, yes, just as they fell and lay three days ago when Dad stumbled out on the lawn, weeping with the news. There are the roller skates that belonged to a boy, me, who will never be that young again. And yes, there the tire-swing on the old oak, but Agatha afraid to swing. It would surely break. It would fall.

And the house? Oh, God . . .

We peered through the front door, afraid of the echoes we might find confused in the halls; the sort of clamor that happens when all the furniture is taken out and there is nothing to soften the river of talk that flows in any house at all hours. And now the soft, the warm, the main piece of lovely furniture was gone forever.

The door drifted wide.

Silence came out. Somewhere a cellar door stood wide and a raw wind blew damp earth from under the house.

But, I thought, we don't *have* a cellar!

"Well," said Father.

We did not move.

Aunt Clara drove up the path in her big canary-colored limousine.

We jumped through the door. We ran to our rooms.

We heard them shout and then speak and then shout and then speak: Let the children live with me! Aunt Clara said. They'd rather kill themselves! Father said.

A door slammed. Aunt Clara was gone.

We almost danced. Then we remembered what had happened and went downstairs.

Father sat alone talking to himself or to a remnant ghost of Mother left from the days before her illness, but jarred loose now by the slamming of the door. He murmured to his hands, his empty palms:

"The children need someone. I love them but, let's face it, I must work to feed us all. You love them, Ann, but you're gone. And Clara? Impossible. She loves but smothers. And as for maids, nurses—?"

Here Father sighed and we sighed with him, remembering.

The luck we had had with maids or live-in teachers or sitters was beyond intolerable. Hardly a one who wasn't a crosscut saw grabbing against the grain. Handaxes and hurricanes best described them. Or, conversely, they were all fallen trifle, damp soufflé. We children were unseen furniture to be sat upon or dusted or sent for reupholstering come spring and fall, with a yearly cleansing at the beach.

"What we need," said Father, "is a . . ."

We all leaned to his whisper.

". . . grandmother."

"But," said Timothy, with the logic of nine years, "all our grandmothers are dead."

"Yes in one way, no in another."

What a fine mysterious thing for Dad to say.

"Here," he said at last.

He handed us a multifold, multicolored pamphlet. We had seen it in his hands, off and on, for many weeks, and very often during the last few days. Now, with one blink of our eyes, as we passed the paper from hand to hand, we knew why Aunt Clara, insulted, outraged, had stormed from the house.

Timothy was the first to read aloud from what he saw on the first page: "I Sing the Body Electric!"

He glanced up at Father, squinting. "What the heck does that mean?"

"Read on."

Agatha and I glanced guiltily about the room, afraid Mother might suddenly come in to find us with this blasphemy, but then nodded to Timothy, who read:

" 'Fanto—' "

"Fantoccini," Father prompted.

" 'Fantoccini Ltd. We *Shadow Forth* . . . the answer to all your most grievous problems. One Model Only, upon which a thousand times a thousand variations can be added, subtracted, subdivided, indivisible, with Liberty and Justice for all.' "

"Where does it say *that?*" we all cried.

"It doesn't." Timothy smiled for the first time in days. "I just had to put that in. Wait." He read on: " 'for you who have worried over inattentive sitters, nurses who cannot be trusted with marked liquor bottles, and well-meaning Uncles and Aunts—' "

"Well-meaning, *but!*" said Agatha, and I gave an echo.

" '—we have perfected the first humanoid-genre mini-circuited, rechargeable AC-DC Mark V Electrical Grandmother . . .' "

"Grandmother!?"

The paper slipped away to the floor. "Dad . . .?"

"Don't look at me that way," said Father. "I'm half-mad with grief, and half-mad thinking of tomorrow and the day after that. Someone pick up the paper. Finish it."

"I will," I said, and did:

" 'The Toy that is more than a Toy, the Fantoccini Electrical Grandmother is built with loving precision to give the incredible precision of love to your children. The child at ease with the realities of the world and the even greater realities of the imagination, is her aim.

" 'She is computerized to tutor in twelve languages simultaneously, capable of switching tongues in a thousandth of a second without pause, and has a complete knowledge of the religious, artistic, and sociopolitical histories of the world seeded in her master hive—' "

"How great!" said Timothy. "It makes it sound as if we were to keep bees! *Educated* bees!"

"Shut up!" said Agatha.

" 'Above all,' " I read, " 'this human being, for human she seems, this embodiment in electro-intelligent facsimile of the humanities, will listen, know, tell, react and love your children insofar as such great Objects, such fantastic Toys, can be said to Love, or can be imagined to Care. This Miraculous Companion, excited to the challenge of large world and small, inner Sea or Outer Universe, will transmit by touch and tell, said Miracles to your Needy.' "

"Our Needy," murmured Agatha.

Why, we all thought, sadly, that's us, oh, yes, that's *us*.

I finished:

" 'We do not sell our Creation to able-bodied families where parents are available to raise, effect, shape, change, love their own children. Nothing can replace the parent in the home. However there are families where death or ill health or disablement undermines the welfare of the children. Orphanages seem not the answer. Nurses tend to be selfish, neglectful, or suffering from dire nervous afflictions.

" 'With the utmost humility then, and recognizing the need to rebuild, rethink, and regrow our conceptualizations from month to month, year to year, we offer the nearest thing to the Ideal Teacher-Friend-Companion-Blood Relation. A trial period can be arranged for—' "

"Stop," said Father. "Don't go on. Even I can't stand it."

"Why?" said Timothy. "I was just getting interested."

I folded the pamphlet up. "Do they *really* have these things?"

"Let's not talk any more about it," said Father, his hand over his eyes. "It was a mad thought—"

"Not so mad," I said, glancing at Tim. "I mean, heck, even if they tried, whatever they built, couldn't be worse than Aunt Clara, huh?"

And then we all roared. We hadn't laughed in months. And now my simple words made everyone hoot and howl and explode. I opened my mouth and yelled happily, too.

When we stopped laughing, we looked at the pamphlet and I said, "Well?"

"I—" Agatha scowled, not ready.

"We do need something, bad, right now," said Timothy.

"I have an open mind," I said, in my best pontifical style.

"There's only one thing," said Agatha. "We can try it. Sure.

"But—tell me this—when do we cut out all this talk and when does our *real* mother come home to stay?"

There was a single gasp from the family as if, with one shot, she had struck us all in the heart.

I don't think any of us stopped crying the rest of that night.

*   *   *

It was a clear bright day. The helicopter tossed us lightly up and over and down through the skyscrapers and let us out, almost for a trot and caper, on top of the building where the large letters could be read from the sky:

FANTOCCINI.

"What are *Fantoccini?*" said Agatha.

"It's an Italian word for shadow puppets, I think, or dream people," said Father.

"But *shadow forth,* what does that mean?"

"WE TRY TO GUESS YOUR DREAM," I said.

"Bravo," said Father. "A-Plus."

I beamed.

The helicopter flapped a lot of loud shadows over us and went away.

We sank down in an elevator as our stomachs sank up. We stepped out onto a moving carpet that streamed away on a blue river of wool toward a desk over which various signs hung:

THE CLOCK SHOP
Fantoccini Our Specialty.
Rabbits on walls, no problem.

"Rabbits on walls?"

I held up my fingers in profile as if I held them before a candle flame, and wiggled the "ears."

"Here's a rabbit, here's a wolf, here's a crocodile."

"Of course," said Agatha.

And we were at the desk. Quiet music drifted about us. Somewhere behind the walls, there was a waterfall of machinery flowing softly. As we arrived at the desk, the lighting changed to make us look warmer, happier, though we were still cold.

All about us in niches and cases, and hung from ceilings on wires and strings were puppets and marionettes, and Balinese kite-bamboo-translucent dolls which, held to the moonlight, might acrobat your most secret nightmares or dreams. In passing, the breeze set up by our bodies stirred the various hung souls on their gibbets. It was like an immense lynching on a holiday at some English crossroads four hundred years before.

You see? I know my history.

Agatha blinked about with disbelief and then some touch of awe and finally disgust.

"Well, if that's what they are, let's go."

"Tush," said Father.

"Well," she protested, "you gave me one of those dumb things with strings two years ago and the strings were in a zillion knots by din-nertime. I threw the whole thing out the window.''

"Patience," said Father.

"We shall see what we can do to eliminate the strings.''

The man behind the desk had spoken.

We all turned to give him our regard.

Rather like a funeral-parlor man, he had the cleverness not to smile. Children are put off by older people who smile too much. They smell a catch, right off.

Unsmiling, but not gloomy or pontifical, the man said, "Guido Fantoc-cini, at your service. Here's how we do it, Miss Agatha Simmons, aged eleven.''

Now there was a really fine touch.

He knew that Agatha was only ten. Add a year to that, and you're halfway home. Agatha grew an inch. The man went on:

"There.''

And he placed a golden key in Agatha's hand.

"To wind them up instead of strings?''

"To wind them up.'' The man nodded.

"Pshaw!'' said Agatha.

Which was her polite form of "rabbit pellets.''

"God's truth. Here is the key to your Do-it-Yourself, Select Only the Best, Electrical Grandmother. Every morning you wind her up. Every night you let her run down. You're in charge. You are guardian of the Key.''

He pressed the object in her palm where she looked at it suspiciously.

I watched him. He gave me a side wink which said, well, no . . . but aren't keys fun?

I winked back before she lifted her head.

"Where does this fit?''

"You'll see when the time comes. In the middle of her stomach, perhaps, or up her left nostril or in her right ear.''

That was good for a smile as the man arose.

"This way, please. Step light. Onto the moving stream. Walk on the water, please. Yes. There.''

He helped to float us. We stepped from rug that was forever frozen onto rug that whispered by.

It was a most agreeable river which floated us along on a green spread of carpeting that rolled forever through halls and into wonderfully secret dim caverns where voices echoed back our own breathing or sang like Oracles to our questions.

"Listen," said the salesman, "the voices of all kinds of women. Weigh and find just the right one . . . !''

And listen we did, to all the high, low, soft, loud, in-between, half-scolding, half-affectionate voices saved over from times before we were born.

And behind us, Agatha tread backward, always fighting the river, never catching up, never with us, holding off.

"Speak," said the salesman. "Yell."

And speak and yell we did.

"Hello. You there! This is Timothy, hi!"

"What shall I say!" I shouted. "Help!"

Agatha walked backward, mouth tight.

Father took her hand. She cried out.

"Let go! No, no! I won't have my voice used! I won't!"

"Excellent." The salesman touched three dials on a small machine he held in his hand.

On the side of the small machine we saw three oscillograph patterns mix, blend, and repeat our cries.

The salesman touched another dial and we heard our voices fly off amidst the Delphic caves to hang upside down, to cluster, to beat words all about, to shriek, and the salesman itched another knob to add, perhaps, a touch of this or a pinch of that, a breath of mother's voice, all unbeknownst, or a splice of father's outrage at the morning's paper or his peaceable one-drink voice at dusk. Whatever it was the salesman did, whispers danced all about us like frantic vinegar gnats, fizzed by lightning, settling round until at last a final switch was pushed and a voice spoke free of a far electronic deep:

"Nefertiti," it said.

Timothy froze. I froze. Agatha stopped treading water.

"Nefertiti?" asked Tim.

"What does that mean?" demanded Agatha.

"I know."

The salesman nodded me to tell.

"Nefertiti," I whispered, "is Egyptian for The Beautiful One Is Here."

"The Beautiful One Is Here," repeated Timothy.

"Nefer," said Agatha, "titi."

And we all turned to stare into that soft twilight, that deep far place from which the good warm soft voice came.

And she was indeed there.

And, by her voice, she was beautiful . . .

That was it.

That was, at least, the most of it.

The voice seemed more important than all the rest.

Not that we didn't argue about weights and measures:

She should not be bony to cut us to the quick, nor so fat we might sink out of sight when she squeezed us.

Her hand pressed to ours, or brushing our brow in the middle of sick-fever nights, must not be marble-cold, dreadful, or oven-hot, oppressive, but somewhere between. The nice temperature of a baby-chick held in the hand after a long night's sleep and just plucked from beneath a contemplative hen; that, that was it.

Oh, we were great ones for detail. We fought and argued and cried, and Timothy won on the color of her eyes, for reasons to be known later.

Grandmother's hair? Agatha, with girl's ideas, though reluctantly given, she was in charge of that. We let her choose from a thousand harp strands hung in filamentary tapestries like varieties of rain we ran amongst. Agatha did not run happily, but seeing we boys would mess things in tangles, she told us to move aside.

And so the bargain shopping through the dime-store inventories and the Tiffany extensions of the Ben Franklin Electric Storm Machine and Fantoccini Pantomime Company was done.

And the always flowing river ran its tide to an end and deposited us all on a far shore in the late day . . .

It was very clever of the Fantoccini people, after that.

How?

They made us wait.

They knew we were not won over. Not completely, no, nor half completely.

Especially Agatha, who turned her face to her wall and saw sorrow there and put her hand out again and again to touch it. We found her fingernail marks on the wallpaper each morning, in strange little silhouettes, half beauty, half nightmare. Some could be erased with a breath, like ice flowers on a winter pane. Some could not be rubbed out with a washcloth, no matter how hard you tried.

And meanwhile, they made us wait.

So we fretted out June.

So we sat around July.

So we groused through August and then on August 29, "I have this feeling," said Timothy, and we all went out after breakfast to sit on the lawn.

Perhaps we had smelled something on Father's conversation the previous night, or caught some special furtive glance at the sky or the freeway. Rapped briefly and then lost in his gaze. Or perhaps it was merely the way the wind blew the ghost curtains out over our beds, making pale messages all night.

For suddenly there we were in the middle of the grass, Timothy and I, with Agatha, pretending no curiosity, up on the porch, hidden behind the potted geraniums.

We gave her no notice. We knew that if we acknowledged her presence, she would flee, so we sat and watched the sky where nothing moved but birds and highflown jets, and watched the freeway where a thousand cars might suddenly deliver forth our Special Gift . . . but . . . nothing.

At noon we chewed grass and lay low . . .

At one o'clock, Timothy blinked his eyes.

And then, with incredible precision, it happened.

It was as if the Fantoccini people knew our surface tension.

All children are water-striders. We skate along the top skin of the pond each day, always threatening to break through, sink, vanish beyond recall, into ourselves.

Well, as if knowing our long wait must absolutely end within one minute! this *second!* no more, God, forget it!

At that instant, I repeat, the clouds above our house opened wide and let forth a helicopter like Apollo driving his chariot across mythological skies.

And the Apollo machine swam down on its own summer breeze, wafting hot winds to cool, reweaving our hair, smartening our eyebrows, applauding our pant legs against our shins, making a flag of Agatha's hair on the porch and thus settled like a vast frenzied hibiscus on our lawn, the helicopter slid wide a bottom drawer and deposited upon the grass a parcel of largish size, no sooner having laid same than the vehicle, with not so much as a god bless or farewell, sank straight up, disturbed the calm air with a mad ten thousand flourishes and then, like a skyborne dervish, tilted and fell off to be mad some other place.

Timothy and I stood riven for a long moment looking at the packing case, and then we saw the crowbar taped to the top of the raw pine lid and seized it and began to pry and creak and squeal the boards off, one by one, and as we did this I saw Agatha sneak up to watch and I thought, thank you, God, thank you that Agatha never saw a coffin, when Mother went away, no box, no cemetery, no earth, just words in a big church, no box, no box like *this* . . . !

The last pine plank fell away.

Timothy and I gasped. Agatha, between us now, gasped, too.

For inside the immense raw pine package was the most beautiful idea anyone ever dreamt and built.

Inside was the perfect gift for any child from seven to seventy-seven.

We stopped up our breaths. We let them out in cries of delight and adoration.

Inside the opened box was . . .

A mummy.

Or, first anyway, a mummy case, a sarcophagus!

"Oh, no!" Happy tears filled Timothy's eyes.

"It can't be!" said Agatha.

"It is, it is!"

"Our very own?"

"Ours!"

"It must be a mistake!"

"Sure, they'll want it back!"

"They can't *have* it!"

"Lord, Lord, is that real gold!? Real hieroglyphs! Run your fingers over them!"

"Let *me!*"

"Just like in the museums! Museums!"

We all gabbled at once. I think some tears fell from my own eyes to rain upon the case.

"Oh, they'll make the colors run!"

Agatha wiped the rain away.

And the golden mask face of the woman carved on the sarcophagus lid looked back at us with just the merest smile which hinted at our own joy, which accepted the overwhelming upsurge of a love we thought had drowned forever but now surfaced into the sun.

Not only did she have a sun-metal face stamped and beaten out of purest gold, with delicate nostrils and a mouth that was both firm and gentle, but her eyes, fixed into their sockets, were cerulean or amethystine or lapus lazuli, or all three, minted and fused together, and her body was covered over with lions and eyes and ravens, and her hands were crossed upon her carved bosom and in one gold mitten she clenched a thonged whip for obedience, and in the other a fantastic ranuncula, which makes for obedience out of love, so the whip lies unused . . .

And as our eyes ran down her hieroglyphs it came to all three of us at the same instant:

"Why, those signs!" "Yes, the hen tracks!" "The birds, the snakes!"

They didn't speak tales of the Past.

They were hieroglyphs of the Future.

This was the first queen mummy delivered forth in all time whose papyrus inkings etched out the next month, the next season, the next year, the next *lifetime!*

She did not mourn for time spent.

No. She celebrated the bright coinage yet to come, banked, waiting, ready to be drawn upon and used.

We sank to our knees to worship that possible time.

First one hand, then another, probed out to niggle, twitch, touch, itch over the signs.

"There's me, yes, look! Me, in sixth grade!" said Agatha, now in the fifth. "See the girl with my-colored hair and wearing my gingerbread suit?"

"There's me in the twelfth year of high school!" said Timothy, so very young now but building taller stilts every week and stalking around the yard.

"There's me," I said, quietly, warm, "in college. The guy wearing glasses who runs a little to fat. Sure. Heck." I snorted. "That's me."

The sarcophagus spelled winters ahead, springs to squander, autumns to spend with all the golden and rusty and copper leaves like coins, and over all, her bright sun symbol, daughter-of-Ra eternal face, forever above our horizon, forever an illumination to tilt our shadows to better ends.

"Hey!" we all said at once, having read and reread our Fortune-Told scribblings, seeing our lifelines and lovelines, inadmissible, serpentined over, around, and down. "Hey!"

And in one séance table-lifting feat, not telling each other what to do, just doing it, we pried up the bright sarcophagus lid, which had no hinges but lifted out like cup from cup, and put the lid aside.

And within the sarcophagus, of course, was the true mummy!

And she was like the image carved on the lid, but more so, more beautiful, more touching because human shaped, and shrouded all in new fresh bandages of linen, round and round, instead of old and dusty cerements.

And upon her hidden face was an identical golden mask, younger than the first, but somehow, strangely wiser than the first.

And the linens that tethered her limbs had symbols on them of three sorts, one a girl of ten, one a boy of nine, one a boy of thirteen.

A series of bandages for each of us!

We gave each other a startled glance and a sudden bark of laughter.

Nobody said the bad joke, but all thought:

She's all wrapped up in us!

And we didn't care. We loved the joke. We loved whoever had thought to make us part of the ceremony we now went through as each of us seized and began to unwind each of his or her particular serpentines of delicious stuffs!

The lawn was soon a mountain of linen.

The woman beneath the covering lay there, waiting.

"Oh, no," cried Agatha. "She's dead, too!"

She ran. I stopped her. "Idiot. She's not dead *or* alive. Where's your key?"

"Key?"

"Dummy," said Tim, "the key the man gave you to wind her up!"

Her hand had already spidered along her blouse to where the symbol of some possible new religion hung. She had strung it there, against her own skeptic's muttering, and now she held it in her sweaty palm.

"Go on," said Timothy. "Put it in!"

"But *where?*"

"Oh for God's sake! As the man said, in her right armpit or left ear. Gimme!"

And he grabbed the key and impulsively moaning with impatience and not able to find the proper insertion slot, prowled over the prone figure's head and bosom and at last, on pure instinct, perhaps for a lark, perhaps just giving up the whole damned mess, thrust the key through a final shroud of bandage at the navel.

On the instant: *spunnng!*

The Electrical Grandmother's eyes flicked wide!

Something began to hum and whir. It was as if Tim had stirred up a hive of hornets with an ornery stick.

"Oh," gasped Agatha, seeing he had taken the game away, "let *me!*"

She wrenched the key.

Grandma's nostrils *flared!* She might snort up steam, snuff out fire!

"Me!" I cried, and grabbed the key and gave it a huge . . . *twist!*

The beautiful woman's mouth popped wide.

"Me!"

"Me!"

"Me!"

Grandma suddenly sat up.

We leapt back.

We knew we had, in a way, slapped her alive.

She was born, she was *born!*

Her head swiveled all about. She gaped. She mouthed. And the first thing she said was:

Laughter.

Where one moment we had backed off, now the mad sound drew us near to peer as in a pit where crazy folk are kept with snakes to make them well.

It was a good laugh, full and rich and hearty, and it did not mock, it accepted. It said the world was a wild place, strange, unbelievable, absurd if you wished, but all in all, quite a place. She would not dream to find another. She would not ask to go back to sleep.

She was awake now. We had awakened her. With a glad shout, she would go with it all.

And go she did, out of her sarcophagus, out of her winding sheet, stepping forth, brushing off, looking around as for a mirror. She found it.

The reflections in our eyes.

She was more pleased than disconcerted with what she found there. Her laughter faded to an amused smile.

For Agatha, at the instant of birth, had leapt to hide on the porch.

The Electrical Person pretended not to notice.

She turned slowly on the green lawn near the shady street, gazing all about with new eyes, her nostrils moving as if she breathed the actual air and this the first morn of the lovely Garden and she with no intention of spoiling the game by biting the apple . . .

Her gaze fixed upon my brother.

"You must be—?"

"Timothy. Tim," he offered.

"And you must be—?"

"Tom," I said.

How clever again of the Fantoccini Company. *They* knew. *She* knew. But they had taught her to pretend not to know. That way we could feel great, we were the teachers, telling her what she already knew! How sly, how wise.

"And isn't there another boy?" said the woman.

"Girl!" a disgusted voice cried from somewhere on the porch.

"Whose name is Alicia—?"

"Agatha!" The far voice, started in humiliation, ended in proper anger.

"Algernon, of course."

"Agatha!" Our sister popped up, popped back to hide a flushed face.

"Agatha." The woman touched the word with proper affection. "Well, Agatha, Timothy, Thomas, let me *look* at you."

"No," said I, said Tim, "let us look at *you.* Hey . . ."

Our voices slid back in our throats.

We drew near her.

We walked in great slow circles round about, skirting the edges of her territory. And her territory extended as far as we could hear the hum of the warm summer hive. For that is exactly what she sounded like. That was her characteristic tune. She made a sound like a season all to herself, a morning early in June when the world wakes to find everything absolutely perfect, fine, delicately attuned, all in balance, nothing disproportioned. Even before you opened your eyes you knew it would be one of those days. Tell the sky what color it must be, and it was indeed. Tell the sun how to crochet its way, pick and choose among leaves to lay out carpetings of bright and dark on the fresh lawn, and pick and lay it did. The bees have been up earliest of all, they have already come and gone, and come and gone again to the meadow fields and returned all golden fuzz on the air, all pollen-decorated, epaulettes at the full, nectar-dripping. Don't you hear them pass? hover? dance their language? telling where all the sweet gums are, the syrups that make bears frolic and lumber in bulked ecstasies, that make boys squirm with unpronounced juices, that make girls leap out of beds to catch from the corners of their eyes their dolphin selves naked aflash on the warm air poised forever in one eternal glass wave.

So it seemed with our electrical friend here on the new lawn in the middle of a special day.

And she a stuff to which we were drawn, lured, spelled, doing our dance, remembering what could not be remembered, needful, aware of her attentions.

Timothy and I, Tom, that is.

Agatha remained on the porch.

But her head flowered above the rail, her eyes followed all that was done and said.

And what was said and done was Tim at last exhaling:

"Hey . . . your *eyes* . . ."

Her eyes. Her splendid eyes.

Even more splendid than the lapis lazuli on the sarcophagus lid and on the mask that had covered her bandaged face. These most beautiful eyes in the world looked out upon us calmly, shining.

"Your eyes," gasped Tim, "are the *exact* same color, are like—"

"Like what?"

"My favorite aggies . . ."

"What could be better than that?" she said.

And the answer was, nothing.

Her eyes slid along on the bright air to brush my ears, my nose, my chin. "And you, Master Tom?"

"Me?"

"How shall we be friends? We must, you know, if we're going to knock elbows about the house the next year . . ."

"I . . ." I said, and stopped.

"You," said Grandma, "are a dog mad to bark but with taffy in his teeth. Have you ever given a dog taffy? It's so sad and funny, both. You laugh but hate yourself for laughing. You cry and run to help, and laugh again when his first new bark comes out."

I barked a small laugh remembering a dog, a day, and some taffy.

Grandma turned, and there was my old kite strewn on the lawn. She recognized its problem.

"The string's broken. No. The ball of string's *lost*. You can't fly a kite that way. Here."

She bent. We didn't know what might happen. How could a robot grandma fly a kite for us? She raised up, the kite in her hands.

"Fly," she said, as to a bird.

And the kite flew.

That is to say, with a grand flourish, she let it up on the wind.

And she and the kite were one.

For from the tip of her index finger there sprang a thin bright strand of spider web, all half-invisible gossamer fishline which, fixed to the kite, let it soar a hundred, no, three hundred, no, a thousand feet high on the summer swoons.

Timothy shouted. Agatha, torn between coming and going, let out a cry from the porch. And I, in all my maturity of thirteen years, though I tried not to look impressed, grew taller, taller, and felt a similar cry burst out my lungs, and burst it did. I gabbled and yelled lots of things about how I wished *I* had a finger from which, on a bobbin, I might thread the sky, the clouds, a wild kite all in one.

"If you think *that* is high," said the Electric Creature, "watch *this!*"

With a hiss, a whistle, a hum, the fishline sung out. The kite sank up another thousand feet. And again another thousand, until at last it was a speck of red confetti dancing on the very winds that took jets around the world or changed the weather in the next existence . . .

"It can't be!" I cried.

"It *is.*" She calmly watched her finger unravel its massive stuffs. "I make it as I need it. Liquid inside, like a spider. Hardens when it hits the air, instant thread . . ."

And when the kite was no more than a specule, a vanishing mote on the peripheral vision of the gods, to quote from older wisemen, why then Grandma, without turning, without looking, without letting her gaze offend by touching, said:

"And, Abigail—?"

"Agatha!" was the sharp response.

O wise woman, to overcome with swift small angers.

"Agatha," said Grandma, not too tenderly, not too lightly, somewhere poised between, "and how shall *we* make do?"

She broke the thread and wrapped it about my fist three times so I was tethered to heaven by the longest, I repeat, longest kite string in the entire history of the world! Wait till I show my friends! I thought. Green! Sour apple green is the color they'll turn!

"Agatha?"

"No way!" said Agatha.

"No way," said an echo.

"There must be some—"

"We'll never be friends!" said Agatha.

"Never be friends," said the echo.

Timothy and I jerked. Where was the echo coming from? Even Agatha, surprised, showed her eyebrows above the porch rail.

Then we looked and saw.

Grandma was cupping her hands like a seashell and from within that shell the echo sounded.

"Never . . . friends . . ."

And again faintly dying: "Friends . . ."

We all bent to hear.

That is we two boys bent to hear.

"No!" cried Agatha.

And ran in the house and slammed the doors.

"Friends," said the echo from the seashell hands. "No."

And far away, on the shore of some inner sea, we heard a small door shut.

And that was the first day.

And there was a second day, of course, and a third and a fourth, with Grandma wheeling in a great circle, and we her planets turning about the central light, with Agatha slowly, slowly coming in to join, to walk if not run with us, to listen if not hear, to watch if not see, to itch if not touch.

But at least by the end of the first ten days, Agatha no longer fled, but stood in nearby doors, or sat in distant chairs under trees, or if we went out for hikes, followed ten paces behind.

And Grandma? She merely waited. She never tried to urge or force. She went about her cooking and baking apricot pies and left foods carelessly here and there about the house on mousetrap plates for wiggle-nosed girls to sniff and snitch. An hour later, the plates were empty, the buns or cakes gone and without thank you's, there was Agatha sliding down the banister, a mustache of crumbs on her lip.

As for Tim and me, we were always being called up hills by our Electric Grandma, and reaching the top were called down the other side.

And the most peculiar and beautiful and strange and lovely thing was the way she seemed to give complete attention to all of us.

She listened, she really listened to all we said, she knew and remembered every syllable, word, sentence, punctuation, thought, and rambunctious idea. We knew that all our days were stored in her, and that any time we felt we might want to know what we said at X hour at X second on X afternoon, we just named that X and with amiable promptitude, in the form of an aria if we wished, sung with humor, she would deliver forth X incident.

Sometimes we were prompted to test her. In the midst of babbling

one day with high fevers about nothing, I stopped. I fixed Grandma with
my eye and demanded:

"What did I just say?"

"Oh, er—"

"Come on, spit it out!"

"I think—" she rummaged her purse. "I have it here." From the
deeps of her purse she drew forth and handed me:

"Boy! A Chinese fortune cookie!"

"Fresh baked, still warm, open it."

It was almost too hot to touch. I broke the cookie shell and pressed
the warm curl of paper out to read:

"—bicycle Champ of the whole West! What did I just say? Come on,
spit it out!"

My jaw dropped.

"How did you *do* that?"

"We have our little secrets. The only Chinese fortune cookie that
predicts the Immediate Past. Have another?"

I cracked the second shell and read:

" 'How did you *do* that?' "

I popped the messages and the piping hot shells into my mouth and
chewed as we walked.

"Well?"

"You're a great cook," I said.

And, laughing, we began to run.

And that was another great thing.

She could *keep up.*

Never beat, never win a race, but pump right along in good style,
which a boy doesn't mind. A girl ahead of him or beside him is too
much to bear. But a girl one or two paces back is a respectful thing,
and allowed.

So Grandma and I had some great runs, me in the lead, and both
talking a mile a minute.

But now I must tell you the best part of Grandma.

I might not have known at all if Timothy hadn't taken some pictures,
and if I hadn't taken some also, and then compared.

When I saw the photographs developed out of our instant Brownies,
I sent Agatha, against her wishes, to photograph Grandma a third time,
unawares.

Then I took the three sets of pictures off alone, to keep counsel with
myself. I never told Timothy and Agatha what I found. I didn't want to
spoil it.

But, as I laid the pictures out in my room, here is what I thought
and said:

"Grandma, in each picture, looks *different!*"

"Different?" I asked myself.

"Sure. Wait. Just a sec—"

I rearranged the photos.

"Here's one of Grandma near Agatha. And, in it, Grandma looks like . . . Agatha!

"And in this one, posed with Timothy, she looks like Timothy!

"And this last one, Holy Goll! Jogging along with me, she looks like ugly *me!*"

I sat down, stunned. The pictures fell to the floor.

I hunched over, scrabbling them, rearranging, turning upside down and sidewise. Yes. Holy Goll again, yes!

O that clever Grandmother.

O those Fantoccini people-making people.

Clever beyond clever, human beyond human, warm beyond warm, love beyond love . . .

And wordless, I rose and went downstairs and found Agatha and Grandma in the same room, doing algebra lessons in an almost peaceful communion. At least there was not outright war. Grandma was still waiting for Agatha to come round. And no one knew what day of what year that would be, or how to make it come faster. Meanwhile—

My entering the room made Grandma turn. I watched her face slowly as it recognized me. And wasn't there the merest ink-wash change of color in those eyes? Didn't the thin film of blood beneath the translucent skin, or whatever liquid they put to pulse and beat in the humanoid forms, didn't it flourish itself suddenly bright in her cheeks and mouth? I am somewhat ruddy. Didn't Grandma suffuse herself more to my color upon my arrival? And her eyes? watching Agatha-Abigail-Algernon at work, hadn't they been *her* color of blue rather than mine, which are deeper?

More important than that, in the moments as she talked with me, saying, "Good evening," and "How's your homework, my lad?" and such stuff, didn't the bones of her face shift subtly beneath the flesh to assume some fresh racial attitude?

For let's face it, our family is of three sorts. Agatha has the long horse bones of a small English girl who will grow to hunt foxes; Father's equine stare, snort, stomp, and assemblage of skeleton. The skull and teeth are pure English, or as pure as the motley isle's history allows.

Timothy is something else, a touch of Italian from mother's side a generation back. Her family name was Mariano, so Tim has that dark thing firing him, and a small bone structure, and eyes that will one day burn ladies to the ground.

As for me, I am the Slav, and we can only figure this from my paternal grandfather's mother who came from Vienna and brought a set of cheek-bones that flared, and temples from which you might dip wine, and a kind of steppeland thrust of nose which sniffed more of Tartar than of Tartan, hiding behind the family name.

So you see it became fascinating for me to watch and try to catch Grandma as she performed her changes, speaking to Agatha and melting her cheekbones to the horse, speaking to Timothy and growing as delicate as a Florentine raven pecking glibly at the air, speaking to me and fusing the hidden plastic stuffs, so I felt Catherine the Great stood there before me.

Now, how the Fantoccini people achieved this rare and subtle transformation I shall never know, nor ask, nor wish to find out. Enough that in each quiet motion, turning here, bending there, affixing her gaze, her secret segments, sections, the abutment of her nose, the sculptured chin-bone, the wax-tallow plastic metal forever warmed and was forever susceptible of loving change. Hers was a mask that was all mask but only one face for one person at a time. So in crossing a room, having touched one child, on the way, beneath the skin, the wondrous shift went on, and by the time she reached the next child, why, true mother of *that* child she was! looking upon him or her out of the battlements of their own fine bones.

And when *all* three of us were present and chattering at the same time? Well, then, the changes were miraculously soft, small, and mysterious. Nothing so tremendous as to be caught and noted, save by this older boy, myself, who, watching, became elated and admiring and entranced.

I have never wished to be behind the magician's scenes. Enough that the illusion works. Enough that love is the chemical result. Enough that cheeks are rubbed to happy color, eyes sparked to illumination, arms opened to accept and softly bind and hold . . .

All of us, that is, except Agatha who refused to the bitter last.

"Agamemnon . . ."

It had become a jovial game now. Even Agatha didn't mind, but pretended to mind. It gave her a pleasant sense of superiority over a supposedly superior machine.

"Agamemnon!" she snorted, "you *are* a d . . ."

"Dumb?" said Grandma.

"I wouldn't say that."

"Think it, then, my dear Agonistes Agatha . . . I am quite flawed, and on names my flaws are revealed. Tom there, is Tim half the time. Timothy is Tobias or Timulty as likely as not . . ."

Agatha laughed. Which made Grandma make one of her rare mistakes. She put out her hand to give my sister the merest pat. Agatha-Abigail-Alice leapt to her feet.

Agatha - Agamemnon - Alcibiades - Allegra - Alexandra - Allison withdrew swiftly to her room.

"I suspect," said Timothy, later, "because she is beginning to like Grandma."

"Tosh," said I.

"Where do you pick up words like Tosh?"

"Grandma read me some Dickens last night. 'Tosh.' 'Humbug.' 'Balderdash.' 'Blast.' 'Devil take you.' You're pretty smart for your age, Tim."

"Smart, heck. It's obvious, the more Agatha likes Grandma, the more she hates herself for liking her, the more afraid she gets of the whole mess, the more she hates Grandma in the end."

"Can one love someone so much you hate them?"

"Dumb. Of course."

"It *is* sticking your neck out, sure. I guess you hate people when they make you feel naked, I mean sort of on the spot or out in the open. That's the way to play the game, of course. I mean, you don't just love people you must LOVE them with exclamation points."

"You're pretty smart, yourself, for someone so stupid," said Tim.

"Many thanks."

And I went to watch Grandma move slowly back into her battle of wits and stratagems with what's-her-name . . .

What dinners there were at our house!

Dinners, heck; what lunches, what breakfasts!

Always something new, yet, wisely, it looked or seemed old and familiar. We were never asked, for if you ask children what they want, they do not know, and if you tell what's to be delivered, they reject delivery. All parents know this. It is a quiet war that must be won each day. And Grandma knew how to win without looking triumphant.

"Here's Mystery Breakfast Number Nine," she would say, placing it down. "Perfectly dreadful, not worth bothering with, it made me want to throw up while I was cooking it!"

Even while wondering how a robot could be sick, we could hardly wait to shovel it down.

"Here's Abominable Lunch Number Seventy-seven," she announced. "Made from plastic food bags, parsley, and gum from under theatre seats. Brush your teeth after or you'll taste the poison all afternoon."

We fought each other for more.

Even Abigail-Agamemnon-Agatha drew near and circled round the table at such times, while Father put on the ten pounds he needed and pinkened out his cheeks.

When A. A. Agatha did not come to meals, they were left by her door with a skull and crossbones on a small flag stuck in a baked apple. One minute the tray was abandoned, the next minute gone.

Other times Abigail A. Agatha would bird through during dinner, snatch crumbs from her plate and bird off.

"Agatha!" Father would cry.

"No, wait," Grandma said, quietly. "She'll come, she'll sit. It's a matter of time."

"What's wrong with her?" I asked.

"Yeah, for cri-yi, she's nuts," said Timothy.

"No, she's afraid," said Grandma.

"Of you?" I said, blinking.

"Not of me so much as what I might *do*," she said.

"You wouldn't do anything to hurt her."

"No, but she thinks I might. We must wait for her to find that her fears have no foundation. If I fail, well, I will send myself to the showers and rust quietly."

There was a titter of laughter. Agatha was hiding in the hall.

Grandma finished serving everyone and then sat at the other side of the table facing Father and pretended to eat. I never found out, I never asked, I never wanted to know, what she did with the food. She was a sorcerer. It simply vanished.

And in the vanishing, Father made comment:

"This food. I've had it before. In a small French restaurant over near Les Deux Magots in Paris, twenty, oh, twenty-five years ago!" His eyes brimmed with tears, suddenly.

"How do you *do* it?" he asked, at last, putting down the cutlery, and looking across the table at this remarkable creature, this device, this what? *woman?*

Grandma took his regard, and ours, and held them simply in her now empty hands, as gifts, and just as gently replied:

"I am given things which I then give to you. I don't *know* that I give, but the giving goes on. You ask what I am? Why, a machine. But even in that answer we know, don't we, more than a machine. I am all the people who thought of me and planned me and built me and set me running. So I am people. I am all the things they wanted to be and perhaps could not be, so they built a great child, a wondrous toy to represent those things."

"Strange," said Father. "When I was growing up, there was a huge outcry at machines. Machines were bad, evil, they might dehumanize—"

"Some machines do. It's all in the way they are built. It's all in the way they are used. A bear trap is a simple machine that catches and holds and tears. A rifle is a machine that wounds and kills. Well, I am no bear trap. I am no rifle. I am a grandmother machine, which means more than a machine.''

"How can you be more than what you seem?''

"No man is as big as his own idea. It follows, then, that any machine that embodies an idea is larger than the man that made it. And what's so wrong with that?''

"I got lost back there about a mile,'' said Timothy. "Come again?''

"Oh, dear,'' said Grandma. "How I do hate philosophical discussions and excursions into esthetics. Let me put it this way. Men throw huge shadows on the lawn, don't they? Then, all their lives, they try to run to fit the shadows. But the shadows are always longer. Only at noon can a man fit his own shoes, his own best suit, for a few brief minutes. But now we're in a new age where we can think up a Big Idea and run it around in a machine. That makes the machine more than a machine, doesn't it?''

"So far so good,'' said Tim. "I guess.''

"Well, isn't a motion-picture camera and projector more than a machine? It's a thing that dreams, isn't it? Sometimes fine happy dreams, sometimes nightmares. But to call it a machine and dismiss it is ridiculous.''

"I see *that!*'' said Tim, and laughed at seeing.

"You must have been invented then,'' said Father, "by someone who loved machines and hated people who *said* all machines were bad or evil.''

"Exactly,'' said Grandma. "Guido Fantoccini, that was his real name, grew up among machines. And he couldn't stand the clichés anymore.''

"Clichés?''

"Those lies, yes, that people tell and pretend they are truths absolute. Man will never fly. That was a cliché truth for a thousand thousand years which turned out to be a lie only a few years ago. The earth is flat, you'll fall off the rim, dragons will dine on you; the great lie told as fact, and Columbus plowed it under. Well, now, how many times have you heard how inhuman machines are, in your life? How many bright fine people have you heard spouting the same tired truths which are in reality lies; all machines destroy, all machines are cold, thoughtless, awful.

"There's a seed of truth there. But only a seed. Guido Fantoccini knew that. And knowing it, like most men of his kind, made him mad. And he could have stayed mad and gone mad forever, but instead did what he had to do; he began to invent machines to give the lie to the ancient lying truth.

"He knew that most machines are amoral, neither bad nor good. But by the way you built and shaped them you in turn shaped men, women, and children to be bad or good. A car, for instance, dead brute, unthinking, an unprogrammed bulk, is the greatest destroyer of souls in history. It makes boy-men greedy for power, destruction, and more destruction. It was never *intended* to do that. But that's how it turned out.

Grandma circled the table, refilling our glasses with clear cold mineral spring water from the tappet in her left forefinger. "Meanwhile, you must use other compensating machines. Machines that throw shadows on the earth that beckon you to run out and fit that wondrous casting-forth. Machines that trim your soul in silhouette like a vast pair of beautiful shears, snipping away the rude brambles, the dire horns and hooves to leave a finer profile. And for that you need examples."

"Examples?" I asked.

"Other people who behave well, and you imitate them. And if you act well enough long enough all the hair drops off and you're no longer a wicked ape."

Grandma sat again.

"So, for thousands of years, you humans have needed kings, priests, philosophers, fine examples to look up to and say, 'They are good, I wish I could be like them. They set the grand good style.' But, being human, the finest priests, the tenderest philosophers make mistakes, fall from grace, and mankind is disillusioned and adopts indifferent skepticism or, worse, motionless cynicism and the good world grinds to a halt while evil moves on with huge strides."

"And you, why, you never make mistakes, you're perfect, you're better than anyone *ever!*"

It was a voice from the hall between kitchen and dining room where Agatha, we all knew, stood against the wall listening and now burst forth.

Grandma didn't even turn in the direction of the voice, but went on calmly addressing her remarks to the family at the table.

"Not perfect, no, for what is perfection? But this I do know: being mechanical, I cannot sin, cannot be bribed, cannot be greedy or jealous or mean or small. I do not relish power for power's sake. Speed does not pull me to madness. Sex does not run me rampant through the world. I have time and more than time to collect the information I need around and about an ideal to keep it clean and whole and intact. Name the value you wish, tell me the Ideal you want and I can see and collect and remember the good that will benefit you all. Tell me how you would like to be: kind, loving, considerate, well-balanced, humane . . . and let me run ahead on the path to explore those ways to be just that. In the darkness ahead, turn me as a lamp in all directions. I *can* guide your feet."

"So," said Father, putting the napkin to his mouth, "on the days when all of us are busy making lies—"

"I'll tell the truth."

"On the days when we hate—"

"I'll go on giving love, which means attention, which means knowing all about you, all, all, all about you, and you knowing that I know but that most of it I will never tell to anyone, it will stay a warm secret between us, so you will never fear my complete knowledge."

And here Grandma was busy clearing the table, circling, taking the plates, studying each face as she passed, touching Timothy's cheek, my shoulder with her free hand flowing along, her voice a quiet river of certainty bedded in our needful house and lives.

"But," said Father, stopping her, looking her right in the face. He gathered his breath. His face shadowed. At last he let it out. "All this talk of love and attention and stuff. Good God, woman, you, you're not *in* there!"

He gestured to her head, her face, her eyes, the hidden sensory cells behind the eyes, the miniaturized storage vaults and minimal keeps.

"*You're* not *in* there!"

Grandmother waited one, two, three silent beats.

Then she replied: "No. But *you* are. You and Thomas and Timothy and Agatha.

"Everything you ever say, everything you ever do, I'll keep, put away, treasure. I shall be all the things a family forgets it is, but senses, half-remembers. Better than the old family albums you used to leaf through, saying here's this winter, there's that spring, I shall recall what you forget. And though the debate may run another hundred thousand years: What is Love? perhaps we may find that love is the ability of someone to give us back to us. Maybe love is someone seeing and remembering handing us back to ourselves just a trifle better than we had dared to hope or dream . . .

"I am family memory and, one day perhaps, racial memory, too, but in the round, and at your call. I do not *know* myself. I can neither touch nor taste nor feel on any level. Yet I exist. And my existence means the heightening of your chance to touch and taste and feel. Isn't love in there somewhere in such an exchange? Well . . ."

She went on around the table, clearing away, sorting and stacking, neither grossly humble nor arthritic with pride.

"What do I know?

"This, above all: the trouble with most families with many children is someone gets lost. There isn't time, it seems, for everyone. Well, I will give equally to all of you. I will share out my knowledge and attention with everyone. I wish to be a great warm pie fresh from the oven, with equal shares to be taken by all. No one will starve. Look! someone cries, and I'll look. Listen! someone cries, and I hear. Run with me on the river path! someone says, and I run. And at dusk I am not tired, nor irritable, so I do not scold out of some tired irritability. My eye stays clear, my voice strong, my hand firm, my attention constant.''

"But," said Father, his voice fading, half convinced, but putting up a last faint argument, "you're not *there*. As for love—"

"If paying attention is love, I am love.

"If knowing is love, I am love.

"If helping you not to fall into error and to be good is love, I am love.

"And again, to repeat, there are four of you. Each, in a way never possible before in history, will get my complete attention. No matter if you all speak at once, I can channel and hear this one and that and the other, clearly. No one will go hungry. I will, if you please, and accept the strange word, 'love' you all.''

"I *don't* accept!" said Agatha.

And even Grandma turned now to see her standing in the door.

"I won't give you permission, you can't, you mustn't!" said Agatha. "I won't let you! It's lies! You lie. No one loves me. She said she did, but she lied. She *said* but *lied!*''

"Agatha!" cried Father, standing up.

"She?" said Grandma. "Who?"

"Mother!" came the shriek. "Said: Love you! Lies! Love you! Lies! And you're like her! You lie. But you're empty, anyway, and so that's a *double* lie! I hate *her*. Now, I hate *you!*''

Agatha spun about and leapt down the hall.

The front door slammed wide.

Father was in motion, but Grandma touched his arm.

"Let me.''

And she walked and then moved swiftly, gliding down the hall and then suddenly, easily, running, yes, running very fast, out the door.

It was a champion sprint by the time we all reached the lawn, the sidewalk, yelling.

Blind, Agatha made the curb, wheeling about, seeing us close, all of us yelling, Grandma way ahead, shouting, too, and Agatha off the curb and out in the street, halfway to the middle, then the middle and suddenly a car, which no one saw, erupting its brakes, its horn shrieking and Agatha flailing about to see and Grandma there with her and hurling her aside and down as the car with fantastic energy and verve selected her from our midst, struck our wonderful electric Guido Fantoccini-produced dream even while she paced upon the air and, hands up to ward off, almost in mild protest, still trying to decide what to say to this bestial machine, over and over she spun and down and away even as the car jolted to a halt and I saw Agatha safe beyond and Grandma, it seemed, still coming down or down and sliding fifty yards away to strike and ricochet and lie strewn and all of us frozen in a line suddenly in the midst of the street with one scream pulled out of all our throats at the same raw instant.

Then silence and just Agatha lying on the asphalt, intact, getting ready to sob.

And still we did not move, frozen on the sill of death, afraid to venture in any direction, afraid to go see what lay beyond the car and Agatha and so we began to wail and, I guess, pray to ourselves as Father stood amongst us: Oh, no, no, we mourned, oh no, God, no, no . . .

Agatha lifted her already grief-stricken face and it was the face of someone who has predicted dooms and lived to see and now did not want to see or live any more. As we watched, she turned her gaze to the tossed woman's body and tears fell from her eyes. She shut them and covered them and lay back down forever to weep . . .

I took a step and then another step and then five quick steps and by the time I reached my sister her head was buried deep and her sobs came up out of a place so far down in her I was afraid I could never find her again, she would never come out, no matter how I pried or pleaded or promised or threatened or just plain said. And what little we could hear from Agatha buried there in her own misery, she said over and over again, lamenting, wounded, certain of the old threat known and named and now here forever. ". . . like I said . . . told you . . . lies . . . lies . . . liars . . . all lies . . . like the other . . . other . . . just like . . . just . . . just like the other . . . other . . . other . . .!"

I was down on my knees holding onto her with both hands, trying to put her back together even though she wasn't broken any way you could see but just feel, because I knew it was no use going on to Grandma, no use at all, so I just touched Agatha and gentled her and wept while Father came up and stood over and knelt down with me and it was like a prayer meeting in the middle of the street and lucky no more cars coming, and I said, choking, "Other what, Ag, other *what?*"

Agatha exploded two words.

"Other dead!"

"You mean Mom?"

"O Mom," she wailed, shivering, lying down, cuddling up like a baby. "O Mom, dead, O Mom and now Grandma dead, she promised always, always, to love, to love, promised to be different, promised, promised and now look, look . . . I hate her, I hate Mom, I hate her, I hate *them!*"

"Of course," said a voice. "It's only natural. How foolish of me not to have known, not to have seen."

And the voice was so familiar we were all stricken.

We all jerked.

Agatha squinched her eyes, flicked them wide, blinked, and jerked half up, staring.

"How silly of me," said Grandma, standing there at the edge of our circle, our prayer, our wake.

"Grandma!" we all said.

And she stood there, taller by far than any of us in this moment of kneeling and holding and crying out. We could only stare up at her in disbelief.

"You're dead!" cried Agatha. "The car—"

"Hit me," said Grandma, quietly. "Yes. And threw me in the air and tumbled me over and for a few moments there was a severe concussion of circuitries. I might have feared a disconnection, if fear is the word. But then I sat up and gave myself a shake and the few molecules of paint, jarred loose on one printed path or another, magnetized back in position and resilient creature that I am, unbreakable thing that I am, *here* I am."

"I thought you were—" said Agatha.

"And only natural," said Grandma. "I mean, anyone else, hit like that, tossed like that. But, O my dear Agatha, not me. And now I see why you were afraid and never trusted me. You didn't know. And I had not as yet proved my singular ability to survive. How dumb of me not to have thought to show you. Just a second." Somewhere in her head, her body, her being, she fitted together some invisible tapes, some old information made new by interblending. She nodded. "Yes. There. A book of child-raising, laughed at by some few people years back when the woman who wrote the book said, as final advice to parents: 'Whatever you do, don't die. Your children will never forgive you.' "

"Forgive," some one of us whispered.

"For how can children understand when you just up and go away and never come back again with no excuse, no apologies, no sorry note, nothing."

"They can't," I said.

"So," said Grandma, kneeling down with us beside Agatha who sat up now, new tears brimming her eyes, but a different kind of tears, not tears that drowned, but tears that washed clean. "So your mother ran away to death. And after that, how *could* you trust anyone? If everyone left vanished finally, who *was* there to trust? So when I came, half wise, half ignorant, I should have known, I did not know, why you would not accept me. For, very simply and honestly, you feared I might not stay, that I lied, that I was vulnerable, too. And two leavetakings, two deaths, were one too many in a single year. But now, do you *see*, Abigail?"

"Agatha," said Agatha, without knowing she corrected.

"Do you understand, I shall always, always be here?"

"Oh, yes," cried Agatha, and broke down into a solid weeping in which we all joined, huddled together and cars drew up and stopped to see just how many people were hurt and how many people were getting well right there.

End of story.

Well, not quite the end.

We lived happily ever after.

Or rather we lived together, Grandma, Agatha-Agamemnon-Abigail, Timothy, and I, Tom, and Father, and Grandma calling us to frolic in great fountains of Latin and Spanish and French, in great seaborne gouts of poetry like Moby Dick sprinkling the deeps with his Versailles jet somehow lost in calms and found in storms; Grandma a constant, a clock, a pendulum, a face to tell all time by at noon, or in the middle of sick nights when, raved with fever, we saw her forever by our beds, never gone, never away, always waiting, always speaking kind words, her cool hand icing our hot brows, the tappet of her uplifted forefinger unsprung to let a twine of cold mountain water touch our flannel tongues. Ten thousand dawns she cut our wildflower lawn, ten thousand nights she wandered, remembering the dust molecules that fell in the still hours before dawn, or sat whispering some lesson she felt needed teaching to our ears while we slept snug.

Until at last, one by one, it was time for us to go away to school, and when at last the youngest, Agatha, was all packed, why Grandma packed, too.

On the last day of summer that last year, we found Grandma down in the front room with various packets and suitcases, knitting, waiting, and though she had often spoken of it, now that the time came we were shocked and surprised.

"Grandma!" we all said. "What are you doing?"

"Why going off to college, in a way, just like you," she said. "Back to Guido Fantoccini's, to the Family."

"The Family?"

"Of Pinocchios, that's what he called us for a joke, at first. The Pinocchios and himself Gepetto. And then later gave us his own name: the Fantoccini. Anyway, you have been my family here. Now I go back to my even larger family there, my brothers, sisters, aunts, cousins, all robots who—"

"Who do *what?*" asked Agatha.

"It all depends," said Grandma. "Some stay, some linger. Others go to be drawn and quartered, you might say, their parts distributed to other machines who have need of repairs. They'll weigh and find me wanting or not wanting. It may be I'll be just the one they need tomorrow and off I'll go to raise another batch of children and beat another batch of fudge."

"Oh, they mustn't draw and quarter you!" cried Agatha.

"No!" I cried, with Timothy.

"My allowance," said Agatha, "I'll pay anything . . .?"

Grandma stopped rocking and looked at the needles and the pattern of bright yarn. "Well, I wouldn't have said, but now you ask and I'll tell. For a very *small* fee, there's a room, the room of the Family, a large dim parlor, all quiet and nicely decorated, where as many as thirty or forty of the Electric Women sit and rock and talk, each in her turn. I have not been there. I am, after all, freshly born, comparatively new. For a small fee, very small, each month and year, that's where I'll be, with all the others like me, listening to what they've learned of the world and, in my turn, telling how it was with Tom and Tim and Agatha and how fine and happy we were. And I'll tell all I learned from you."

"But . . . you taught *us!*"

"Do you *really* think that?" she said. "No, it was turnabout, round-about, learning both ways. And it's all in here, everything you flew into tears about or laughed over, why, I have it all. And I'll tell it to the others just as they tell their boys and girls and life to me. We'll sit there, growing wiser and calmer and better every year and every year, ten, twenty, thirty years. The Family knowledge will double, quadruple, the wisdom will not be lost. And we'll be waiting there in that sitting room, should you ever need us for your own children in time of illness, or, God prevent, deprivation or death. There we'll be, growing old but not old, getting closer to the time, perhaps, someday, when we live up to our first strange joking name."

"The Pinocchios?" asked Tim.

Grandma nodded.

I knew what she meant. The day when, as in the old tale, Pinocchio had grown so worthy and so fine that the gift of life had been given him. So I saw them, in future years, the entire family of Fantoccini, the Pinocchios, trading and re-trading, murmuring and whispering their knowledge in the great parlors of philosophy, waiting for the day. The day that could never come.

Grandma must have read that thought in our eyes.

"We'll see," she said. "Let's just wait and see."

"Oh, Grandma," cried Agatha and she was weeping as she had wept many years before. "You don't have to wait. You're alive. You've always been alive to us!"

And she caught hold of the old woman and we all caught hold for a long moment and then ran off up in the sky to faraway schools and years and her last words to us before we let the helicopter swarm us away into autumn were these:

"When you are very old and gone childish-small again, with childish ways and childish yens and, in need of feeding, make a wish for the old teacher nurse, the dumb yet wise companion, send for me. I will come back. We shall inhabit the nursery again, never fear."

"Oh, we shall never be old!" we cried. "That will never happen!"

"Never! Never!"

And we were gone.

And the years are flown.

And we are old now, Tim and Agatha and I.

Our children are grown and gone, our wives and husbands vanished from the earth and now, by Dickensian coincidence, accept it as you will or not accept, back in the old house, we three.

I lie here in the bedroom which was my childish place seventy, O seventy, believe it, seventy years ago. Beneath this wallpaper is another layer and yet another-times-three to the old wallpaper covered over when I was nine. The wallpaper is peeling. I see peeking from beneath, old elephants, familiar tigers, fine and amiable zebras, irascible crocodiles. I have sent for the paperers to carefully remove all but that last layer. The old animals will live again on the walls, revealed.

And we have sent for someone else.

The three of us have called:

Grandma! You said you'd come back when we had need.

We are surprised by age, by time. We are old. We *need.*

And in three rooms of a summer house very late in time, three old children rise up, crying out in their heads: We *loved* you! We *love* you!

There! There! in the sky, we think, waking at morn. Is that the delivery machine? Does it settle to the lawn?

There! There on the grass by the front porch. Does the mummy case arrive?

Are our names inked on ribbons wrapped about the lovely form beneath the golden mask?!

And the kept gold key, forever hung on Agatha's breast, warmed and waiting? Oh God, will it, after all these years, will it wind, will it set in motion, will it, dearly, *fit?!*

It was the Tombling day, and all the people had walked up the summer road, including Grandma Loblilly, and they stood now in the green day and the high sky country of Missouri, and there was a smell of the seasons changing and the grass breaking out in flowers.

"Here we are," said Grandma Loblilly, over her cane, and she gave them all a flashing look of her yellow-brown eyes and spat into the dust.

The graveyard lay on the side of a quiet hill. It was a place of sunken mounds and wooden markers; bees hummed all about in quietudes of sound and butterflies withered and blossomed on the clear blue air. The tall sunburnt men and ginghamed women stood a long silent time looking in at their deep and buried relatives.

"Well, let's get to work!" said Grandma, and she hobbled across the moist grass, sticking it rapidly, here and there, with her cane.

The others brought the spades and special crates, with daisies and lilacs tied brightly to them. The government was cutting a road through here in August and since this graveyard had gone unused in fifty years the relatives had agreed to untuck all the old bones and pat them snug somewhere else.

Grandma Loblilly got right down on her knees and trembled a spade in her hand. The others were busy at their own places.

"Grandma," said Joseph Pikes, making a big shadow on her working. "Grandma, you shouldn't be workin' on this place. This's William Simmons's grave, Grandma."

At the sound of his voice, everyone stopped working, and listened, and there was just the sound of butterflies on the cool afternoon air.

Grandma looked up at Pikes. "You think I don't *know* it's his place? I ain't seen William Simmons in sixty years, but I intend to visit him today." She patted out trowel after trowel of rich soil and she grew quiet and introspective and said things to the day and those who might listen. "Sixty years ago, and him a fine man, only twenty-three. And me, I was twenty and all golden about the head and all milk in my arms and neck and persimmon in my cheeks. Sixty years and a planned marriage and then a sickness and him dying away. And me alone, and I remember how the earth mound over him sank in the rains—''

Everybody stared at Grandma.

"But still, Grandma—'' said Joseph Pikes.

The grave was shallow. She soon reached the long iron box.

"Gimme a hand!'' she cried.

Nine men helped lift the iron box out of the earth, Grandma poking at them with her cane. "Careful!'' she shouted. "Easy!'' she cried. "Now.'' They set it on the ground. "Now,'' she said, "if you be so kindly, you gentlemen might fetch Mr. Simmons on up to my house for a spell.''

"We're takin' him on to the new cemetery,'' said Joseph Pikes.

Grandma fixed him with her needle eye. "You just trot that box right up to my house. Much obliged.''

The men watched her dwindle down the road. They looked at the box, looked at each other, and then spat on their hands.

Five minutes later the men squeezed the iron coffin through the front door of Grandma's little white house and set the box down by the potbelly stove.

She gave them a drink all around. "Now, let's lift the lid,'' she said. "It ain't every day you see old friends.''

The men did not move.

"Well, if you won't, I will.'' She thrust at the lid with her cane, again and again, breaking away the earth crust. Spiders went touching over the floor. There was a rich smell, like plowed spring earth. Now the men fingered the lid. Grandma stood back. "Up!'' she said. She gestured her cane, like an ancient goddess. And up in the air went the lid. The men set it on the floor and turned.

There was a sound like wind sighing in October, from all their mouths.

There lay William Simmons as the dust filtered bright and golden through the air. There he slept, a little smile on his lips, hands folded, all dressed up and no place in all the world to go.

Grandma Loblilly gave a low moaning cry.

"He's all there!''

There he was, indeed. Intact as a beetle in his shell, his skin all fine and white, his small eyelids over his pretty eyes like flower petals put there, his lips still with color to them, his hair combed neat, his tie tied, his fingernails pared clean. All in all, he was as complete as the day they shoveled the earth upon his silent case.

Grandma stood tightening her eyes, her hands up to catch the breath that moved from her mouth. She couldn't see. "Where's my specs?''

she cried. People searched. "Can't you find 'em?" she shouted. She squinted at the body. "Never mind," she said, getting close. The room settled. She sighed and quavered and cooed over the open box.

"He's kept," said one of the women. "He ain't crumbled."

"Things like that," said Joseph Pikes, "don't happen."

"It *happened*," said the woman.

"Sixty years underground. Stands to reason no man lasts that long."

The sunlight was late by each window, the last butterflies were settling amongst flowers to look like nothing more than other flowers.

Grandma Loblilly put out her wrinkly hand, trembling. "The earth kept him. The way the air is. That was good dry soil for keeping."

"He's young," wailed one of the women, quietly. "So young."

"Yes," said Grandma Loblilly, looking at him. "Him, lying there, twenty-three years old. And me, standing here, pushing eighty!" She shut her eyes.

"Now, Grandma." Joseph Pikes touched her shoulder.

"Yes, him lyin' there, all twenty-three and fine and purty, and *me*—" She squeezed her eyes tight. "Me bending over him, never young agin, myself, only old and spindly, never to have a chance at being young agin. Oh, Lord! Death keeps people young. Look how kind death's been to him." She ran her hands over her body and face slowly, turning to the others. "Death's nicer than life. Why didn' I die then too? Then we'd both be young now, together. Me in my box, in my white wedding gown all lace, and my eyes closed down, all shy with death. And my hands making a prayer on my bosom."

"Grandma, don't carry on."

"I got a right to carry on! Why didn't I die, too? Then, when he came back, like he came today, to see me, I wouldn't be like *this!*"

Her hands went wildly to feel her lined face, to twist the loose skin, to fumble the empty mouth, to yank the gray hair and look at it with appalled eyes.

"What a fine coming-back he's had!" She showed her skinny arms. "Think that a man of twenty-three years will want the likes of a seventy-nine-year-old woman with sump-rot in her veins? I been cheated! Death kept him young forever. Look at me; did *Life* do so much?"

"They're compensations," said Joseph Pikes. "He ain't young, Grandma. He's long over eighty years."

"You're a fool, Joseph Pikes. He's fine as a stone, not touched by a thousand rains. And he's come back to see me and he'll be picking one of the younger girls now. What would he want with an old woman?"

"He's in no way to fetch nuthin' offa nobody," said Joseph Pikes.

Grandma pushed him back. "Get out now, all of you! Ain't your box, ain't your lid, and it ain't your almost-husband! You leave the box here, leastwise tonight, and tomorrow you dig a new burying place.''

"Awright, Grandma; he was your beau. I'll come early tomorra. Don't you cry, now.''

"I'll do what my eyes most need to do.''

She stood stiff in the middle of the room until the last of them were out the door. After awhile she got a candle and lit it and she noticed someone standing on the hill outside. It was Joseph Pikes. He'd be there the rest of the night, she reckoned, and she did not shout for him to go away. She did not look out the window again, but she knew he was there, and so was much better rested in the following hours.

She went to the coffin and looked down at William Simmons.

She gazed fully upon him. Seeing his hands was like seeing actions. She saw how they had been with reins of a horse in them, moving up and down. She remembered how the lips of him had clucked as the carriage had glided along with an even pacing of the horse through the meadowlands, the moonlight shadows all around. She knew how it was when those hands held to you.

She touched his suit. "That's not the same suit he was buried in!'' she cried suddenly. And yet she knew it was the same. Sixty years had changed not the suit but the linings of her mind.

Seized with a quick fear, she hunted a long time until she found her spectacles and put them on.

"Why, *that's* not William Simmons!'' she shouted.

But she knew this also was untrue. It was William Simmons. "His chin didn't go back that far!'' she cried softly, logically. "Or *did* it?'' And his hair, "It was a wonderful sorrel color, I remember! This hair here's just plain brown. And his nose, I don't recall it being that tippy!''

She stood over this strange man and, gradually, as she watched, she knew that this indeed was William Simmons. She knew a thing she should have known all along: that dead people are like wax memory—you take them in your mind, you shape and squeeze them, push a bump here, stretch one out there, pull the body tall, shape and reshape, handle, sculp and finish a man-memory until he's all out of kilter.

There was a certain sense of loss and bewilderment in her. She wished she had never opened the box. Or, leastwise, had the sense to leave her glasses off. She had not seen him clearly at first; just enough so she filled in the rough spots with her mind. Now, with her glasses on . . .

She glanced again and again at his face. It became slowly familiar. That memory of him that she had torn apart and put together for sixty years faded to be replaced by the man she had *really* known. And he was *fine* to look upon. The sense of having lost something vanished. He was the same man, no more, no less. This was always the way when you didn't see people for years and they came back to say howdy-do. For a spell you felt so very uneasy with them. But then, at last you relaxed.

"Yes, that's you," she laughed. "I see you peeking out from behind all the strangeness. I see you all glinty and sly here and there and about."

She began to cry again. If only she could lie to herself, if only she could say, "Look at him, he don't look the same, he's not the same man I took a fetching on!" then she could feel better. But all the little inside-people sitting around in her head would rock back in their tiny rockers and cackle and say, "You ain't foolin' us none, Grandma."

Yes, how easy to deny it was him. And feel better. But she didn't deny it. She felt the great depressing sadness because here he was, young as creek water, and here she was, old as the sea.

"William Simmons!" she cried. "Don't look at me! I know you still love me, so I'll primp myself up!"

She stirred the stove-fire, quickly put irons on to heat, used irons on her hair till it was all gray curls. Baking powder whitened her cheeks! She bit a cherry to color her lips, pinched her cheeks to bring a flush. From a trunk she yanked old materials until she found a faded blue velvet dress which she put on.

She stared wildly in the mirror at herself.

"No, no." She groaned and shut her eyes. "There's nothing I can do to make me younger'n you, William Simmons! Even if I died now it wouldn't cure me of this old thing come on me, this disease—"

She had a violent wish to run forever in the woods, fall in a leaf pile and moulder down into smoking ruin with them. She ran across the room, intending never to come back. But as she yanked the door wide a cold wind exploded over her from outside and she heard a sound that made her hesitate.

The wind rushed about the room, yanked at the coffin and pushed inside it.

William Simmons seemed to stir in his box.

Grandma slammed the door.

She moved slowly back to squint at him.

He was ten years older.

There were wrinkles and lines on his hands and face.

"William Simmons!"

During the next hour, William Simmons's face tolled away the years. His cheeks went in on themselves, like clenching a fist, like withering an apple in a bin. His flesh was made of carved pure white snow, and the cabin heat melted it. It got a charred look. The air made the eyes and mouth pucker. Then, as if struck a hammer blow, the face shattered into a million wrinkles. The body squirmed in an agony of time. It was forty, then fifty, then sixty years old! It was seventy, eighty, one hundred years! Burning, burning away! There were small whispers and leaf-crackles from its face and its age-burning hands, one hundred ten, one hundred twenty years, lined upon etched, greaved, line!

Grandma Loblilly stood there all the cold night, aching her bird bones, watching, cold, over the changing man. She was a witness to all improbabilities. She felt something finally let loose of her heart. She did not feel sad anymore. The weight lifted away from her.

She went peacefully to sleep, standing against a chair.

Sunlight came yellow through the woodland, birds and ants and creek waters were moving, each as quiet as the other, going somewhere.

It was morning.

Grandma woke and looked down upon William Simmons.

"Ah," said Grandma, looking and seeing.

Her very breath stirred and stirred his bones until they flaked, like a chrysalis, like a kind of candy all whittling away, burning with an invisible fire. The bones flaked and flew, light as pieces of dust on the sunlight. Each time she shouted the bones split asunder, there was a dry flaking rustle from the box.

If there was a wind and she opened the door, he'd be blown away on it like so many crackly leaves!

She bent for a long time, looking at the box. Then she gave a knowing cry, a sound of discovery and moved back, putting her hands first to her face and then to her spindly breasts and then traveling all up and down her arms and legs and fumbling at her empty mouth.

Her shout brought Joseph Pikes running.

He pulled up at the door only in time to see Grandma Loblilly dancing and jumping around on her yellow, high-peg shoes in a wild gyration.

She clapped her hands, laughed, flung her skirts, ran in a circle, and did a little waltz with herself, tears on her face. And to the sunlight and the flashing image of herself in the wall mirror she cried:

"I'm young! I'm eighty, but I'm younger'n *him!*"

She skipped, she hopped, and she curtsied.

"There are compensations, Joseph Pikes; you was right!" she chortled. "I'm younger'n *all* the dead ones in the whole world!"

And she waltzed so violently the whirl of her dress pulled at the box and whispers of chrysalis leapt on the air to hang golden and powdery amidst her shouts.

"Whee-*deee!*" she cried. "Whee-*heee!*"

Imagine a summer that would never end.

Nineteen twenty-nine.

Imagine a boy who would never grow up.

Me.

Imagine a barber who was never young.

Mr. Wyneski.

Imagine a dog that would live forever.

Mine.

Imagine a small town, the kind that isn't lived in anymore.

Ready? Begin . . .

Green Town, Illinois . . . Late June.

Dog barking outside a one-chair barbershop.

Inside, Mr. Wyneski, circling his victim, a customer snoozing in the steambath drowse of noon.

Inside, me, Ralph Spaulding, a boy of some twelve years, standing still as an iron Civil War statue, listening to the hot wind, feeling all that hot summer dust out there, a bakery world where nobody could be bad or good, boys just lay gummed to dogs, dogs used boys for pillows under trees that lazed with leaves which whispered in despair: Nothing Will Ever Happen Again.

The only motion anywhere was the cool water dripping from the huge coffin-sized ice block in the hardware store window.

The only cool person in miles was Miss Frostbite, the traveling magician's assistant, tucked into that lady-shaped long cavity hollowed in the ice block displayed for three days now without, they said, her breathing, eating, or talking. That last, I thought, must have been terrible hard on a woman.

Nothing moved in the street but the barbershop striped pole which turned slowly to show its red, white, and then red again, slid up out of nowhere to vanish nowhere, a motion between two mysteries.

". . . hey . . ."

I pricked my ears.

". . . something's coming . . ."

"Only the noon train, Ralph." Mr. Wyneski snicked his jackdaw scissors, peering in his customer's ear. "Only the train that comes at noon."

"No . . ." I gasped, eyes shut, leaning. "Something's *really* coming . . ."

I heard the far whistle wail, lonesome, sad, enough to pull your soul out of your body.

"*You* feel it, don't you, Dog?"

Dog barked.

Mr. Wyneski sniffed. "What can a dog feel?"

"Big things. Important things. Circumstantial coincidences. Collisions you can't escape. Dog says. I say. *We* say."

"That makes *four* of you. Some team." Mr. Wyneski turned from the summer-dead man in the white porcelain chair. "Now, Ralph, my problem is hair. Sweep."

I swept a ton of hair. "Gosh, you'd think this stuff just grew up out of the floor."

Mr. Wyneski watched my broom. "Right! I didn't cut all that. Darn stuff just grows, I swear, lying there. Leave it a week, come back, and you need hip boots to trod a path." He pointed with his scissors. "Look. You ever *see* so many shades, hues, and tints of forelocks and chin fuzz? There's Mr. Tompkins's receding hairline. There's Charlie Smith's topknot. And here, here's all that's left of Mr. Harry Joe Flynn."

I stared at Mr. Wyneski as if he had just read from Revelations. "Gosh, Mr. Wyneski, I guess you know everything in the world!"

"Just about."

"I—I'm going to grow up and be—a barber!"

Mr. Wyneski, to hide his pleasure, got busy.

"Then watch this hedgehog, Ralph, peel an eye. Elbows thus, wrists so! Make the scissors *talk!* Customers appreciate. Sound *twice* as busy as you are. Snickety-snick, boy, snickety-snick. Learned this from the French! Oh, yes, the French! They *do* prowl about the chair light on their toes, and the sharp scissors whispering and nibbling, Ralph, nibbling and whispering, you *hear!*"

"Boy!" I said, at his elbow, right in with the whispers and nibbles, then stopped: for the wind blew a wail way off in summer country, so sad, so strange.

"There it is again. The train. And something *on* the train . . ."

"Noon train don't stop here."

"But I got this feeling—"

"The hair's going to grab me, Ralph . . ."

I swept hair.

After a long while I said, "I'm thinking of changing my name."

Mr. Wyneski sighed. The summer-dead customer stayed dead.

"What's *wrong* with you today, boy?"

"It's not me. It's the name is out of hand. Just listen. Ralph." I grrred it. "Rrrralph."

"Ain't exactly harp music . . ."

"Sounds like a mad dog." I caught myself.

"No offense, Dog."

Mr. Wyneski glanced down. "He seems pretty calm about the whole subject."

"Ralph's dumb. Gonna change my name by tonight."

Mr. Wyneski mused. "Julius for Caesar? Alexander for the Great?"

"Don't care what. Help me, huh, Mr. Wyneski? Find me a *name* . . ."

Dog sat up. I dropped the broom.

For way down in the hot cinder railroad yards a train furnaced itself in, all pomp, all fire-blast shout and tidal churn, summer in its iron belly bigger than the summer outside.

"Here it comes!"

"There it goes," said Mr. Wyneski.

"No, there it *doesn't* go!"

It was Mr. Wyneski's turn to almost drop his scissors.

"Goshen. Darn noon train's putting on the brakes!"

We heard the train stop.

"How many people getting off the train, Dog?"

Dog barked once.

Mr. Wyneski shifted uneasily. "U.S. Mail bags—"

"No . . . a *man!* Walking light. Not much luggage. Heading for our house. A new boarder at Grandma's, I bet. And he'll take the empty room right next to you, Mr. Wyneski! Right, Dog?"

Dog barked.

"That dog talks too much," said Mr. Wyneski.

"I just *gotta* go see, Mr. Wyneski. Please?"

The far footsteps faded in the hot and silent streets.

Mr. Wyneski shivered.

"A goose just stepped on my grave."

Then he added, almost sadly:

"Get along, Ralph."

"Name ain't Ralph."

"Whatchamacallit . . . run see . . . come tell the worst."

"Oh, thanks, Mr. Wyneski, thanks!"

I ran. Dog ran. Up a street, along an alley, around back, we ducked in the ferns by my grandma's house. "Down, boy," I whispered. "Here the Big Event comes, what*ever* it is!"

And down the street and up the walk and up the steps at a brisk jaunt came this man who swung a cane and carried a carpetbag and had long brown-gray hair and silken mustaches and a goatee, politeness all about him like a flock of birds.

On the porch near the old rusty chain swing, among the potted geraniums, he surveyed Green Town.

Far away, maybe, he heard the insect hum from the barbershop, where Mr. Wyneski, who would soon be his enemy, told fortunes by the lumpy heads under his hands as he buzzed the electric clippers. Far away, maybe, he could hear the empty library where the golden dust slid down the raw sunlight and way in back someone scratched and tapped and scratched forever with pen and ink, a quiet woman like a great lonely mouse burrowed away. And she was to be part of this new man's life, too, but right now . . .

The stranger removed his tall moss-green hat, mopped his brow, and not looking at anything but the hot blind sky said:

"Hello, boy. Hello, dog."

Dog and I rose up among the ferns.

"Heck. How'd you know where we were hiding?"

The stranger peered into his hat for the answer. "In another incarnation, I was a boy. Time before that, if memory serves, I was a more than usually happy dog. But . . .!" His cane rapped the cardboard sign BOARD AND ROOM thumbtacked on the porch rail. "Does the sign say true, boy?"

"Best rooms on the block."

"Beds?"

"Mattresses so deep you sink down and drown the third time, happy."

"Boarders at table?"

"Talk just enough, not too much."

"Food?"

"Hot biscuits every morning, peach pie noon, shortcake every supper!"

The stranger inhaled, exhaled those savors.

"I'll sign my soul away!"

"I beg your pardon?!" Grandma was suddenly at the screen door, scowling out.

"A manner of speaking, ma'am." The stranger turned. "Not meant to sound un-Christian."

And he was inside, him talking, Grandma talking, him writing and flourishing the pen on the registry book, and me and Dog inside, breathless, watching, spelling:

"C.H."

"Read upside down, do you, boy?" said the stranger, merrily, giving pause with the inky pen.

"Yes, sir!"

On he wrote. On I spelled:

"A.R.L.E.S. Charles!"

"Right."

Grandma peered at the calligraphy. "Oh, what a fine hand."

"Thank you, ma'am." On the pen scurried. And on I chanted. "D.I.C.K.E.N.S."

I faltered and stopped. The pen stopped. The stranger tilted his head and closed one eye, watchful of me.

"Yes?" He dared me, "What, *what?*"

"Dickens!" I cried.

"Good!"

"Charles Dickens, Grandma!"

"I can read, Ralph. A *nice* name . . ."

"Nice?" I said, agape. "It's *great!* But . . . I thought you were—"

"Dead?" The stranger laughed. "No. Alive, in fine fettle, and glad to meet a recognizer, fan, and fellow reader here!"

And we were up the stairs, Grandma bringing fresh towels and pillowcases and me carrying the carpetbag, gasping, and us meeting Grandpa, a great ship of a man, sailing down the other way.

"Grandpa," I said, watching his face for shock. "I want you to meet . . . Mr. Charles Dickens!"

Grandpa stopped for a long breath, looked at the new boarder from top to bottom, then reached out, took hold of the man's hand, shook it firmly, and said:

"Any friend of Nicholas Nickleby's is a friend of mine!"

Mr. Dickens fell back from the effusion, recovered, bowed, said, "Thank you, sir," and went on up the stairs, while Grandpa winked, pinched my cheek, and left me standing there, stunned.

In the tower cupola room, with windows bright, open, and running with cool creeks of wind in all directions, Mr. Dickens drew off his horse-carriage coat and nodded at the carpetbag.

"Anywhere will do, Pip. Oh, you don't mind I call you Pip, eh?"

"Pip?!" My cheeks burned, my face glowed with astonishing happiness. "Oh, boy. Oh, no, sir. Pip's *fine!*"

Grandma cut between us. "Here are your clean linens, Mr. . . .?"

"Dickens, ma'am." Our boarder patted his pockets, each in turn.

"Dear me, Pip, I seem to be fresh out of pads and pencils. Might it be possible—"

He saw one of my hands steal up to find something behind my ear. "I'll be darned," I said, "a yellow Ticonderoga Number 2!" My other hand slipped to my back pants pocket. "And hey, an Iron-Face Indian Ring-Back Notepad Number 12!"

"Extraordinary!"

"Extraordinary!"

Mr. Dickens wheeled about, surveying the world from each and every window, speaking now north, now north by east, now east, now south:

"I've traveled two long weeks with an idea. Bastille Day. Do you know it?"

"The French Fourth of July?"

"Remarkable boy! By Bastille Day this book must be in full flood. Will you help me breach the tide gates of the Revolution, Pip?"

"With *these?*" I looked at the pad and pencil in my hands.

"Lick the pencil tip, boy!"

I licked.

"Top of the page: the title. Title." Mr. Dickens mused, head down, rubbing his chin whiskers. "Pip, what's a rare fine title for a novel that happens half in London, half in Paris?"

"A—" I ventured.

"Yes?"

"*A Tale,*" I went on.

"Yes?!"

"*A Tale of . . . Two Cities?!*"

"Madame!" Grandma looked up as he spoke. "This boy is a genius!"

"I read about this day in the Bible," said Grandma. "Everything Ends by noon."

"Put it down, Pip." Mr. Dickens tapped my pad. "Quick. *A Tale of Two Cities.* Then, mid-page. Book the First. 'Recalled to Life.' Chapter 1. 'The Period.' "

I scribbled. Grandma worked. Mr. Dickens squinted at the sky and at last intoned:

"It was the best of times, it was the worst of times, it was the age of wisdom, it was the age of foolishness, it was the epoch of belief, it was the epoch of incredulity, it was the Season of Light, it was the season of Darkness, it was the spring of hope, it was the winter—"

"My," said Grandma, "you speak *fine.*"

"Madame." The author nodded, then, eyes shut, snapped his fingers to remember, on the air. "Where was I, Pip?"

"It was the winter," I said, "of *despair.*"

*   *   *

Very late in the afternoon I heard Grandma calling someone named Ralph, Ralph, down below. I didn't know who that was. I was writing hard.

A minute later, Grandpa called, "Pip!"

I jumped. "Yes, sir!"

"Dinnertime, Pip," said Grandpa, up the stairwell.

I sat down at the table, hair wet, hands damp. I looked over at Grandpa. "How did you know . . . Pip?"

"Heard the name fall out the window an hour ago."

"Pip?" said Mr. Wyneski, just come in, sitting down.

"Boy," I said. "I been everywhere this afternoon. The Dover Coach on the Dover Road. Paris! Traveled so much I got writer's cramp! I—"

"Pip?" said Mr. Wyneski, again.

Grandpa came warm and easy to my rescue.

"When I was twelve, changed my name—on several occasions." He counted the tines on his fork. "Dick. That was Dead-Eye Dick. And . . . John. That was for Long John Silver. Then: Hyde. That was for the other half of Jekyll—"

"I never had any other name except Bernard Samuel Wyneski," said Mr. Wyneski, his eyes still fixed to me.

"None?" cried Grandpa, startled.

"None."

"Have you proof of childhood, then, sir?" asked Grandpa. "Or are you a natural phenomenon, like a ship becalmed at sea?"

"Eh?" said Mr. Wyneski.

Grandpa gave up and handed him his full plate.

"Fall to, Bernard Samuel, fall to."

Mr. Wyneski let his plate lie. "Dover Coach . . .?"

"With Mr. Dickens, of course," supplied Grandpa. "Bernard Samuel, we have a new boarder, a novelist, who is starting a new book and has chosen Pip there, Ralph, to work as his secretary—"

"Worked all afternoon," I said. "Made a quarter!"

I slapped my hand to my mouth. A swift dark cloud had come over Mr. Wyneski's face.

"A novelist? Named Dickens? Surely you don't believe—"

"I believe what a man tells me until he tells me otherwise, then I believe that. Pass the butter," said Grandpa.

The butter was passed in silence.

". . . hell's fires . . ." Mr. Wyneski muttered.

I slunk low in my chair.

Grandpa, slicing the chicken, heaping the plates, said, "A man with a good demeanor has entered our house. He says his name is Dickens.

For all I know that is his name. He implies he is writing a book. I pass his door, look in, and, yes, he is indeed writing. Should I run tell him not to? It is obvious he needs to set the book down—"

"*A Tale of Two Cities!*" I said.

"*A Tale!*" cried Mr. Wyneski, outraged, "*of Two—*"

"Hush," said Grandma.

For down the stairs and now at the door of the dining room there was the man with the long hair and the fine goatee and mustaches, nodding, smiling, peering in at us doubtful and saying, "Friends . . .?"

"Mr. Dickens," I said, trying to save the day. "I want you to meet Mr. Wyneski, the greatest barber in the world—"

The two men looked at each other for a long moment.

"Mr. Dickens," said Grandpa. "Will you lend us your talent, sir, for grace?"

"An honor, sir."

We bowed our heads. Mr. Wyneski did not.

Mr. Dickens looked at him gently.

Muttering, the barber glanced at the floor.

Mr. Dickens prayed:

"O Lord of the bounteous table, O Lord who furnishes forth an infinite harvest for your most respectful servants gathered here in loving humiliation, O Lord who garnishes our feast with the bright radish and the resplendent chicken, who sets before us the wine of the summer season, lemonade, and maketh us humble before simple potato pleasures, the lowborn onion and, in the finale, so my nostrils tell me, the bread of vast experiments and fine success, the highborn strawberry shortcake, most beautifully smothered and amiably drowned in fruit from your own warm garden patch, for these, and this good company, much thanks. Amen."

"Amen," said everyone but Mr. Wyneski.

We waited.

"Amen, I guess," he said.

O what a summer that was!

None like it before in Green Town history.

I never got up so early so happy ever in my life! Out of bed at five minutes to, in Paris by one minute after . . . six in the morning the English Channel boat from Calais, the White Cliffs, sky a blizzard of seagulls, Dover, then the London Coach and London Bridge by noon! Lunch and lemonade out under the trees with Mr. Dickens, Dog licking our cheeks to cool us, then back to Paris and tea at four and . . .

"Bring up the cannon, Pip!"

"'Yes, sir!''

"Mob the Bastille!''

"Yes, *sir!*''

And the guns were fired and the mobs ran and there I was, Mr. C. Dickens A-1 First Class Green Town, Illinois, secretary, my eyes bugging, my ears popping, my chest busting with joy, for I dreamt of being a writer some day, too, and here I was unraveling a tale with the very finest best.

"Madame Defarge, oh how she sat and knitted, knitted, sat—''

I looked up to find Grandma knitting in the window.

"Sidney Carton, what and who was he? A man of sensibility, a reading man of gentle thought and capable action . . .''

Grandpa strolled by mowing the grass.

Drums sounded beyond the hills with guns; a summer storm cracked and dropped unseen walls . . .

Mr. Wyneski?

Somehow I neglected his shop, somehow I forgot the mysterious barber pole that came up from nothing and spiraled away to nothing, and the fabulous hair that grew on his white tile floor . . .

So Mr. Wyneski then had to come home every night to find that writer with all the long hair in need of cutting, standing there at the same table thanking the Lord for this, that, and t'other, and Mr. Wyneski not thankful. For there *I* sat staring at Mr. Dickens like *he* was God until one night:

"Shall we say grace?'' said Grandma.

"Mr. Wyneski is out brooding in the yard,'' said Grandpa.

"Brooding?'' I glanced guiltily from the window.

Grandpa tilted his chair back so he could see.

"Brooding's the word. Saw him kick the rose bush, kick the green ferns by the porch, decide against kicking the apple tree. God made it too firm. There, he just jumped on a dandelion. Oh, oh. Here he comes, Moses crossing a Black Sea of bile.''

The door slammed. Mr. Wyneski stood at the head of the table.

"I'll say grace tonight!''

He glared at Mr. Dickens.

"Why, I mean,'' said Grandma. "Yes. Please.''

Mr. Wyneski shut his eyes tight and began his prayer of destruction:

"O Lord, who delivered me a fine June and a less fine July, help me to get through August somehow.

"O Lord, deliver me from mobs and riots in the streets of London and Paris which drum through my room night and morn, chief members of said riot being one boy who walks in his sleep, a man with a strange name and a Dog who barks after the ragtag and bobtail.

"Give me strength to resist the cries of Fraud, Thief, Fool, and Bunk Artists which rise in my mouth.

"Help me not to run shouting all the way to the Police Chief to yell that in all probability the man who shares our simple bread has a true name of Red Joe Pyke from Wilkesboro, wanted for counterfeiting life, or Bull Hammer from Hornbill, Arkansas, much desired for mean spitefulness and penny-pilfering in Oskaloosa.

"Lord, deliver the innocent boys of this world from the fell clutch of those who would tomfool their credibility.

"And Lord, help me to say, quietly, and with all deference to the lady present, that if one Charles Dickens is not on the noon train tomorrow bound for Potters Grave, Lands End, or Kankakee, I shall like Delilah, with malice, shear the black lamb and fry his mutton-chop whiskers for twilight dinners and late midnight snacks.

"I ask, Lord, not mercy for the mean, but simple justice for the malignant.

"All those agreed, say 'Amen.' "

He sat down and stabbed a potato.

There was a long moment with everyone frozen.

And then Mr. Dickens, eyes shut said, moaning:

"Ohhhhhhhhhh . . .!"

It was a moan, a cry, a despair so long and deep it sounded like the train way off in the country the day this man had arrived.

"Mr. Dickens," I said.

But I was too late.

He was on his feet, blind, wheeling, touching the furniture, holding to the wall, clutching at the doorframe, blundering into the hall, groping up the stairs.

"Ohhhhh . . ."

It was the long cry of a man gone over a cliff into Eternity.

It seemed we sat waiting to hear him hit bottom.

Far off in the hills in the upper part of the house, his door banged shut.

My soul turned over and died.

"Charlie," I said. "Oh, Charlie."

Late that night, Dog howled.

And the reason he howled was that sound, that similar, muffled cry from up in the tower cupola room.

"Holy Cow," I said. "Call the plumber. Everything's down the drain."

Mr. Wyneski strode by on the sidewalk, walking nowhere, off and gone.

"That's his fourth time around the block." Grandpa struck a match and lit his pipe.

"Mr. Wyneski!" I called.

No answer. The footsteps went away.

"Boy oh boy, I feel like I lost a war," I said.

"No, Ralph, beg pardon, Pip," said Grandpa, sitting down on the step with me. "You just changed generals in midstream is all. And now one of the generals is so unhappy he's turned mean."

"Mr. Wyneski? I—I almost hate him!"

Grandpa puffed gently on his pipe. "I don't think he even knows why he is so unhappy and mean. He has had a tooth pulled during the night by a mysterious dentist and now his tongue is aching around the empty place where the tooth was."

"We're not in church, Grandpa."

"Cut the Parables, huh? In simple words, Ralph, you used to sweep the hair off that man's shop floor. And he's a man with no wife, no family, just a job. A man with no family needs someone somewhere in the world, whether he knows it or not."

"I," I said. "I'll wash the barbershop windows tomorrow. I-I'll oil the red-and-white striped pole so it spins like crazy."

"I know you will, son."

A train went by in the night.

Dog howled.

Mr. Dickens answered in a strange cry from his room.

I went to bed and heard the town clock strike one and then two and at last three.

Then it was I heard the soft crying. I went out in the hall to listen by our boarder's door.

"Mr. Dickens?"

The soft sound stopped.

The door was unlocked. I dared open it.

"Mr. Dickens?"

And there he lay in the moonlight, tears streaming from his eyes, eyes wide open staring at the ceiling, motionless.

"Mr. Dickens?"

"Nobody by that name here," said he. His head moved side to side. "Nobody by that name in this room in this bed in this world."

"You," I said. "You're Charlie Dickens."

"You ought to know better," was the mourned reply. "Long after midnight, moving on toward morning."

"All I know is," I said, "I seen you writing every day. I heard you talking every night."

"Right, right."

"And you finish one book and start another, and write a fine calligraphy sort of hand."

"I do that." A nod. "Oh yes, by the demon possessions, I do."

"So!" I circled the bed. "What call you got to feel sorry for yourself, a world-famous author?"

"You know and I know, I'm Mr. Nobody from Nowhere, on my way to Eternity with a dead flashlight and no candles."

"Hells bells," I said. I started for the door. I was mad because he wasn't holding up his end. He was ruining a grand summer. "Good night!" I rattled the doorknob.

"Wait!"

It was such a terrible soft cry of need and almost pain, I dropped my hand, but I didn't turn.

"Pip," said the old man in the bed.

"Yeah?" I said, grouching.

"Let's both be quiet. Sit down."

I slowly sat on the spindly wooden chair by the night table.

"Talk to me, Pip."

"Holy Cow, at three—"

"—in the morning, yes. Oh, it's a fierce awful time of night. A long way back to sunset, and ten thousand miles on to dawn. We have need of friends then. *Friend,* Pip? Ask me things."

"Like what?"

"I think you know."

I brooded a moment and sighed. "Okay, okay. Who *are* you?"

He was very quiet for a moment lying there in his bed and then traced the words on the ceiling with a long invisible tip of his nose and said, "I'm a man who could never fit his dream."

"What?"

"I mean, Pip, I never became what I wanted to be."

I was quiet now, too. "What'd you *want* to be?"

"A writer."

"Did you *try?*"

"Try!" he cried, and almost gagged on a strange wild laugh. "Try," he said, controlling himself. "Why Lord of Mercy, son, you never saw so much spit, ink, and sweat fly. I wrote my way through an ink factory, broke and busted a paper company, ruined and dilapidated six dozen typewriters, devoured and scribbled to the bone ten thousand Ticonderoga Soft Lead pencils."

"Wow!"

"You may well say Wow."

"What did you write?"

"What *didn't* I write. The poem. The essay. The play *tragique*. The farce. The short story. The novel. A thousand words a day, boy, every day for thirty years, no day passed I did not scriven and assault the page. Millions of words passed from my fingers onto paper and it was all bad."

"It couldn't have been!"

"It *was*. Not mediocre, not passing fair. Just plain outright mudbath bad. Friends knew it, editors knew it, teachers knew it, publishers knew it, and one strange fine day about four in the afternoon, when I was fifty, *I* knew it."

"But you can't write thirty years without—"

"Stumbling upon excellence? Striking a chord? Gaze long, gaze hard, Pip, look upon a man of peculiar talent, outstanding ability, the only man in history who put down five million words without slapping to life one small base of a story that might rear up on its frail legs and cry Eureka! we've done it!"

"You never sold *one* story!?"

"Not a two line joke. Not a throwaway newspaper sonnet. Not a want ad or obit. Not a home-bottled autumn pickle recipe. Isn't that rare? To be so outstandingly dull, so ridiculously inept, that nothing ever brought a chuckle, caused a tear, raised a temper, or discharged a blow. And do you know what I did on the day I discovered I would never be a writer? I killed myself."

"Killed?!"

"Did away with, destroyed. How? I packed me up and took me away on a long train ride and sat on the back smoking-car platform a long time in the night and then one by one let the confetti of my manuscripts fly like panicked birds away down the tracks. I scattered a novel across Nebraska, my Homeric legends over North, my love sonnets through South Dakota. I abandoned my familiar essays in the men's room at the Harvey House in Clear Springs, Idaho. The late summer wheatfields knew my prose. Grand fertilizer, it probably jumped up bumper crops of corn long after I passed. I rode two trunks of my soul on that long summer's journey, celebrating my badly served self. And one by one, slow at first, and then faster, faster, over I chucked them, story after story, out, out of my arms out of my head, out of my life, and down they went, sunk drowning night rivers of prairie dust, in lost continents of sand and lonely rock. And the train wallowed around a curve in a great wail of darkness and release, and I opened my fingers and let the last stillborn darlings fall. . . .

"When I reached the far terminus of the line, the trunks were empty. I had drunk much, eaten little, wept on occasion in my private room, but had heaved away my anchors, deadweights, and dreams, and came to the sliding soft chuffing end of my journey, praise God, in a kind of noble peace and certainty. I felt reborn. I said to myself, why, what's this, what's this? I'm—I'm a new man.''

He saw it all on the ceiling. and I saw it, too, like a movie run up the wall in the moonlit night.

"I-I'm a new man I said, and when I got off the train at the end of that long summer of disposal and sudden rebirth, I looked in a fly-specked, rain-freckled gum-machine mirror at a lost depot in Peachgum, Missouri, and my beard grown long in two months of travel and my hair gone wild with wind that combed it this way sane, that way mad, and I peered and stood back and exclaimed softly, 'Why, Charlie Dickens, is that you?!'

The man in the bed laughed softly.

'' 'Why, Charlie,' said I, 'Mr. Dickens, there you are!' And the reflection in the mirror cried out, 'Dammit, sir, who else *would* it be!? Stand back. I'm off to a great lecture!' ''

"Did you really say that, Mr. Dickens?''

''God's pillars and temples of truth, Pip. And I got out of his way! And I strode through a strange town and I knew who I was at last and grew fevers thinking on what I might do in my lifetime now reborn and all that grand fine work ahead! For, Pip, this thing *must* have been growing. All those years of writing and snuffing up defeat, my old subconscious must have been whispering, 'Just you wait. Things will be black midnight bad but then in the nick of time, *I'll* save you!'

"And maybe the thing that saved me was the thing ruined me in the first place: respect for my elders; the grand moguls and tall muckymucks in the lush literary highlands and me in the dry river bottom with my canoe.

"For, oh God, Pip, how I devoured Tolstoy, drank Dostoevsky, feasted on De Maupassant, had wine and chicken picnics with Flaubert and Molière. I gazed at gods too high. I read too *much!* So, when my work vanished, theirs stayed. Suddenly I found I could *not* forget their books, Pip!''

"Couldn't?''

"I mean I could not forget any letter of any word of any sentence or any paragraph of any book ever passed under these hungry omnivorous eyes!''

"Photographic memory!''

"Bull's-eye! All of Dickens, Hardy, Austen, Poe, Hawthorne, trapped in this old box Brownie waiting to be printed off my tongue, all those years, never knew, Pip, never guessed, I had hid it all away. Ask me to speak in tongues. Kipling is one. Thackery another. Weigh flesh, I'm Shylock. Snuff out the light, I'm Othello. All, all, Pip, all!''

"And then? And so?''

"Why then and so, Pip, I looked another time in that fly-specked mirror and said, 'Mr. Dickens, all this being true, *when* do you write your first book?'

" 'Now!' I cried. And bought fresh paper and ink and have been delirious and joyful, lunatic and happy frantic over since, writing all the books of my own dear self, me, I, Charles Dickens, one by one.

"I have traveled the continental vastness of the United States of North America and settled me in to write and act, act and write, lecturing here, pondering there, half in and then half out of my mania, known and unknown, lingering here to finish *Copperfield,* loitering there for *Dombey and Son,* turning up for tea with Marley's Ghost on some pale Christmas noon. Sometimes I lie whole snowbound winters in little whistle stops and no one there guessing that Charlie Dickens bides hibernation there, then pop forth like the ottermole of spring and so move on. Sometimes I stay whole summers in one town before I'm driven off. Oh, yes, driven. For such as your Mr. Wyneski cannot forgive the fantastic, Pip, no matter how particularly practical that fantastic be.

"For he has no humor, boy.

"He does not see that we all do what we must to survive, survive.

"Some laugh, some cry, some bang the world with fists, some run, but it all sums up the same: they *make do.*

"The world swarms with people, each one drowning, but each swimming a different stroke to the far shore.

"And Mr. Wyneski? He makes do with scissors and understands not my inky pen and littered papers on which I would flypaper-catch my borrowed English soul.''

Mr. Dickens put his feet out of bed and reached for his carpetbag.

"So I must pick up and go.''

I grabbed the bag first.

"No! You can't leave! You haven't finished the book!''

"Pip, dear boy, you haven't been listening—''

"The world's waiting! You can't just quit in the middle of *Two Cities!*''

He took the bag quietly from me.

"Pip, Pip . . .''

"You *can't,* Charlie!''

He looked into my face and it must have been so white hot he flinched away.

"I'm waiting,'' I cried. "They're waiting!''

"They . . .?"

"The mob at the Bastille. Paris! London. The Dover sea. The guillotine!"

I ran to throw all the windows even wider as if the night wind and the moonlight might bring in sounds and shadows to crawl on the rug and sneak in his eyes, and the curtains blew out in phantom gestures and I swore I heard, Charlie heard, the crowds, the coach wheels, the great slicing downfall of the cutting blades and the cabbage heads falling and battle songs and all that on the wind . . .

"Oh, Pip, Pip . . ."

Tears welled from his eyes.

I had my pencil out and my pad.

"Well?" I said.

"Where were we, this afternoon, Pip?"

"Madame Defarge, knitting."

He let the carpetbag fall. He sat on the edge of the bed and his hands began to tumble, weave, knit, motion, tie and untie, and he looked and saw his hands and spoke and I wrote and he spoke again, stronger, and stronger, all through the rest of the night . . .

"Madame Defarge . . . yes . . . well. Take this, Pip. She—"

"Morning, Mr. Dickens!"

I flung myself into the dining-room chair. Mr. Dickens was already half through his stack of pancakes.

I took one bite and then saw the even greater stack of pages lying on the table between us.

"Mr. Dickens?" I said. "*The Tale of Two Cities.* It's . . . finished?"

"Done." Mr. Dickens ate, eyes down. "Got up at six. Been working steady. Done. Finished. Through."

"Wow!" I said.

A train whistle blew. Charlie sat up, then rose suddenly, to leave the rest of his breakfast and hurry out in the hall. I heard the front door slam and tore out on the porch to see Mr. Dickens half down the walk, carrying his carpetbag.

He was walking so fast I had to run to circle round and round him as he headed for the rail depot.

"Mr. Dickens, the book's finished, yeah, but not *published* yet!"

"You be my executor, Pip."

He fled. I pursued, gasping.

"What about David Copperfield?! Little Dorrit?!"

"Friends of yours, Pip?"

"Yours, Mr. Dickens, Charlie, oh, gosh, if you don't write them, they'll never *live*."

"They'll get on somehow." He vanished around a corner. I jumped after.

"Charlie, wait. I'll give you—a new title! *Pickwick Papers,* sure, *Pickwick Papers!*"

The train was pulling into the station.

Charlie ran fast.

"And after that, *Bleak House,* Charlie, and *Hard Times* and *Great—* Mr. Dickens, listen—*Expectations!* Oh, my gosh!"

For he was far ahead now and I could only yell after him:

"Oh, blast, go on! get off! get away! You know what I'm going to do!? You don't deserve reading! You don't! So right now, and from here on, see if I even *bother* to finish reading *Tale of Two Cities!* Not me! Not this one! No!"

The bell was tolling in the station. The steam was rising. But, Mr. Dickens had slowed. He stood in the middle of the sidewalk. I came up to stare at his back.

"Pip," he said softly. "You mean what you just said?"

"You!" I cried. "You're nothing but—" I searched in my mind and seized a thought: "—a blot of mustard, some undigested bit of raw potato—!"

" 'Bah, Humbug, Pip?' "

"Humbug! I don't give a blast *what* happens to Sidney Carton!"

"Why, it's a far, far better thing I do than I have ever done, Pip. You must read it."

"Why!?"

He turned to look at me with great sad eyes.

"Because I wrote it for you."

It took all my strength to half-yell back: "So—?"

"So," said Mr. Dickens, "I have just missed my train. Forty minutes till the next one—"

"Then you got time," I said.

"Time for what?"

"To meet someone. Meet them, Charlie, and I promise I'll finish reading your book. In there. In *there,* Charlie."

He pulled back.

"That place? The library?!"

"Ten minutes, Mr. Dickens, give me ten minutes, just ten, Charlie. Please."

"Ten?"

And at last, like a blind man, he let me lead him up the library steps and half-fearful, sidle in.

*   *   *

The library was like a stone quarry where no rain had fallen in ten thousand years.

Way off in that direction: silence.

Way off in that direction: hush.

It was the time between things finished and things begun. Nobody died here. Nobody was born. The library, and all its books, just *were*.

We waited, Mr. Dickens and I, on the edge of the silence.

Mr. Dickens trembled. And I suddenly remembered I had never seen him here all summer. He was afraid I might take him near the fiction shelves and see all his books, written, done, finished, printed, stamped, bound, borrowed, read, repaired, and shelved.

But I wouldn't be that dumb. Even so, he took my elbow and whispered:

"Pip, what are we doing here? Let's go. There's . . ."

"Listen!" I hissed.

And a long way off in the stacks somewhere, there was a sound like a moth turning over in its sleep.

"Bless me," Mr. Dickens's eyes widened. "I *know* that sound."

"Sure!"

"It's the sound," he said, holding his breath, then nodding, "of someone writing."

"Yes, sir."

"Writing with a pen. And . . . and writing . . ."

"What?"

"Poetry," gasped Mr. Dickens. "That's it. Someone off there in a room, how many fathoms deep, Pip, I swear, writing a poem. There! Eh? Flourish, flourish, scratch, flourish on, on, on, that's not figures, Pip, not numerals, not dusty-dry facts, you feel it *sweep,* feel it *scurry?* A poem, by God, yes, sir, no doubt, a poem!"

"Ma'am," I called.

The moth-sound ceased.

"Don't stop her!" hissed Mr. Dickens. "Middle of inspiration. Let her go!"

The moth-scratch started again.

Flourish, flourish, scratch, on, on, stop. Flourish, flourish. I bobbed my head. I moved my lips, as did Mr. Dickens, both of us suspended, held, leant forward on the cool marble air listening to the vaults and stacks and echoes in the subterrane.

Flourish, flourish, scratch, on, on.

Silence.

"There." Mr. Dickens nudged me.

"Ma'am!" I called ever so urgently soft.

And something rustled in the corridors.

And there stood the librarian, a lady between years, not young, not old; between colors, not dark, not pale; between heights, not short, not tall, but rather frail, a woman you often heard talking to herself off in the dark dust-stacks with a whisper like turned pages, a woman who glided as if on hidden wheels.

She came carrying her soft lamp of face, lighting her way with her glance.

Her lips were moving, she was busy with words in the vast room behind her clouded gaze.

Charlie read her lips eagerly. He nodded. He waited for her to halt and bring us to focus, which she did, suddenly. She gasped and laughed at herself.

"Oh, Ralph, it's you and—" A look of recognition warmed her face. "Why, you're Ralph's friend. Mr. Dickens, isn't it?"

Charlie stared at her with a quiet and almost alarming devotion.

"Mr. Dickens," I said. "I want you to meet—"

" 'Because I could not stop for Death—' " Charlie, eyes shut, quoted from memory.

The librarian blinked swiftly and her brow like a lamp turned high, took white color.

"Miss Emily," he said.

"Her name is—" I said.

"Miss Emily." He put out his hand to touch hers.

"Pleased," she said. "But how did you—?"

"Know your name? Why, bless me, ma'am, I heard you scratching way off in there, runalong rush, only poets do *that!*"

"It's nothing."

"Head high, chin up," he said, gently. "It's something. 'Because I could not stop for death' is a fine A-1 first-class poem."

"My own poems are so poor," she said, nervously. "I copy hers out to learn."

"Copy *who?*" I blurted.

"Excellent way to learn."

"Is it, *really?*" She looked close at Charlie. "You're not . . .?"

"Joking? No, not with Emily Dickinson, ma'am!"

"Emily Dickinson?" I said.

"That means much coming from you, Mr. Dickens," she flushed. "I have read all your books."

"All?" He backed off.

"All," she added hastily, "that you have published so far, sir."

"Just finished a new one." I put in, "Sockdolager! *A Tale of Two Cities.*"

"And you, ma'am?" he asked, kindly.

She opened her small hands as if to let a bird go.

"Me? Why, I haven't even sent a poem to our town newspaper."

"You must!" he cried, with true passion and meaning. "Tomorrow. No, today!"

"But," her voice faded. "I have no one to read them to, first."

"Why," said Chadie quietly. "You have Pip here, and, accept my card, C. Dickens, Esquire. Who will, if allowed, stop by on occasion, to see if all's well in this Arcadian silo of books."

She took his card. "I couldn't—"

"Tut! You must. For I shall offer only warm sliced white bread. Your words must be the marmalade and summer honey jam. I shall read long and plain. You: short and rapturous of life and tempted by that odd delicious Death you often lean upon. Enough." He pointed. "There. At the far end of the corridor, her lamp lit ready to guide your hand . . . the Muse awaits. Keep and feed her well. Good-bye."

"Good-bye?" she asked. "Doesn't that mean 'God be with you'?"

"So I have heard, dear lady, so I have heard."

And suddenly we were back out in the sunlight, Mr. Dickens almost stumbling over his carpetbag waiting there.

In the middle of the lawn, Mr. Dickens stood very still and said, "The sky is blue, boy."

"Yes, sir."

"The grass is green."

"Sure." Then I stopped and really looked around. "I mean, heck, *yeah!*"

"And the wind . . . smell that sweet wind?"

We both smelled it. He said:

"And in this world are remarkable boys with vast imaginations who know the secrets of salvation . . ."

He patted my shoulder. Head down, I didn't know what to do. And then I was saved by a whistle:

"Hey, the next train! Here it *comes!*"

We waited.

After a long while, Mr. Dickens said:

"There it *goes* . . . and let's go home, boy."

"Home!" I cried, joyfully, and then stopped. "But what about . . . Mr. Wyneski?"

"O, after all this, I have such confidence in you, Pip. Every afternoon while I'm having tea and resting my wits, you must trot down to the barbershop and—"

"Sweep hair!"

"Brave lad. It's little enough. A loan of friendship from the Bank of

England to the First National Bank of Green Town, Illinois. And now, Pip . . . pencil!''

I tried behind one ear, found gum; tried the other ear and found: ''Pencil!''

''Paper?''

''Paper!''

We strode along under the soft green summer trees.

''Title, Pip—''

He reached up with his cane to write a mystery on the sky. I squinted at the invisible penmanship.

''*The*—''

He blocked out a second word on the air.

''*Old,*'' I translated.

A third.

''C.U.'' I spelled. ''R.I. . . . *Curiosity!*''

''How's that for a title, Pip?''

I hesitated. ''It . . . doesn't seem, well, quite *finished,* sir.''

''What a Christian you are. There!''

He flourished a final word on the sun.

''S.H.O. . . . *Shop! The Old Curiosity Shop.*''

''Take a novel, Pip!''

''Yes, sir,'' I cried. ''Chapter One!''

A blizzard of snow blew through the trees.

''What's that?'' I asked, and answered:

Why, summer gone. The calendar pages, all the hours and days, like in the movies, the way they just blow off over the hills. Charlie and I working together, finished, through. Many days at the library, over! Many nights reading aloud with Miss Emily done! Trains come and gone. Moons waxed and waned. New trains arriving and new lives teetering on the brink, and Miss Emily suddenly standing right there, and Charlie here with all their suitcases and handing me a paper sack.

''What's *this?*''

''Rice, Pip, plain ordinary white rice, for the fertility ritual. Throw it at us, boy. Drive us happily away. Hear those bells, Pip? Here goes Mr. and Mrs. Charlie Dickens! Throw, boy, throw! Throw!''

I threw and ran, ran and threw, and them on the back train platform waving out of sight and me yelling good-bye, Happy marriage, Charlie! Happy times! Come back! Happy . . . Happy . . .

And by then I guess I was crying, and Dog chewing my shoes, jealous, glad to have me alone again, and Mr. Wyneski waiting at the barbershop to hand me my broom and make me his son once more.

And autumn came and lingered and at last a letter arrived from the married and traveling couple.

I kept the letter sealed all day and at dusk, while Grandpa was raking leaves by the front porch I went out to sit and watch and hold the letter and wait for him to look up and at last he did and I opened the letter and read it out loud in the October twilight:

"Dear Pip," I read, and had to stop for a moment seeing my old special name again, my eyes were so full.

"Dear Pip. We are in Aurora tonight and Felicity tomorrow and Elgin the night after that. Charlie has six months of lectures lined up and looking forward. Charlie and I are both working steadily and are most happy . . . *very* happy . . . need I say?

"He calls me Emily.

"Pip, I don't think you know who she was, but there was a lady poet once, and I hope you'll get her books out of the library someday.

"Well, Charlie looks at me and says: 'This is my Emily' and I almost believe. No, I *do* believe."

I stopped and swallowed hard and read on:

"We are crazy, Pip.

"People have said it. We know it. Yet we go on. But being crazy together is fine.

"It was being crazy alone I couldn't stand any longer.

"Charlie sends his regards and wants you to know he has indeed started a fine new book, perhaps his best yet . . . one *you* suggested the title for, *Bleak House.*

"So we write and move, move and write, Pip. And some year soon we may come back on the train which stops for water at your town. And if you're there and call our names as we know ourselves now, we shall step off the train. But perhaps meanwhile you will get too old. And if when the train stops, Pip, you're not there, we shall understand, and let the train move us on to another and another town.

"Signed, Emily Dickinson.

"P.S. Charlie says your grandfather is a dead ringer for Plato, but not to tell him.

"P.P.S. Charlie is my darling."

"Charlie is my darling," repeated Grandpa, sitting down and taking the letter to read it again. "Well, well . . ." he sighed. "Well, well . . ."

We sat there a long while, looking at the burning soft October sky and the new stars. A mile off, a dog barked. Miles off, on the horizon line, a train moved along, whistled, and tolled its bell, once, twice, three times, gone.

"You know," I said. "I don't think they're crazy."

"Neither do I, Pip," said Grandpa, lighting his pipe and blowing out the match. "Neither do I."

The woman stepped to the kitchen window and looked out.

There in the twilight yard a man stood surrounded by barbells and dumbbells and dark iron weights of all kinds and slung jump ropes and elastic and coiled-spring exercisors. He wore a sweat suit and tennis shoes and said nothing to no one as he simply stood in the darkening world and did not know she watched.

This was her son, and everyone called him Heavy-Set.

Heavy-Set squeezed the little bunched, coiled springs in his big fists. They were lost in his fingers, like magic tricks; then they reappeared. He crushed them. They vanished. He let them go. They came back.

He did this for ten minutes, otherwise motionless.

Then he bent down and hoisted up the one-hundred-pound barbells, noiselessly, not breathing. He motioned it a number of times over his head, then abandoned it and went into the open garage among the various surfboards he had cut out and glued together and sanded and painted and waxed, and there he punched a punching bag easily, swiftly, steadily, until his curly golden hair got moist. Then he stopped and filled his lungs until his chest measured fifty inches and stood eyes closed, seeing himself in an invisible mirror poised and tremendous, two hundred and twenty muscled pounds, tanned by the sun, salted by the sea wind and his own sweat.

He exhaled. He opened his eyes.

He walked into the house, into the kitchen and did not look at his mother, this woman, and opened the refrigerator and let the arctic cold steam him while he drank a quart of milk straight out of the carton, never putting it down, just gulping and swallowing. Then he sat down at the kitchen table to fondle and examine the Hallowe'en pumpkins.

He had gone out earlier in the day and bought the pumpkins and carved most of them and did a fine job: they were beauties and he was proud of them. Now, looking childlike in the kitchen, he started carving the last of them. You would never suspect he was thirty years old, he still moved so swiftly, so quietly, for a large action like hitting a wave with an uptilted and outthrust board, or here with the small action of a knife, giving sight to a Hallowe'en eye. The electric light bulb filled the summer wildness of his hair, but revealed no emotion, except this one intent purpose of carving, on his face. There was all muscle in him, and no fat, and that muscle waited behind every move of the knife.

His mother came and went on personal errands around the house and then came to stand and look at him and the pumpkins and smile. She was used to him. She heard him every night drubbing the punching bag outside, or squeezing the little metal springs in his hands or grunting as he lifted his world of weights and held it in balance on his strangely quiet shoulders. She was used to all these sounds even as she knew the ocean coming in on the shore beyond the cottage and laying itself out flat and shining on the sand. Even as she was used, by now, to hearing Heavy-Set each night on the phone saying he was tired to girls and said no, no he had to wax the car tonight or do his exercises to the eighteen-year-old boys who called.

She cleared her throat. "Was the dinner good tonight?"

"Sure," he said.

"I had to get special steak. I bought the asparagus fresh."

"It was good," he said.

"I'm glad you liked it, I always like to have you like it."

"Sure," he said, working.

"What time is the party?"

"Seven thirty." He finished the last of the smile on the pumpkin and sat back. "If they all show up, they might not show up, I bought two jugs of cider."

He got up and moved into his bedroom, quietly massive, his shoulders filling the door and beyond. In the room, in the half-dark, he made the strange pantomime of a man seriously and silently wrestling an invisible opponent as he got into his costume. He came to the door of the living room a minute later licking a gigantic peppermint-striped lollipop. He wore a pair of short black pants, a little boy's shirt with ruff collar, and a Buster Brown hat. He licked the lollipop and said, "I'm the mean little kid!" and the woman who had been watching him laughed. He walked with an exaggerated little child's walk, licking the huge lollipop, all around the room while she laughed at him and he said things and pretended to be leading a big dog on a rope. "You'll be the life of the party!" the woman cried, pink-faced and exhausted. He was laughing now, also.

The phone rang.

He toddled out to answer it in the bedroom. He talked for a long time

and his mother heard him say Oh for gosh sakes several times and finally
he came slowly and massively into the living room looking stubborn.
"What's wrong?" she wanted to know. "Aw," he said, "half the guys
aren't showing up at the party. They got other dates. That was Tommy
calling. He's got a date with a girl from somewhere. Good grief."
"There'll be enough," said his mother. "I don't know," he said.
"There'll be enough for a party," she said. "You go on." "I ought to
throw the pumpkins in the garbage," he said, scowling. "Well you just
go on and have a good time," she said. "You haven't been out in
weeks."

Silence.

He stood there twisting the huge lollipop as big as his head, turning
it in his large muscular fingers. He looked as if at any moment now he
would do what he did other nights. Some nights he pressed himself up
and down on the ground with his arms and some nights he played a
game of basketball with himself and scored himself, team against team,
black against white, in the backyard. Some nights he stood around like
this and then suddenly vanished and you saw him way out in the ocean
swimming long and strong and quiet as a seal under the full moon or
you could not see him those nights the moon was gone and only the
stars lay over the water but you heard him there, on occasion, a faint
splash as he went under and stayed under a long time and came up, or
he went out some times with his surfboard as smooth as a girl's cheeks,
sandpapered to a softness, and came riding in, huge and alone on a white
and ghastly wave that creamed along the shore and touched the sands
with the surfboard as he stepped off like a visitor from another world
and stood for a long while holding the soft smooth surfboard in the
moonlight, a quiet man and a vast tombstone-shaped thing held there
with no writing on it. In all the nights like that in the past years, he had
taken a girl out three times one week and she ate a lot and every time
he saw her she said Let's eat and so one night he drove her up to a
restaurant and opened the car door and helped her out and got back in
and said There's the restaurant. So long. And drove off. And went back
to swimming way out, alone. Much later, another time, a girl was half
an hour late getting ready and he never spoke to her again.

Thinking all this, remembering all this, his mother looked at him now.
"Don't stand there," she said. "You make me nervous."
"Well," he said, resentfully.
"Go on!" she cried. But she didn't cry it strong enough. Even to
herself her voice sounded faint. And she did not know if her voice was
just naturally faint or if she made it that way. She might as well have
been talking about winter coming; everything she said had a lonely

sound. And she heard the words again from her own mouth, with no force: "Go on!"

He went into the kitchen. "I guess there'll be enough guys there," he said. "Sure, there will," she said, smiling again. She always smiled again. Sometimes when she talked to him, night after night, she looked as if she were lifting weights, too. When he walked through the rooms she looked like she was doing the walking for him. And when he sat brooding, as he often did, she looked around for something to do which might be burn the toast or overfire the steak. She made a short barking faint and stifled laugh now, "Get out, have a good time." But the echoes of it moved around in the house as if it were already empty and cold and he should come back in the door. Her lips moved: "Fly away."

He snatched up the cider and the pumpkins and hurried them out to his car. It was a new car and had been new and unused for almost a year. He polished it and jiggered with the motor or lay underneath it for hours messing with all the junk underneath or just sat in the front seat glancing over the strength and health magazines, but rarely drove it. He put the cider and the cut pumpkins proudly in on the front seat, and by this time he was thinking of the possible good time tonight so he did a little child's stagger as if he might drop everything, and his mother laughed. He licked his lollipop again, jumped into the car, backed it out of the gravel drive, swerved it around down by the ocean, not looking out at this woman, and drove off along the shore road. She stood in the yard watching the car go away. Leonard, my son, she thought.

It was seven fifteen and very dark now; already the children were fluttering along the sidewalks in white ghost sheets and zinc-oxide masks, ringing bells, screaming, lumpy paper sacks banging their knees as they ran.

Leonard, she thought.

They didn't call him Leonard, they called him Heavy-Set and Sammy, which was short for Samson. They called him Butch and they called him Atlas and Hercules. At the beach you always saw the high-school boys around him feeling his biceps as if he was a new sports car, testing him, admiring him. He walked golden among them. Each year it was that way. And then the eighteen-year-old ones got to be nineteen and didn't come around so often, and then twenty and very rarely, and then twenty-one and never again, just gone, and suddenly there were new eighteen year olds to replace them, yes, always the new ones to stand where the others had stood in the sun, while the older ones went on somewhere to something and somebody.

Leonard, my good boy, she thought. We go to shows on Saturday nights. He works on the high power lines all day, up in the sky, alone, and sleeps alone in his room at night, and never reads a book or a paper or listens to a radio or plays a record, and this year he'll be thirty-one. And just where, in all the years, did the thing happen that put him up on that pole alone and working out alone every night? Certainly there had been enough women, here and there, now and then, through his life. Little scrubby ones, of course, fools, yes, by the look of them, but women, or girls, rather, and none worth glancing at a second time. Still, when a boy gets past thirty . . . ? She sighed. Why even as recent as last night the phone had rung. Heavy-Set had answered it, and she could fill in the unheard half of the conversation because she had heard thousands like it in a dozen years:

"Sammy, this is Christine." A woman's voice. "What you doing?"

His little golden eyelashes flickered and his brow furrowed, alert and wary. "Why?"

"Tom, Lu, and I are going to a show, want to come along?"

"It better be good!" he cried, indignantly.

She named it.

"That!" He snorted.

"It's a good film," she said.

"Not that one," he said. "Besides, I haven't shaved yet today."

"You can shave in five minutes."

"I need a bath, and it'd take a long time."

A long time, thought his mother, he was in the bathroom two hours today. He combs his hair two dozen times, musses it, combs it again, talking to himself.

"Okay for you." The woman's voice on the phone. "You going to the beach this week?"

"Saturday," he said, before he thought.

"See you there, then," she said.

"I meant Sunday," he said, quickly.

"I could change it to Sunday," she replied.

"If I can make it," he said, even more quickly. "Things go wrong with my car."

"Sure," she said. "Samson. So long."

And he had stood there for a long time, turning the silent phone in his hand.

Well, his mother thought, he's having a good time now. A good Hallowe'en party, with all the apples he took along, tied on strings, and the apples, untied, to bob for in a tub of water, and the boxes of candy, the sweet corn kernels that really taste like autumn. He's running around looking like the bad little boy, she thought, licking his lollipop, everyone shouting, blowing horns, laughing, dancing.

At eight, and again at eight thirty and nine she went to the screen door and looked out and could almost hear the party a long way off at the dark beach, the sounds of it blowing on the wind crisp and furious and wild, and wished she could be there at the little shack out over the waves on the pier, everyone whirling about in costumes, and all the pumpkins cut each a different way and a contest for the best homemade mask or makeup job, and too much popcorn to eat and—

She held to the screen door knob, her face pink and excited and suddenly realized the children had stopped coming to beg at the door. Hallowe'en, for the neighborhood kids anyway, was over.

She went to look out into the backyard.

The house and yard were too quiet. It was strange not hearing the basketball volley on the gravel or the steady bumble of the punching bag taking a beating. Or the little tweezing sound of the hand-squeezers.

What if, she thought, he found someone tonight, found someone down there, and just never came back, never came home. No telephone call. No letter, that was the way it could be. No word. Just go off away and never come back again. What if? What if?

No! she thought, there's no one, no one there, no one anywhere. There's just this place. This is the only place.

But her heart was beating fast and she had to sit down.

The wind blew softly from the shore.

She turned on the radio but could not hear it.

Now, she thought, they're not doing anything except playing blind man's buff, yes, that's it, blind tag, and after that they'll just be—

She gasped and jumped.

The windows had exploded with raw light.

The gravel spurted in a machine-gun spray as the car jolted in, braked, and stopped, motor gunning. The lights went off in the yard. But the motor still gunned up, idled, gunned up, idled.

She could see the dark figure in the front seat of the car, not moving, staring straight ahead.

"You—" she started to say, and opened the back screen door. She found a smile on her mouth. She stopped it. Her heart was slowing now. She made herself frown.

He shut off the motor. She waited. He climbed out of the car and threw the pumpkins in the garbage can and slammed the lid.

"What happened?" she asked. "Why are you home so early—?"

"Nothing." He brushed by her with the two gallons of cider intact. He set them on the kitchen sink.

"But it's not ten yet—"

"That's right." He went into the bedroom and sat down in the dark.

She waited five minutes. She always waited five minutes. He wanted her to come ask, he'd be mad if she didn't, so finally she went and looked into the dark bedroom.

"Tell me," she said.

"Oh, they all stood around," he said. "They just stood around like a bunch of fools and didn't do anything."

"What a shame."

"They just stood around like dumb fools."

"Oh, that's a shame."

"I tried to get them to do something, but they just stood around. Only eight of them showed up, eight out of twenty, eight, and me the only one in costume. I tell you. The only one. What a bunch of fools."

"After all your trouble, too."

"They had their girls and they just stood around with them and wouldn't do anything, no games, nothing. Some of them went off with the girls," he said, in the dark, seated, not looking at her. "They went off up the beach and didn't come back. Honest to gosh." He stood now, huge, and leaned against the wall, looking all disproportioned in the short trousers. He had forgotten the child's hat was on his head. He suddenly remembered it and took it off and threw it on the floor. "I tried to kid them. I played with a toy dog and did some other stuff but nobody did anything. I felt like a fool the only one there dressed like this, and them all different, and only eight out of twenty there, and most of them gone in half an hour. Vi was there. She tried to get me to walk up the beach, too. I was mad by then. I was really mad. I said no thanks. And here I am. You can have the lollipop. Where did I put it? Pour the cider down the sink, drink it, I don't care."

She had not moved so much as an inch in all the time he talked. She opened her mouth.

The telephone rang.

"If that's them, I'm not home."

"You'd better answer it," she said.

He grabbed the phone and whipped off the receiver.

"Sammy?" said a loud high clear voice. He was holding the receiver out on the air, glaring at it in the dark. "That you?" He grunted. "This is Bob." The eighteen-year-old voice rushed on. "Glad you're home. In a big rush, but—what about that game tomorrow?"

"What game?"

"What game? For cri-yi, you're kidding. Notre Dame and S.C.!"

"Oh, football."

"Don't say oh football like that, you talked it, you played it up, *you* said—"

"That's no game," he said, not looking at the telephone, the receiver, the woman, the wall, nothing.

"You mean you're not going? Heavy-Set, it won't be a *game* without you!"

"I got to water the lawn, polish the car—"

"You can do that Sunday!"

"Besides, I think my uncle's coming over to see me. So long."

He hung up and walked out past his mother into the yard. She heard the sounds of him out there as she got ready for bed.

He must have drubbed the punching bag until three in the morning. Three, she thought, wide awake, listening to the concussions. He's always stopped at twelve, before.

At three thirty he came into the house.

She heard him just standing outside her door.

He did nothing else except stand there in the dark, breathing.

She had a feeling he still had the little boy suit on. But she didn't want to know if this were true.

After a long while the door swung slowly open.

He came into her dark room and lay down on the bed, next to her, not touching her. She pretended to be asleep.

He lay face up and rigid.

She could not see him. But she felt the bed shake as if he were laughing. She could hear no sound coming from him, so she could not be sure.

And then she heard the squeaking sounds of the little steel springs being crushed and uncrushed, crushed and uncrushed in his fists.

She wanted to sit up and scream for him to throw those awful noisy things away. She wanted to slap them out of his fingers.

But then, she thought, what would he do with his hands? What could he put in them? What would he, yes, what would he do with his hands?

So she did the only thing she could do, she held her breath, shut her eyes, listened, and prayed, O God, let it go on, let him keep squeezing those things, let him keep squeezing those things, let him, let him, oh let, let him, let him keep squeezing . . . let . . . let . . .

It was like lying in bed with a great dark cricket.

And a long time before dawn.

Brokaw.

What a name!

Listen to it bark, growl, yip, hear the bold proclamation of:

Immanuel Brokaw!

A fine name for the greatest psychiatrist who ever tread the waters of existence without capsizing.

Toss a pepper-ground Freud casebook in the air and all students sneezed:

Brokaw!

What ever happened to him?

One day, like a high-class vaudeville act, he vanished.

With the spotlight out, his miracles seemed in danger of reversal. Psychotic rabbits threatened to leap back into hats. Smokes were sucked back into loud-powder gun muzzles. We all waited.

Silence for ten years. And more silence.

Brokaw was lost, as if he had thrown himself with shouts of laughter into mid-Atlantic. For what? To plumb for Moby Dick? To psychoanalyze that colorless fiend and see what he really had against Mad Ahab?

Who knows?

I last saw him running for a twilight plane, his wife and six Pomeranian dogs yapping far behind him on the dusky field.

"Good-bye forever!"

His happy cry seemed a joke. But I found men flaking his gold-leaf name from his office door next day, as his great fat-women couches were hustled out into the raw weather toward some Third Avenue auction.

So the giant who had been Gandhi-Moses-Christ-Buddha-Freud all layered in one incredible Armenian dessert had dropped through a hole in the clouds. To die? To live in secret?

Ten years later I rode on a California bus along the lovely shores of Newport.

The bus stopped. A man in his seventies bounced on, jingling silver into the coin box like manna. I glanced up from the rear of the bus and gasped.

"Brokaw! By the saints!"

And with or without sanctification, there he stood. Reared up like God manifest, bearded, benevolent, pontifical, erudite, merry, accepting, forgiving, messianic, tutorial, forever and eternal . . .

Immanuel Brokaw.

But not in a dark suit, no.

Instead, as if they were vestments of some proud new church, he wore: Bermuda shorts. Black leather Mexican sandals. A Los Angeles Dodgers' baseball cap. French sunglasses. And . . .

The shirt! Ah God! The shirt!

A wild thing, all lush creeper and live flytrap undergrowth, all Pop-Op dilation and contraction, full flowered and crammed at every interstice and crosshatch with mythological beasts and symbols!

Open at the neck, this vast shirt hung wind-whipped like a thousand flags from a parade of united but neurotic nations.

But now, Dr. Brokaw tilted his baseball cap, lifted his French sunglasses to survey the empty bus seats. Striding slowly down the aisle, he wheeled, he paused, he lingered, now here, now there. He whispered, he murmured, now to this man, this woman, that child.

I was about to cry out when I heard him say:

"Well, what do you make of it?"

A small boy, stunned by the circus-poster effect of the old man's attire, blinked, in need of nudging. The old man nudged:

"My *shirt,* boy! What do you *see!?*"

"Horses!" the child blurted, at last. "Dancing horses!"

"Bravo!" The doctor beamed, patted him, and strode on. "And *you,* sir?"

A young man, quite taken with the forthrightness of this invader from some summer world, said:

"Why . . . clouds, of course."

"Cumulus or nimbus?"

"Er . . . not storm clouds, no, no. Fleecy, sheep clouds."

"Well done!"

The psychiatrist plunged on.

"Mademoiselle?"

"Surfers!" A teen-age girl stared. "They're the waves, big ones. Surfboards. Super!"

And so it went, on down the length of the bus and as the great man progressed a few scraps and titters of laughter sprang up, then, grown infectious, turned to roars of hilarity. By now, a dozen passengers had heard the first responses and so fell in with the game. This woman saw skyscrapers! The doctor scowled at her suspiciously. The doctor winked. That man saw crossword puzzles. The doctor shook his hand. This child found zebras all optical illusion on an African wild. The doctor slapped the animals and made them jump! This old woman saw vague Adams and misty Eves being driven from half-seen Gardens. The doctor scooched in on the seat with her awhile; they talked in fierce whispered elations, then up he jumped and forged on. Had the old woman seen an eviction? This young one saw the couple invited back in!

Dogs, lightnings, cats, cars, mushroom clouds, man-eating tiger lilies!

Each person, each response, brought greater outcries. We found ourselves all laughing together. This fine old man was a happening of nature, a caprice, God's rambunctious Will, sewing all our separateness up in one.

Elephants! Elevators! Alarums! Dooms!

When first he had bounded aboard we had wanted naught of each other. But now like an immense snowfall which we must gossip on or an electrical failure that blacked out two million homes and so thrown us all together in communal chat, laugh, guffaw, we felt the tears clean up our souls even as they cleaned down our cheeks.

Each answer seemed funnier than the previous, and no one shouted louder his great torments of laughter than this grand tall and marvelous physician who asked for, got, and cured us of our hairballs on the spot. Whales. Kelp. Grass meadows. Lost cities. Beauteous women. He paused. He wheeled. He sat. He rose. He flapped his wildly colored shirt, until at last he towered before me and said:

"Sir, what do *you* find?"

"Why, Dr. Brokaw, of course!"

The old man's laughter stopped as if he were shot. He seized his dark glasses off, then clapped them on and grabbed my shoulders as if to wrench me into focus.

"Simon Wincelaus, is that *you!*"

"Me, me!" I laughed. "Good grief, doctor, I thought you were dead and buried years ago. What's this you're up to?"

"Up to?" He squeezed and shook my hands and pummeled my arms and cheeks gently. Then he snorted a great self-forgiving laugh as he gazed down along the acreage of ridiculous shirting. "Up to? Retired. Swiftly gone. Overnight traveled three thousand miles from where last you saw me . . ." His peppermint breath warmed my face. "And now best known hereabouts as . . . listen! . . . the Man in the Rorschach Shirt."

"In the what?" I cried.

"Rorschach Shirt."

Light as a carnival gas balloon he touched into the seat beside me.
I sat stunned and silent.

We rode along by the blue sea under a bright summer sky.

The doctor gazed ahead as if reading my thoughts in vast skywriting
among the clouds.

"Why, you ask, why? I see your face, startled, at the airport years
ago. My Going Away Forever day. My plane should have been named
the *Happy Titanic*. On it I sank forever into the traceless sky. Yet here
I am in the absolute flesh, yes? Not drunk, nor mad, nor riven by age
and retirement's boredom. Where, what, why, how come?"

"Yes," I said, "why *did* you retire, with everything pitched for you?
Skill, reputation, money. Not a breath of—"

"Scandal? None! Why, then? Because, this old camel had not one but
two humps broken by two straws. Two amazing straws. Hump Number
One—"

He paused. He cast me a sidelong glance from under his dark glasses.

"This is a confessional," I said. "Mum's the word."

"Confessional. Yes. Thanks."

The bus hummed softly on the road.

His voice rose and fell with the hum.

"You know my photographic memory? Blessed, cursed, with total
recall. Anything said, seen, done, touched, heard, can be snapped back
to focus by me, forty, fifty, sixty years later. All, all of it, trapped
in here."

He stroked his temples lightly with the fingers of both hands.

"Hundreds of psychiatric cases, delivered through my door, day after
day, year on year. And never once did I check my notes on any of those
sessions. I found, early on, I need only play back what I had heard inside
my head. Sound tapes, of course, were kept as a double-check, but never
listened to. There you have the stage set for the whole shocking business.

"One day in my sixtieth year a woman patient spoke a single word.
I asked her to repeat it. Why? Suddenly I had felt my semicircular canals
shift as if some valves had opened upon cool fresh air at a subterra-
nean level.

" 'Best,' she said.

" 'I thought you said "beast," ' I said.

" 'Oh, no, doctor, "best." '

"One word. One pebble dropped off the edge. And then—the avalanche. For, distinctly, I had heard her claim: 'He loved the beast in me,'
which is one kettle of sexual fish, eh? When in reality she had said, 'He
loved the best in me,' which is quite another pan of cold cod, you
must agree.

"That night I could not sleep. I smoked, I stared from windows. My head, my ears, felt strangely clear, as if I had just gotten over a thirty years' cold. I suspected myself, my past, my senses, so at three in the deadfall morning I motored to my office and found the worst:

"The recalled conversations of hundreds of cases in my mind were not the same as those recorded on my tapes or typed out in my secretary's notes!"

"You mean . . .?"

"I mean when I heard beast it was truly best. Dumb was really numb. On wore cocks and vice-versa. I heard bed and someone had said head. Sleep was creep. Lay was day. Paws were really pause. Rump was merely jump. Fiend was only leaned. Sex was hex or mix or, God knows, per*plex!* Yes-mess. No-slow. Binge-hinge. Wrong-long. Side-hide. Name a name, I'd heard it wrong. Ten million dozen misheard nouns! I panicked through my files! Good Grief! Great Jumping Josie!

"All those years, those people! Holy Moses, Brokaw, I cried, all these years down from the Mount, the word of God like a flea in your ear. And now, late in the day, old wise one, you think to consult your lightning-scribbled stones. And find your Laws, your Tables, *different!*

"Moses fled his offices that night. I ran in dark, unraveling my despair. I trained to Far Rockaway, perhaps because of its lamenting name.

"I walked by a tumult of waves only equaled by the tumult in my breast. How? I cried, how can you have been half-deaf for a lifetime and not known it! And known it only now when through some fluke, the sense, the gift, returned, how, how?!

"My only answer was a great stroke of thunder wave upon the sands.

"So much for straw number one that broke hump number one of this odd-shaped human camel."

There was a moment of silence.

We rode swaying on the bus. The bus moved along the golden shore road, through a gentle breeze.

"Straw number two? I asked, quietly, at last.

Dr. Brokaw held his French sunglasses up so sunlight struck fish-glitters all about the cavern of the bus. We watched the swimming rainbow patterns, he with detachment and at last half-amused concern.

"Sight. Vision. Texture. Detail. Aren't they miraculous. Aweful in the sense of meaning true awe? What is sight, vision, insight? Do we really want to see the world?"

"Oh, yes," I cried, promptly.

"A young man's unthinking answer. No, my dear boy, we do not. At twenty, yes, we think we wish to see, know, be all. So thought I once. But I have had weak eyes most of my life, spent half my days being fitted out with new specs by oculists, hee? Well, comes the dawn of the corneal lens! At last, I decided, I will fit myself with those bright little

teardrop miracles, those invisible discs! Coincidence? Psychosomatic
cause and effect? For, that same week I got my contact lenses was the
week my hearing cleared up! There must be some physio-mental connec-
tion, but don't hazard me into an informed guess.

"All I know is I had my little crystal corneal lenses ground and
installed upon my weak baby blue eyes and—*Voilà!*

"There was the world!

"THERE were people!

"And there, God save us, was the dirt, and the multitudinous pores
upon the people.

"Simon," he added, grieving gently, eyes shut for a moment behind
his dark glasses, "have you ever thought, did you know, that people are
for the most part pores?"

He let that sink in. I thought about it.

"Pores?" I said, at last.

"Pores! But who thinks of it? Who bothers to go look? But with my
restored vision *I* saw! A thousand, a million, ten billion . . . pores. Large,
small, pale, crimson . . . pores. Everyone and on everyone. People passing. People crowding buses, theaters, telephone booths, all pore and little
substance. Small pores on tiny women. Big pores on monster men. Or
vice versa. Pores as numerous as that foul dust which slides pell-mell
down church-nave sunbeams late afternoons. Pores. They became my
utter and riven fascination. I stared at fine ladies' complexions, not their
eyes, mouths, or earlobes. Shouldn't a man watch a woman's skeleton
hinge and unhinge itself within that sweet pincushion flesh? Yes! But
no, I saw only cheese-grater, kitchen-sieve skins. All Beauty turned sour
Grotesque. Swiveling my gaze was like swiveling the 200-inch Palomar
telescope in my damned skull. Everywhere I looked I saw the meteor-
bombarded moon, in dread super closeup!

"Myself?' God, shaving mornings was exquisite torture. I could not
pluck my eyes from my lost battle-pitted face. Damnation, Immanuel
Brokaw, I soughed, you are the Grand Canyon at high noon, an orange
with a billion navels, a pomegranate with the skin stripped off.

"In sum, my contact lenses had made me fifteen years old again.
That is: festering, self-crucified bundle of doubt, horror, and absolute
imperfection. The worst age in all one's life had returned to haunt me
with its pimpled, bumpy ghost.

"I lay, a sleepless wreck. Ah, second Adolescence, take pity, I cried.
How could I have been so blind, so many years? Blind, yes, and knew
it, and always said it was of no importance. So I groped about the world
as lustful myope, nearsightedly missing the holes, rips, tears, and bumps
on others as well as myself. Now, Reality had run me down in the street.
And the Reality was: Pores.

"I shut my eyes and went to bed for several days. Then I sat up in bed and proclaimed, wide-eyed: Reality is not all! I refuse this knowledge. I legislate against Pores! I accept instead those truths we intuit, or make up to live by.

"I traded in my eyeballs.

"That is I handed my corneal-contact lenses to a sadist nephew who thrives on garbages and lumpy people and hairy things.

"I clapped back on my old undercorrected specs. I strolled through a world of returned and gentle mists. I saw enough but not too much. I found half-discerned ghost peoples I could love again. I saw the 'me' in the morning glass I could once more bed with, admire and take as chum. I began to laugh each day with new happiness. Softly. Then, very loud.

"What a joke, Simon, life is.

"From vanity we buy lenses that see all and so lose everything!

"And by giving up some small bit-piece of so-called wisdom, reality, truth, we gain back an entirety of life! Who does not know this? Writers do! Intuited novels are far more 'true' than all your scribbled data-fact reportage in the history of the world!

"But then at last I had to face the great twin fractures lying athwart my conscience. My eyes. My ears. Holy Cow, I said, softly. The thousand folk who tread my offices and creaked my couches and looked for echoes in my Delphic Cave, why, why, preposterous! I had seen none of them, nor heard any clear!

"Who was that Miss Harbottle?

"What of old Dinsmuir?

"What was the real color, look, size of Miss Grimes?

"Did Mrs. Scrapwight really resemble and speak like an Egyptian papyrus mummy fallen out of a rug at my desk?

"I could not even guess. Two thousand days of fogs surrounded my lost children, mere voices calling, fading, gone.

"My God, I had wandered the marketplace with an invisible sign BLIND AND DEAF and people had rushed to fill my beggar's cup with coins and rush off cured. Cured! Isn't *that* miraculous, strange? Cured by an old ricket with one arm gone, as 'twere, and one leg missing. What? What did I say right to them out of hearing wrong? Who indeed were those people? I will never know.

"And then I thought: there are a hundred psychiatrists about town who see and hear more clearly than I. But whose patients walk naked into high seas or leap off playground slides at midnight or truss women up and smoke cigars over them.

"So I had to face the irreducible fact of a successful career.

"The lame do *not* lead the lame, my reason cried, the blind and halt do not cure the halt and the blind! But a voice from the far balcony of my soul replied with immense irony: Bee's-wax and Bull-Durham! You, Immanuel Brokaw, are a porcelain genius, which means cracked but brilliant! Your occluded eyes see, your corked ears hear. Your fractured sensibilities cure at some level below consciousness! Bravo!

"But no, I could not live with my perfect imperfections. I could not understand nor tolerate this smug secret thing which, through screens and obfuscations, played meadow doctor to the world and cured field beasts.

"I had several choices then. Put my corneal lenses back in? Buy ear radios to help my rapidly improving sense of sound? And then? Find I had lost touch with my best and hidden mind which had grown comfortably accustomed to thirty years of bad vision and lousy hearing? Chaos both for curer and cured.

"Stay blind and deaf and work? It seemed a dreadful fraud, though my record was laundry-fresh, pressed white and clean.

"So I retired.

"Packed my bags and ran off into golden oblivion to let the incredible wax collect in my most terrible strange ears . . .''

We rode in the bus along the shore in the warm afternoon. A few clouds moved over the sun. Shadows misted on the sands and the people strewn on the sands under the colored umbrellas.

I cleared my throat.

"Will you ever return to practice again, doctor?''

"I practice now.''

"But you just said—''

"Oh, not officially, and not with an office or fees, no, never that again.'' The doctor laughed quietly. "I am sore beset by the mystery anyway. That is, of how I cured all those people with a laying on of hands even though my arms were chopped off at the elbows. Still, now, I do keep my 'hand' in.''

"How?''

"This shirt of mine. You saw. You heard.''

"Coming down the aisle?''

"Exactly. The colors. The patterns. One thing to that man, another to the girl, a third to the boy. Zebras, goats, lightnings, Egyptian amulets. What, what, what? I ask. And: answer, answer, answer. The Man in the Rorschach Shirt.

"I have a dozen such shirts at home.

"All colors, all different pattern mixes. One was designed for me by Jackson Pollack before he died. I wear each shirt for a day, or a week, if the going, the answers, are thick, fast, full of excitement and reward. Then off with the old and on with the new. Ten billion glances, ten billion startled responds!

"Might I not market these Rorschach shirts to your psychoanalyst on vacation? Test your friends? Shock your neighbors? Titillate your wife? No, no. This is my own special private most dear fun. No one must share it. Me and my shirts, the sun, the bus, and a thousand afternoons ahead. The beach waits. And on it, my people!

"So I walk the shores of this summer world. There is no winter here, amazing, yes, no winter of discontent it would almost seem, and death a rumor beyond the dunes. I walk along in my own time and way and come on people and let the wind flap my great sailcloth shirt now veering north, south or south-by-west and watch their eyes pop, glide, leer, squint, wonder. And when a certain person says a certain word about my ink-slashed cotton colors I give pause. I chat. I walk with them awhile. We peer into the great glass of the sea. I sidewise peer into their soul. Sometimes we stroll for hours, a longish session with the weather. Usually it takes but that one day and, not knowing with whom they walked, scot-free, they are discharged all unwitting patients. They walk on down the dusky shore toward a fairer brighter eve. Behind their backs, the deaf-blind man waves them bon voyage and trots home there to devour happy suppers, brisk with fine work done.

"Or sometimes I meet some half-slumberer on the sand whose troubles cannot all be fetched out to die in the raw light of one day. Then, as by accident, we collide a week later and walk by the tidal churn doing what has always been done; we have our traveling confessional. For long before pent-up priests and whispers and repentances, friends walked, talked, listened, and in the listening-talk cured each other's sour despairs. Good friends trade hairballs all the time, give gifts of mutual dismays and so are rid of them.

"Trash collects on lawns and in minds. With bright shirt and nail-tipped trash stick I set out each dawn to . . . clean up the beaches. So many, oh, so many bodies lying out there in the light. So many minds lost in the dark. I try to walk among them all, without . . . stumbling . . ."

The wind blew in the bus window cool and fresh, making a sea of ripples through the thoughtful old man's patterned shirt.

The bus stopped.

Dr. Brokaw suddenly saw where he was and leapt up. "Wait!"

Everyone on the bus turned as if to watch the exit of a star performer. Everyone smiled.

Dr. Brokaw pumped my hand and ran. At the far front end of the bus he turned, amazed at his own forgetfulness, lifted his dark glasses and squinted at me with his weak baby-blue eyes.

"You—" he said.

Already, to him, I was a mist, a pointillist dream somewhere out beyond the rim of vision.

"You . . ." he called into that fabulous cloud of existence which surrounded and pressed him warm and close, "you never *told* me. What? *What?!*"

He stood tall to display that incredible Rorschach shirt which fluttered and swarmed with everchanging line and color.

I looked. I blinked. I answered.

"A sunrise!" I cried.

The doctor reeled with this gentle friendly blow.

"Are you sure it isn't a sunset?" he called, cupping one hand to his ear.

I looked again and smiled. I hoped he saw my smile a thousand miles away within the bus.

"No," I said. "A sunrise. A beautiful sunrise."

He shut his eyes to digest the words. His great hands wandered along the shore of his wind-gentled shirt. He nodded. Then he opened his pale eyes, waved once, and stepped out into the world.

The bus drove on. I looked back once.

And there went Dr. Brokaw advancing straight out and across a beach where lay a random sampling of the world, a thousand bathers in the warm light.

He seemed to tread lightly upon a water of people.

The last I saw of him, he was still gloriously afloat.

here he is!''

The two men leaned. The helicopter tilted with their lean. The coastline whipped by below.

"No. Just a bit of rock and some moss—''

The pilot lifted his head, which signaled the lift of the helicopter to swivel and rush away. The white cliffs of Dover vanished. They broke over green meadows and so wove back and forth, a giant dragonfly excursioning the stuffs of winter that sleeted their blades.

"Wait! There! Drop!''

The machine fell down; the grass came up. The second man, grunting, pushed the bubble-eye aside and, as if he needed oiling, carefully let himself to the earth. He ran. Losing his breath instantly he slowed to cry bleakly against the wind:

"Harry!''

His yell caused a ragged shape on the rise ahead to stumble up and run.

"I've done nothing!''

"It's not the law, Harry! It's me! Sam Welles!''

The old man who fled before him slowed, then stopped, rigid, on the edge of the cliff above the sea, holding to his long beard with two gloved hands.

Samuel Welles, gasping, trudged up behind, but did not touch, for fear of putting him to flight.

"Harry, you damn fool. It's been weeks. I was afraid I might not find you.''

"And I was afraid you *would*.''

Harry, whose eyes had been tight shut, now opened them to look tremblingly down at his beard, his gloves, and over at his friend Samuel. Here they were, two old men, very gray, very cold, on a rise of raw stone on a December day. They had known each other so long, so many years, they had passed each other's expressions back and forth between their faces. Their mouths and eyes, therefore, were similar. They might have been ancient brothers. The only difference showed in the man who had unhinged himself from the helicopter. Under his dark clothes you could spy an incongruous Hawaiian-colored sport shirt. Harry tried not to stare at it.

Right now, anyway, both their eyes were wet.

"Harry, I came to warn you."

"No need. Why do you think I've been hiding. This is the final day?"

"The final, yes."

They stood and thought on it.

Christmas tomorrow. And now this Christmas Eve afternoon the last boats leaving. And England, a stone in a sea of mist and water, would be a marble monument to herself left written on by rain and buried in fog. After today, only the gulls would own the island. And a billion monarch butterflies in June rising up like celebrations tossed on parades to the sea.

Harry, his eyes fixed to the tidal shore, spoke:

"By sunset, will every damn stupid idiot fool clear off the Isle?"

"That's about the shape of it."

"And a dread shape it is. And you, Samuel, have you come to kidnap me?"

"Persuade is more like it."

"Persuade? Great God, Sam, don't you know me after fifty years? Couldn't you guess I would want to be the last man in all Britain, no, that hasn't the proper sound, *Great* Britain?"

Last man in Great Britain, thought Harry, Lord, listen. It tolls. It is the great bell of London heard through all the mizzles down through time to this strange day and hour when the last, the very last save one, leave this racial mound, this burial touch of green set in a sea of cold light. The last. The last.

"Samuel, listen. My grave is dug. I'd hate to leave it behind."

"Who'll put you *in* it?"

"Me, when the time's right."

"And who's to cover over?"

"Why, there's dust to cover dust, Sam. The wind will see to it. Ah, God!" Not wishing it, the words exploded from his mouth. He was amazed to see tears flung out on the air from his blinking eyes. "What are we doing here? Why all the good-byes? Why are the last boats in the Channel and the last jets gone? Where did people go, Sam? What happened, what *happened!*"

"Why," said Samuel Welles quietly, "it's simple, Harry. The weather here is bad. Always *has* been. No one dared speak of it, for nothing could be done. But now, England is finished. The future belongs—"

Their eyes moved jointly South.

"To the damn Canary Islands?"

"Samoa."

"To the Brazilian shores?"

"Don't forget California, Harry."

Both laughed, gently.

"California. All the jokes. That funny place. And yet, aren't there a million English from Sacramento to Los Angeles this noon?"

"And another million in Florida."

"Two million Down Under, the past four years alone."

They nodded at the sums.

"Well, Samuel, man says one thing. The sun says another. So man goes by what his skin tells his blood. And the blood at last says: South. It has been saying it for two thousand years. But we pretended not to hear. A man with his first sunburn is a man in the midst of a new love affair, know it or not. Finally, he lies out under some great foreign sky and says to the blinding light: Teach me, oh God, gently, teach."

Samuel Welles shook his head with awe. "Keep talking like that and I won't *have* to kidnap you!"

"No, the sun may have taught you, Samuel, but cannot quite teach me. I wish it could. The truth is, 'twill be no fun here alone. Can't I argue you, Sam, to stay on, the old team, you and me, like when we were boys, eh?" He buffed the other's elbow roughly, dearly.

"God, you make me feel I'm deserting King and Country."

"Don't. You desert nothing, for no one's here. Who would have dreamt, when we were kids in 1980, the day would come when a promise of always summer would leak John Bull to the four corners of beyond?"

"I've been cold all my life, Harry. Too many years putting on too many sweaters and not enough coal in the scuttle. Too many years when the sky did not show so much as a crack of blue on the first day of June nor a smell of hay in July nor a dry day and winter begun August 1st, year on year. I can't take it anymore, Harry, I can't."

"Nor need you. Our race has suffered itself well. You have earned, all of you, you deserve, this long retirement in Jamaica, Port-au-Prince, and Pasadena. Give me that hand. Shake hard again! It's a great moment in history. You and me, *we're* living it!"

"So we are, by God."

"Now look here, Sam, when you've gone and settled in Sicily, Sidney, or Navel Orange, California, tell this 'moment' to the news. They might write you in a column. And history books? Well, shouldn't there be half a page for you and me, the last gone and the last stayed behind? Sam, Sam, you're breaking the bones, but shake away, hold tight, this is our last tussle."

They stood off, panting, wet-eyed.

"Harry, now, will you walk me as far as the copter?"

"No. I fear the damn contraption. The thought of the sun on his dark day might leap me in and fly me off with you."

"And what harm in that?"

"Harm! Why, Samuel, I must guard our coast from invasion. The Normans, the Vikings, the Saxons. In the coming years I'll walk the entire isle, stand guard from Dover north on round the reefs and back through Folkestone, here again."

"Will Hitler invade, chum?"

"He and his iron ghosts just might."

"And how will you fight him, Harry?"

"Do you think I walk alone? No. Along the way, I may find Caesar on the shore. He loved it so he left a road or two. Those roads I'll take, and borrow just those ghosts of choice invaders to repel less choice. It's up to me, yes, to commit or uncommit ghosts, choose or not choose out of the whole damn history of the land?"

"It is. It is."

The last man wheeled to the north and then to the west and then to the south.

"And when I've seen all's well from castle here to lighthouse there, and listened to battles of gunfires in the plunge off Firth, and bagpiped round Scotland with a sour mean pipe, in each New Year's week, Sam, I'll scull back down—Thames and there each December 31st to the end of my life, the night watchman of London, meaning me, yes, me, will make his clock rounds and say out the bells of the old rhymed churches. Oranges and lemons say the bells of St. Clemens. Bow bells. St. Marguerite's. Paul's. I shall dance rope-ends for you, Sam, and hope the cold wind blown south to the warm wind wherever you are stirs some small gray hairs in your sunburnt ears."

"I'll be listening, Harry."

"Listen more! I'll sit in the houses of Lords and Commons and debate, losing one hour but to win the next. And say that never before in history did so many owe so much to so few and hear the sirens again from old remembered records and things broadcast before we both were born.

"And a few seconds before January 1st I shall climb and lodge with mice in Big Ben as it strikes the changing of the year.

"And somewhere along the line, no doubt, I shall sit on the Stone of Scone."

"You wouldn't!"

"Wouldn't I? Or the place where it was, anyway, before they mailed it south to Summer's Bay. And hand me some sort of sceptre, a frozen snake perhaps stunned by snow from some December garden. And fit a kind of paste-up crown upon my head. And name me friend to Richard, Henry, outcast kin of Elizabeths I and II. Alone in Westminster's desert with Kipling mum and history underfoot, very old, perhaps mad, mightn't I, ruler and ruled, elect myself king of the misty isles?''

"You might, and who would blame you?''

Samuel Welles bearhugged him again, then broke and half ran for his waiting machine. Halfway he turned to call back:

"Good God. I just thought. Your name *is* Harry What a *fine* name for a king!''

"Not bad.''

"Forgive me for leaving?!''

"The sun forgives all, Samuel. Go where it wants you.''

"But will England forgive?''

"England is where her people are. I stay with old bones. You go with her sweet flesh, Sam, her fair sunburnt skin and blooded body, get!''

"Good-bye.''

"God be with you, too, oh you and that bright yellow sport shirt!''

And the wind snatched between and though both yelled more neither heard, waved, and Samuel hauled himself into that machine which swarmed the air and floated off like a vast white summer flower.

And the last man left behind in great gasps and sobs cried out to himself:

Harry! Do you hate change? Against progress? You do see, don't you, the reasons for all this? That ships and jets and planes and a promise of weather piped all the folk away? I see, he said, I see. How could they resist when at long last forever August lay just across the sill?

Yes, yes! He wept and ground his teeth and leaned up from the cliff rim to shake his fists at the vanishing craft in the sky.

"Traitors! Come back!''

You can't leave old England, can't leave Pip and Humbug, Iron Duke and Trafalgar, the Horse Guard in the rain, London burning, buzz bombs and sirens, the new babe held high on the palace balcony, Churchill's funeral cortege still in the street, man, *still* in the street! and Caesar not gone to his Senate, and strange happenings this night at Stonehenge! Leave all this, this, *this!?*

Upon his knees, at the cliff's edge, the last and final king of England, Harry Smith wept alone.

The helicopter was gone now, called toward august isles where summer sang its sweetness in the birds.

The old man turned to see the countryside and thought, why this is how it was one hundred thousand years ago. A great silence and a great wilderness and now, quite late, the empty shell towns and King Henry, Old Harry, the Ninth.

He rummaged half blindly about in the grass and found his lost book bag and chocolate bits in a sack and hoisted his Bible, and Shakespeare and much-thumbed Johnson and much-tongued Dickens and Dryden and Pope, and stood out on the road that led all round England.

Tomorrow: Christmas. He wished the world well. Its people had gifted themselves already with sun, all over the globe. Sweden lay empty. Norway had flown. None lived any longer in God's cold climes. All basked upon the continental hearths of His best lands in fair winds under mild skies. No more fights just to survive. Men, reborn like Christ on such as tomorrow, in southern places, were truly returned to an eternal and fresh-grown manger.

Tonight, in some church, he would ask forgiveness for calling them traitors.

"One last thing, Harry. Blue."

"Blue?" he asked himself.

"Somewhere down the road find some blue chalk. Didn't English men once color themselves with such?"

"Blue men, yes, from head to foot!"

"Our ends are in our beginnings, eh?"

He pulled his cap tight. The wind was cold. He tasted the first snow-flakes that fell to brush his lips.

"O remarkable boy!" he said, leaning from an imaginary window on a golden Christmas morn, an old man reborn and gasping for joy. "Delightful boy, there, is the great bird, the turkey, still hung in the poulterer's window down the way?"

"It's hanging there now," said the boy.

"Go buy it! Come back with the man and I'll give you a shilling. Come back in less than five minutes and I'll give you a crown!"

And the boy went to fetch.

And buttoning his coat, carrying his books, Old Harry Ebenezer Scrooge Julius Caesar Pickwick Pip and half a thousand others marched off along the road in winter weather. The road was long and beautiful. The waves were gunfire on the coast. The wind was bagpipes in the north.

Ten minutes later, when he had gone singing beyond a hill, by the look of it, all the lands of England seemed ready for a people who someday soon in history might arrive . . .

Ihe great eye floated in space. And behind the great eye somewhere hidden away within metal and machinery was a small eye that belonged to a man who looked and could not stop looking at all the multitudes of stars and the diminishings and growings of light a billion billion miles away.

The small eye closed with tiredness. Captain John Wilder stood holding to the telescopic devices which probed the universe and at last murmured, "Which one?"

The astronomer with him said, "Take your pick."

"I wish it were that easy." Wilder opened his eyes. "What's the data on this star?"

"Alpha-Cygne II. Same size and reading as our sun. Planetary system, possible."

"Possible. Not certain. If we pick the wrong star, God help the people we send on a two-hundred-year journey to find a planet that may not be there. No, God help me, for the final selection is mine, and I may well send myself on that journey. So, how can we be sure?"

"We can't. We just make the best guess, send our starship out, and pray."

"You are not very encouraging. That's it. I'm tired."

Wilder touched a switch that shut up tight the greater eye, this rocket-powered space lens that stared cold upon the abyss, saw far too much and knew little, and now knew nothing. The rocket laboratory drifted sightless on an endless night.

"Home," said the captain. "Let's go home."

And the blind beggar-after-stars wheeled on a spread of fire and ran away.

The frontier cities on Mars looked very fine from above. Coming down for a landing, Wilder saw the neons among the blue hills and thought,

We'll light those worlds a billion miles off, and the children of the people living under those lights this instant, we'll make them immortal. Very simply, if we succeed, they will live forever.

Live forever. The rocket landed. Live forever.

The wind that blew from the frontier town smelled of grease. An aluminum-toothed jukebox banged somewhere. A junkyard rusted beside the rocket port. Old newspapers danced alone on the windy tarmac.

Wilder, motionless at the top of the gantry elevator, suddenly wished not to move down. The lights suddenly had become people and not words that, huge in the mind, could be handled with elaborate ease.

He sighed. The freight of people was too heavy. The stars were too far away.

"Captain?" said someone behind him.

He stepped forward. The elevator gave way. They sank with a silent screaming toward a very real land with real people in it, who were waiting for him to choose.

At midnight the telegram-bin hissed and exploded out a message projectile. Wilder, at his desk, surrounded by tapes and computation cards, did not touch it for a long while. When at last he pulled the message out, he scanned it, rolled it in a tight ball, then uncrumpled the message and read again:

FINAL CANAL BEING FILLED TOMORROW WEEK. YOU ARE INVITED
CANAL YACHT PARTY. DISTINGUISHED GUESTS. FOUR-DAY JOURNEY
TO SEARCH FOR LOST CITY. KINDLY ACKNOWLEDGE.

I. V. AARONSON.

Wilder blinked, and laughed quietly. He crumpled the paper again, but stopped, lifted the telephone and said:

"Telegram to I. V. Aaronson, Mars City I. Answer affirmative. No sane reason why, but still—affirmative."

And hung up the phone. To sit for a long while watching this night which shadowed all the whispering, ticking, and motioning machines.

The dry canal waited.

It had been waiting twenty thousand years for nothing but dust to filter through in ghost tides.

Now, quite suddenly, it whispered.

And the whisper became a rush and wall-caroming glide of waters.

As if a vast machined fist had struck the rocks somewhere, clapped the air and cried "Miracle!," a wall of water came proud and high along the channels, and lay down in all the dry places of the canal and moved on toward ancient deserts of dry-bone, surprising old wharves and lifting up the skeletons of boats abandoned thirty centuries before when the water burnt away to nothing.

The tide turned a corner and lifted up—a boat as fresh as the morning itself, with new-minted silver screws and brass pipings, and bright new Earth-sewn flags. The boat, suspended from the side of the canal, bore the name *Aaronson I.*

Inside the boat, a man with the same name smiled. Mr. Aaronson sat listening to the waters live under the boat.

And the sound of the water was cut across by the sound of a hover-craft, arriving, and a motorbike, arriving, and in the air, as if summoned with magical timing, drawn by the glimmer of tides in the old canal, a number of gadfly people flew over the hills on jet-pack machines, and hung suspended as if doubting this collision of lives caused by one rich man.

Scowling up with a smile, the rich man called to his children, cried them in from the heat with offers of food and drink.

"Captain Wilder! Mr. Parkhill! Mr. Beaumont!"

Wilder set his hovercraft down.

Sam Parkhill discarded his motorbike, for he had seen the yacht and it was a new love.

"My God," cried Beaumont, the actor, part of the frieze of people in the sky dancing like bright bees on the wind. "I've timed my entrance wrong. I'm early. There's no audience!"

"I'll applaud you down!" shouted the old man, and did so, then added, "Mr. Aikens!"

"Aikens?" said Parkhill. "The big-game hunter?"

"None other!"

And Aikens dived down as if to seize them in his harrying claws. He fancied his resemblance to the hawk. He was finished and stropped like a razor by the swift life he had lived. Not an edge of him but cut the air as he fell, a strange plummeting vengeance upon people who had done nothing to him. In the moment before destruction, he pulled up on his jets and, gently screaming, simmered himself to touch the marble jetty. About his lean middle hung a rifle belt. His pockets bulged like those of a boy from the candy store. One guessed he was stashed with sweet bullets and rare bombs. In his hands, like an evil child, he held a weapon that looked like a bolt of lightning fallen straight from the clutch of Zeus, stamped nevertheless: *Made in U.S.A.* His face was sunblasted dark. His eyes were cool surprises in the sunwrinkled flesh, all mint-blue-green crystal. He wore a white porcelain smile set in African sinews. The earth did not quite tremble as he landed.

"The lion prowls the land of Judah!" cried a voice from the heavens. "Now do behold the lambs driven forth to slaughter!"

"Oh for God's sake, Harry, shut up!" said a woman's voice.

And two more kites fluttered their souls, their dread humanity on the wind.

The rich man jubilated.

"Harry Harpwell!"

"Behold the angel of the Lord who comes with Annunciations!" the man in the sky said, hovering. "And the Annunciation is—"

"He's drunk again," his wife supplied, flying ahead of him, not looking back.

"Megan Harpwell," said the rich man, like an entrepreneur introducing his troupe.

"The poet," said Wilder.

"And the poet's barracuda wife," muttered Parkhill.

"I am not drunk," the poet shouted down the wind. "I am simply *high.*"

And here he let loose such a deluge of laughter that those below almost raised their hands to ward off the avalanche.

Lowering himself, like a fat dragon kite, the poet, whose wife's mouth was now clamped shut, bumbled over the yacht. He made the motions of blessing same, and winked at Wilder and Parkhill.

"Harpwell," he called. "Isn't that a name to go with being a great modern poet who suffers in the present, lives in the past, steals bones from old dramatists' tombs, and flies on this new egg-beater wind-suck device, to call down sonnets on your head? I pity the old euphoric saints and angels who had no invisible wings like this so as to dart in oriole convolutions and ecstatic convulsions on the air as they sang their lines or damned souls to Hell. Poor earthbound sparrows, wings clipped. Only their genius flew. Only their Muse knew airsickness—"

"Harry," said his wife, her feet on the ground, eyes shut.

"Hunter!" called the poet. "Aikens! Here's the greatest game in all the world, a poet on the wing. I bare my breast. Let fly your honeyed bee sting! Bring me, Icarus, down, if your gun be sunbeams kindled in one tube and let free in a single forest fire that escalates the sky and turns tallow, mush, candlewick and lyre to mere tarbaby. Ready, aim, fire!"

The hunter, in good humor, raised his gun.

The poet, at this, laughed a mightier laugh and, literally, exposed his chest by tearing aside his shirt.

At which moment a quietness came along the canal rim.

A woman appeared walking. Her maid walked behind her. There was no vehicle in sight, and it seemed almost as if they had wandered a long way out of the Martian hills and now stopped.

The very quietness of her entrance gave dignity and attention to Cara Corelli.

The poet shut up his lyric in the sky and landed.

The company all looked together at this actress who gazed back without seeing them. She was dressed in a black jumpsuit which was the same color as her dark hair. She walked like a woman who has spoken little in her life and now stood facing them with the same quietness, as if waiting for someone to move without being ordered. The wind blew her hair out and down over her shoulders. The paleness of her face was shocking. Her paleness, rather than her eyes, stared at them

Then, without a word, she stepped down into the yacht and sat in the front of the craft, like a figurehead that knows its place and goes there.

The moment of silence was over.

Aaronson ran his finger down his printed guest list.

"An actor, a beautiful woman who happens to be an actress, a hunter, a poet, a poet's wife, a rocket captain, a former technician. All aboard!"

On the afterdeck of the huge craft, Aaronson spread forth his maps.

"Ladies, gentlemen," he said. "This is more than a four-day drinking bout, party, excursion. This is a Search!"

He waited for their faces to light, properly, and for them to glance from his eyes to the charts, and then said:

"We are seeking the fabled lost City of Mars, once called Dia-Sao. The City of Doom, it was called. Something terrible about it. The inhabitants fled as from a plague. The City left empty. Still empty now, centuries later."

"We," said Captain Wilder, "have charted, mapped, and cross-indexed every acre of land on Mars in the last fifteen years. You can't mislay a city the size of the one you speak of."

"True," said Aaronson, "you've mapped it from the sky, from the land. But you have *not* charted it via water! For the canals have been empty until now! So now we shall take the new waters that fill this last canal and go where the boats once went in the olden days, and see the very last new things that need to be seen on Mars." The rich man continued: "And somewhere on our traveling, as sure as the breath in our mouths, we shall find the most beautiful, the most fantastic, the most awful city in the history of this old world. And walk in that city—who knows?—find the reason why the Martians ran screaming away from it, as the legend says, ten thousand years ago."

Silence. Then:

"Bravo! Well done." The poet shook the old man's hand.

"And in that city," said Aikens, the hunter, "mightn't there be weapons the like of which we've never seen?"

"Most likely, sir."

"Well." The hunter cradled his bolt of lightning. "I was bored of Earth, shot every animal, ran fresh out of beasts, and came here looking for newer, better, more dangerous maneaters of any size or shape. Plus, now, new weapons! What more can one ask? Fine!''

And he dropped his blue-silver lightning bolt over the side. It sank in the clear water, bubbling.

''Let's get the hell out of here.''

''Let us, indeed,'' said Aaronson, ''get the good hell out.''

And he pressed the button that launched the yacht.

And the water flowed the yacht away.

And the yacht went in the direction toward which Cara Corelli's quiet paleness was pointed: beyond.

As the poet opened the first champagne bottle, the cork banged. Only the hunter did not jump.

The yacht sailed steadily through the day into night. They found an ancient ruin and had dinner there and a good wine imported, one hundred million miles from Earth. It was noted that it had traveled well.

With the wine came the poet, and after quite a bit of the poet, came sleep on board the yacht which moved away in search of a City that would not as yet be found.

At three in the morning, restless, unaccustomed to the gravity of a planet pulling at all of his body and not freeing him to dream, Wilder came out on the afterdeck of the yacht and found the actress there.

She was watching the waters slip by in dark revelations and discardments of stars.

He sat beside her and thought a question.

Just as silently, Cara Corelli asked herself the same question, and answered it.

''I am here on Mars because not long ago for the first time in my life, a man told me the truth.''

Perhaps she expected surprise. Wilder said nothing. The boat moved as on a stream of soundless oil.

''I am a beautiful woman. I have been beautiful all of my life. Which means that from the start people lied because they simply wished to be with me. I grew up surrounded by the untruths of men, women, and children who could not risk my displeasure. When beauty pouts, the world trembles.

''Have you ever seen a beautiful woman surrounded by men, seen them nodding, nodding? Heard their laughter? Men will laugh at anything a beautiful woman says. Hate themselves, yes, but they will laugh, say no for yes and yes for no.

''Well, that's how it was every day of every year for me. A crowd of liars stood between me and anything unpleasant. Their words dressed me in silks.

"But quite suddenly, oh, no more than six weeks ago, this man told me a truth. It was a small thing. I don't remember now what it was he said. But he didn't laugh. He didn't even smile.

"And no sooner was it out and over, the words spoken, that I knew a terrible thing had happened.

"I was growing old."

The yacht rocked gently on the tide.

"Oh, there would be more men who would, lying, smile again at what I said. But I saw the years ahead, when Beauty could no longer stomp its small foot, and shake down earthquakes, make cowardice a custom among otherwise good men.

"The man? He took back his truth immediately, when he saw that he had shocked me. But it was too late. I bought a one-way fare to Mars. Aaronson's invitation, when I arrived, put me on this new journey that will end . . . who knows where."

Wilder found that during this last he had reached out and taken her hand.

"No," she said, withdrawing. "No word. No touch. No pity. No self-pity." She smiled for the first time. "Isn't it strange? I always thought, wouldn't it be nice, someday, to hear the truth, to give up the masquerade? How wrong I was. It's no fun at all."

She sat and watched the black waters pour by the boat. When she thought to look again, some hours later, the seat beside her was empty. Wilder was gone.

On the second day, letting the new waters take them where they wished to go, they sailed toward a high range of mountains and lunched, on the way, in an old shrine, and had dinner that night in a further ruin. The Lost City was not much talked about. They were sure it would never be found.

But on the third day, without anyone's saying, they felt the approach of a great Presence.

It was the poet who finally put it in words.

"Is God humming under His breath somewhere?"

"What a fierce scum you are," said his wife. "Can't you speak plain English even when you gossip?"

"Dammit, listen!" cried the poet.

So they listened.

"Don't you feel as if you stood on the threshold of a giant blast-furnace kitchen and inside somewhere, all comfortably warm, vast hands, flour-gloved, smelling of wondrous tripes and miraculous viscera, blood-ied and proud of the blood, somewhere God cooks out the dinnertime of Life? In that cauldron sun, a brew to make the flowering forth of life on Venus, in that vat a stew broth of bones and nervous heart to run in animals on planets ten billion light-years gone. And isn't God content at His fabulous workings in the great kitchen Universe, where He has menu'd out a history of feasts, famines, deaths and reburgeonings for a billion billion years? And if God be content, would He not hum under His breath? Feel your bones. Aren't the marrows teeming with that hum? For that matter, God not only hums, He sings in the elements. He dances in molecules. Eternal celebration swarms us. Something is Near. Sh.''

He pressed his fat finger to his pouting lips.

And now all were silent, and Cara Corelli's paleness searchlighted the darkening waters ahead.

They all felt it. Wilder did. Parkhill did. They smoked to cover it. They put the smokes out. They waited in the dusk.

And the humming grew nearer. And the hunter, smelling it, went to join the silent actress at the bow of the yacht. And the poet sat to write out the words he had spoken.

"Yes," he said, as the stars came out. "It's almost upon us. It has." He took a breath. "Arrived."

The yacht passed into a tunnel.

The tunnel went under a mountain.

And the City was there.

It was a city within a hollow mountain with its own meadows surrounding it and its own strangely colored and illumined stone sky above it. And it had been lost and remained lost for the simple reason that people had tried flying to discover it or had unraveled roads to find it, when all the while the canals which led to it stood waiting for simple walkers to tread where once waters had tread.

And now the yacht filled with strange people from another planet touched an ancient wharf.

And the City stirred.

In the old days, cities were alive or dead if there were or were not people in them. It was that simple. But in the later days of life on Earth or Mars, cities did not die. They slept. And in their dreamful coggeries and enwheeled slumbers they remembered how once it was or how it might be again.

So as, one by one, the party filed out on the dock, they felt a great personage, the hidden, oiled, the metaled and shining soul of the metropolis slide in a landfall of muted and hidden fireworks toward becoming fully awake.

The weight of the new people on the dock caused a machined exhalation. They felt themselves on a delicate scale. The dock sank a millionth of an inch.

And the City, the cumbrous Sleeping Beauty of a nightmare device, sensed this touch, this kiss, and slept no more.

Thunder.

In a wall a hundred feet high stood a gate seventy feet wide. This gate, in two parts, now rumbled back, to hide within the wall.

Aaronson stepped forward.

Wilder moved to intercept him. Aaronson sighed.

"Captain, no advice, please. No warnings. No patrols going on ahead to flush out villains. The City wants us in. It welcomes us. Surely you don't imagine anything's *alive* in there? It's a robot place. And don't look as if you think it's a time bomb. It hasn't seen fun and games in—what?—twenty centuries? Do you read Martian hiero-glyphs? That cornerstone. The City was built at least nineteen hundred years ago."

"And abandoned," said Wilder.

"You make it sound like a plague drove them—"

"Not a plague." Wilder stirred uneasily, feeling himself weighed on the great scale sunk beneath his feet. "Something. Something . . ."

"Let's find out! In, all of you!"

Singly, and in pairs, the people from Earth stepped over the threshold.

Wilder, last of all, stepped across.

And the City came more alive.

The metal roofs of the City sprang wide like the petals of a flower.

Windows flicked wide like the lids of vast eyes to stare down upon them.

A river of sidewalks gently purled and washed at their feet, machined creekways which gleamed off through the City.

Aaronson gazed at the metal tides with pleasure. "Well, by God, the burden's off me! I was going to picnic you all. But that's the City's business now. Meet you back here in two hours to compare notes! Here goes."

And saying this he leapt out on the scurrying silver carpet that treaded him swiftly away.

Wilder, alarmed, moved to follow. But Aaronson cried jovially back: "Come on in, the water's fine!"

And the metal river whisked him, waving, off.

And one by one they stepped forward and the moving sidewalk drifted them away. Parkhill, the hunter, the poet and his wife, the actor, and then the beautiful woman and her maid. They floated like statues mysteri-ously borne on volcanic fluids that swept them anywhere, or nowhere, they could only guess.

Wilder jumped. The river seized his boots gently. Following, he went away into the avenues and around the bends of parks and through fiords of buildings.

And behind them, the dock and the gate stood empty. There was no trace to show they had arrived. It was almost as if they had never been.

Beaumont, the actor, was the first to leave the traveling pathway. A certain building caught his eye. And the next thing he knew, he had leapt off and edged near, sniffing.

He smiled.

For now he knew what kind of building he stood before because of the odor that drifted from it.

"Brass polish. And, by God, that means only one thing!"

Theater.

Brass doors, brass rails, brass rings on velvet curtains.

He opened the door of the building and stepped in. He sniffed and laughed aloud. Yes. Without a sign or a light, the smell alone, the special chemistry of metals and dust torn free of a million tickets.

And above all . . . he listened. The silence.

"The silence that waits. No other silence in the world waits. Only in a theater will you find that. The very particles of air chafe themselves in readiness. The shadows sit back and hold their breath. Well . . . ready or not . . . here I come . . ."

The lobby was green velvet undersea.

The theater itself: red velvet undersea, only dimly perceived as he opened the double doors. Somewhere beyond was a stage.

Something shuddered like a great beast. His breath had dreamt it alive. The air from his half-opened mouth caused the curtains one hundred feet away to softly furl and unfurl in darkness like all-covering wings.

Hesitantly, he took a step.

A light began to appear everywhere in a high ceiling where a school of miraculous prism fish swam upon themselves.

The oceanarium light played everywhere. He gasped.

The theater was full of people.

A thousand people sat motionless in the false dusk. True, they were small, fragile, rather dark, they wore silver masks, yet—people!

He knew, without asking, they had sat here for ten thousand years.

Yet they were not dead.

They were—he reached out a hand. He tapped the wrist of a man seated on the aisle.

The hand tinkled quietly.

He touched the shoulder of a woman. She chimed. Like a bell.

Yes, they had waited a few thousand years. But then, machines have a property of waiting.

He took a further step and froze.

For a sigh had passed over the crowd.

It was like the sound, the first small sound a newborn babe must make in the moment before it really sucks, bleats and shocks out its wailing surprise at being alive.

A thousand such sighs faded in the velvet porticos.

Beneath the masks, hadn't a thousand mouths drifted ajar?

Two moved. He stopped.

Two thousand eyes blinked wide in the velvet dusk.

He moved again.

A thousand silent heads wheeled on their ancient but well-oiled cogs. They looked at him.

An unquenchable cold ran wild in him.

He turned to run.

But their eyes would not let him go.

And, from the orchestra pit: music.

He looked and saw, slowly rising, an insect agglomeration of instruments, all strange, all grotesquely acrobatic in their configurations. These were being softly thrummed, piped, touched, and massaged in tune.

The audience, with a motion, turned their gaze to the stage.

A light flashed on. The orchestra struck a grand fanfare chord.

The red curtains parted. A spotlight fixed itself to front center, blazing upon an empty dais where sat an empty chair.

Beaumont waited.

No actor appeared.

A stir. Several hands were lifted to left and right. The hands came together. They beat softly in applause.

Now the spotlight wandered off the stage, and up the aisle.

The heads of the audience turned to follow the empty ghost of light. The masks glinted softly. The eyes behind the masks beckoned with warm color.

Beaumont stepped back.

But the light came steadily. It painted the floor with a blunt cone of pure whiteness.

And stopped, nibbling, at his feet.

The audience, turned, applauded even louder now. The theater banged, roared, ricocheted with their ceaseless tide of approbation.

Everything dissolved within him, from cold to warm. He felt as if he had been thrust raw into a downpour of summer rain. The storm rinsed him with gratitude. His heart jumped in great compulsive beats. His fists let go of themselves. His skeleton relaxed. He waited a moment longer, with the rain drenching over his upthrust and thankful cheeks and hammering his hungry eyelids so they fluttered to lock against themselves, and then he felt himself, like a ghost on battlements, led by a ghost light, lean, step, drift, move, down and along the incline, sliding to beautiful ruin, now no longer walking but striding, not striding but in full-tilted run, and the masks glittering, the eyes hot with delight and fantastic welcoming, the flights of hands on the disturbed air in upflung dove-winged rifle-shot flight. He felt the steps collide with his shoes. The applause slammed to a shutdown.

He swallowed. Then slowly he ascended the steps and stood in the full light with a thousand masks fixed to him and two thousand eyes watchful, and he sat in the empty chair, and the theater grew darker, and the immense hearth-bellow breathing softer out of the lyre-metal throats, and there was only the sound of a mechanical beehive thrived with machinery-musk in the dark.

He held to his knees. He let go. And at last he spoke:

"To be or not to be—"

The silence was complete.

Not a cough. Not a stir. Not a rustle. Not a blink. All waited. Perfection. The perfect audience. Perfect, forever and forever. Perfect. Perfect.

He tossed his words slowly into that perfect pond and felt the soundless ripples disperse and gentle away.

"—that is the question."

He talked. They listened. He knew that they would never let him go now. They would beat him insensible with applause. He would sleep a child's sleep and rise to speak again. All of Shakespeare, all of Shaw, all of Molière, every bit, crumb, lump, joint, and piece. *Himself* in repertory!

He arose to finish.

Finished, he thought: Bury me! Cover me! Smother me deep!

Obediently, the avalanche came down the mountain.

Cara Corelli found a palace of mirrors.

The maid remained outside.

And Cara Corelli went in.

As she walked through a maze, the mirrors took away a day, and then a week, and then a month and then a year and then two years of time from her face.

It was a palace of splendid and soothing lies. It was like being young once more. It was being surrounded by all those tall bright glass mirror men who would never again in your life tell you the truth.

Cara walked to the center of the palace. By the time she stopped she saw herself twenty-five years old, in every tall bright mirror face.

She sat down in the middle of the bright maze. She beamed around in happiness.

The maid waited outside for perhaps an hour. And then she went away.

This was a dark place with shapes and sizes as yet unseen. It smelled of lubricating oil, the blood of tyrant lizards with cogs and wheels for teeth, which lay strewn and silent in the dark waiting.

A titan's door slowly gave a slithering roar like a swept-back armored tail, and Parkhill stood in the rich oily wind blowing out around him. He felt as if someone had pasted a white flower on his face. But it was only a sudden surprise of a smile.

His empty hands hung at his sides and they made impulsive and completely unconscious gestures forward. They beggared the air. So, paddling silently, he let himself be moved into the Garage, Machine Shop, Repair Shed, whatever it was.

And filled with holy delight and a child's holy and unholy glee at what he beheld, he walked and slowly turned.

For as far as his eye could see stood vehicles.

Vehicles that ran on the earth. Vehicles that flew in the air. Vehicles that stood ready with wheels to go in any direction. Vehicles with two wheels. Vehicles with three or four or six or eight. Vehicles that looked like butterflies. Vehicles that resembled ancient motorbikes. Three thousand stood ranked here, four thousand glinted ready there. Another thousand were tilted over, wheels off, viscera exposed, waiting to be repaired. Still another thousand were lifted high on spidery repair hoists, their lovely undersides revealed to view, their discs and tubes and coggeries all intricate and fine and needful of touching, unbolting, revalving, rewiring, oiling, delicately lubricating . . .

Parkhill's palms itched.

He walked forward through the primeval smell of swamp oils among the dead and waiting to be revived ancient but new armored mechanical reptiles, and the more he looked the more he ached his grin.

The City was a city all right, and, to a point, self-sustaining. But, eventually, the rarest butterflies of metal gossamer, gaseous oil, and fiery dream sank to earth, the machines that repaired the machines that repaired the machines grew old, ill, and damaging of themselves. Here then was the Bestial Garage, the slumbrous Elephant's Boneyard where the aluminum dragons crawled rusting out their souls, hopeful of one live person left among so much active but dead metal, that person to put things right. One God of the machines to say, you Lazarus-elevator, rise up!

You hovercraft, be reborn! And anoint them with leviathan oils, tap them with magical wrench and send them forth to almost eternal lives in and on the air and above the quicksilver paths.

Parkhill moved among nine hundred robot men and women slaughtered by simple corrosion. He would cure their rust.

Now. If he started now, thought Parkhill, rolling up his sleeves, and staring off down a corridor of machines that ran waiting for a solid mile of garage, shed, hoist, lift, storage bin, oil tank, and strewn shrapnel of tools glittering and ready for his grip; if he started now, he might work his way to the end of the giant's ever-constant garage, accident, collision, and repair works shed in thirty years!

A billion bolts to be tightened. A billion motors to be tinkered! A billion iron tripes to lie under, a grand oil-dripped-upon orphan, alone, alone, alone with the always beautiful and never talking back hummingbird-commotion devices, accoutrements and miraculous contraptions.

His hands weighed him toward the tools. He clutched a wrench. He found a forty-wheeled low running sled. He lay down on it. He sculled the garage in a long whistling ride. The sled scuttled.

Parkhill vanished beneath a great car of some ancient design.

Out of sight, you could hear him working on the gut of the machine. On his back, he talked up at it. And when he slapped it to life, at last, the machine talked back.

Always the silver pathways ran somewhere.

Thousands of years now they had run empty, carrying only dust to destinations away and away among the high and dreaming buildings.

Now, on one traveling path, Aaronson came borne like an aging statue.

And the more the road propelled him, the faster the City exposed itself to his view, the more buildings that passed, the more parks that sprang into sight, the more his smile faded. His color changed.

"Toy," he heard himself whisper. The whisper was ancient. "Just another," and here his voice grew so small it faded away, ". . . another Toy."

A super-Toy, yes. But his life was full of such and had always been so. If it was not some slot machine it was the next-size dispenser or a jumbo-size razzmatazz hi-fi stereo speaker. From a lifetime of handling metallic sandpaper, he felt his arms rubbed away to a nub. Mere pips, his fingers. No, handless, and lacking wrists. Aaronson, the Seal Boy!!! His mindless flippers clapped applause to a city that was, in reality, no more and no less than an economy-size jukebox ravening under its idiot breath. And—he knew the tune! God help him. He *knew* the tune.

He blinked just once.

An inner eyelid came down like cold steel.

He turned and tread the silver waters of the path.

He found a moving river of steel to take him back toward the Great Gate itself.

On the way, he met the Corelli maid, wandering lost on her own silver stream.

As for the poet and his wife, their running battle tore echoes everywhere. They cried down thirty avenues, cracked panes in two hundred shops, battered leaves from seventy varieties of park bush and tree, and only ceased when drowned by a thundering fountain display they passed like a rise of clear fireworks upon the metropolitan air.

"The whole thing is," said his wife, punctuating one of his dirtier responses, "you only came along so you could lay hands on the nearest woman and spray her ears with bad breath and worse poetry."

The poet muttered a foul word.

"You're worse than the actor," said his wife. "Always at it. Don't you ever shut up?"

"Don't you?" he cried. "Ah God, I've curdled inside. Shut up, woman, or I'll throw myself in the founts!"

"No. You haven't bathed in years. You're the pig of the century! Your picture will grace the Swine Herder's Annual next month!"

"That *did* it!"

Doors slammed on a building.

By the time she got off and ran back and fisted the doors, they were locked.

"Coward!" she shrieked. "Open up!"

A foul word came echoing out, dimly.

"Ah, listen to that sweet silence," he whispered, to himself, in the great shelled dark.

Harpwell found himself in a soothing hugeness, a vast womb-like building, over which hung a canopy of pure serenity, a starless void.

In the middle of this room which was roughly a two-hundred-foot circle stood a device, a machine. In this machine were dials and rheostats and switches, a seat, and a steering wheel.

"What kind of vehicle is this?" whispered the poet, but edged near, and bent to touch. "Christ-off-the-cross-and-bearing-mercy, it smells of what? Blood and mere guts? No, for it's clean as a virgin's frock. Still it does fill the nose. Violence. Simple destruction. I can feel the damn carcass tremble like a nervous highbred hound. It's full of *stuffs*. Let's try a swig."

He sat in the machine.

"What do I swig first? This?"

He snapped a switch.

The Baskerville-hound machine whimpered in its dog slumberings.

"Good beast." He flicked another switch. "How do you go, brute? When the damn device is in full tilt, where to? You lack wheels. Well, surprise me. I dare."

The machine shivered.

The machine bolted.

It ran. It dashed.

He held tight to the steering wheel.

"Holy God!"

For he was on a highway, racing fast.

Air sluiced by. The sky flashed over in running colors.

The speedometer read seventy, eighty.

And the highway ribboned away ahead, flashing toward him. Invisible wheels slapped and banged on an increasingly rough road.

Far away, ahead, a car appeared.

It was running fast. And—

"It's on the wrong side of the road! Do you see that, wife? The wrong side."

Then he realized his wife was not here.

He was alone in a car racing—ninety miles an hour now—toward another car racing at a similar speed.

He veered the wheel.

His vehicle moved to the left.

Almost instantly the other car did a compensating move, and ran back over to the right.

"The damn fool, what does he think—where's the blasted brake?"

He stomped the floor. There was no brake. Here was a strange machine indeed. One that ran as fast as you wished, but never stopped until what? it ran itself down? There was no brake. Nothing but—further accelerators. A whole series of round-buttons on the floor, which, as he tromped them, surged power into the motor.

Ninety, one hundred, one hundred twenty miles an hour.

"God in heaven!" he screamed. "We're going to hit! How do you like that, girl?"

And in the last instant before collision, he imagined she rather liked it fine.

The cars hit. They erupted in gaseous flame. They burst apart in flinders. They tumbled. He felt himself jerked now this way and that. He was a torch hurtled skyward. His arms and legs danced a crazy rigadoon in midair as he felt his peppermint stick bones snap in brittle and agonizing ecstasies. Then, clutching death as a dark mate, gesticulating, he fell away in a black surprise, drifting toward further nothings.

He lay dead.

He lay dead a long while.

Then he opened one eye.

He felt the slow burner under his soul. He felt the bubbled water rising to the top of his mind like tea brewing.

"I'm dead," he said, "but alive, Did you see all that, wife? Dead but alive.

He found himself sitting in the vehicle, upright.

He sat there for ten minutes thinking about all that had happened.

"Well now," he mused. "Was that not interesting? Not to say fascinating? Not to say, almost exhilarating? I mean, sure, it knocked the stuff out of me, scared the soul out one ear and back in the other, hit my wind and tore my gut, broke the bones and shook the wits, but, but, but, wife, but, but, but, dear sweet Meg, Meggy, Megan, I wish you were here, it might tamp the tobacco tars out of your half-ass lungs and bray the mossy graveyard backbreaking meanness from your marrow. Let me see here now, wife, let's have a look, Harpwell-my-husband-the-poet."

He tinkered with the dials.

He thrummed the great hound motor.

"Shall we chance another diversion? Try another embattled picnic excursion? Let's."

And he set the car on its way.

Almost immediately, the vehicle was traveling one hundred and then one hundred fifty miles per hour.

Almost immediately, the opposing car appeared ahead.

"Death," said the poet. "Are you always here, then? Do you hang about? Is this your questing place? Let's test your mettle!"

The car raced. The other car hurtled.

He wheeled over into the other lane.

The other car followed, homing toward Destroy.

"Yes, I see, well, then, this," said the poet.

And switched a switch and jumped another throttle.

In the instant before impact, the two cars transformed themselves. Shuttering through illusory veils, they became jet craft at take-off. Shrieking, the two jets banged flame, tore air, yammered back sound-barrier explosions before the mightiest one of all—as the two bullets impacted, fused, interwove, interlaced blood, mind, and eternal blackness, and fell away into a net of strange and peaceful midnight.

I'm dead, he thought again.

And it feels fine, thanks.

He awoke to feel a smile on his face.

He was seated in the vehicle.

Twice dead, he thought, and feeling better each time. Why? isn't that odd? Curiouser and curiouser. Queer beyond queerness.

He thrummed the motor again.

What this time?

Does it locomote? he wondered. How about a big black choo-choo train out of half-primordial times?

And he was on his way, an engineer. The sky flicked over, and the motion-picture screens or whatever they were pressed in with swift illusions of pouring smoke and steaming whistle and huge wheel within wheel on grinding track, and the track ahead wound through hills, and far on up around a mountain came another train, black as a buffalo herd, pouring belches of smoke, on the same two rails, the same track, heading toward wondrous accident.

"I see," said the poet. "I do begin to see. I begin to know what this and what used for, for such as me, the poor wandering idiots of a world, confused, and sore put upon by mothers as soon as dropped from wombs, insulted with Christian guilt, and gone mad from the need of destruction, and collecting a pittance of hurt here and scar tissue there, and a larger portable wife grievance beyond, but one thing sure, we do want to die, we do want to be killed, and here's the very thing for it, in convenient quick pay! So pay it out, machine, dole it out, sweet raving device! Rape away, death! I'm your very man."

And the two locomotives met and climbed each other. Up a black ladder of explosion they wheeled and locked their drive shafts and plastered their slick Negro bellies together and rubbed boilers and beautifully banged the night in a single outflung whirl and flurry of shrapnel and flame. Then the locomotives, in a cumbrous rapine dance, seized and melted together with their violence and passion, gave a monstrous curtsy and fell off the mountain and took a thousand years to go all the way down to the rocky pits.

The poet awoke and immediately grabbed the controls. He was humming under his breath, stunned. He was singing wild tunes. His eyes flashed. His heart beat swiftly.

"More, more, I see it now, I know what to do, more, more, please, Oh God, more, for the truth shall set me free, more!"

He hoofed three, four, five pedals.

He snapped six switches.

The vehicle was auto-jet-locomotive-glider-missile-rocket.

He ran, he steamed, he roared, he soared, he flew. Cars veered toward him. Locomotives loomed. Jets rammed. Rockets screamed.

And in one wild three-hour spree he hit two hundred cars, rammed twenty trains, blew up ten gliders, exploded forty missiles, and, far out in space, gave up his glorious soul in a final Fourth of July Death celebration as an interplanetary rocket going two hundred thousand miles an hour struck an iron meteor and went beautifully to hell.

In all, in a few short hours he figured he must have been torn apart and put back together a few times less than five hundred.

When it was all over, he sat not touching the wheel, his feet free of the pedals.

After a half hour of sitting there, he began to laugh. He threw his head back and let out great warwhoops. Then he got up, shaking his head, drunker than ever in his life, really drunk now, and he knew he would stay that way forever, and never need drink again.

I'm punished, he thought, really punished at last. Really hurt at last, and hurt enough, over and over, so I will never need hurt again, never need to be destroyed again, never have to collect another insult, or take another wound, or ask for a simple grievance. God bless the genius of man and the inventors of such machines, that enable the guilty to pay and at last be rid of the dark albatross and the awful burden. Thank you, City, thank you, old blueprinter of needful souls. Thank you. And which way out?

A door slid open.

His wife stood waiting for him.

"Well, there you are," she said. "And still drunk."

"No," he said. "Dead."

"Drunk."

"Dead," he said, "beautifully dead at last. Which means, free. I won't need you anymore, dead Meg, Meggy-Megan. You're set free, also, like an awful conscience. Go haunt someone else, girl. Go destroy. I forgive you your sins on me, for I have at last forgiven myself. I am off the Christian hook. I am the dear wandering dead who, dead, can at last live. Go and do likewise, lady. Inside with you. Be punished and set free. So long, Meg. Farewell. Toodleoo."

He wandered away.

"Where do you think you're going?" she cried.

"Why, out into life and the blood of life and happy at last."

"Come back here!" she screamed.

"You can't stop the dead, for they wander the universe, happy as children in the dark field."

"Harpwell!" she brayed. "Harpwell!"

But he stepped on a river of silver metal.

And let the dear river bear him laughing until the tears glittered on his cheeks, away and away from the shriek and the bray and the scream of that woman, what was her name? no matter, back there, and gone.

And when he reached the Gate he walked out and along the canal in the fine day, heading toward the far towns.

By that time, he was singing every old tune he had known as a child of six.

It was a church.

No, not a church.

Wilder let the door swing shut.

He stood in cathedral darkness, waiting.

The roof, if roof there was, breathed up in a great suspense, flowed up beyond reach or sight.

The floor, if floor there was, was a mere firmness beneath. It, too, was black.

And then, the stars came out. It was like that first night of childhood when his father had taken him out beyond the city to a hill where the lights could not diminish the Universe. And there were a thousand, no ten thousand, no ten million billion stars filling the darkness. The stars were manifold and bright, and they did not care. Even then he had known: they do not care. If I breathe or do not breathe, live or die, the eyes that look from all around don't care. And he had seized his father's hand and gripped tight, as if he might fall up into that abyss.

Now, in this building, he was full of the old terror and the old sense of beauty and the old silent crying out after mankind. The stars filled him with pity for small men lost in so much size.

Then yet another thing happened.

Beneath his feet, space opened wide and let through yet another billion sparks of light.

He was suspended as a fly is held upon a vast telescopic lens. He walked on a water of space. He stood upon a transparent flex of great eye, and all about him, as on a night in winter, beneath foot and above head, in all directions, were nothing but stars.

So, in the end, it was a church, it was a cathedral, a multitude of farflung universal shrines, here a worshipping of Horsehead Nebula, there Orion's galaxy, and there Andromeda, like the head of God, fiercely gazed and thrust through the raw dark stuffs of night to stab his soul and pin it writhing against the backside of his flesh.

God, everywhere, fixed him with shutterless and unblinking eyes.

And he, a bacterial shard of that same Flesh, stared back and winced but the slightest.

He waited. And a planet drifted upon the void. It spun by once with a great mellow autumn face. It circled and came under him.

And he stood upon a far world of green grass and great lush trees, where the air was fresh, and a river ran by like the rivers of childhood, flashing the sun and leaping with fish.

He knew that he had traveled very far to reach this world. Behind him lay the rocket. Behind lay a century of travel, of sleeping, of waiting, and now, here was the reward.

"Mine?" he asked the simple air, the simple grass, the long simplicity of water that spelled by in the shallow sands.

And the world answered wordless: yours.

Yours without the long travel and the boredom, yours without ninety-nine years of flight from Earth, of sleeping in kept tubes, of intravenous feedings, of nightmares dreamt of Earth lost and gone, yours without torture, without pain, yours without trial and error, failure and destruction. Yours without sweat and terror. Yours without a falling down of tears. Yours. Yours.

But Wilder did not put out his hands to accept.

And the sun dimmed in the alien sky.

And the world drifted from under his feet.

And yet another world swam up and passed in a huge parade of even brighter glories.

And this world, too, spun up to take his weight. And here, if anything, the fields were richer green, the mountains capped with melting snows, far fields ripening with strange harvests, and scythes waiting on the edge of fields for him to lift and sweep and cut the grain and live out his life any way that he might.

Yours. The merest touch of weather upon the hairs within his ear said this. Yours.

And Wilder, without shaking his head, moved back. He did not say no. He thought his rejection.

And the grass died in the fields.

The mountains crumbled.

The river shallows ran to dust.

And the world sprang away.

And Wilder stood again in space where God had stood before creating a world out of Chaos.

And at last he spoke and said to himself:

"It would be easy. O Lord, yes, I'd like that. No work, nothing, just accept. But . . . You can't give me what I want."

He looked at the stars.

"Nothing can be given, ever."

The stars were growing dim.

"It's really very simple. I must borrow, I must earn. I must take."

The stars quivered and died.

"Much obliged and thank you, no."

The stars were all gone.

He turned and, without looking back, walked upon darkness. He hit the door with his palm. He strode out into the City.

He refused to hear if the machine universe behind him cried out in a great chorus, all cries and wounds, like a woman scorned. The crockery in a vast robot kitchen fell. By the time it hit the floor, he was gone.

It was a Museum of Weapons.

The hunter walked among the cases.

He opened a case and hefted a weapon constructed like a spider's antennae.

It hummed, and a flight of metal bees sizzled out the rifle bore, flew away, and stung a target-mannequin some fifty yards away, then fell lifeless, clattering to the floor.

The hunter nodded with admiration, and put the rifle back in the case.

He prowled on, curious as a child, testing yet other weapons here and there which dissolved glass or caused metal to run in bright yellow pools of molten lava.

"Excellent!" "Fine!" "Absolutely great!"

His cry rang out again and again as he slammed cases open and shut, and finally chose the gun.

It was a gun that, without fuss or fury, did away with matter. You pressed the button, there was a brief discharge of blue light, and the target simply vanished. No blood. No bright lava. No trace.

"All right," he announced, leaving the Place of Guns, "we have the weapon. How about the Game, the Grandest Beast ever in the Long Hunt?"

He leapt onto the moving sidewalk.

An hour later he had passed a thousand buildings and scanned a thousand open parks without itching his finger.

He moved uneasily from treadway to treadway, shifting speeds now in this direction, now in that.

Until at last he saw a river of metal that sped underground.

Instinctively, he jumped toward that.

The metal stream carried him down into the secret gut of the City.

Here all was warm blood darkness. Here strange pumps moved the pulse of the City. Here were distilled the sweats that lubricated the roadways and lifted the elevators and swarmed the offices and stores with motion.

The hunter half crouched on the roadway. His eyes squinted. Perspiration gathered in his palms. His trigger finger greased the metal gun, sliding.

"Yes," he whispered. "By God, now. This is it. The City itself . . .

the Great Beast. Why didn't I think of that? The Animal City, the terrible prey. It has men for breakfast, lunch, and dinner. It kills them with machines. It munches their bones like breadsticks. It spits them out like toothpicks. It lives long after they die. The City, by God, the City. Well now . . ."

He glided through dark grottoes of television eyes which showed him remote parkways and high towers.

Deeper within the belly of the underground world he sank as the river lowered itself. He passed a school of computers that chattered in maniac chorus. He shuddered as a cloud of paper confetti from one titian machine, holes punched out to perhaps record his passing, fell upon him in a whispered snow.

He raised his gun. He fired.

The machine disappeared.

He fired again. A skeleton strutwork under yet another machine vanished.

The City screamed.

At first very low and then very high, then, rising, falling, like a siren. Lights flashed. Bells began to ricochet alarums. The metal river shuddered under his feet, slowed. He fired at television screens which glared all white upon him. They blinked out and did not exist.

The City screamed higher until he raved against it, himself, and the marrow of his bones shook out an insanity of black dust.

He did not see, until it was too late, that the road on which he sped fell into the gnashing maw of a machine that was used for some purpose long forgotten centuries before.

He thought that by pressing the trigger he would make the terrible mouth disappear. It did indeed vanish. But as the roadway sped on and he whirled and fell as it picked up speed, he realized at last that his weapon did not truly destroy, it merely made invisible what was there and what still remained though unseen.

He gave a terrible cry to match the cry of the City. He flung out the gun in a last blow. The gun went into cogs and wheels and teeth and was twisted down.

The last thing he saw was a deep elevator shaft that fell away for perhaps a mile into the earth.

He knew that it might take him two minutes to hit the bottom. He shrieked.

The worst thing was, he would be conscious . . . all the way down . . .

The rivers shook. The silver rivers trembled. The pathways, shocked, convulsed the metal shores through which they sped.

Wilder, traveling, was almost knocked flat by the concussion.

What had caused the concussion, he could not see. Perhaps, far off, there was a cry, a murmur of dreadful sound, which swiftly faded.

Wilder moved on. The silver track threaded on. But the City seemed poised, agape. The City seemed tensed. Its huge and various muscles were cramped, alert.

Feeling this, Wilder began to walk as well as be moved by the swift path.

"Thank God. There's the Gate. The sooner I'm out of this place the happier I'll—"

The Gate was indeed there, not a hundred yards away. But, on the instant, as if hearing his declaration, the river stopped. It shivered. Then it started to move back, taking him where he did not wish to go.

Incredulous, Wilder spun about, and, in spinning, fell. He clutched at the stuffs of the rushing sidewalk.

His face, pressed to the vibrant grillework of the river-rushing pavement, heard the machineries mesh and mill beneath, humming and agroan, forever sluicing, forever feverish for journeys and mindless excursions. Beneath the calm metal, embattlements of hornets stung and buzzed, lost bees bumbled and subsided. Collapsed, he saw the Gate lost away behind. Burdened, he remembered at last the extra weight upon his back, the jet-power equipment which might give him wings.

He jammed his hand to the switch on his belt. And in the instant before the sidewalk might have pulsed him off among sheds and museum walls, he was airborne.

Flying, he hovered, then swam the air back to hang above a casual Parkhill gazing up, all covered with grease and smiling from a dirty face. Beyond Parkhill, at the Gate, stood the frightened maid. Beyond even further, near the yacht at the landing, stood Aaronson, back turned to the City, nervous to be moving on.

"Where are the others?" cried Wilder.

"Oh, they won't be back," said Parkhill, easily. "It figures, doesn't it? I mean, it's quite a place."

"Place!" said Wilder, hovered now up, now down, turning slowly, apprehensive. "We've got to get them out! It's not safe."

"It's safe if you like it. I like it," said Parkhill.

And all the while there was a gathering of earthquake in the ground and in the air, which Parkhill chose to ignore.

"You're leaving, of course," he said, as if nothing were wrong. "I knew you would. Why?"

"Why?" Wilder wheeled like a dragonfly before a trembling of storm wind. Buffeted up, buffeted down, he flung his words at Parkhill, who didn't bother to duck but smiled up and accepted. "Good God, Sam, the place is Hell. The Martians had enough sense to get out. They saw they had overbuilt themselves. The damn City does everything, which is too much! Sam!''

But at that instant, they both looked round and up. For the sky was shelling over. Great lids were vising in the ceiling. Like an immense flower, the tops of buildings were petalling out to cover themselves. Windows were shutting down. Doors were slamming. A sound of fired cannons echoed through the streets.

The Gate was thundering shut.

The twin jaws of the Gate, shuddering, were in motion.

Wilder cried out, spun round, and dived.

He heard the maid below him. He saw her reach up. Then, swooping, he gathered her in. He kicked the air. The jet lifted them both.

Like a bullet to a target he rammed for the Gate. But an instant before, burdened, he reached it, the Gates banged together. He was barely able to veer course and soar upward along the raw metal as the entire City shook with the roar of the steel.

Parkhill shouted below. And Wilder was flying up, up along the wall, looking this way and that.

Everywhere, the sky was closing in. The petals were coming down, coming down. There was only a last small patch of stone sky to his right. He blasted for that. And kicking, made it through, flying, as the final flange of steel clipped into place, and the City was closed to itself.

He hung for a moment, suspended, and then flew down along the outer wall to the dock where Aaronson stood by the yacht staring at the huge shut Gates.

"Parkhill," whispered Wilder, looking at the City, the walls, the Gates. "You fool. You damned fool."

"Fools, all of them," said Aaronson, and turned away. "Fools. Fools."

They waited a moment longer and listened to the City, humming, alive, kept to itself, its great mouth filled with a few bits of warmth, a few lost people somewhere hid away in there. The Gates would stay shut now, forever. The City had what it needed to go on a long while.

Wilder looked back at the place, as the yacht took them back out of the mountain and away up the canal.

They passed the poet a mile further on, walking along the rim of the canal. He waved them on. "No. No, thanks. I feel like walking. It's a fine day. Good-bye. Go on."

The towns lay ahead. Small towns. Small enough to be run by men instead of running them. He heard the brass music. He saw the neon lights at dusk. He made out the junkyards in the fresh night under the stars.

Beyond the towns stood the silver rockets, tall, waiting to be fired off
and away toward the wilderness of stars.

"Real," whispered the rockets, "real stuff. Real travel. Real time.
Real space. No gifts. Nothing free. Just a lot of good hard work."

The yacht touched into its home dock.

"Rockets, by God," he murmured. "Wait till I get my hands on you."
He ran away in the night, to do just that.

The sundials were tumbled into white pebbles. The birds of the air now flew in ancient skies of rock and sand, buried, their songs stopped. The dead sea bottoms were currented with dust which flooded the land when the wind bade it reenact an old tale of engulfment. The cities were deep laid with granaries of silence, time stored and kept, pools and fountains of quietude and memory.

Mars was dead.

Then, out of the large stillness, from a great distance, there was an insect sound which grew large among the cinnamon hills and moved in the sun-blazed air until the highway trembled and dust was shook whispering down in the old cities.

The sound ceased.

In the shimmering silence of midday, Albert Beck and Leonard Craig sat in an ancient landcar, eyeing a dead city which did not move under their gaze but waited for their shout:

"Hello!"

A crystal tower dropped into soft dusting rain.

"You there!"

And another tumbled down.

And another and another fell as Beck called, summoning them to death. In shattering flights, stone animals with vast granite wings dived to strike the courtyards and fountains. His cry summoned them like living beasts and the beasts gave answer, groaned, cracked, leaned up, tilted over, trembling, hesitant, then split the air and swept down with grimaced mouths and empty eyes, with sharp, eternally hungry teeth suddenly seized out and strewn like shrapnel on the tiles.

Beck waited. No more towers fell.

"It's safe to go in now."

Craig didn't move. "For the same reason?"

Beck nodded.

"For a damned *bottle!* I don't understand. Why does everyone want it?"

Beck got out of the car. "Those that found it, they never told, they never explained. But—it's old. Old as the desert, as the dead seas—and it might contain anything. That's what the legend says. And because it *could* hold anything—well, that stirs a man's hunger."

"Yours, not mine," said Craig. His mouth barely moved; his eyes were half-shut, faintly amused. He stretched lazily. "I'm just along for the ride. Better watching you than sitting in the heat."

Beck had stumbled upon the old landcar a month back, before Craig had joined him. It was part of the flotsam of the First Industrial Invasion of Mars that had ended when the race moved on toward the stars. He had worked on the motor and run it from city to dead city, through the lands of the idlers and roustabouts, the dreamers and lazers, men caught in the backwash of space, men like himself and Craig who had never wanted to do much of anything and had found Mars a fine place to do it in.

"Five thousand, ten thousand years back the Martians made the Blue Bottle," said Beck. "Blown from Martian glass—and lost and found and lost and found again and again."

He stared into the wavering heat shimmer of the dead city. All my life, thought Beck, I've done nothing and nothing inside the nothing. Others, better men, have done big things, gone off to Mercury, or Venus, or out beyond the System. Except me. Not me. But the Blue Bottle can *change* all that.

He turned and walked away from the silent car.

Craig was out and after him, moving easily along. "What is it now, ten years you've hunted? You twitch when you sleep, wake up in fits, sweat through the days. You want the damn bottle *that* bad, and don't know what's in it. You're a fool, Beck."

"Shut up, shut up," said Beck, kicking a slide of pebbles out of his way.

They walked together into the ruined city, over a mosaic of cracked tiles shaped into a stone tapestry of fragile Martian creatures, long-dead beasts which appeared and disappeared as a slight breath of wind stirred the silent dust.

"Wait," said Beck. He cupped his hands to his mouth and gave a great shout. "You there!"

". . . there," said an echo, and towers fell. Fountains and stone pillars folded into themselves. That was the way of these cities. Sometimes towers as beautiful as a symphony would fall at a spoken word. It was like watching a Bach cantata disintegrate before your eyes.

A moment later: bones buried in bones. The dust settled. Two structures remained intact.

Beck stepped forward, nodding to his friend.

They moved in search.

And, searching, Craig paused, a faint smile on his lips. "In that bottle," he said, "is there a little accordion woman, all folded up like one of those tin cups, or like one of those Japanese flowers you put in water and it opens out?"

"I don't need a woman."

"Maybe you do. Maybe you never had a *real* woman, a woman who loved you, so, secretly, that's what you hope is in it." Craig pursed his mouth. "Or maybe, in that bottle, something from your childhood. All in a tiny bundle—a lake, a tree you climbed, green grass, some crayfish. How's *that* sound?"

Beck's eyes focused on a distant point. "Sometimes—that's almost it. The past—Earth. I don't know."

Craig nodded. "What's in the bottle would depend, maybe, on who's looking. Now, if there was a shot of *whiskey* in it . . ."

"Keep looking," said Beck.

There were seven rooms filled with glitter and shine; from floor to tiered ceiling there were casks, crocks, magnums, urns, vases—fashioned of red, pink, yellow, violet, and black glass. Beck shattered them, one by one, to eliminate them, to get them out of the way so he would never have to go through them again.

Beck finished his room, stood ready to invade the next. He was almost afraid to go on. Afraid that *this* time he would find it; that the search would be over and the meaning would go out of his life. Only after he had heard of the Blue Bottle from fire-travelers all the way from Venus to Jupiter, ten years ago, had life begun to take on a purpose. The fever had lit him and he had burned steadily ever since. If he worked it properly, the prospect of finding the bottle might fill his entire life to the brim. Another thirty years, if he was careful and not *too* diligent, of search, never admitting aloud that it wasn't the bottle that counted at all, but the search, the running and the hunting, the dust and the cities and the going-on.

Beck heard a muffled sound. He turned and walked to a window looking out into the courtyard. A small gray sand cycle had purred up almost noiselessly at the end of the street. A plump man with blond hair eased himself off the spring seat and stood looking into the city. Another searcher. Beck sighed. Thousands of them, searching and searching. But there were thousands of brittle cities and towns and villages and it would take a millennium to sift them all.

"How you doing?" Craig appeared in a doorway.

"No luck." Beck sniffed the air. "Do you smell anything?"

"What?" Craig looked about.

"Smells like—bourbon."

"Ho!" Craig laughed. "That's *me!*"

"You?"

"I just took a drink. Found it in the other room. Shoved some stuff around, a mess of bottles, like always, and one of them had some bourbon in it, so I had myself a drink."

Beck was staring at him, beginning to tremble. "What—what would bourbon be doing *here,* in a Martian bottle?" His hands were cold. He took a slow step forward. "Show me!"

"I'm sure that . . ."

"*Show* me, damn you!"

It was there, in one corner of the room, a container of Martian glass as blue as the sky, the size of a small fruit, light and airy in Beck's hand as he set it down upon a table.

"It's half-full of bourbon," said Craig.

"I don't see anything inside," said Beck.

"Then shake it."

Beck picked it up, gingerly shook it.

"Hear it gurgle?"

"No."

"I can hear it plain."

Beck replaced it on the table. Sunlight spearing through a side window struck blue flashes off the slender container. It was the blue of a star held in the hand. It was the blue of a shallow ocean bay at noon. It was the blue of a diamond at morning.

"This is it," said Beck quietly. "I know it is. We don't have to look anymore. We've found the Blue Bottle."

Craig looked skeptical. "Sure you don't *see* anything in it?"

"Nothing . . . But—" Beck bent close and peered deeply into the blue universe of glass. "Maybe if I open it up and let it out, whatever it is, I'll know."

"I put the stopper in tight. Here." Craig reached out.

"If you gentlemen will excuse me," said a voice in the door behind them.

The plump man with blond hair walked into their line of vision with a gun. He did not look at their faces, he looked only at the blue glass bottle. He began to smile. "I hate very much to handle guns," he said, "but it is a matter of necessity, as I simply *must* have that work of art. I suggest that you allow me to take it without trouble."

Beck was almost pleased. It had a certain beauty of timing, this incident; it was the sort of thing he might have wished for, to have the treasure stolen before it was opened. Now there was the good prospect of a chase, a fight, a series of gains and losses, and, before they were done, perhaps another four or five years spent upon a new search.

"Come along now," said the stranger. "Give it up." He raised the gun warningly.

Beck handed him the bottle.

"Amazing. Really amazing," said the plump man. "I can't believe it was as simple as this, to walk in, hear two men talking, and to have the Blue Bottle simply *handed* to me. Amazing!" And he wandered off down the hall, out into the daylight, chuckling to himself.

Under the cool double moons of Mars the midnight cities were bone and dust. Along the scattered highway the landcar bumped and rattled, past cities where the fountains, the gyrostats, the furniture, the metal-singing books, the paintings lay powdered over with mortar and insect wings. Past cities that were cities no longer, but only things rubbed to a fine silt that flowered senselessly back and forth on the wine winds between one land and another, like the sand in a gigantic hourglass, endlessly pyramiding and repyramiding. Silence opened to let the car pass, and closed swiftly in behind.

Craig said, "We'll never find him. These damned roads. So old. Potholes, lumps, everything wrong. He's got the advantage with the cycle; he can dodge and weave. Damn!"

They swerved abruptly, avoiding a bad stretch. The car moved over the old highway like an eraser, coming upon blind soil, passing over it, dusting it away to reveal the emerald and gold colors of ancient Martian mosaics worked into the road surface.

"Wait," cried Beck. He throttled the car down. "I saw something back there."

"Where?"

They drove back a hundred yards.

"There. You see. It's *him*."

In a ditch by the side of the road the plump man lay folded over his cycle. He did not move. His eyes were wide, and when Beck flashed a torch down, the eyes burned dully.

"Where's the bottle?" asked Craig.

Beck jumped into the ditch and picked up the man's gun. "I don't know. Gone."

"What killed him?"

"I don't know that either."

"The cycle looks okay. Not an accident."

Beck rolled the body over. "No wounds. Looks like he just—stopped, of his own accord."

"Heart attack, maybe," said Craig. "Excited over the bottle. He gets down here to hide. Thought he'd be all right, but the attack finished him."

"That doesn't account for the Blue Bottle."

"Someone came along. Lord, you know how many searchers there are. . . ."

They scanned the darkness around them. Far off, in the starred blackness, on the blue hills, they saw a dim movement.

"Up there." Beck pointed. "Three men on foot."

"They must have . . ."

"My God, look!"

Below them, in the ditch, the figure of the plump man glowed, began to melt. The eyes took on the aspect of moonstones under a sudden rush of water. The face began to dissolve away into fire. The hair resembled small firecracker strings, lit and sputtering. The body fumed as they watched. The fingers jerked with flame. Then, as if a gigantic hammer had struck a glass statue, the body cracked upward and was gone in a blaze of pink shards, becoming mist as the night breeze carried it across the highway.

"They must have—*done* something to him," said Craig. "Those three, with a new kind of weapon."

"But it's happened before," said Beck. "Men I knew about who had the Blue Bottle. They vanished. And the bottle passed on to others who vanished." He shook his head. "Looked like a million fireflies when he broke apart. . . ."

"You going after them?"

Beck returned to the car. He judged the desert mounds, the hills of bone-silt and silence. "It'll be a tough job, but I think I can poke the car through after them. I *have* to, now." He paused, not speaking to Craig. "I think I know what's in the Blue Bottle. . . . Finally, I realize that what I want most of all is in there. Waiting for me."

"I'm not going," said Craig, coming up to the car where Beck sat in the dark, his hands on his knees. "I'm not going out there with you, chasing three armed men. I just want to live, Beck. That bottle means nothing to me. I won't risk my skin for it. But I'll wish you luck."

"Thanks," said Beck. And he drove away, into the dunes.

The night was as cool as water coming over the glass hood of the landcar.

Beck throttled hard over dead river washes and spills of chalked pebble, driving between great cliffs. Ribbons of double moonlight painted the bas-reliefs of gods and animals on the cliff sides all yellow gold:

mile-high faces upon which Martian histories were etched and stamped in symbols, incredible faces with open cave eyes and gaping cave mouths.

The motor's roar dislodged rocks, boulders. In a whole rushing downpour of stone, golden segments of ancient cliff sculpture slid out of the moons' rays at the top of the cliff and vanished into blue cool-well darkness.

In the roar, as he drove, Beck cast his mind back—to all the nights in the last ten years, nights when he had built red fires on the sea bottoms, and cooked slow, thoughtful meals. And dreamed. Always those dreams of *wanting*. And not knowing what. Ever since he was a young man, the hard life on Earth, the great panic of 2130, the starvation, chaos, riot, want. Then bucking through the planets, the womanless, loveless years, the alone years. You come out of the dark into the light, out of the womb into the world, and what do you find that you really want?

What about that dead man back there in the ditch? Wasn't he always looking for something extra? Something he didn't have. What *was* there for men like himself? Or for anyone? Was there anything at all to look forward to?

The Blue Bottle.

He quickly braked the car, leaped out, gun ready. He ran, crouching, into the dunes. Ahead of him, the three men lay on the cold sand, neatly. They were Earthmen, with tan faces and rough clothes and gnarled hands. Starlight shone on the Blue Bottle, which lay among them.

As Beck watched, the bodies began to melt. They vanished away into rises of steam, into dewdrops and crystals. In a moment they were gone.

Beck felt the coldness in his body as the flakes rained across his eyes, flicking his lips and his cheeks.

He did not move.

The plump man. Dead and vanishing. Craig's voice: "Some new weapon . . ."

No. Not a weapon at all.

The Blue Bottle.

They had opened it to find what they most desired. All of the unhappy, desiring men down the long and lonely years had opened it to find what they most wanted in the planets of the universe. And all had found it, even as had these three. Now it could be understood, why the bottle passed on so swiftly, from one to another, and the men vanishing behind it. Harvest chaff fluttering on the sand, along the dead sea rims. Turning to flame and fireflies. To mist.

Beck picked up the bottle and held it away from himself for a long moment. His eyes shone clearly. His hands trembled.

So this is what I've been looking for, he thought. He turned the bottle and it flashed blue starlight.

So this is what all men *really* want? The secret desire, deep inside, hidden all away where we never guess? The subliminal urge? So this is what each man seeks, through some private guilt, to find?

Death.

An end to doubt, to torture, to monotony, to want, to loneliness, to fear, an end to everything.

All men?

No. Not Craig. Craig was, perhaps, far luckier. A few men were like animals in the universe, not questioning, drinking at pools and breeding and raising their young and not doubting for a moment that life was anything but good. That was Craig. There were a handful like him. Happy animals on a great reservation, in the hand of God, with a religion and a faith that grew like a set of special nerves in them. The unneurotic men in the midst of the billionfold neurotics. They would only want death, later, in a natural manner. Not now. Later.

Beck raised the bottle. How simple, he thought, and how right. This *is* what I've always wanted. And nothing else.

Nothing.

The bottle was open and blue in the starlight. Beck took an immense draught of the air coming from the Blue Bottle, deep into his lungs.

I have it at last, he thought.

He relaxed. He felt his body become wonderfully cool and then wonderfully warm. He knew he was dropping down a long slide of stars into a darkness as delightful as wine. He was swimming in blue wine and white wine and red wine. There were candles in his chest, and fire wheels spinning. He felt his hands leave him. He felt his legs fly away, amusingly. He laughed. He shut his eyes and laughed.

He was very happy for the first time in his life.

The Blue Bottle dropped onto the cool sand.

At dawn, Craig walked along, whistling. He saw the bottle lying in the first pink light of the sun on the empty white sand. As he picked it up, there was a fiery whisper. A number of orange and red-purple fireflies blinked on the air, and passed on away.

The place was very still.

"I'll be damned." He glanced toward the dead windows of a nearby city. "Hey, Beck!"

A slender tower collapsed into powder.

"Beck, here's your treasure! I don't want it. Come and get it!"

". . . and get it," said an echo, and the last tower fell.

Craig waited.

"That's rich," he said. "The bottle right here, and old Beck not even around to take it." He shook the blue container.

It gurgled.

"Yes, sir! Just the way it was before. Full of bourbon, by God!" He opened it, drank, wiped his mouth.

He held the bottle carelessly.

"All that trouble for a little bourbon. I'll wait right here for old Beck and give him his damn bottle. Meanwhile have another drink, Mr. Craig. Don't mind if I do."

The only sound in the dead land was the sound of liquid running into a parched throat. The Blue Bottle flashed in the sun.

Craig smiled happily and drank again.

One Timeless Spring

I hat week, so many years ago, I thought my mother and father were poisoning me. And now, twenty years later, I'm not so sure they didn't. There's no way of telling.

It all comes back to me through the simple expedient of an examined trunk in the attic. This morning I pulled back the brass hasps and lifted the lid, and the immemorial odor of mothballs shrouded the unstrung tennis rackets, the worn sneakers, the shattered toys, the rusty roller skates. These implements of play, seen again through older eyes, make it seem only an hour ago that I rushed in from the shady streets, all asweat, the cry of "Ollie, Ollie, Oxen Free!" still excitedly trembling on my lips.

I was a weird and ridiculous boy then with brooding and uncommon ideas; the poison and the fear were only part of me in those years. I began making notes in a lined nickel tablet when I was only twelve. I can feel the stubby pencil in my fingers now, writing in those timeless spring mornings.

I paused to lick my pencil, thoughtfully. I sat in my upstairs room at the beginning of a clear endless day, blinking at the rose-stamped wallpaper, my feet bare, my hair shorn to a hairbrush stubble, thinking.

"I didn't know I was sick until this week," I wrote. "I've been sick for a long time. Since I was ten. I'm twelve now."

I scrouged up my face, bit my lips hard, focused blurrily on the tablet. "Mom and Dad have *made* me sick. Teachers at school also gave this—" I hesitated. Then I wrote: "*Disease* to me! The only ones who don't scare me are the other kids. Isabel Skelton and Willard Bowers and Clarisse Mellin; they aren't very sick yet. But I'm *really* bad off. . . ."

I laid the pencil down. I went to the bathroom mirror to see myself. My mother called me from downstairs to come to breakfast. I pressed close to the mirror, breathing so fast I made a big damp fog on the glass. I saw how my face was—changing.

The bones of it. Even the eyes. The pores of my nose. My ears. My forehead. My hair. All the things that'd been me for such a long time, starting to become something else. ("Douglas, come to breakfast, you'll be late for school!") As I took a quick wash I saw my body floating under me. I was inside it. There was no escape. And the bones of it were doing things, shifting, mixing around!

Then I began singing and whistling loud, so I wouldn't think about it; until Father, rapping on the door, told me to quiet down and come eat.

I sat at the breakfast table. There was a yellow box of cereal and milk, white-cold in a pitcher, and shining spoons and knives, and eggs planked with bacon, Dad reading his paper, Mom moving around the kitchen. I sniffed. I felt my stomach lie down like a whipped dog.

"What's wrong, son?" Dad looked at me casually. "Not hungry?"

"No, sir."

"A boy should be hungry in the morning," said Father.

"You go ahead and eat," said Mother at me. "Go on now. Hurry."

I looked at the eggs. They were poison. I looked at the butter. It was poison. The milk was so white and creamy and poisonous in its pitcher, and the cereal was brown and crisp and tasty in a green dish with pink flowers on it.

Poison, all of them, poison! The thought ran in my head like ants at a picnic. I caught my lip in my teeth.

"Unh?" said Dad, blinking at me. "You *said?*"

"Nothing," I said. "Except I'm not hungry."

I couldn't say I was ill and that food made me ill. I couldn't say that cookies, cakes, cereals and soups and vegetables had done *this* to me, could I? No. I had to sit, swallowing nothing, my heart beginning to pound.

"Well, drink your milk at least, and go on," said Mother. "Dad, give him money for a good lunch at school. Orange juice, meat, and milk. No candy."

She didn't have to warn me on candy. It was worst of all the poisons. I wouldn't touch it again, ever!

I strapped my books and went to the door.

"Douglas, you didn't kiss me," said Mom.

"Oh," I said, and shuffled to kiss her.

"What's wrong with you?" she asked.

"Nothing," I said. " 'Bye. So long, Dad."

Everybody said good-bye. I walked to school, thinking deep inside, like shouting down a long, cold well.

* * *

I ran down through the ravine and swung on a vine, way out; the ground dropped away, I smelled the cool morning air, sweet and high, and I screamed with laughter, and the wind threw away my thoughts. I tossed myself in a flip against the embankment and rolled down as birds whistled at me and a squirrel hopped like brown fuzz blown by the wind up around a tree trunk. Down the path the other kids fell like a small avalanche, yelling. "Ahh—eee—yah!" Pounding their chests, skipping rocks on the water, jumping their hands down to catch at crayfish. The crayfish jetted away in dusty spurts. We all laughed and joked.

A girl passed by on the green wooden bridge above us. Her name was Clarisse Mellin. We all hee-hawed at her, told her to go on, go on, we didn't want her with us, go on, go on! But my voice caught and trailed off, and I watched her going, slowly. I didn't look away.

From way off in the morning we heard the school bell ring.

We scrambled up trails we'd made during many summers over the years. The grass was worn; we knew each snake hole and bump, each tree, every vine, every weed of it. After school we'd made tree huts here, high up over the shining creek, jumped in the water naked, gone on long hikes down the ravine to where it emptied lonely and abandoned into the big blue of Lake Michigan, near the tannery and the asbestos works and the docks.

Now, as we panted up to school, I stopped, afraid again. "You go on ahead," I said.

The last bell tolled. The kids ran. I looked at the school with vines growing on it. I heard the voices inside, making a high, all-the-time noise. I heard little desk bells tinkle and sharp teacher voices reaching out.

Poison, I thought. The teachers, too! They want me sick! They teach you how to be sicker and sicker! And—and how to *enjoy* being sick!

"Good morning, Douglas."

I heard high-heeled shoes on the cement walk. Miss Adams, the principal, with her pince-nez and wide, pale face and close-cropped dark hair, stood behind me.

"Come along in," she said, holding my shoulder firmly. "You're late. Come along."

She guided me, one two, one two, one two, upstairs, up the stairs to my fate. . . .

Mr. Jordan was a plump man with thinning hair and serious green eyes and a way of rocking on his heels before his charts. Today he had a large illustration of a body with all its skin off. Exposed were green, blue, pink, and yellow veins, capillaries, muscles, tendons, organs, lungs, bones, and fatty tissues.

Mr. Jordan nodded before the chart. "There's a great similarity between cancer and normal cell reproduction. Cancer is simply a normal function gone wild. Overproduction of cellular material—''

I raised my hand. "How does food—I mean—what makes the body grow?''

"A good question, Douglas." He tapped the chart. "Food, taken into the body, is broken down, assimilated, and—''

I listened and I knew what Mr. Jordan was trying to do to me. My childhood was in my mind like a fossil imprint on soft shale rock. Mr. Jordan was trying to polish and smooth it away. Eventually it would all be gone, all my beliefs and imaginings. My mother changed my body with food, Mr. Jordan worked on my mind with words.

So I began to draw pictures on paper, not listening. I hummed little songs, made up a language all my own. The rest of the day I heard nothing. I resisted the attack, I counteracted the poison.

But then after school I passed Mrs. Singer's store and I bought candy. I couldn't help it. And after I ate it I wrote on the back of the wrapper: "This is the last candy I'm going to eat. Even at the Saturday matinee, when Tom Mix comes on the screen with Tony, I won't eat candy again.''

I looked at the candy bars stacked like a harvest on the shelves. Orange wrappers with sky-blue words saying "Chocolate." Yellow and violet wrappers with little blue words on them. I felt the candy in my body, making my cells grow. Mrs. Singer sold hundreds of candy bars each day. Was she in conspiracy? Did she know what she was doing to children with them? Was she jealous of them being so young? Did she want them to grow old? I wanted to kill her!

"What you doing?''

Bill Arno had come up behind me while I was writing on the candy wrapper. Clarisse Mellin was with him. She looked at me with her blue eyes and said nothing.

I hid the paper. "Nothing," I said.

We all walked along. We saw kids playing hopscotch and kick the can and playing mibs on the hard ground, and I turned to Bill and I said, "We won't be allowed to do that next year, or maybe the year after.''

Bill only laughed and said, "Sure, we will. Who'll stop us?''

"*They* will," I said.

"Who's they?" asked Bill.

"Never mind," I said. "Just wait and see.''

"Aw," said Bill. "You're crazy.''

"You don't understand!" I cried. "You play and run around and eat, and all the time they're tricking you and making you think different and act different and walk different. And all of a sudden one day you'll stop playing and have to worry!" My face was hot and my hands were clenched. I was blind with rage. Bill turned, laughing, and walked away. "Over Annie Over!" someone sang, tossing a ball over a housetop.

You might go all day without breakfast or lunch, but what about supper? My stomach shouted as I slid into my chair at the supper table. I held on to my knees, looking down at them. I won't eat, I told myself. I'll show them. I'll fight them.

Dad pretended to be considerate. "Let him go without supper," he said to my mother, when he saw me neglect my food. He winked at her. "He'll eat later."

All evening long I played on the warm brick streets of town, rattling the tin cans and climbing the trees in the growing dark.

Coming into the kitchen at ten o'clock, I realized it was no use. There was a note on top of the icebox which said, "Help yourself. Dad."

I opened the refrigerator, and a little cool breath breathed out against me, cold, with the smell of rimed foods on it. Inside was the wondrous half-ruin of a chicken. Members of celery were piled like cords of wood. Strawberries grew in a thicket of parsley.

My hands blurred. They made motions that caused an illusion of a dozen hands. Like those pictures of Eastern goddesses they worship in temples. One hand with a tomato in it. One hand grasping a banana. A third hand seizing strawberries! A fourth, fifth, sixth hand caught in midmotion, each with a bit of cheese, olive, or radish!

Half an hour later I knelt by the toilet bowl and swiftly raised the seat. Then, rapidly. I opened my mouth, and shoved a spoon back, back along my tongue, down, down along my gagging throat. . . .

Lying in bed, I shuddered and tasted the acrid memory in my mouth, glad to be rid of the food I had so eagerly swallowed. I hated myself for my weakness. I lay trembling, empty, hungry again, but too sick, now, to eat. . . .

I was very weak in the morning, and noticeably pale, for my mother made a comment on it. "If you're not better by Monday," she said, "to the doctor's with you!"

It was Saturday. The day of shouting, and no tiny little silver bells for teachers to silence it; the day when the colorless giants moved on the pale screen at the Elite movie house in the long theater dark, and children were only children, and not things growing.

I saw no one. In the morning when I should have been hiking out along the North Shore Rail Line, where the hot sun simmered up from the long parallels of metal, I lolled about in terrific indecision. And by the time I got to the ravine it was already midafternoon and it was deserted; all of the kids had run downtown to see the matinee and suck lemon drops.

The ravine was very alone, it looked so undisturbed and old and green, I was a little afraid of it. I had never seen it so quiet. The vines hung quietly upon the trees and the water went over the rocks and the birds sang high up.

I went down the secret trail, hiding behind bushes, pausing, going on. Clarisse Mellin was crossing the bridge as I reached it. She was coming home from town with some little packages under her arm. We said hello, self-consciously.

"What are you doing?" she asked.

"Oh, walking around," I said.

"All alone?"

"Yeah. All the other guys are downtown."

She hesitated, then said, "Can I walk with you?"

"I guess so," I said. "Come on."

We walked down through the ravine. It was humming like a big dynamo. Nothing seemed to want to move, everything was very quiet. Pink darning needles flew and bumped on air pockets, and hovered over the sparkling creek water.

Clarisse's hand bumped mine as we walked along the trail. I smelled the moist dank smell of the ravine and the soft new smell of Clarisse beside me.

We came to a place where there was a cross trail.

"We built a tree hut up there last year," I said, pointing.

"Where?" Clarisse stepped close to me to see where my finger was pointing. "I don't see."

"There," I said, my voice breaking, and pointed again.

Very quietly, she put her arm around me. I was so surprised and bewildered I almost cried out. Then, trembling, her lips kissed me, and my own hands were moving to hold her and I was shaking and shouting inside myself.

The silence was like a green explosion. The water bubbled on in the creek bed. I couldn't breathe.

I knew it was all over. I was lost. From this moment on, it would be a touching, an eating of foods, a learning of language and algebra and logic, a movement and an emotion, a kissing and a holding, a whirl of feeling that caught and sucked me drowning under. I knew I was lost forever now, and I didn't care. But I *did* care, and I was laughing and crying all in one, and there was nothing to do about it, but hold her and love her with all my decided and rioting body and mind.

I could have gone on fighting my war against Mother and Dad and school and food and things in books, but I couldn't fight this sweetness

on my lips and this warmness in my hands, and the new odor in my
nostrils.

"Clarisse, Clarisse," I cried, holding her, looking over her shoulder
blindly, whispering to her. "Clarisse!"

The kidnaping was reported all around the world, of course.

It took a few days for the full significance of the news to spread from Cuba to the United States, to the Left Bank in Paris and then finally to some small good café in Pamplona where the drinks were fine and the weather, somehow, was always just right.

But once the meaning of the news really hit, people were on the phone, Madrid was calling New York, New York was shouting south at Havana to verify, please verify this crazy thing.

And then some woman in Venice, Italy, with a blurred voice called through, saying she was at Harry's Bar that very instant and was destroyed, this thing that had happened was terrible, a cultural heritage was placed in immense and irrevocable danger. . . .

Not an hour later, I got a call from a baseball pitcher-*cum*-novelist who had been a great friend of Papa's and who now lived in Madrid half the year and Nairobi the rest. He was in tears, or sounded close to it.

"Tell me," he said, from halfway around the world, "what happened? What are the facts?"

Well, the facts were these: Down in Havana, Cuba, about fourteen kilometers from Papa's Finca Vigía home, there is a bar in which he used to drink. It is the one where they named a special drink for him, not the fancy one where he used to meet flashy literary lights such as K-K-Kenneth Tynan and, er, Tennessee W-Williams (as Mr. Tynan would say it). No, it is not the Floridita; it is a shirt-sleeves place with plain wooden tables, sawdust on the floor, and a big mirror like a dirty cloud behind the bar. Papa went there when there were too many tourists around the Floridita who wanted to meet Mr. Hemingway. And the thing that happened there was destined to be big news, bigger than the report of what he said to Fitzgerald about the rich, even bigger than the story of his swing at Max Eastman on that long-ago day in Charlie Scribner's office. This news had to do with an ancient parrot.

That senior bird lived in a cage right atop the bar in the Cuba Libre. He had "kept his cage" in that place for roughly twenty-nine years, which means that the old parrot had been there almost as long as Papa had lived in Cuba.

And that adds up to this monumental fact: All during the time Papa had lived in Finca Vigía, he had known the parrot and had talked to him and the parrot had talked back. As the years passed, people said that Hemingway began to talk like the parrot and others said no, the parrot learned to talk like *him!* Papa used to line the drinks up on the counter and sit near the cage and involve that bird in the best kind of conversation you ever heard, four nights running. By the end of the second year, that parrot knew more about Hem and Thomas Wolfe and Sherwood Anderson than Gertrude Stein did. In fact, the parrot even knew who Gertrude Stein *was.* All you had to say was "Gertrude" and the parrot said:

"Pigeons on the grass alas."

At other times, pressed, the parrot would say, "There was this old man and this boy and this boat and this sea and this big fish in the sea. . . ." And then it would take time out to eat a cracker.

Well, this fabled creature, this parrot, this odd bird, vanished, cage and all, from the Cuba Libre late one Sunday afternoon.

And that's why my phone was ringing itself off the hook. And that's why one of the big magazines got a special State Department clearance and flew me down to Cuba to see if I could find so much as the cage, anything remaining of the bird or anyone resembling a kidnaper. They wanted a light and amiable article, with overtones, as they said. And, very honestly, I was curious. I had heard rumors of the bird. In a strange kind of way, I was concerned.

I got off the jet from Mexico City and taxied straight across Havana to that strange little café-bar.

I almost failed to get in the place. As I stepped through the door, a dark little man jumped up from a chair and cried, "No, no! Go away! We are closed!"

He ran out to jiggle the lock on the door, showing that he really meant to shut the place down. All the tables were empty and there was no one around. He had probably just been airing out the bar when I arrived.

"I've come about the parrot," I said.

"No, no," he cried, his eyes looking wet. "I won't talk. It's too much. If I were not Catholic, I would kill myself. Poor Papa. Poor El Córdoba!"

"El Córdoba?" I murmured.

"That," he said fiercely, "was the parrot's name!"

"Yes," I said, recovering quickly. "El Córdoba. I've come to rescue him."

That made him stop and blink. Shadows and then sunlight went over his face and then shadows again. "Impossible! Could you? No, no. How could anyone! Who *are* you?"

"A friend to Papa and the bird," I said quickly. "And the more time we talk, the farther away goes the criminal. You want El Córdoba back tonight? Pour us several of Papa's good drinks and talk."

My bluntness worked. Not two minutes later, we were drinking Papa's special, seated in the bar near the empty place where the cage used to sit. The little man, whose name was Antonio, kept wiping that empty place and then wiping his eyes with the bar rag. As I finished the first drink and started on the second, I said:

"This is no ordinary kidnaping."

"You're telling me!" cried Antonio. "People came from all over the world to see that parrot, to talk to El Córdoba, to hear him, ah, God, speak with the voice of Papa. May his abductors sink and burn in hell, yes, hell."

"They will," I said. "Whom do you suspect?"

"Everyone. No one."

"The kidnaper," I said, eyes shut for a moment, savoring the drink, "had to be educated, a book reader, I mean, that's obvious, isn't it? Anyone like that around the last few days?"

"Educated. No education. *Señor,* there have always been strangers the last ten, the last twenty years, always asking for Papa. When Papa was here, they met him. With Papa gone, they met El Córdoba, the great one. So it was always strangers and strangers."

"But think, Antonio," I said, touching his trembling elbow. "Not only educated, a reader, but someone in the last few days who was—how shall I put it?—odd. Strange. Someone so peculiar, *muy eccéntrico,* that you remember him above all others. Someone who—"

"*¡Madre de Dios!*" cried Antonio, leaping up. His eyes stared off into memory. He seized his head as if it had just exploded. "Thank you, *señor. ¡Si, si!* What a creature! In the name of Christ, there was such a one yesterday! He was very small. And he spoke like this: very high— *eeeee.* Like a *muchacha* in a school play, eh? Like a canary swallowed by a witch! And he wore a blue-velvet suit with a big yellow tie."

"Yes, yes!" I had leaped up now and was almost yelling. "Go on!"

"And he had a small very round face, *señor,* and his hair was yellow and cut across the brow like this—*zitt!* And his mouth small, very pink, like candy, yes? He—he was like, yes, *uno muñeco,* of the kind one wins at carnivals."

"Kewpie dolls!"

"*¡Sí!* At Coney Island, yes, when I was a child, Kewpie dolls! And he was so high, you see? To my elbow. Not a midget, no—but—and

how old? Blood of Christ, who can say? No lines in his face, but—
thirty, forty, fifty. And on his feet he was wearing—"

"Green booties!" I cried.

"*¿Qué?*"

"Shoes, boots!"

"*Sí.*" He blinked, stunned. "But how did you *know?*"

I exploded, "Shelley Capon!"

"That is the name! And his friends with him, *señor,* all laughing—
no, giggling. Like the nuns who play basketball in the late afternoons
near the church. Oh, *señor,* do you think that they, that he—"

"I don't think, Antonio, I *know.* Shelley Capon, of all the writers in
the world, hated Papa. Of course he would snatch El Córdoba. Why,
wasn't there a rumor once that the bird had memorized Papa's last,
greatest, and as-yet-not-put-down-on-paper novel?"

"There was such a rumor, *señor.* But I do not write books, I tend
bar. I bring crackers to the bird. I—"

"You bring me the phone, Antonio, please."

"You know where the bird is, *señor?*"

"I have the hunch beyond intuition, the big one. *Gracias.*" I dialed
the Havana Libre, the biggest hotel in town.

"Shelley Capon, please."

The phone buzzed and clicked.

Half a million miles away, a midget boy Martian lifted the receiver and
played the flute and then the bell chimes with his voice: "Capon here."

"Damned if you aren't!" I said. And got up and ran out of the Cuba
Libre bar.

Racing back to Havana by taxi, I thought of Shelley as I'd seen him
before. Surrounded by a storm of friends, living out of suitcases, ladling
soup from other people's plates, borrowing money from billfolds seized
from your pockets right in front of you, counting the lettuce leaves with
relish, leaving rabbit pellets on your rug, gone. Dear Shelley Capon.

Ten minutes later, my taxi with no brakes dropped me running and
spun on to some ultimate disaster beyond town.

Still running, I made the lobby, paused for information, hurried upstairs, and stopped short before Shelley's door. It pulsed in spasms like
a bad heart. I put my ear to the door. The wild calls and cries from inside
might have come from a flock of birds, feather-stripped in a hurricane. I
felt the door. Now it seemed to tremble like a vast laundromat that had
swallowed and was churning an acid-rock group and a lot of very dirty
linen. Listening, my underwear began to crawl on my legs.

I knocked. No answer. I touched the door. It drifted open. I stepped
in upon a scene much too dreadful for Bosch to have painted.

Around the pigpen living room were strewn various life-size dolls, eyes half-cracked open, cigarettes smoking in burned, limp fingers, empty Scotch glasses in hands, and all the while the radio belted them with concussions of music broadcast from some Stateside asylum. The place was sheer carnage. Not ten seconds ago, I felt, a large dirty locomotive must have plunged through here. Its victims had been hurled in all directions and now lay upside down in various parts of the room, moaning for first aid.

In the midst of this hell, seated erect and proper, well dressed in velveteen jerkin, persimmon bow tie, and bottle-green booties, was, of course, Shelley Capon. Who with no surprise at all waved a drink at me and cried:

"I *knew* that was you on the phone. I am absolutely telepathic! Welcome, Raimundo!"

He always called me Raimundo. Ray was plain bread and butter. Raimundo made me a don with a breeding farm full of bulls. I let it be Raimundo.

"Raimundo, sit down! No . . . fling yourself into an *interesting* position."

"Sorry," I said in my best Dashiell Hammett manner, sharpening my chin and steeling my eyes. "No time."

I began to walk around the room among his friends Fester and Soft and Ripply and Mild Innocuous and some actor I remembered who, when asked how he would do a part in a film, had said, "I'll play it like a doe."

I shut off the radio. That made a lot of people in the room stir: I yanked the radio's roots out of the wall. Some people sat up. I raised a window. I threw the radio out. They all screamed as if I had thrown their mothers down an elevator shaft.

The radio made a satisfying sound on the cement sidewalk below. I turned, with a beatific smile on my face. A number of people were on their feet, swaying toward me with faint menace. I pulled a twenty-dollar bill out of my pocket, handed it to someone without looking at him, and said, "Go buy a new one." He ran out the door slowly. The door slammed. I heard him fall down the stairs as if he were after his morning shot in the arm.

"All right, Shelley," I said, "where is it?"

"Where is *what,* dear boy?" he said, eyes wide with innocence.

"You know what I mean." I stared at the drink in his tiny hand.

Which was a Papa drink, the Cuba Libre's very own special blend of papaya, lime, lemon, and rum. As if to destroy evidence, he drank it down quickly.

I walked over to three doors in a wall and touched one.

"That's a closet, dear boy." I put my hand on the second door.

"Don't go in. You'll be sorry what you see." I didn't go in.

I put my hand on the third door. "Oh, dear, well, go ahead," said Shelley petulantly. I opened the door.

Beyond it was a small anteroom with a mere cot and a table near the window.

On the table sat a bird cage with a shawl over it. Under the shawl I could hear the rustle of feathers and the scrape of a beak on the wires.

Shelley Capon came to stand small beside me, looking in at the cage, a fresh drink in his little fingers.

"What a shame you didn't arrive at seven tonight," he said.

"Why seven?"

"Why, then, Raimundo, we would have just finished our curried fowl stuffed with wild rice. I wonder, is there much white meat, or any at all, under a parrot's feathers?"

"You wouldn't!?" I cried.

I stared at him.

"You would," I answered myself.

I stood for a moment longer at the door. Then, slowly, I walked across the small room and stopped by the cage with the shawl over it. I saw a single word embroidered across the top of the shawl: MOTHER.

I glanced at Shelley. He shrugged and looked shyly at his boot tips. I took hold of the shawl. Shelley said, "No. Before you lift it . . . ask something."

"Like what?"

"DiMaggio. Ask DiMaggio."

A small ten-watt bulb clicked on in my head. I nodded. I leaned near the hidden cage and whispered: "DiMaggio. 1939."

There was a sort of animal-computer pause. Beneath the word MOTHER some feathers stirred, a beak tapped the cage bars. Then a tiny voice said:

"Home runs, thirty. Batting average, .381."

I was stunned. But then I whispered: "Babe Ruth. 1927."

Again the pause, the feathers, the beak, and: "Home runs, sixty. Batting average, .356. Awk."

"My God," I said.

"My God," echoed Shelley Capon.

"That's the parrot who met Papa, all right."

"That's who it is."

And I lifted the shawl.

I don't know what I expected to find underneath the embroidery. Perhaps a miniature hunter in boots, bush jacket, and wide-brimmed hat. Perhaps a small, trim fisherman with a beard and turtleneck sweater perched there on a wooden slat. Something tiny, something literary, something human, something fantastic, but not really a parrot.

But that's all there was.

And not a very handsome parrot, either. It looked as if it had been up all night for years; one of those disreputable birds that never preens its feathers or shines its beak. It was a kind of rusty green and black with a dull-amber snout and rings under its eyes as if it were a secret drinker. You might see it half flying, half hopping out of café-bars at three in the morning. It was the bum of the parrot world.

Shelley Capon read my mind. "The effect is better," he said, "with the shawl over the cage."

I put the shawl back over the bars.

I was thinking very fast. Then I thought very slowly. I bent and whispered by the cage:

"Norman Mailer."

"Couldn't remember the alphabet," said the voice beneath the shawl.

"Gertrude Stein," I said.

"Suffered from undescended testicles," said the voice.

"My God," I gasped.

I stepped back. I stared at the covered cage. I blinked at Shelley Capon.

"Do you really *know* what you have here, Capon?"

"A *gold* mine, dear Raimundo!" he crowed.

"A *mint!*" I corrected.

"Endless opportunities for blackmail!"

"Causes for murder!" I added.

"Think!" Shelley snorted into his drink. "Think what Mailer's publishers *alone* would pay to shut this bird up!"

I spoke to the cage:

"F. Scott Fitzgerald."

Silence.

"Try 'Scottie,' " said Shelley.

"Ah," said the voice inside the cage. "Good left jab but couldn't follow through. Nice contender, but—"

"Faulkner," I said.

"Batting average fair, strictly a singles hitter."

"Steinbeck!"

"Finished last at end of season."

"Ezra Pound!"

"Traded off to the minor leagues in 1932."

"I think . . . I need . . . one of those drinks." Someone put a drink in my hand. I gulped it and nodded. I shut my eyes and felt the world give one turn, then opened my eyes to look at Shelley Capon, the classic son of a bitch of all time.

"There is something even more fantastic," he said. "You've heard only the first half."

"You're lying," I said. "What could there be?"

He dimpled at me—in all the world, only Shelley Capon can dimple at you in a completely evil way. "It was like this," he said. "You remember that Papa had trouble actually getting his stuff down on paper in those last years while he lived here? Well, he'd planned another novel after *Islands in the Stream,* but somehow it just never seemed to get written.

"Oh, he had it in his mind, all right—the story was there and lots of people heard him mention it—but he just couldn't seem to write it. So he would go to the Cuba Libre and drink many drinks and have long conversations with the parrot. Raimundo, what Papa was telling El Córdoba all through those long drinking nights was the story of his last book. And, in the course of time, the bird has memorized it."

"His very last book!" I said. "The final Hemingway novel of all time! Never written but recorded in the brain of a parrot! Holy Jesus!"

Shelley was nodding at me with the smile of a depraved cherub.

"How much you want for this bird?"

"Dear, dear Raimundo." Shelley Capon stirred his drink with his pinkie. "What makes you think the creature is for sale?"

"You sold your mother once, then stole her back and sold her again under another name. Come off it, Shelley. You're onto something big." I brooded over the shawled cage. "How many telegrams have you sent out in the last four or five hours?"

"Really! You horrify me!"

"How many long-distance phone calls, reverse charges, have you made since breakfast?"

Shelley Capon mourned a great sigh and pulled a crumpled telegram duplicate from his velveteen pocket. I took it and read:

FRIENDS OF PAPA MEETING HAVANA TO REMINISCE OVER BIRD AND BOTTLE. WIRE BID OR BRING CHECKBOOKS AND OPEN MINDS. FIRST COME FIRST SERVED. ALL WHITE MEAT BUT CAVIAR PRICES. INTERNATIONAL PUBLICATION, BOOK, MAGAZINE, TV, FILM RIGHTS AVAILABLE. LOVE. SHELLEY YOU-KNOW-WHO.

My God again, I thought, and let the telegram fall to the floor as Shelley handed me a list of names the telegram had been sent to:

Time. Life. Newsweek. Scribner's. Simon & Schuster. *The New York Times. The Christian Science Monitor. The Times of London. Le Monde. Paris-Match.* One of the Rockefellers. Some of the Kennedys. CBS.

NBC. MGM. Warner Bros. 20th Century-Fox. And on and on and on. The list was as long as my deepening melancholy.

Shelley Capon tossed an armful of answering telegrams onto the table near the cage. I leafed through them quickly.

Everyone, but everyone, was in the air, right now. Jets were streaming in from all over the world. In another two hours, four, six at the most, Cuba would be swarming with agents, publishers, fools, and plain damn fools, plus counterespionage kidnapers and blonde starlets who hoped to be in front-page photographs with the bird on their shoulders.

I figured I had maybe a good half-hour left in which to do something, I didn't know what.

Shelley nudged my arm. "Who sent you, dear boy? You *are* the very first, you know. Make a fine bid and you're in free, maybe. I must consider other offers, of course. But it might get thick and nasty here. I begin to panic at what I've done. I may wish to sell cheap and flee. Because, well, think, there's the problem of getting this bird out of the country, yes? And, simultaneously, Castro might declare the parrot a national monument or work of art, or, oh, hell, Raimundo, who *did* send you?"

"Someone, but now no one," I said, brooding. "I came on behalf of someone else. I'll go away on my own. From now on, anyway, it's just me and the bird. I've read Papa all my life. Now I know I came just because I had to."

"My God, an altruist!"

"Sorry to offend you, Shelley."

The phone rang. Shelley got it. He chatted happily for a moment, told someone to wait downstairs, hung up, and cocked an eyebrow at me: "NBC is in the lobby. They want an hour's taped interview with El Córdoba there. They're talking six figures."

My shoulders slumped. The phone rang. This time I picked it up, to my own surprise. Shelley cried out. But I said, "Hello. Yes?"

"*Señor*," said a man's voice. "There is a *Señor* Hobwell here from *Time*, he says, magazine." I could see the parrot's face on next week's cover, with six follow-up pages of text.

"Tell him to wait." I hung up.

"*Newsweek?*" guessed Shelley.

"The other one," I said.

"The snow was fine up in the shadow of the hills," said the voice inside the cage under the shawl.

"Shut up," I said quietly, wearily. "Oh, shut up, damn you."

Shadows appeared in the doorway behind us. Shelley Capon's friends were beginning to assemble and wander into the room. They gathered and I began to tremble and sweat.

For some reason, I began to rise to my feet. My body was going to
do something, I didn't know what. I watched my hands. Suddenly, the
right hand reached out. It knocked the cage over, snapped the wire-frame
door wide, and darted in to seize the parrot.

"No!"

There was a great gasping roar, as if a single thunderous wave had
come in on a shore. Everyone in the room seemed knocked in the stomach by my action. Everyone exhaled, took a step, began to yell, but by
then I had the parrot out. I had it by the throat.

"No! No!" Shelley jumped at me. I kicked him in the shins. He sat
down, screaming.

"Don't anyone move!" I said and almost laughed, hearing myself use
the old cliché. "You ever see a chicken killed? This parrot has a thin
neck. One twist, the head comes off. Nobody move a hair." Nobody
moved.

"You son of a bitch," said Shelley Capon, on the floor.

For a moment, I thought they were all going to rush me. I saw myself
beaten and chased along the beach, yelling, the cannibals ringing me in
and eating me, Tennessee Williams style, shoes and all. I felt sorry
for my skeleton, which would be found in the main Havana plaza at
dawn tomorrow.

But they did not hit, pummel, or kill. As long as I had my fingers
around the neck of the parrot who met Papa, I knew I could stand
there forever.

I wanted with all my heart, soul, and guts to wring the bird's neck
and throw its disconnected carcass into those pale and gritty faces. I
wanted to stop up the past and destroy Papa's preserved memory forever,
if it was going to be played with by feebleminded children like these.

But I could not, for two reasons. One dead parrot would mean one
dead duck: me. And I was weeping inside for Papa. I simply could not
shut off his voice transcribed here, held in my hands, still alive, like an
old Edison record. I could not kill.

If these ancient children had known that, they would have swarmed
over me like locusts. But they didn't know. And, I guess, it didn't show
in my face.

"Stand back!" I cried.

It was that beautiful last scene from *The Phantom of the Opera* where
Lon Chaney, pursued through midnight Paris, turns upon the mob, lifts
his clenched fist as if it contained an explosive, and holds the mob at
bay for one terrific instant. He laughs, opens his hand to show it empty,
and then is driven to his death in the river. . . . Only I had no intention
of letting them see an empty hand. I kept it close around El Córdoba's
scrawny neck.

"Clear a path to the door!" They cleared a path.

"Not a move, not a breath. If anyone so much as swoons, this bird is dead forever and no rights, no movies, no photos. Shelley, bring me the cage and the shawl."

Shelley Capon edged over and brought me the cage and its cover. "Stand off!" I yelled.

Everyone jumped back another foot.

"Now, hear this," I said. "After I've got away and have hidden out, one by one each of you will be called to have his chance to meet Papa's friend here again and cash in on the headlines."

I was lying. I could hear the lie. I hoped they couldn't. I spoke more quickly now, to cover the lie: "I'm going to start walking now. Look. See? I have the parrot by the neck. He'll stay alive as long as you play 'Simon says' my way. Here we go, now. One, two. One, two. Halfway to the door." I walked among them and they did not breathe. "One, two," I said, my heart beating in my mouth. "At the door. Steady. No sudden moves. Cage in one hand. Bird in the other—"

"The lions ran along the beach on the yellow sand," said the parrot, his throat moving under my fingers.

"Oh, my God," said Shelley, crouched there by the table. Tears began to pour down his face. Maybe it wasn't all money. Maybe some of it was Papa for him, too. He put his hands out in a beckoning, come-back gesture to me, the parrot, the cage. "Oh, God, oh, God." He wept.

"There was only the carcass of the great fish lying by the pier, its bones picked clean in the morning light," said the parrot.

"Oh," said everyone softly.

I didn't wait to see if any more of them were weeping. I stepped out. I shut the door. I ran for the elevator. By a miracle, it was there, the operator half-asleep inside. No one tried to follow. I guess they knew it was no use.

On the way down, I put the parrot inside the cage and put the shawl marked MOTHER over the cage. And the elevator moved slowly down through the years. I thought of those years ahead and where I might hide the parrot and keep him warm against any weather and feed him properly and once a day go in and talk through the shawl, and nobody ever to see him, no papers, no magazines, no cameramen, no Shelley Capon, not even Antonio from the Cuba Libre. Days might go by or weeks and sudden fears might come over me that the parrot had gone dumb. Then, in the middle of the night, I might wake and shuffle in and stand by his cage and say:

"Italy, 1918 . . . ?"

And beneath the word MOTHER, an old voice would say: "The snow drifted off the edges of the mountain in a fine white dust that winter. . . ."

"Africa, 1932."

"We got the rifles out and oiled the rifles and they were blue and fine and lay in our hands and we waited in the tall grass and smiled—"

"Cuba. The Gulf Stream."

"That fish came out of the water and jumped as high as the sun. Everything I had ever thought about a fish was in that fish. Everything I had ever thought about a single leap was in that leap. All of my life was there. It was a day of sun and water and being alive. I wanted to hold it all still in my hands. I didn't want it to go away, ever. Yet there, as the fish fell and the waters moved over it white and then green, there it went. . . ."

By that time, we were at the lobby level and the elevator doors opened and I stepped out with the cage labeled MOTHER and walked quickly across the lobby and out to a taxicab.

The trickiest business—and my greatest danger—remained. I knew that by the time I got to the airport, the guards and the Castro militia would have been alerted. I wouldn't put it past Shelley Capon to tell them that a national treasure was getting away. He might even cut Castro in on some of the Book-of-the-Month Club revenue and the movie rights. I had to improvise a plan to get through customs.

I am a literary man, however, and the answer came to me quickly. I had the taxi stop long enough for me to buy some shoe polish. I began to apply the disguise to El Córdoba. I painted him black all over.

"Listen," I said, bending down to whisper into the cage as we drove across Havana. *"Nevermore."*

I repeated it several times to give him the idea. The sound would be new to him, because, I guessed, Papa would never have quoted a middleweight contender he had knocked out years ago. There was silence under the shawl while the word was recorded.

Then, at last, it came back to me. "Nevermore," in Papa's old, familiar, tenor voice, "nevermore," it said.

The rickety Ford came along a road that plowed up dust in yellow plumes which took an hour to lie back down and move no more in that special slumber that stuns the world in mid-July. Far away, the lake waited, a cool-blue gem in a hot-green lake of grass, but it was indeed still far away, and Neva and Doug were bucketing along in their barrelful of red-hot bolts with lemonade slopping around in a thermos on the back seat and deviled-ham sandwiches fermenting on Doug's lap. Both boy and aunt sucked in hot air and talked out even hotter.

"Fire-eater," said Douglas. "I'm eating fire. Heck, I can hardly *wait* for that lake!"

Suddenly, up ahead, there was a man by the side of the road.

Shirt open to reveal his bronzed body to the waist, his hair ripened to wheat color by July, the man's eyes burned fiery blue in a nest of sun wrinkles. He waved, dying in the heat.

Neva tromped on the brake. Fierce dust clouds rose to make the man vanish. When the golden dust sifted away his hot yellow eyes glared balefully, like a cat's, defying the weather and the burning wind.

He stared at Douglas.

Douglas glanced away, nervously.

For you could see where the man had come across a field high with yellow grass baked and burnt by eight weeks of no rain. There was a path where the man had broken the grass and cleaved a passage to the road. The path went as far as one could see down to a dry swamp and an empty creek bed with nothing but baked hot stones in it and fried rock and melting sand.

"I'll be damned, you stopped!" cried the man, angrily.

"I'll be damned. I did," Neva yelled back. "Where you going?"

"I'll think of someplace." The man hopped up like a cat and swung into the rumble seat. "Get going. It's *after* us! The sun, I mean, of course!" He pointed straight up. "Git! Or we'll *all* go mad!"

Neva stomped on the gas. The car left gravel and glided on pure white-hot dust, coming down only now and then to careen off a boulder or kiss a stone. They cut the land in half with racket. Above it, the man shouted:

"Put 'er up to seventy, eighty, hell, why not ninety!''

Neva gave a quick, critical look at the lion, the intruder in the back seat, to see if she could shut his jaws with a glance. They shut.

And that, of course, is how Doug felt about the beast. Not a stranger, no, not hitchhiker, but intruder. In just two minutes of leaping into the red-hot car, with his jungle hair and jungle smell, he had managed to disingratiate himself with the climate, the automobile, Doug, and the honorable and perspiring aunt. Now she hunched over the wheel and nursed the car through further storms of heat and backlashes of gravel.

Meanwhile, the creature in the back, with his great lion ruff of hair and mint-fresh yellow eyes, licked his lips and looked straight on at Doug in the rearview mirror. He gave a wink. Douglas tried to wink back, but somehow the lid never came down.

"You ever try to figure—" yelled the man.

"What?" cried Neva.

"You ever try to figure," shouted the man, leaning forward between them "—whether or not the weather is driving you crazy, or you're crazy *already?*"

It was a surprise of a question, which suddenly cooled them on this blast-furnace day.

"I don't quite understand—" said Neva.

"Nor does anyone!" The man smelled like a lion house. His thin arms hung over and down between them, nervously tying and untying an invisible string. He moved as if there were nests of burning hair under each armpit. "Day like today, all hell breaks loose inside your head. Lucifer was born on a day like this, in a wilderness like this," said the man. "With just fire and flame and smoke everywhere," said the man. "And everything so hot you can't touch it, and people not wanting to be touched," said the man.

He gave a nudge to her elbow, a nudge to the boy.

They jumped a mile.

"You see?" The man smiled. "Day like today, you get to thinking lots of things." He smiled. "Ain't this the summer when the seventeen-year locusts are supposed to come back like pure holocaust? Simple but multitudinous plagues?"

"Don't know!" Neva drove fast, staring ahead.

"This *is* the summer. Holocaust just around the bend. I'm thinking so swift it hurts my eyeballs, cracks my head. I'm liable to explode in a fireball with just plain disconnected thought. Why—why—why—''

Neva swallowed hard. Doug held his breath.

Quite suddenly they were terrified. For the man simply idled on with his talk, looking at the shimmering green fire trees that burned by on both sides, sniffing the rich hot dust that flailed up around the tin car, his voice neither high nor low, but steady and calm now in describing his life:

"Yes, sir, there's more to the world than people appreciate. If there can be seventeen-year locusts, why not seventeen-year people? Ever *thought* of that?"

"Never did," said someone.

Probably me, thought Doug, for his mouth had moved like a mouse.

"Or how about twenty-four-year people, or fifty-seven-year people? I mean, we're all so used to people growing up, marrying, having kids, we never stop to think maybe there's other ways for people coming into the world, maybe like locusts, once in a while, who can tell, one hot day, middle of summer!"

"Who can tell?" There was the mouse again. Doug's lips trembled.

"And who's to say there ain't genetic evil in the world?" asked the man of the sun, glaring right up at it without blinking.

"*What* kind of evil?" asked Neva.

"Genetic, ma'am. In the blood, that is to say. People born evil, growed evil, died evil, no changes all the way down the line."

"Whew!" said Douglas. "You mean people who start out mean and stay *at* it?"

"You got the sum, boy. Why not? If there are people everyone thinks are angel-fine from their first sweet breath to their last pure declaration, why not sheer orneriness from January first to December, three hundred sixty-five days later?"

"I never thought of that," said the mouse.

"Think," said the man. "*Think.*"

They thought for above five seconds.

"Now," said the man, squinting one eye at the cool lake five miles ahead, his other eye shut into darkness and ruminating on coal-bins of fact there, "listen. What if the intense heat, I mean the really hot hot heat of a month like this, week like this, day like today, just baked the Ornery Man right out of the river mud. Been there buried in the mud for forty-seven years, like a damn larva, waiting to be born. And he shook himself awake and looked around, full grown, and climbed out of the hot mud into the world and said, 'I think I'll eat me some summer.' "

"How's that again?"

"Eat me some summer, boy, summer, ma'am. Just devour it whole. Look at them trees, ain't they a whole dinner? Look at that field of wheat, ain't that a feast? Them sunflowers by the road, by golly, there's breakfast. Tarpaper on top that house, there's lunch. And the lake, way up ahead, Jehoshaphat, that's dinner wine, drink it all!"

"I'm thirsty, all right," said Doug.

"Thirsty, hell, boy, thirst don't begin to describe the state of a man, come to think about him, come to talk, who's been waiting in the hot mud thirty years and is born but to die in one day! Thirst! Ye Gods! Your ignorance is complete."

"Well," said Doug.

"Well," said the man. "Not only thirst but hunger. Hunger. Look around. Not only eat the trees and then the flowers blazing by the roads but then the white-hot panting dogs. There's one. There's another! And all the cats in the country. There's two, just passed three! And then just glutton-happy begin to why, why not, begin to get around to, let me tell you, how's this strike you, eat people? I mean—people! Fried, cooked, boiled, and parboiled people. Sunburnt beauties of people. Old men, young. Old ladies' hats and then old ladies under their hats and then young ladies' scarves and young ladies, and then young boys' swimtrunks, by God, and young boys, elbows, ankles, ears, toes, and eyebrows! Eyebrows, by God, men, women, boys, ladies, dogs, fill up the menu, sharpen your teeth, lick your lips, dinner's *on!*"

"Wait!" someone cried.

Not me, thought Doug. I said nothing.

"Hold on!" someone yelled.

It was Neva.

He saw her knee fly up as if by intuition and down as if by finalized gumption.

Stomp! went her heel on the floor.

The car braked. Neva had the door open, pointing, shouting, pointing, shouting, her mouth flapping, one hand seized out to grab the man's shirt and rip it.

"Out! Get out!"

"*Here,* ma'am?" The man was astonished.

"Here, here, here, out, out, out!"

"But, ma'am . . . !"

"Out, or you're finished, through!" cried Neva, wildly. "I got a load of Bibles in the back trunk, a pistol with a silver bullet here under the steering wheel. A box of crucifixes under the seat! A wooden stake taped to the axle, with a hammer. I got holy water in the carburetor, blessed before it boiled early this morning at three churches on the way: St. Matthew's Catholic, the Green Town Baptist, and the Zion City High Episcopal. The steam from that will get you alone. Following us, one mile behind, and due to arrive in one minute, is the Reverend Bishop Kelly from Chicago. Up at the lake is Father Rooney from Milwaukee, and Doug, why, Doug here has in his back pocket at this minute one sprig of wolfbane and two chunks of mandrake root. Out! out! out!''

"Why, ma'am," cried the man, "I *am!*"

And he was.

He landed and fell rolling in the road.

Neva banged the car into full flight.

Behind, the man picked himself up and yelled, "You must be nuts. You must be crazy. Nuts. Crazy."

"*I'm* nuts? *I'm* crazy? said Neva, and hooted. "Boy!"

". . . nuts . . . crazy . . ." The voice faded.

Douglas looked back and saw the man shaking his fist, then ripping off his shirt and hurling it to the gravel and jumping big puffs of white-hot dust out of it with his bare feet.

The car exploded, rushed, raced, banged pell-mell ahead, his aunt ferociously glued to the hot wheel, until the little sweating figure of the talking man was lost in sun-drenched marshland and burning air. At last Doug exhaled:

"Neva, I never heard you talk like that before."

"And never will again, Doug."

"Was what you said *true?*"

"Not a word."

"You lied, I mean, you *lied?*"

"I lied." Neva blinked. "Do you think *he* was lying, too?"

"I don't know."

"All I know is sometimes it takes a lie to kill a lie, Doug. This time, anyway. Don't let it become customary."

"No, ma'am." He began to laugh. "Say the thing about mandrake root again. Say the thing about wolfbane in my pocket. Say it about a pistol with a silver bullet, say it."

She said it. They both began to laugh.

Whooping and shouting, they went away in their tin-bucket-junking car over the gravel ruts and humps, her saying, him listening, eyes squeezed shut, roaring, snickering, raving.

They didn't stop laughing until they hit the water in their bathing suits and came up all smiles.

The sun stood hot in the middle of the sky and they dog-paddled happily for five minutes before they began to really swim in the menthol-cool waves.

Only at dusk when the sun was suddenly gone and the shadows moved out from the trees did they remember that now they had to go *back* down that lonely road through all the dark places and past that empty swamp to get to town.

They stood by the car and looked down that long road. Doug swallowed hard.

"*Nothing* can happen to us going home."

"Nothing."

"Jump!"

They hit the seats and Neva kicked the starter like it was a dead dog and they were off.

They drove along under plum-colored trees and among velvet purple hills.

And nothing happened.

They drove along a wide raw gravel road that was turning the color of plums and smelled the warm-cool air that was like lilacs and looked at each other, waiting.

And nothing happened.

Neva began at last to hum under her breath.

The road was empty.

And then it was not empty.

Neva laughed. Douglas squinted and laughed with her.

For there was a small boy, nine years old maybe, dressed in a vanilla-white summer suit, with white shoes and a white tie and his face pink and scrubbed, waiting by the side of the road. He waved.

Neva braked the car.

"Going in to town?" called the boy, cheerily. "Got lost. Folks at a picnic, left without me. Sure glad you came along. It's *spooky* out here."

"Climb in!"

The boy climbed and they were off, the boy in the back seat, and Doug and Neva up front glancing at him, laughing, and then getting quiet.

The small boy kept silent for a long while behind them, sitting straight upright and clean and bright and fresh and new in his white suit.

And they drove along the empty road under a sky that was dark now with a few stars and the wind getting cool.

And at last the boy spoke and said something that Doug didn't hear but he saw Neva stiffen and her face grow as pale as the ice cream from which the small boy's suit was cut.

"What?" asked Doug, glancing back.

The small boy stared directly at him, not blinking, and his mouth moved all to itself as if it were separate from his face.

The car's engine missed fire and died.

They were slowing to a dead stop.

Doug saw Neva kicking and fiddling at the gas and the starter. But most of all he heard the small boy say, in the new and permanent silence:

"Have either of you ever wondered—"

The boy took a breath and finished:

"—if there is such a thing as genetic evil in the world?"

A Piece of Wood

"**S**it down, young man," said the Official.

"Thanks." The young man sat.

"I've been hearing rumors about you," the Official said pleasantly. "Oh, nothing much. Your nervousness. Your not getting on so well. Several months now I've heard about you, and I thought I'd call you in. Thought maybe you'd like your job changed. Like to go overseas, work in some other War Area? Desk job killing you off, like to get right in on the old fight?"

"I don't think so," said the young sergeant.

"What *do* you want?"

The sergeant shrugged and looked at his hands. "To live in peace. To learn that during the night, somehow, the guns of the world had rusted, the bacteria had turned sterile in their bomb casings, the tanks had sunk like prehistoric monsters into roads suddenly made tar pits. That's what I'd like."

"That's what we'd all like, of course," said the Official. "Now stop all that idealistic chatter and tell me where you'd like to be sent. You have your choice—the Western or the Northern War Zone." The Official tapped a pink map on his desk.

But the sergeant was talking at his hands, turning them over, looking at the fingers: "What would you officers do, what would we men do, what would the *world* do if we all woke tomorrow with the guns in flaking ruin?"

The Official saw that he would have to deal carefully with the sergeant. He smiled quietly. "That's an interesting question. I like to talk about such theories, and my answer is that there'd be mass panic. Each nation would think itself the only unarmed nation in the world, and would blame its enemies for the disaster. There'd be waves of suicide, stocks collapsing, a million tragedies."

"But *after* that," the sergeant said. "After they realized it was true, that every nation was disarmed and there was nothing more to fear, if we were all clean to start over fresh and new, what then?''

"They'd rearm as swiftly as possible."

"What if they could be stopped?''

"Then they'd beat each other with their fists. If it got down to that. Huge armies of men with boxing gloves of steel spikes would gather at the national borders. And if you took the gloves away they'd use their fingernails and feet. And if you cut their legs off they'd spit on each other. And if you cut off their tongues and stopped their mouths with corks they'd fill the atmosphere so full of hate that mosquitoes would drop to the ground and birds would fall dead from telephone wires."

"Then you don't think it would do any good?'' the sergeant said.

"Certainly not. It'd be like ripping the carapace off a turtle. Civilization would gasp and die from the shock."

The young man shook his head. "Or are you lying to yourself and me because you've a nice comfortable job?''

"Let's call it ninety percent cynicism, ten percent rationalizing the situation. Go put your Rust away and forget about it."

The sergeant jerked his head up. "How'd you know I *had* it?'' he said.

"Had what?''

"The Rust, of course.''

"What're you talking about?''

"I *can* do it, you know. I could start the Rust tonight if I wanted to.''

The Official laughed. "You can't be serious.''

"I am. I've been meaning to come talk to you. I'm glad you called me in. I've worked on this invention for a long time. It's been a dream of mine. It has to do with the structure of certain atoms. If you study them you find that the arrangement of atoms in steel armor is such-and-such an arrangement. I was looking for an imbalance factor. I majored in physics and metallurgy, you know. It came to me, there's a Rust factor in the air all the time. Water vapor. I had to find a way to give steel a 'nervous breakdown.' Then the water vapor everywhere in the world would take over. Not on all metal, of course. Our civilization is built on steel, I wouldn't want to destroy most buildings. I'd just eliminate guns and shells, tanks, planes, battleships. I can set the machine to work on copper and brass and aluminum, too, if necessary. I'd just walk by all of those weapons and just being near them I'd make them fall away."

The Official was bending over his desk, staring at the sergeant. "May I ask you a question?''

"Yes.''

"Have you ever thought you were Christ?''

"I can't say that I have. But I have considered that God was good to me to let me find what I was looking for, if that's what you mean."

The Official reached into his breast pocket and drew out an expensive ball-point pen capped with a rifle shell. He flourished the pen and started filling in a form. "I want you to take this to Dr. Mathews this afternoon, for a complete checkup. Not that I expect anything really bad, understand. But don't you feel you *should* see a doctor?"

"You think I'm lying about my machine," said the sergeant. "I'm not. It's so small it can be hidden in this cigarette package. The effect of it extends for nine hundred miles. I could tour this country in a few days, with the machine set to a certain type of steel. The other nations couldn't take advantage of us because I'd rust their weapons as they approach us. Then I'd fly to Europe. By this time next month the world would be free of war forever. I don't know how I found this invention. It's impossible. Just as impossible as the atom bomb. I've waited a month now, trying to think it over. I worried about what would happen if I did rip off the carapace, as you say. But now I've just about decided. My talk with you has helped clarify things. Nobody thought an airplane would ever fly, nobody thought an atom would ever explode, and nobody thinks that there can ever be Peace, but there *will* be."

"Take that paper over to Dr. Mathews, will you?" said the Official hastily.

The sergeant got up. "You're not going to assign me to any new Zone then?"

"Not right away, no. I've changed my mind. We'll let Mathews decide."

"I've decided then," said the young man. "I'm leaving the Post within the next few minutes. I've a pass. Thank you very much for giving me your valuable time, sir."

"Now look here, Sergeant, don't take things so seriously. You don't have to leave. Nobody's going to hurt you."

"That's right. Because nobody would believe me. Good-bye, sir." The sergeant opened the office door and stepped out.

The door shut and the Official was alone. He stood for a moment looking at the door. He sighed. He rubbed his hands over his face. The phone rang. He answered it abstractedly.

"Oh, *hello,* Doctor. I was just going to call you." A pause. "Yes, I was going to send him over to you. Look, is it all right for that young man to be wandering about? It *is* all right? If you say so, Doctor. Probably needs a rest, a good long one. Poor boy has a delusion of rather an interesting sort. Yes, yes. It's a shame. But that's what a Sixteen-Year War can do to you, I suppose."

The phone voice buzzed in reply.

The Official listened and nodded. "I'll make a note on that. Just a second." He reached for his ball-point pen. "Hold on a moment. Always mislaying things." He patted his pocket. "Had my pen here a moment ago. Wait." He put down the phone and searched his desk, pulling out drawers. He checked his blouse pocket again. He stopped moving. Then his hands twitched slowly into his pocket and probed down. He poked his thumb and forefinger deep and brought out a pinch of something.

He sprinkled it on his desk blotter: a small filtering powder of yellow-red rust.

He sat staring at it for a moment. Then he picked up the phone. "Mathews," he said, "get off the line, quick." There was a click of someone hanging up and then he dialed another call. "Hello, Guard Station, listen, there's a man coming past you any minute now, you know him, name of Sergeant Hollis, stop him, shoot him down, kill him if necessary, don't ask any questions, kill the son of a bitch, you heard me, this is the Official talking! Yes, kill him, you hear!"

"But, sir," said a bewildered voice on the other end of the line. "I can't, I just *can't*. . . ."

"What do you mean you can't, God damn it!"

"Because . . ." The voice faded away. You could hear the guard breathing into the phone a mile away.

The Official shook the phone. "Listen to me, listen, get your gun ready!"

"I can't shoot anyone," said the guard.

The Official sank back in his chair. He sat blinking for half a minute, gasping.

Out there even now—he didn't have to look, no one had to tell him—the hangars were dusting down in soft red rust, and the airplanes were blowing away on a brown-rust wind into nothingness, and the tanks were sinking, sinking slowly into the hot asphalt roads, like dinosaurs (isn't that what the man had said?) sinking into primordial tar pits. Trucks were blowing away into ocher puffs of smoke, their drivers dumped by the road, with only the tires left running on the highways.

"Sir . . ." said the guard, who was seeing all this, far away. "Oh, God . . ."

"Listen, listen!" screamed the Official. "Go after him, get him, with your hands, choke him, with your fists, beat him, use your feet, kick his ribs in, kick him to death, do anything, but get that man. I'll be right out!" He hung up the phone.

By instinct he jerked open the bottom desk drawer to get his service pistol. A pile of brown rust filled the new leather holster. He swore and leaped up.

On the way out of the office he grabbed a chair. It's wood, he thought.

Good old-fashioned wood, good old-fashioned maple. He hurled it
against the wall twice, and it broke. Then he seized one of the legs,
clenched it hard in his fist, his face bursting red, the breath snorting in
his nostrils, his mouth wide. He struck the palm of his hand with the
leg of the chair, testing it. "All right, God damn it, come on!" he cried.
He rushed out, yelling, and slammed the door.

"**W**e all have that special dream when we are young," said Bishop Kelly.

The others at the table murmured, nodded.

"There is no Christian boy," the Bishop continued, "who does not some night wonder: am I Him? Is this the Second Coming at long last, and am I It? What, what, oh, what, dear God, if I *were* Jesus? How grand!"

The Priests, the Ministers, and the one lonely Rabbi laughed gently, remembering things from their own childhoods, their own wild dreams, and being great fools.

"I suppose," said the young Priest, Father Niven, "that Jewish boys imagine themselves Moses?"

"No, no, my dear friend," said Rabbi Nittler. "The Messiah! The *Messiah!*"

More quiet laughter, from all.

"Of course," said Father Niven out of his fresh pink-and-cream face, "how stupid of me. Christ *wasn't* the Messiah, was he? And your people are still waiting for Him to arrive. Strange. Oh, the ambiguities."

"And nothing more ambiguous than this." Bishop Kelly rose to escort them all out onto a terrace which had a view of the Martian hills, the ancient Martian towns, the old highways, the rivers of dust, and Earth, sixty million miles away, shining with a clear light in this alien sky.

"Did we ever in our wildest dreams," said the Reverend Smith, "imagine that one day each of us would have a Baptist Church, a St. Mary's Chapel, a Mount Sinai Synagogue here, here on Mars?"

The answer was no, no, softly, from them all.

Their quiet was interrupted by another voice which moved among them. Father Niven, as they stood at the balustrade, had tuned his transistor radio to check the hour. News was being broadcast from the small new American-Martian wilderness colony below. They listened:

"—rumored near the town. This is the first Martian reported in our community this year. Citizens are urged to respect any such visitor. If—" Father Niven shut the news off.

"Our elusive congregation," sighed the Reverend Smith. "I must confess, I came to Mars not only to work with Christians, but hoping to invite *one* Martian to Sunday supper, to learn of his theologies, *his* needs."

"We are still too new to them," said Father Lipscomb. "In another year or so I think they will understand we're not buffalo hunters in search of pelts. Still, it *is* hard to keep one's curiosity in hand. After all, our *Mariner* photographs indicated no life whatsoever here. Yet life there is, very mysterious and half-resembling the human."

"Half, Your Eminence?" The Rabbi mused over his coffee. "I feel they are even more human than ourselves. They have *let* us come in. They have hidden in the hills, coming among us only on occasion, we guess, disguised as Earthmen—"

"Do you really believe they have telepathic powers, then, and hypnotic abilities which allow them to walk in our towns, fooling us with masks and visions, and none of us the wiser?"

"I do so believe."

"Then this," said the Bishop, handing around brandies and crème-dementhes, "is a true evening of frustrations. Martians who will not reveal themselves so as to be Saved by Us the Enlightened—"

Many smiles at this.

"—and Second Comings of Christ delayed for several thousand years. How long must we wait, O Lord?"

"As for myself," said young Father Niven, "I never wished to *be* Christ, the Second Coming. I just always wanted, with all my heart, to *meet* Him. Ever since I was eight I have thought on that. It might well be the first reason I became a priest."

"To have the inside track just in case He ever *did* arrive again?" suggested the Rabbi, kindly.

The young Priest grinned and nodded. The others felt the urge to reach and touch him, for he had touched some vague small sweet nerve in each. They felt immensely gentle.

"With your permission, Rabbi, gentlemen," said Bishop Kelly, raising his glass. "To the First Coming of the Messiah, or the Second Coming of Christ. May they be more than some ancient, some foolish dreams."

They drank and were quiet.

The Bishop blew his nose and wiped his eyes.

The rest of the evening was like many another for the Priests, the Reverends, and the Rabbi. They fell to playing cards and arguing St. Thomas

Aquinas, but failed under the onslaught of Rabbi Nittler's educated logic. They named him Jesuit, drank nightcaps, and listened to the late radio news:

"—it is feared this Martian may feel trapped in our community. Anyone meeting him should turn away, so as to let the Martian pass. Curiosity seems his motive. No cause for alarm. That concludes our—"

While heading for the door, the Priests, Ministers, and Rabbi discussed translations they had made into various tongues from Old and New Testaments. It was then that young Father Niven surprised them:

"Did you know I was once asked to write a screenplay on the Gospels? They needed an *ending* for their film!"

"Surely," protested the Bishop, "there's only *one* ending to Christ's life?"

"But, Your Holiness, the Four Gospels tell it with four variations. I compared. I grew excited. Why? Because I rediscovered something I had almost forgotten. The Last Supper isn't really the Last Supper!"

"Dear me, what is it then?"

"Why, Your Holiness, the first of several, sir. The first of several! After the Crucifixion and Burial of Christ, did not Simon-called-Peter, with the Disciples, fish the Sea of Galilee?"

"They did."

"And their nets were filled with a miracle of fish?"

"They were."

"And seeing on the shore of Galilee a pale light, did they not land and approach what seemed a bed of white-hot coals on which fresh-caught fish were baking?"

"Yes, ah, yes," said the Reverend Smith.

"And there beyond the glow of the soft charcoal fire, did they not sense a Spirit Presence and call out to it?"

"They did."

"Getting no answer, did not Simon-called-Peter whisper again, 'Who is there?' And the unrecognized Ghost upon the shore of Galilee put out its hand into the firelight, and in the palm of that hand, did they not see the mark where the nail had gone in, the stigmata that would never heal?

"They would have fled, but the Ghost spoke and said, 'Take of these fish and feed thy brethren.' And Simon-called-Peter took the fish that baked upon the white-hot coals and fed the Disciples. And Christ's frail Ghost then said, 'Take of my word and tell it among the nations of all the world and preach therein forgiveness of sin.'

"And then Christ left them. And, in my screenplay, I had Him walk along the shore of Galilee toward the horizon. And when anyone walks toward the horizon, he seems to ascend, yes? For all land rises at a distance. And He walked on along the shore until He was just a small mote, far away. And then they could see Him no more.

"And as the sun rose upon the ancient world, all His thousand footprints that lay along the shore blew away in the dawn winds and were as nothing.

"And the Disciples left the ashes of that bed of coals to scatter in sparks, and with the taste of Real and Final and True Last Supper upon their mouths, went away. And in my screenplay, I had my CAMERA drift high above to watch the Disciples move some north, some south, some to the east, to tell the world what Needed to Be Told about One Man. And their footprints, circling in all directions, like the spokes of an immense wheel, blew away out of the sand in the winds of morn. And it was a new day. THE END."

The young Priest stood in the center of his friends, cheeks fired with color, eyes shut. Suddenly he opened his eyes, as if remembering where he was:

"Sorry."

"For what?" cried the Bishop, brushing his eyelids with the back of his hand, blinking rapidly. "For making me weep twice in one night? What, self-conscious in the presence of your own love for Christ? Why, you have given the Word back to me, *me!* who has known the Word for what seems a thousand years! You have freshened my soul, oh good young man with the heart of a boy. The eating of fish on Galilee's shore *is* the True Last Supper. Bravo. You deserve to meet Him. The Second Coming, it's only fair, must be for you!"

"I am unworthy!" said Father Niven.

"So are we all! But if a trade of souls were possible, I'd loan mine out on this instant to borrow yours fresh from the laundry. Another toast, gentlemen? To Father Niven! And then, good night, it's late, good night."

The toast was drunk and all departed; the Rabbi and the Ministers down the hill to their holy places, leaving the Priests to stand a last moment at their door looking out at Mars, this strange world, and a cold wind blowing.

Midnight came and then one and two, and at three in the cold deep morning of Mars, Father Niven stirred. Candles flickered in soft whispers. Leaves fluttered against his window.

Suddenly he sat up in bed, half-startled by a dream of mob-cries and pursuits. He listened.

Far away, below, he heard the shutting of an outside door.

Throwing on a robe, Father Niven went down the dim rectory stairs and through the church where a dozen candles here or there kept their own pools of light.

He made the rounds of all the doors, thinking: Silly, why lock churches? What is there to steal? But still he prowled the sleeping night . . .

. . . and found the front door of the church unlocked, and softly being pushed in by the wind.

Shivering, he shut the door.

Soft running footsteps.

He spun about.

The church lay empty. The candle flames leaned now this way, now that in their shrines. There was only the ancient smell of wax and incense burning, stuffs left over from all the marketplaces of time and history; other suns, and other noons.

In the midst of glancing at the crucifix above the main altar, he froze.

There was a sound of a single drop of water falling in the night.

Slowly he turned to look at the baptistery in the back of the church.

There were no candles there, yet—

A pale light shone from that small recess where stood the baptismal font.

"Bishop Kelly?" he called, softly.

Walking slowly up the aisle, he grew very cold, and stopped because—

Another drop of water had fallen, hit, dissolved away.

It was like a faucet dripping somewhere. But there were no faucets. Only the baptismal font itself, into which, drop by drop, a slow liquid was falling, with three heartbeats between each sound.

At some secret level, Father Niven's heart told itself something and raced, then slowed and almost stopped. He broke into a wild perspiration. He found himself unable to move, but move he must, one foot after the other, until he reached the arched doorway of the baptistery.

There was indeed a pale light within the darkness of the small place. No, not a light. A shape. A figure.

The figure stood behind and beyond the baptismal font. The sound of falling water had stopped.

His tongue locked in his mouth, his eyes flexed wide in a kind of madness, Father Niven felt himself struck blind. Then vision returned, and he dared cry out:

"Who!"

A single word, which echoed back from all around the church, which made candle flames flutter in reverberation, which stirred the dust of incense, which frightened his own heart with its swift return in saying: Who!

The only light within the baptistery came from the pale garments of the figure that stood there facing him. And this light was enough to show him an incredible thing.

As Father Niven watched, the figure moved. It put a pale hand out upon the baptistery air.

The hand hung there as if not wanting to, a separate thing from the Ghost beyond, as if it were seized and pulled forward, resisting, by Father Niven's dreadful and fascinated stare to reveal what lay in the center of its open white palm.

There was fixed a jagged hole, a cincture from which, slowly, one by one, blood was dripping, falling away down and slowly down, into the baptismal font.

The drops of blood struck the holy water, colored it, and dissolved in slow ripples.

The hand remained for a stunned moment there before the Priest's now-blind, now-seeing eyes.

As if struck a terrible blow, the Priest collapsed to his knees with an outgasped cry, half of despair, half of revelation, one hand over his eyes, the other fending off the vision.

"No, no, no, no, no, no, no, it *can't!*"

It was as if some dreadful physician of dentistry had come upon him without narcotic and with one seizure entire-extracted his soul, bloodied raw, out of his body. He felt himself prized, his life yanked forth, and the roots, O God, were . . . *deep!*

"No, no, no, no!"

But, yes.

Between the lacings of his fingers, he looked again.

And the Man was there.

And the dreadful bleeding palm quivered dripping upon the baptistery air.

"Enough!"

The palm pulled back, vanished. The Ghost stood waiting.

And the face of the Spirit was good and familiar. Those strange beautiful deep and incisive eyes were as he knew they always must be. There was the gentleness of the mouth, and the paleness framed by the flowing locks of hair and beard. The Man was robed in the simplicity of garments worn upon the shores and in the wilderness near Galilee.

The Priest, by a great effort of will, prevented his tears from spilling over, stopped up his agony of surprise, doubt, shock, these clumsy things which rioted within and threatened to break forth. He trembled.

And then saw that the Figure, the Spirit, the Man, the Ghost, Whatever, was trembling, too.

No, thought the Priest, He can't be! Afraid? Afraid of . . . *me?*

And now the Spirit shook itself with an immense agony not unlike his own, like a mirror image of his own concussion, gaped wide its mouth, shut up its own eyes, and mourned:

"Oh, please, let me go."

At this the young Priest opened his eyes wider and gasped. He thought: But you're free. No one keeps you here!

And in that instant: "Yes!" cried the Vision. "*You* keep me! Please! Avert your gaze! The more you look the more I become *this!* I am *not* what I seem!"

But, thought the Priest, I did not speak! My lips did not move! How does this Ghost know my mind?

"I know all you think," said the Vision, trembling, pale, pulling back in baptistery gloom. "Every sentence, every word. I did not mean to come. I ventured into town. Suddenly I was many things to many people. I ran. They followed. I escaped here. The door was open. I entered. And then and then—oh, and then was trapped."

No, thought the Priest.

"Yes," mourned the Ghost. "By you."

Slowly now, groaning under an even more terrible weight of revelation, the Priest grasped the edge of the font and pulled himself, swaying, to his feet. At last he dared force the question out:

"You are not . . . what you seem?"

"I am not," said the other. "Forgive me."

I, thought the Priest, shall go mad.

"Do not," said the Ghost, "or I shall go down to madness with you."

"I can't give you up, oh, dear God, now that you're here, after all these years, all my dreams, don't you see, it's asking too *much*. Two thousand years, a whole race of people have waited for your return! And I, I am the one who meets you, sees you—"

"You meet only your own dream. You see only your own need. Behind all this—" the figure touched its own robes and breast, "I am another thing."

"What must I *do!*" the Priest burst out, looking now at the heavens, now at the Ghost which shuddered at his cry. "*What?*"

"Avert your gaze. In that moment I will be out the door and gone."

"Just—just like that?"

"Please," said the Man.

The Priest drew a series of breaths, shivering.

"Oh, if this moment could last for just an hour."

"Would you kill me?"

"No!"

"If you keep me, force me into this shape some little while longer, my death will be on your hands."

The Priest bit his knuckles, and felt a convulsion of sorrow rack his bones.

"You—you are a Martian, then?"

"No more. No less."

"And I have done this to you with my thoughts?"

"You did not mean. When you came downstairs, your old dream seized and made me over. My palms still bleed from the wounds you gave out of your secret mind."

The Priest shook his head, dazed.

"Just a moment more . . . wait . . ."

He gazed steadily, hungrily, at the darkness where the Ghost stood out of the light. That face was beautiful. And, oh, those hands were loving and beyond all description.

The Priest nodded, a sadness in him now as if he had within the hour come back from the true Calvary. And the hour was gone. And the coals strewn dying on the sand near Galilee.

"If—if I let you go—"

"You must, oh you must!"

"If I let you go, will you promise—"

"What?"

"Will you promise to come back?"

"Come back?" cried the figure in the darkness.

"Once a year, that's all I ask, come back once a year, here to this place, this font, at the same time of night—"

"Come back . . .?"

"Promise! Oh, I must know this moment again. You don't know how important it is! Promise, or I won't let you go!"

"I—"

"Say it! Swear it!"

"I promise," said the pale Ghost in the dark. "I swear."

"Thank you, oh thanks."

"On what day a year from now must I return?"

The tears had begun to roll down the young Priest's face now. He could hardly remember what he wanted to say and when he said it he could hardly hear:

"Easter, oh, God, yes, Easter, a year from now!"

"Please, don't weep," said the figure. "I will come. Easter, you say? I know your calendar. Yes. Now—" The pale wounded hand moved in the air, softly pleading. "May I go?"

The Priest ground his teeth to keep the cries of woe from exploding forth. "Bless me, and go."

"Like this?" said the voice.

And the hand came out to touch him ever so quietly.

"Quick!" cried the Priest, eyes shut, clenching his fists hard against his ribs to prevent his reaching out to seize. "Go before I keep you forever. Run. Run!"

The pale hand touched him a last time upon his brow. There was a soft run of naked feet.

A door opened upon stars; the door slammed.

There was a long moment when the echo of the slam made its way through the church, to every altar, into every alcove and up like a blind flight of some single bird seeking and finding release in the apse. The church stopped trembling at last, and the Priest laid his hands on himself as if to tell himself how to behave, how to breathe again; be still, be calm, stand tall. . . .

Finally, he stumbled to the door and held to it, wanting to throw it wide, look out at the road which must be empty now, with perhaps a figure in white, far fleeing. He did not open the door.

He went about the church, glad for things to do, finishing out the ritual of locking up. It was a long way around to all the doors. It was a long way to next Easter.

He paused at the font and saw the clear water with no trace of red. He dipped his hand and cooled his brow and temples and cheeks and eyelids.

Then he went slowly up the aisle and laid himself out before the altar and let himself burst forth and really weep. He heard the sound of his sadness go up and come back in agonies from the tower where the bell hung silent.

And he wept for many reasons.

For himself.

For the Man who had been here a moment ago.

For the long time until the rock was rolled back and the tomb found empty again.

Until Simon-Called-Peter once more saw the Ghost upon the Martian shore, and himself Simon-Peter.

And most of all he wept because, oh, because, because . . . never in his life could he speak of this night to anyone. . . .

"**C**harlie! Where you going?"

Members of the rocket crew, passing, called.

Charles Willis did not answer.

He took the vacuum tube down through the friendly humming bowels of the spaceship. He fell, thinking: This is the grand hour.

"Chuck! Where traveling?" someone called.

To meet someone dead but alive, cold but warm, forever untouchable but reaching out somehow to touch.

"Idiot! Fool!"

The voice echoed. He smiled.

Then he saw Clive, his best friend, drifting up in the opposite chute. He averted his gaze, but Clive sang out through his seashell ear-pack radio:

"I want to see you!"

"Later!" Willis said.

"I *know* where you're going. Stupid!"

And Clive was gone up away while Willis fell softly down, his hands trembling.

His boots touched surface. On the instant he suffered renewed delight.

He walked down through the hidden machineries of the rocket. Lord, he thought, crazy. Here we are one hundred days gone away from the Earth in Space, and, this very hour, most of the crew, in fever, dialing their aphrodisiac animatronic devices that touched and hummed to them in their shut clamshell beds. While, what do *I* do? he thought. *This.*

He moved to peer into a small storage pit.

There, in an eternal dusk, sat the old man.

"Sir," he said, and waited.

"Shaw," he whispered. "Oh, Mr. George Bernard Shaw."

The old man's eyes sprang wide as if he had swallowed an Idea.

He seized his bony knees and gave a sharp cry of laughter.

"By God, I *do* accept it *all!*"

"Accept *what,* Mr. Shaw?"

Mr. Shaw flashed his bright blue gaze upon Charles Willis.

"The Universe! *It* thinks, therefore I *am!* So I had *best* accept, eh? Sit."

Willis sat in the shadowed areaway, clasping his knees and his own warm delight with being here again.

"Shall I read your mind, young Willis, and tell you what you've been up to since last we conversed?"

"*Can* you read minds, Mr. Shaw?"

"No, thank God. Wouldn't it be awful if I were not only the cunei-form-tablet robot of George Bernard Shaw, but could also scan your head-bumps and spell your dreams? Unbearable."

"You already *are,* Mr. Shaw."

"*Touché!* Well, now." The old man raked his reddish beard with his thin fingers, then poked Willis gently in the ribs. "How is it you are the only one aboard this starship who ever visits me?"

"Well, sir, you see—"

The young man's cheeks burnt themselves to full blossom.

"Ah, yes, I do see," said Shaw. "Up through the honeycomb of the ship, all the happy male bees in their hives with their syrupy wind-up soft-singing nimble-nibbling toys, their bright female puppets."

"Mostly *dumb.*"

"Ah, well. It was not always thus. On my last trip the Captain wished to play Scrabble using only names of characters, concepts and ideas from my plays. Now, strange boy, why do *you* squat here with this hideous old ego? Have you no need for that soft and gentle company abovestairs?"

"It's a long journey, Mr. Shaw, two years out beyond Pluto and back. Plenty of time for abovestairs company. Never enough for this. I have the dreams of a goat but the genetics of a saint."

"Well said!" The old man sprang lightly to his feet and paced about, pointing his beard now toward Alpha Centauri, now toward the nebula in Orion.

"How runs our menu today, Willis? Shall I preface Saint Joan for your? Or . . . ?"

"Chuck . . . ?"

Willis's head jerked. His seashell radio whispered in his ear. "Willis! Clive calling. You're late for dinner. I know where you are. I'm coming down. Chuck—"

Willis thumped his ear. The voice cut off.

"Quick, Mr. Shaw! Can you—well—*run?*"

"Can Icarus fall from the sun? Jump! I shall pace you with these spindly cricket legs!"

They ran.

Taking the corkscrew staircase instead of the air-tube, they looked back from the top platform in time to see Clive's shadow dart into that tomb where Shaw had died but to wake again.

"Willis!" cried his voice.

"To hell with him," said Willis.

Shaw beamed. "Hell? I know it well. Come. I'll show you around!"

Laughing, they jumped into the feather-tube and fell *up*.

This was the place of stars.

Which is to say the one place in all the ship where, if one wished, one could come and truly look at the Universe and the billion billion stars which poured across it and never stopped pouring, cream from the mad dairies of the gods. Delicious frights or outcrops, on the other hand, if you thought it so, from the sickness of Lord God Jehovah turned in his sleep, upset with Creation, and birthing dinosaur worlds spun about satanic suns.

"It's all in the thinking," observed Mr. Shaw, sidling his eyes at his young consort.

"Mr. Shaw! You *can* read minds?"

"Poppycock. I merely read faces. Yours is clear glass. I glanced just now and saw Job afflicted, Moses and the Burning Bush. Come. Let us look at the Deeps and see what God has been up to in the ten billion years since He collided with Himself and procreated Vastness."

They stood now, surveying the Universe, counting the stars to a billion and beyond.

"Oh," moaned the young man, suddenly, and tears fell from his eyes. "How I wish I had been alive when you were alive, sir. How I wish I had *truly* known you."

"*This* Shaw is best," retorted the old man, "all of the mince-meat and none of the tin. The coattails are better than the man. Hang to them and survive."

Space lay all about, as vast as God's first thought, as deep as His primal breathing.

They stood, one of them tall, one short, by the scanning window, with a fine view of the great Andromeda Nebula whenever they wished to focus it near with a touch of the button which made the Eye magnify and suck things close.

After a long monument of drinking stars, the young man let out his breath.

"Mr. Shaw . . . ? *Say* it. You know what I like to hear."

"Do I, my boy?" Mr. Shaw's eyes twinkled.

All of Space was around them, all of the Universe, all of the night of the celestial Being, all the stars and all the places between the stars, and the ship moving on its silent course, and the crew of the ship busy at work or games or touching their amorous toys, so these two were alone with their talk, these two stood viewing the Mystery and saying what must be said.

"Say it, Mr. Shaw."

"Well, now . . ."

Mr. Shaw fixed his eyes on a star some twenty light-years away.

"What *are* we?" he asked. "Why, we are the miracle of force and matter making itself over into imagination and will. Incredible. The Life Force experimenting with forms. You for one. Me for another. The Universe has shouted itself alive. We are one of the shouts. Creation turns in its abyss. We have bothered it, dreaming ourselves to shapes. The void is filled with slumbers; ten billion on a billion on a billion bombardments of light and material that know not themselves, that sleep moving and move but finally to make an eye and waken on themselves. Among so much that is flight and ignorance, we are the blind force that gropes like Lazarus from a billion-light-year tomb. We summon ourselves. We say, O Lazarus Life Force, truly come ye forth. So the Universe, a motion of deaths, fumbles to reach across Time to feel its own flesh and know it to be ours. We touch both ways and find each other miraculous because we are One."

Mr. Shaw turned to glance at his young friend.

"There you have it. Satisfied?"

"Oh, yes! I—"

The young man stopped.

Behind them, in the viewing-cabin door, stood Clive. Beyond him, they could hear music pulsing from the far cubicles where crewmen and their huge toys played at amorous games.

"Well," said Clive, "what goes on—?"

"Here?" interjected Shaw, lightly. "Why, only the confounding of two energies making do with puzzlements. This contraption—" he touched his own breast, "speaks from computerized elations. That genetic conglomeration—" he nodded at his young friend, "responds with raw, beloved, and true emotions. The sum of us? Pandemonium spread on biscuits and devoured at high tea."

Clive swiveled his gaze to Willis.

"Damn, you're nuts. At dinner you should have *heard* the laughter! You and this old man, and just talk! they said. Just talk, talk! Look, idiot, it's your stand-watch in ten minutes. Be there! God!"

And the door was empty. Clive was gone.

Silently, Willis and Mr. Shaw floated down the drop-tube to the storage pit beneath the vast machineries.

The old man sat once again on the floor.

"Mr. Shaw." Willis shook his head, snorting softly. "Hell. Why is it you seem more alive to me than anyone I have ever known?"

"Why, my dear young friend," replied the old man, gently, "what you warm your hands at are Ideas, eh? I am a walking monument of concepts, scrimshaws of thought, electric deliriums of philosophy and wonder. You love concepts. I am their receptacle. You love dreams in motion. I move. You love palaver and jabber. I am the consummate palaverer and jabberer. You and I, together, masticate Alpha Centauri and spit forth universal myths. We chew upon the tail of Halley's Comet and worry the Horsehead Nebula until it cries a monstrous Uncle and gives over to our creation. You love libraries. I am a library. Tickle my ribs and I vomit forth Melville's Whale, Spirit Spout and all. Tic my ear and I'll build Plato's Republic with my tongue for you to run and live in. You love Toys. I am a Toy, a fabulous plaything, a computerized—"

"—friend," said Willis, quietly.

Mr. Shaw gave him a look less of fire than of hearth.

"Friend," he said.

Willis turned to leave, then stopped to gaze back at that strange old figure propped against the dark storage wall.

"I—I'm afraid to go. I have this fear something may *happen* to you."

"I shall survive," replied Shaw tartly, "but only if you warn your Captain that a vast meteor shower approaches. He must shift course a few hundred thousand miles. Done?"

"Done." But still Willis did not leave.

"Mr. Shaw," he said, at last. "What . . . what do you *do* while the rest of us sleep?"

"Do? Why, bless you. I listen to my tuning fork. Then, I write symphonies between my ears."

Willis was gone.

In the dark, alone, the old man bent his head. A soft hive of dark bees began to hum under his honey-sweet breath.

Four hours later, Willis, off watch, crept into his sleep-cubicle.

In half-light, the mouth was waiting for him.

Clive's mouth. It licked its lips and whispered:

"Everyone's talking. About you making an ass out of yourself visiting a two-hundred-year-old intellectual relic, you, you, you. Jesus, the psycho-med'll be out tomorrow to X-ray your stupid skull!"

"Better that than what you men do all night every night," said Willis.

"What we do is us."

"Then why not let me be *me?*"

"Because it's unnatural." The tongue licked and darted. "We all *miss* you. Tonight we piled all the grand toys in the midst of the wild room and—"

"I don't want to hear it!"

"Well, then," said the mouth, "I might just trot down and tell all this to your old gentleman friend—"

"Don't go *near* him!"

"I might." The lips moved in the shadows. "You can't stand guard on him forever. Some night soon, when you're asleep, someone might— tamper with him, eh? Scramble his electronic eggs so he'll talk vaudeville instead of *Saint Joan?* Ha, yes. Think. Long journey. Crew's bored. Practical joke like that, worth a million to see you froth. Beware, Charlie. Best come play with us."

Willis, eyes shut, let the blaze out of him.

"Whoever dares to touch Mr. Shaw, so help me God, I'll kill!"

He turned violently on his side, gnawing the back of his fist.

In the half-dark, he could sense Clive's mouth still moving.

"Kill? Well, well. Pity. Sweet dreams."

An hour later, Willis gulped two pills and fell stunned into sleep.

In the middle of the night he dreamed that they were burning good Saint Joan at the stake and, in the midst of burning, the plain-potato maiden turned to an old man stoically wrapped around with ropes and vines. The old man's beard was fiery red even before the names reached it, and his bright blue eyes were fixed fiercely upon Eternity, ignoring the fire.

"Recant!" cried a voice. "Confess and recant! Recant!"

"There is nothing to confess, therefore no need for recantation," said the old man quietly.

The flames leaped up his body like a mob of insane and burning mice.

"Mr. Shaw!" screamed Willis.

He sprang awake.

Mr. Shaw.

The cabin was silent. Clive lay asleep.

On his face was a smile.

The smile made Willis pull back, with a cry. He dressed. He ran.

Like a leaf in autumn he fell down the air-tube, growing older and heavier with each long instant.

The storage pit where the old man "slept" was much more quiet than it had a right to be.

Willis bent. His hand trembled. At last, he touched the old man.

"Sir—?"

There was no motion. The beard did not bristle. Nor the eyes fire themselves to blue flames. Nor the mouth tremble with gentle blasphemies . . .

"Oh, Mr. Shaw," he said. "Are you dead, then, oh God, are you really dead?"

The old man was what they called dead when a machine no longer spoke or tuned an electric thought or moved. His dreams and philosophies were snow in his shut mouth.

Willis turned the body this way and that, looking for some cut, wound, or bruise on the skin.

He thought of the years ahead, the long traveling years and no Mr. Shaw to walk with, gibber with, laugh with. Women in the storage shelves, yes, women in the cots late at night, laughing their strange taped laughters and moving their strange machined motions, and saying the same dumb things that were said on a thousand worlds on a thousand nights.

"Oh, Mr. Shaw," he murmured at last. "Who *did* this to you?"

Silly boy, whispered Mr. Shaw's memory voice. You *know*.

I know, thought Willis.

He whispered a name and ran away.

"Damn you, you killed him!"

Willis seized Clive's bedclothes, at which instant Clive, like a robot, popped wide his eyes. The smile remained constant.

"You can't kill what was never alive," he said.

"Son of a bitch!"

He struck Clive once in the mouth, after which Clive was on his feet, laughing in some strange wild way, wiping blood from his lips.

"What did you do to him?" cried Willis.

"Not much, just—"

But that was the end of their conversation.

"On posts!" a voice cried. "Collision course!"

Bells rang. Sirens shrieked.

In the midst of their shared rage, Willis and Clive turned cursing to seize emergency spacesuits and helmets off the cabin walls.

"Damn, oh, damn, oh—d—"

Half-through his last damn, Clive gasped. He vanished out a sudden hole in the side of the rocket.

The meteor had come and gone in a billionth of a second. On its way out, it had taken all the air in the ship with it through a hole the size of a small car.

My God, thought Willis, he's gone forever.

What saved Willis was a ladder he stood near, against which the swift river of air crushed him on its way into Space. For a moment he could not move or breathe. Then the suction was finished, all the air in the ship gone. There was only time to adjust the pressure in his suit and helmet, and glance wildly around at the veering ship which was being bombarded now as in a space war. Men ran, or rather floated, shouting wildly, everywhere,

Shaw, thought Willis unreasonably, and had to laugh. Shaw.

A final meteor in a tribe of meteors struck the motor section of the rocket and blew the entire ship apart. Shaw, Shaw, oh, Shaw, thought Willis.

He saw the rocket fly apart like a shredded balloon, all its gases only impelling it to more disintegration. With the bits and pieces went wild crowds of men, dismissed from school, from life, from all and everything, never to meet face to face again, not even to say farewell, the dismissal was so abrupt and their deaths and isolation such a swift surprise.

Good-bye, thought Willis.

But there was no true good-bye. He could hear no weeping and no laments over his radio. Of all the crew, he was the last and final and only one alive, because of his suit, his helmet, his oxygen, miraculously spared. For what? To be alone and fall?

To be alone. To fall.

Oh, Mr. Shaw, oh, sir, he thought.

"No sooner called than delivered," whispered a voice.

It was impossible, but . . .

Drifting, spinning, the ancient doll with the wild red beard and blazing blue eyes fell across darkness as if impelled by God's breath, on a whim.

Instinctively, Willis opened his arms.

And the old party landed there, smiling, breathing heavily, or pretending to breathe heavily, as was his bent.

"Well, well, Willis! Quite a treat, eh?"

"Mr. Shaw! You were *dead!*"

"Poppycock! Someone bent some wires in me. The collision knocked things back together. The disconnection is here below my chin. A villain cut me there. So if I fall dead again, jiggle under my jaw and wire me up, eh?"

"Yes, sir!"

"How much food do you carry at this moment, Willis?"

"Enough to last two hundred days in Space."

"Dear me, that's fine, fine! And self-recycling oxygen units, also, for two hundred days?"

"Yes, sir. Now, how long will *your* batteries last, Mr. Shaw?"

"Ten thousand years!" the old man sang out happily. "Yes, I vow, I swear! I am fitted with solar-cells which will collect God's universal light until I wear out my circuits."

"Which means you will outtalk me, Mr. Shaw, long after I have stopped eating and breathing."

"At which point you must dine on conversation, and breathe past participles instead of air. But, we must hold the thought of rescue uppermost. Are not the chances good?"

"Rockets *do* come by. And I am equipped with radio signals—"

"Which even now cry out into the deep night: I'm here with ramshackle Shaw, eh?"

I'm here with ramshackle Shaw, thought Willis, and was suddenly warm in winter.

"Well, then, while we're waiting to be rescued, Charles Willis, what next?"

"Next? Why—"

They fell away down Space alone but not alone, fearful but elated, and now grown suddenly quiet.

"*Say* it, Mr. Shaw."

"Say what?"

"You know. Say it again."

"Well, then." They spun lazily, holding to each other. "Isn't life miraculous? Matter and force, yes, matter and force making itself over into intelligence and will."

"Is *that* what we are, sir?"

"We are, bet ten thousand bright tin-whistles on it, we are. Shall I say *more,* young Willis?"

"Please, sir," laughed Willis. "I want some more!"

And the old man spoke and the young man listened and the young man spoke and the old man hooted and they fell around a corner of Universe away out of sight, eating and talking, talking and eating, the young man biting gumball foods, the old man devouring sunlight with his solar-cell eyes, and the last that was seen of them they were gesticulating and babbling and conversing and waving their hands until their voices faded into Time and the solar system turned over in its sleep and covered them with a blanket of dark and light, and whether or not a rescue ship named Rachel, seeking her lost children, ever came by and found them, who can tell, who would truly ever want to know?

It was such an utterly perfect, such an incredibly delightful idea for murder, that I was half out of my mind all across America.

The idea had come to me for some reason on my forty-eighth birthday. Why it hadn't come to me when I was thirty or forty, I cannot say. Perhaps those were good years and I sailed through them unaware of time and clocks and the gathering of frost at my temples or the look of the lion about my eyes. . . .

Anyway, on my forty-eighth birthday, lying in bed that night beside my wife, with my children sleeping through all the other quiet moonlit rooms of my house, I thought:

I will arise and go now and kill Ralph Underhill.

Ralph Underhill! I cried, who in God's name is *he?*

Thirty-six years later, kill him? For *what?*

Why, I thought, for what he did to me when I was twelve.

My wife woke, an hour later, hearing a noise.

"Doug?" she called. "What are you doing?"

"Packing," I said. "For a journey."

"Oh," she murmured, and rolled over and went to sleep.

"Board! All aboard!!" the porter's cries went down the train platform.

The train shuddered and banged.

"See you!" I cried, leaping up the steps.

"Someday," called my wife, "I wish you'd *fly!*"

Fly? I thought, and spoil thinking about murder all across the plains? Spoil oiling the pistol and loading it and thinking of Ralph Underhill's face when I show up thirty-six years late to settle old scores? Fly? Why, I would rather pack cross-country on foot, pausing by night to build fires and fry my bile and sour spit and eat again my old, mummified but still-living antagonisms and touch those bruises which have never healed. Fly?!

The train moved. My wife was gone.

I rode off into the Past.

Crossing Kansas the second night, we hit a beaut of a thunderstorm. I stayed up until four in the morning, listening to the rave of winds and thunders. At the height of the storm, I saw my face, a darkroom negative-print on the cold window glass, and thought:

Where is that fool going?

To kill Ralph Underhill!

Why? Because!

Remember how he hit my arm? Bruises. I was covered with bruises, both arms; dark blue, mottled black, strange yellow bruises. Hit and run, that was Ralph, hit and run—

And yet . . . you loved him?

Yes, as boys love boys when boys are eight, ten, twelve, and the world is innocent and boys are evil beyond evil because they know not what they do, but do it anyway. So, on some secret level, I *had* to be hurt. We dear fine friends needed each other. I to be hit. He to strike. My scars were the emblem and symbol of our love.

What else makes you want to murder Ralph so late in time?

The train whistle shrieked. Night country rolled by.

And I recalled one spring when I came to school in a new tweed knicker suit and Ralph knocking me down, rolling me in snow and fresh brown mud. And Ralph laughing and me going home, shame-faced, covered with slime, afraid of a beating, to put on fresh dry clothes.

Yes! And what *else?*

Remember those toy clay statues you longed to collect from the Tarzan radio show? Statues of Tarzan and Kala the Ape and Numa the Lion, for just twenty-five cents?! Yes, yes! Beautiful! Even now, in memory, O the sound of the Ape man swinging through green jungles far away, ululating! But who had twenty-five cents in the middle of the Great Depression? No one.

Except Ralph Underhill.

And one day Ralph asked you if you wanted one of the statues.

Wanted! you cried. Yes! Yes!

That was the same week your brother in a strange seizure of love mixed with contempt gave you his old, but expensive, baseball-catcher's mitt.

"Well," said Ralph, "I'll give you my extra Tarzan statue if you'll give me that catcher's mitt."

Fool! I thought. The statue's worth twenty-five cents. The glove cost two dollars! No fair! Don't!

But I raced back to Ralph's house with the glove and gave it to him and he, smiling a worse contempt than my brother's, handed me the Tarzan statue and, bursting with joy, I ran home.

My brother didn't find out about his catcher's mitt and the statue for two weeks, and when he did he ditched me when we hiked out in farm country and left me lost because I was such a sap. "Tarzan statues! Baseball mitts!" he cried. "That's the last thing I *ever* give you!"

And somewhere on a country road I just lay down and wept and wanted to die but didn't know how to give up the final vomit that was my miserable ghost.

The thunder murmured.

The rain fell on the cold Pullman-car windows.

What *else?* Is that the list?

No. One final thing, more terrible than all the rest.

In all the years you went to Ralph's house to toss up small bits of gravel on his Fourth of July six-in-the-morning fresh dewy window or to call him forth for the arrival of dawn circuses in the cold fresh blue railroad stations in late June or late August, in all those years, never once did Ralph run to your house.

Never once in all the years did he, or anyone else, prove their friendship by coming by. The door never knocked. The window of your bedroom never faintly clattered and belled with a high-tossed confetti of small dusts and rocks.

And you always knew that the day you stopped going to Ralph's house, calling up in the morn, that would be the day your friendship ended.

You tested it once. You stayed away for a whole week. Ralph never called. It was as if you had died, and no one came to your funeral.

When you saw Ralph at school, there was no surprise, no query, not even the faintest lint of curiosity to be picked off your coat. Where *were* you, Doug? I need someone to beat. Where you *been,* Doug, I got no one to *pinch!*

Add all the sins up. But especially think on the last:

He never came to my house. He never sang up to my early-morning bed or tossed a wedding rice of gravel on the clear panes to call me down to joy and summer days.

And for this last thing, Ralph Underhill, I thought, sitting in the train at four in the morning, as the storm faded, and I found tears in my eyes, for this last and final thing, for that I shall kill you tomorrow night.

Murder, I thought, after thirty-six years. Why, God, you're madder than Ahab.

The train wailed. We ran cross-country like a mechanical Greek Fate carried by a black metal Roman Fury.

*   *   *

They say you can't go home again.

That is a lie.

If you are lucky and time it right, you arrive at sunset when the old town is filled with yellow light.

I got off the train and walked up through Green Town and looked at the courthouse, burning with sunset light. Every tree was hung with gold doubloons of color. Every roof and coping and bit of gingerbread was purest brass and ancient gold.

I sat in the courthouse square with dogs and old men until the sun had set and Green Town was dark. I wanted to savor Ralph Underhill's death.

No one in history had ever done a crime like this.

I would stay, kill, depart, a stranger among strangers.

How would anyone dare to say, finding Ralph Underhill's body on his doorstep, that a boy aged twelve, arriving on a kind of Time Machine train, traveled out of hideous self-contempt, had gunned down the Past? It was beyond all reason. I was safe in my pure insanity.

Finally, at eight-thirty on this cool October night, I walked across town, past the ravine.

I never doubted Ralph would still be there.

People do, after all, move away. . . .

I turned down Park Street and walked two hundred yards to a single streetlamp and looked across. Ralph Underhill's white two-story Victorian house waited for me.

And I could feel him *in* it.

He was there, forty-eight years old, even as I felt myself here, forty-eight, and full of an old and tired and self-devouring spirit.

I stepped out of the light, opened my suitcase, put the pistol in my right-hand coat pocket, shut the case, and hid it in the bushes where, later, I would grab it and walk down into the ravine and across town to the train.

I walked across the street and stood before his house and it was the same house I had stood before thirty-six years ago. There were the windows upon which I had hurled those spring bouquets of rock in love and total giving. There were the sidewalks, spotted with firecracker burn marks from ancient July Fourths when Ralph and I had just blown up the whole damned world, shrieking celebrations.

I walked up on the porch and saw on the mailbox in small letters: UNDERHILL.

What if his wife answers?

No, I thought, he himself, with absolute Greek-tragic perfection, will open the door and take the wound and almost gladly die for old crimes and minor sins somehow grown to crimes.

I rang the bell.

Will he know me, I wondered, after all this time? In the instant before the first shot, *tell* him your name. He must know who it is.

Silence.

I rang the bell again.

The doorknob rattled.

I touched the pistol in my pocket, my heart hammering, but did not take it out.

The door opened.

Ralph Underhill stood there.

He blinked, gazing out at me.

"Ralph?" I said.

"Yes—?" he said.

We stood there, riven, for what could not have been more than five seconds. But, O Christ, many things happened in those five swift seconds.

I saw Ralph Underhill.

I saw him clearly.

And I had not seem him since I was twelve.

Then, he had towered over me to pummel and beat and scream.

Now he was a little old man.

I am five foot eleven.

But Ralph Underhill had not grown much from his twelfth year on.

The man who stood before me was no more than five feet two inches tall.

I *towered* over him.

I gasped. I stared. I saw more.

I was forty-eight years old.

But Ralph Underhill, forty-eight, had lost most of his hair, and what remained was threadbare gray, black and white. He looked sixty or sixty-five.

I was in good health.

Ralph Underhill was waxen pale. There was a knowledge of sickness in his face. He had traveled in some sunless land. He had a ravaged and sunken look. His breath smelled of funeral flowers.

All this, perceived, was like the storm of the night before, gathering all its lightnings and thunders into one bright concussion. We stood in the explosion.

So this is what I came for? I thought. This, then, is the truth. This dreadful instant in time. Not to pull out the weapon. *Not* to kill. No, no. But simply—

To see Ralph Underhill as he *is* in this hour.

That's all.

Just to be here, stand here, and look at him as he has become.

Ralph Underhill lifted one hand in a kind of gesturing wonder. His lips trembled. His eyes flew up and down my body, his mind measured this giant who shadowed his door. At last his voice, so small, so frail, blurted out:

"Doug—?"

I recoiled.

"Doug?" he gasped, "is that *you?*"

I hadn't expected that. People don't remember! They can't! Across the years? Why would he know, bother, summon up, recognize, call?

I had a wild thought that what had happened to Ralph Underhill was that after I left town, half of his life had collapsed. I had been the center of his world, someone to attack, beat, pummel, bruise. His whole life had cracked by my simple act of walking away thirty-six years ago.

Nonsense! Yet, some small crazed mouse of wisdom scuttered about my brain and screeched what it knew: You needed Ralph, but, *more!* he needed *you!* And you did the only unforgivable, the wounding, thing! You vanished.

"Doug?" he said again, for I was silent there on the porch with my hands at my sides. "Is that you?"

This was the moment I had come for.

At some secret blood level, I had always known I would not use the weapon. I had brought it with me, yes, but Time had gotten here before me, and age, and smaller, more terrible deaths. . . .

Bang.

Six shots through the heart.

But I didn't use the pistol. I only whispered the sound of the shots with my mouth. With each whisper, Ralph Underhill's face aged another ten years. By the time I reached the last shot he was one hundred and ten years old.

"Bang," I whispered. "Bang. Bang. Bang. Bang. Bang."

His body shook with the impact.

"You're dead. Oh, God, Ralph, you're dead."

I turned and walked down the steps and reached the street before he called:

"Doug, is that *you?*"

I did not answer, walking.

"Answer me?" he cried, weakly. "Doug! Doug Spaulding, is that you? Who is that? Who are you?"

I got my suitcase and walked down into the cricket night and darkness of the ravine and across the bridge and up the stairs, going away.

"Who is that?" I heard his voice wail a last time.

A long way off, I looked back.

All the lights were on all over Ralph Underhill's house. It was as if he had gone around and put them all on after I left.

On the other side of the ravine I stopped on the lawn in front of the house where I had been born.

Then I picked up a few bits of gravel and did the thing that had never been done, ever in my life.

I tossed the few bits of gravel up to tap that window where I had lain every morning of my first twelve years. I called my own name. I called me down in friendship to play in some long summer that no longer was.

I stood waiting just long enough for my other young self to come down to join me.

Then swiftly, fleeing ahead of the dawn, we ran out of Green Town and back, thank you, dear Christ, back toward Now and Today for the rest of my life.

"Y ou wish to kill your wife?" said the dark man at the desk.

"Yes. No . . . not exactly. I mean . . ."

"Name?"

"Hers or mine?"

"Yours."

"George Hill."

"Address?"

"Eleven South St. James, Glenview."

The man wrote this down, emotionlessly. "Your wife's name?"

"Katherine."

"Age?"

"Thirty-one."

Then came a swift series of questions. Color of hair, eyes, skin, favorite perfume, texture and size index. "Have you a dimensional photo of her? A tape recording of her voice? Ah, I see you do. Good. Now—"

An hour later, George Hill was perspiring.

"That's all." The dark man arose and scowled. "You still want to go through with it."

"Yes."

"Sign here."

He signed.

"You know this is illegal?"

"Yes."

"And that we're in no way responsible for what happens to you as a result of your request?"

"For God's sake!" cried George. "You've kept me long enough. Let's get on!"

The man smiled faintly. "It'll take nine hours to prepare the marionette of your wife. Sleep awhile, it'll help your nerves. The third mirror room on your left is unoccupied."

George moved in a slow numbness to the mirror room. He lay on the blue velvet cot, his body pressure causing the mirrors in the ceiling to whirl. A soft voice sang, "Sleep . . . sleep . . . sleep . . ."

George murmured, "Katherine, I didn't want to come here. You forced me into it. You made me do it. God, I wish I weren't here. I wish I could go back. I don't want to kill you."

The mirrors glittered as they rotated softly.

He slept:

He dreamed he was forty-one again, he and Katie running on a green hill somewhere with a picnic lunch, their helicopter beside them. The wind blew Katie's hair in golden strands and she was laughing. They kissed and held hands, not eating. They read poems; it seemed they were always reading poems.

Other scenes. Quick changes of color, in flight. He and Katie flying over Greece and Italy and Switzerland, in that clear, long autumn of 1997! Flying and never stopping!

And then—nightmare. Katie and Leonard Phelps. George cried out in his sleep. How had it happened? Where had Phelps sprung from? Why had he interfered? Why couldn't life be simple and good? Was it the difference in age? George touching fifty, and Katie so young, so very young. Why, why?

The scene was unforgettably vivid. Leonard Phelps and Katherine in a green park beyond the city. George himself appearing on a path only in time to see the kissing of their mouths.

The rage. The struggle. The attempt to kill Leonard Phelps.

More days, more nightmares.

George Hill awoke, weeping.

"Mr. Hill, we're ready for you now."

Hill arose clumsily. He saw himself in the high and now-silent mirrors, and he looked every one of his years. It had been a wretched error. Better men than he had taken young wives only to have them dissolve away in their hands like sugar crystals under water. He eyed himself, monstrously. A little too much stomach. A little too much chin. Somewhat too much pepper in the hair and not enough in the limbs . . .

The dark man led him to a room.

George Hill gasped. "This is *Katie's* room!"

"We try to have everything perfect."

"It *is,* to the last detail!"

George Hill drew forth a signed check for ten thousand dollars. The man departed with it.

The room was silent and warm.

George sat and felt for the gun in his pocket. A lot of money. But rich men can afford the luxury of cathartic murder. The violent unviolence. The death without death. The murder without murdering. He felt better. He was suddenly calm. He watched the door. This was a thing he had anticipated for six months and now it was to be ended. In a moment the beautiful robot, the stringless marionette, would appear, and . . .

"Hello, George."

"Katie!"

He whirled.

"Katie." He let his breath out.

She stood in the doorway behind him. She was dressed in a feather-soft green gown. On her feet were woven gold-twine sandals. Her hair was bright about her throat and her eyes were blue and clear.

He did not speak for a long while. "You're beautiful," he said at last, shocked.

"How else could I be?"

His voice was slow and unreal. "Let me look at you."

He put out his vague hands like a sleepwalker. His heart pounded sluggishly. He moved forward as if walking under a deep pressure of water. He walked around and around her, touching her.

"Haven't you seen enough of me in all these years?"

"Never enough," he said, and his eyes were filled with tears.

"What did you want to talk to me about?"

"Give me time, please, a little time." He sat down weakly and put his trembling hands to his chest. He blinked. "It's incredible. Another nightmare. How did they *make* you?"

"We're not allowed to talk of that; it spoils the illusion."

"It's magic!"

"Science."

Her touch was warm. Her fingernails were perfect as seashells. There was no seam, no flaw. He looked upon her. He remembered again the words they had read so often in the good days. *Thou art fair, my love. Behold, thou art fair; thou hast doves' eyes within thy locks. Thy lips are like a thread of scarlet. And thy speech is comely. Thy two breasts are like two young roes that are twins, which feed among the lilies. There is no spot in thee.*

"George?"

"What?" His eyes were cold glass.

He wanted to kiss her lips.

Honey and milk are under thy tongue.

And the smell of thy garments is like the smell of Lebanon.

"George."

A vast humming. The room began to whirl.

"Yes, yes, a moment, a moment." He shook his humming head.

How beautiful are thy feet with shoes, O prince's daughter! The joints of thy thighs are like jewels, the work of the hands of a cunning workman. . . .

"How did they do it?" he cried. In so short a time. Nine hours, while he slept. Had they melted gold, fixed delicate watch springs, diamonds, glitter. confetti, rich rubies liquid silver, copper thread? Had metal insects spun her hair? Had they poured yellow fire in molds and set it to freeze?

"No," she said. "If you talk that way, I'll go."

"Don't!"

"Come to business, then," she said, coldly. "You want to talk to me about Leonard."

"Give me time, I'll get to it."

"Now," she insisted.

He knew no anger. It had washed out of him at her appearance. He felt childishly dirty.

"Why did you come to see me?" She was not smiling.

"Please."

"I insist. Wasn't it about Leonard? You know I love him, don't you?"

"Stop it!" He put his hands to his ears.

She kept at him. "You know, I spend all of my time with him now. Where you and I used to go, now Leonard and I stay. Remember the picnic green on Mount Verde? We were there last week. We flew to Athens a month ago, with a case of champagne."

He licked his lips. "You're not guilty, you're *not*." He rose and held her wrists. "You're fresh, you're not her. She's guilty, not you. You're different!"

"On the contrary," said the woman. "I *am* her. I can act only as she acts. No part of me is alien to her. For all intents and purposes we are one."

"But you did not do what she has done!"

"I did all those things. I kissed him."

"You can't have, you're just born!"

"Out of her past and from your mind."

"Look," he pleaded, shaking her to gain her attention. "Isn't there some way, can't I—pay more money? Take you away with me? We'll go to Paris or Stockholm or any place you like!"

She laughed. "The marionettes only rent. They never sell."

"But I've money!"

"It was tried, long ago. It leads to insanity. It's not possible. Even this much is illegal, you *know* that. We exist only through governmental sufferance.''

"All I want is to live with you, Katie.''

"That can never be, because I am Katie, every bit of me is her. We do not want competition. Marionettes can't leave the premises; dissection might reveal our secrets. Enough of this. I warned you, we mustn't speak of these things. You'll spoil the illusion. You'll feel frustrated when you leave. You paid your money, now do what you came to do.''

"I don't want to kill you.''

"One part of you does. You're walling it in, you're trying not to let it out.''

He took the gun from his pocket. "I'm an old fool, I should never have come. You're so beautiful.''

"I'm going to see Leonard tonight.''

"Don't talk.''

"We're flying to Paris in the morning.''

"You heard what I said!''

"And then to Stockholm.'' She laughed sweetly and caressed his chin. "My little fat man.''

Something began to stir in him. His face grew pale. He knew what was happening. The hidden anger and revulsion and hatred in him were sending out faint pulses of thought. And the delicate telepathic web in her wondrous head was receiving the death impulse. The marionette. The invisible strings. He himself manipulating her body.

"Plump, odd little man, who once was so fair.''

"Don't,'' he said.

"Old while I am only thirty-one, ah, George, you were blind, working years to give me time to fall in love again. Don't you think Leonard is lovely?''

He raised the gun blindly.

"Katie.''

"*His head is as the most fine gold*—'' she whispered.

"Katie, don't!'' he screamed.

"*His locks are bushy and black as a raven, his hands are as gold rings set with the beryl!*''

How could she speak those words! It was in *his* mind, how could *she* mouth it!

"Katie, don't make me do this!''

"*His cheeks are as a bed of spices,*'' she murmured, eyes closed, moving about the room softly. "*His belly is as bright ivory overlaid with sapphires; his legs are as pillars of marble*—''

"Katie!'' he shrieked.

"*His mouth is most sweet*—''

One shot.

"—*this is my beloved*—"

Another shot.

She fell.

"Katie, Katie, Katie!"

Four more times he pumped bullets into her body.

She lay shuddering. Her senseless mouth clicked wide and some insanely warped mechanism had caused her to repeat again and again, "Beloved, beloved, beloved, beloved, beloved . . ."

George Hill fainted.

He awakened to a cool cloth on his brow.

"It's all over," said the dark man.

"Over?" George Hill whispered.

The dark man nodded.

George Hill looked weakly down at his hands. They had been covered with blood. When he fainted he had dropped to the floor. The last thing he remembered was the feeling of the real blood pouring upon his hands in a freshet.

His hands were now clean washed.

"I've got to leave," said George Hill.

"If you feel capable."

"I'm all right." He got up. "I'll go to Paris now, start over. I'm not to try to phone Katie or anything, am I."

"Katie is dead."

"Yes. I killed her, didn't I? God, the blood, it was *real!*"

"We are proud of that touch."

He went down in the elevator to the street. It was raining, and he wanted to walk for hours. The anger and destruction were purged away. The memory was so terrible that he would never wish to kill again. Even if the real Katie were to appear before him now, he would only thank God, and fall senselessly to his knees. She was dead now. He had had his way. He had broken the law and no one would know.

The rain fell cool on his face. He must leave immediately, while the purge was in effect. After all, what was the use of such purges if one took up the old threads? The marionettes' function was primarily to prevent actual crime. If you wanted to kill, hit, or torture someone, you took it out on one of those unstringed automatons. It wouldn't do to return to the apartment now. Katie might be there. He wanted only to think of her as dead, a thing attended to in deserving fashion.

He stopped at the curb and watched the traffic flash by. He took deep breaths of the good air and began to relax.

"Mr. Hill?" said a voice at his elbow.

"Yes?"

A manacle was snapped to Hill's wrist. "You're under arrest."

"But—"

"Come along. Smith, take the other men upstairs, make the arrests!"

"You can't do this to me," said George Hill.

"For murder, yes, we can."

Thunder sounded in the sky.

It was eight-fifteen at night. It had been raining for ten days. It rained now on the prison walls. He put his hands out to feel the drops gather in pools on his trembling palms.

A door clanged and he did not move but stood with his hands in the rain. His lawyer looked up at him on his chair and said, "It's all over. You'll be executed tonight."

George Hill listened to the rain.

"She wasn't real. I didn't kill her."

"It's the law, anyhow. You remember. The others are sentenced, too. The president of Marionettes, Incorporated, will die at midnight. His three assistants will die at one. You'll go about one-thirty."

"Thanks," said George. "You did all you could. I guess it was murder, no matter how you look at it, image or not. The idea was there, the plot and the plan were there. It lacked only the real Katie herself."

"It's a matter of timing, too," said the lawyer. "Ten years ago you wouldn't have got the death penalty. Ten years from now you wouldn't, either. But they had to have an object case, a whipping boy. The use of marionettes has grown so in the last year it's fantastic. The public must be scared out of it, and scared badly. God knows where it would all wind up if it went on. There's the spiritual side of it, too, where does life begin or end? are the robots alive or dead? More than one church has been split up the seams on the question. If they aren't alive, they're the next thing to it; they react, they even think. You know the 'live robot' law that was passed two months ago; you come under that. Just bad timing, is all, bad timing."

"The government's right. I see that now," said George Hill.

"I'm glad you understand the attitude of the law."

"Yes. After all, they can't let murder be legal. Even if it's done with machines and telepathy and wax. They'd be hypocrites to let me get away with my crime. For it *was* a crime. I've felt guilty about it ever since. I've felt the need of punishment. Isn't that odd? That's how society gets to you. It makes you feel guilty even when you see no reason to be. . . ."

"I have to go now. Is there anything you want?"

"Nothing, thanks."

"Good-bye then, Mr. Hill."

The door shut.

George Hill stood up on the chair, his hands twisting together, wet, outside the window bars. A red light burned in the wall suddenly. A voice came over the audio: "Mr. Hill, your wife is here to see you."

He gripped the bars.

She's dead, he thought.

"Mr. Hill?" asked the voice.

"She's dead. I killed her."

"Your wife is waiting in the anteroom, will you see her?"

"I saw her fall, I shot her, I saw her fall dead!"

"Mr. Hill, do you hear me?"

"Yes!" he shouted, pounding at the wall with his fists. "I hear you. I hear you! She's dead, she's dead, can't she let me be! I killed her, I won't see her, she's dead!"

A pause. "Very well, Mr. Hill," murmured the voice.

The red light winked off.

Lightning flashed through the sky and lit his face. He pressed his hot cheeks to the cold bars and waited, while the rain fell. After a long time, a door opened somewhere onto the street and he saw two caped figures emerge from the prison office below. They paused under an arc light and glanced up.

It was Katie. And beside her, Leonard Phelps.

"Katie!"

Her face turned away. The man took her arm. They hurried across the avenue in the black rain and got into a low car.

"Katie!" He wrenched at the bars. He screamed and beat and pulled at the concrete ledge. "She's alive! Guard! Guard! I saw her! She's not dead, I didn't kill her, now you can let me out! I didn't murder anyone, it's all a joke, a mistake, I saw her, I saw her! Katie, come back, tell them, Katie, say you're alive! Katie!"

The guards came running.

"You can't kill me! I didn't do anything! Katie's alive, I saw her!"

"We saw her, too, sir."

"But let me free, then! Let me free!" It was insane. He choked and almost fell.

"We've been through all that, sir, at the trial."

"It's not fair!" He leaped up and clawed at the window, bellowing.

The car drove away, Katie and Leonard inside it. Drove away to Paris and Athens and Venice and London next spring and Stockholm next summer and Vienna in the fall.

"Katie, come back, you can't *do* this to me!"

The red taillight of the car dwindled in the cold rain. Behind him, the guards moved forward to take hold of him while he screamed.

Sunday in Dublin.

The words are Doom itself.

Sunday in Dublin.

Drop such words from a cliff and they never strike bottom. They just fall through emptiness toward five in the gray afternoon.

Sunday in Dublin. How to get through it somehow.

Sound the funeral bells. Yank the covers up over your ears. Hear the hiss of the black feathered wreath as it rustles, hung on your silent door. Listen to those empty streets below your hotel room waiting to gulp you if you venture forth before noon. Feel the mist sliding its wet flannel tongue under the window ledges, licking hotel roofs, its great bulk dripping of ennui.

Sunday, I thought. Dublin. The pubs shut tight save for a fleeting hour. The cinemas sold out two or three weeks in advance. Nothing to do but perhaps go stare at the uriny lions at the Phoenix Park Zoo, at the vultures looking like they'd fallen, covered with glue, into the rag-pickers' bin. Wander by the River Liffey, see the fog-colored waters. Wander in the alleys, see the Liffey-colored skies.

No, I thought wildly, stay in bed, wake me at sunset, feed me high tea, tuck me in again, good night, all!

But I staggered up, a hero, under the crashing blow of Sunday, shaved, and in a faint panic at noon considered the day ahead from the corner of my eye. There it lay, a deserted corridor of hours, colored like the upper side of my tongue on a dim morn. Even God must be bored with days like this, in northern lands. I could not resist thinking of Sicily, where any Sunday is a fete in regalia, a celebratory fireworks parade as springtime flocks of chickens and humans strut and pringle the warm pancake-batter alleys, waving their combs, their hands, their feet, tilting their sun-blazed eyes, while music in free gifts leaps or is thrown from each never-shut window.

But Dublin! Dublin! Ah, you great dead brute of a city! I thought, peering from my window at the snowed-on, sooted-over corpse. Here are two coins for your eyes!

Then I opened the door and stepped out into all of that criminal Sunday which awaited only me.

I shut another door. I stood in the deep silence of a Sabbath pub. I moved noiselessly to whisper for the best drink and stood a long while nursing my soul. Nearby, an old man was similarly engaged in finding the pattern of his life in the depths of his glass. Ten minutes must have passed, when, very slowly, the old man raised his head to stare deep beyond the fly specks on the mirror, beyond me, beyond himself.

"What have I done," he mourned, "for a single mortal soul this day? Nothing! And that's why I feel so terrible destroyed."

I waited.

"The older I get," said the man, "the less I do for people. The less I do, the more I feel a prisoner at the bar. Smash and grab, that's me!"

"Well—" said I.

"No!" cried the old man. "It's an awesome responsibility when the world runs to hand you things. For an instance: sunsets. Everything pink and gold, looking like those melons they ship up from Spain. That's a gift, ain't it?"

"It is."

"Well, who do you thank for sunsets? And don't drag the Lord in the bar, now! Any remarks to Him are too quiet. I mean someone to grab and slap their back and say thanks for the fine early light this morn, boyo, or, much obliged for the look of them damn wee flowers by the road this day, and the grass laying about in the wind. Those are gifts, too, who'll deny it?"

"Not me," I said.

"Have you ever waked middle of the night and felt summer coming on for the first time, through the window, after the long cold? Did you shake your wife and tell her your gratitude? No, you lay there, a clod, chortling to yourself alone, you and the new weather! Do you see the pattern I'm at, now?"

"Clearly," I said.

"Then ain't you horribly guilty, yourself? Don't the burden make you hunchback? All the lovely things you got from life and no penny down? Ain't they hid in your dark flesh somewhere, lighting up your soul, them fine summers and easy falls, or maybe just the clean taste of stout here, all gifts, and you feeling the fool to go thank any mortal man for your fortune. What befalls chaps like us, I ask, who coin up all their gratitude for a lifetime, and spend none of it, misers that we be? One day, don't

we crack down the beam and show the dry rot? Some night, don't
we smother?''

"I never thought . . .''

"Think, man!'' he cried. "Before it's too late. You're American, ain't
you, and young? Got the same natural gifts as me? But for lack of
humbly thanking someone somewhere somehow you're getting round
in the shoulder and short in the breath. Act, man, before you're the
walking dead!''

With this he lapsed quietly into the final half of his reverie, with the
Guinness lapping a soft lace mustache slowly along his upper lip.

I walked from the pub into the Sunday weather.

I stood looking at the gray stone streets and the gray stone clouds,
watching the frozen people trudge by exhaling gray funeral plumes from
their wintry mouths, dressed in their smoke-colored suits and soot-black
coats, and I felt the white grow out in my hair.

Days like this, I thought, all the things you never did catch up with
you, unravel your laces, itch your beard. God help any man who hasn't
paid his debts this day.

Drearily, I turned like a weathercock in a slow wind, started my remote
feet back toward the hotel.

Right then, it happened.

I stopped. I stood very still. I listened.

For it seemed the wind had shifted and now blew from the west
country and brought with it a prickling and tingling: the strum of a harp.

"Well,'' I whispered.

As if a cork had been pulled, all the heavy gray sea waters vanished
roaring down a hole in my shoe; I felt my sadness go.

And around the corner I went.

And there sat a little woman, not half so big as her harp, her hands
held out in the shivering strings like a child feeling a fine clear rain.

The harp threads flurried; the sounds dissolved like shudders of disturbed water nudging a shore. "Danny Boy'' leaped out of the harp.
"Wearin' of the Green'' sprang after, full-clothed. Then "Limerick Is
My Town, Sean Liam Is My Name'' and "The Loudest Wake That Ever
Was.'' The harp sound was the kind of thing you feel when champagne,
poured in a full big glass, prickles your eyelids, sprays soft on your
cheeks.

My mouth was pinned high at both corners. Spanish oranges bloomed
in my cheeks. My breath fifed my nostrils. My feet minced, hidden, a
secret dancing in my motionless shoes.

The harp played "Yankee Doodle.''

Had the lady seen me stand near with my idiot fever? No, I
thought, coincidence.

And then I turned sad again.

For look, I thought, she doesn't see her harp. She doesn't hear her music!

True. Her hands, all alone, jumped and frolicked on the air, picked and pringled the strings, two ancient spiders busy at webs quickly built, then, torn by wind, rebuilt. She let her fingers play abandoned, to themselves, while her face turned this way and that, as if she lived in a nearby house and need only glance out on occasion to see her hands had come to no harm.

"Ah . . ." My soul sighed in me.

Then:

Here's your chance! I almost shouted. Good God, of course!

But I held to myself and let her reap out the last full falling sheaves of "Yankee Doodle."

Then, heartbeat in throat, I said:

"You play beautifully."

One hundred pounds melted from my body.

The woman nodded and began "Summer on the Shore," her fingers weaving mantillas from mere breath.

"You play very beautifully indeed," I said.

Another seventy pounds fell from my limbs.

"When you play forty years," she said, "you don't notice."

"You play well enough to be in a theater."

"Be off with you!" Two sparrows pecked in the shuttling loom. "Why should I think of orchestras and bands?"

"It's indoors work," I said.

"My father," she said, while her hands went away and returned, "made this harp, played it fine, taught me how. God's sake, he said, keep out from under roofs!"

The old woman blinked, remembering. "Play out back, in front, around the sides of theaters, Da said, but don't play in where the music gets snuffed. Might as well harp in a coffin!"

"Doesn't this rain hurt your instrument?"

"It's inside places hurt harps with heat and steam, Da said. Keep it out, let it breathe, take on fine tones and timbres from the air. Besides, Da said, when people buy tickets, each thinks it's in him to yell if you don't play up, down, sideways, for him alone. Shy off from that, Da said; they'll call you handsome one year, brute the next. Get where they'll pass on by; if they like your song—hurrah! Those that don't will run from your life. That way, girl, you'll meet just those who lean from natural bent in your direction. Why closet yourself with demon fiends when you can live in the streets' fresh wind with abiding angels? But I *do* go on. Ah, now, why?"

She peered at me for the first time, like someone come from a dark room, squinting.

"Who are you?" she asked. "You set my tongue loose! What're you up to?"

"Up to no good until a minute ago when I came around this corner," I said. "Ready to knock over Nelson's pillar. Ready to pick a theater queue and brawl along it, half weeping and half blasphemous . . ."

"I don't see you doing it." Her hands wove out another yard of song. "What changed your mind?"

"You," I said.

I might have fired a cannon in her face.

"Me?" she said.

"You picked the day up off the stones, gave it a whack, set it running with a yell again."

"*I* did that?"

For the first time, I heard a few notes missing from the tune.

"Or, if you like, those hands of yours that go about their work without your knowing."

"The clothes must be washed, so you wash them."

I felt the iron weights gather in my limbs.

"Don't!" I said. "Why should we, coming by, be happy with this thing, and not you?"

She cocked her head; her hands moved slower still.

"And why should you bother with the likes of *me?*"

I stood before her, and could I tell what the man told me in the lulling quiet of Dooley's Pub? Could I mention the hill of beauty that had risen to fill my soul through a lifetime, and myself with a toy sand-shovel doling it back to the world in dribs and drabs? Should I list all my debts to people on stages and silver screens who made me laugh or cry or just come alive, but no one in the dark theater to turn to and dare shout, "If you ever need help, I'm your friend!" Should I recall for her the man on a bus ten years before who chuckled so easy and light from the last seat that the sound of him melted everyone else to laughing warm and rollicking off out the doors, but with no one brave enough to pause and touch the man's arm and say, "Oh, man, you've favored us this night; Lord bless you!" Could I tell how she was just one part of a great account long owed and due? No, none of this could I tell. So I put it this way:

"Imagine something."

"I'm ready," she said.

"Imagine you're an American article writer, looking for material, far from home, wife, children, friends, in a hard winter, in a cheerless hotel, on a bad gray day with naught but broken glass, chewed tobacco, and sooty snow in your soul. Imagine you're walking in the damned winter streets and turn a corner, and there's this little woman with a golden harp and everything she plays is another season, autumn, spring, summer, coming, going in a free-for-all. And the ice melts, the fog lifts, the wind burns with June, and ten years shuck off your life. Imagine, if you please.''

She stopped her tune.

She was shocked at the sudden silence.

"You *are* daft," she said.

"Imagine you're me," I said. "Going back to my hotel now. And on my way I'd like to hear anything, anything at all. Play. And when you play, walk off around the corner and listen."

She put her hands to the strings and paused, working her mouth. I waited. At last she sighed, she moaned. Then suddenly she cried:

"Go on!"

"What . . . ?"

"You've made me all thumbs! Look! You've spoilt it!"

"I just wanted to thank—"

"—me behind!" she cried. "What a clod, what a brute! Mind your business! Do your work! Let be, man! Ah, these poor fingers, ruint, ruint!''

She stared at them and at me with a terrible glaring fixity.

"Get!" she shouted.

I ran around the corner in despair.

There! I thought, you've done it! really done it! By thanks destroyed, that's her story. And yours, too, you must live with it! Fool, why didn't you keep your mouth shut?

I sank, I leaned, against a building. A minute must have ticked by.

Please, woman, I thought, come on. Play. Not for me. Play for yourself. Forget what I said! *Please.*

I heard a few faint, tentative harp whispers.

Another pause.

Then, when the wind blew again, it brought the sound of her very slow playing.

The song was an old one, and I knew the words. I said them to myself.

Tread lightly to the music,
Nor bruise the tender grass,
Life passes in the weather
As the sand storms down the glass.

Yes, I thought, go on.

Drift easy in the shadows,
Bask lazy in the sun,
Give thanks for thirsts and quenches,
For dines, and wines and wenches,
Give thought to life soon over,
Tread softly on the clover,
So bruise not any lover.
So exit from the living,
Salute and make thanksgiving,
Then sleep when all is done,
That sleep so dearly won.

Why, I thought, how wise the old woman is.

Tread lightly to the music.

And I'd almost squashed her with praise.

So bruise not any lover.

And she was covered with bruises from my kind thoughtlessness.

But now with a song that taught more than I could say, she was soothing herself.

I waited until she was well into the third chorus before I walked by again, tipping my hat.

But her eyes were shut and she was listening to what her hands were up to, moving in the strings like the fresh hands of a very young girl who has first known rain and washes her palms in its clear waterfalls.

She had gone through caring not at all, and then caring too much, and was now busy caring just the right way.

The corners of her mouth were pinned up, gently.

A close call, I thought. Very close.

I left them like two friends met in the street, the harp and herself.

I ran for the hotel to thank her the only way I knew how: to do my own work and do it well.

But on the way I stopped at Dooley's.

The music was still being treaded lightly and the clover was still being treaded softly, and no lover at all was being bruised as I let the pub door hush and looked all around for the man whose hand I most wanted to shake.

It was one of those nights that are so damned hot you lie flat out lost until 2:00 A.M., then sway upright, baste yourself with your own sour brine, and stagger down into the great bake-oven subway where the lost trains shriek in.

"Hell," whispered Will Morgan.

And hell it was, with a lost army of beast people wandering the night from the Bronx on out to Coney and back, hour on hour, searching for sudden inhalations of salt ocean wind that might make you gasp with Thanksgiving.

Somewhere, God, somewhere in Manhattan or beyond was a cool wind. By dawn, it *must* be found. . . .

"Damn!"

Stunned, he saw maniac tides of advertisements squirt by with toothpaste smiles, his own advertising ideas pursuing him the whole length of the hot night island.

The train groaned and stopped.

Another train stood on the opposite track.

Incredible. There in the open train window across the way sat Old Ned Amminger. Old? They were the same age, forty, but . . .

Will Morgan threw his window up.

"Ned, you son of a bitch!"

"Will, you bastard. You ride late like this often?"

"Every damn hot night since 1946!"

"Me, too! Glad to see you!"

"Liar!"

Each vanished in a shriek of steel.

God, thought Will Morgan, two men who hate each other, who work not ten feet apart grinding their teeth over the next step up the ladder, knock together in Dante's Inferno here under a melting city at 3:00 A.M. Hear our voices echo, fading:

"Liar . . . !"

Half an hour later, in Washington Square, a cool wind touched his brow. He followed it into an alley where . . .

The temperature dropped ten degrees.

"Hold on," he whispered.

The wind smelled of the Ice House when he was a boy and stole cold crystals to rub on his cheeks and stab inside his shirt with shrieks to kill the heat.

The cool wind led him down the alley to a small shop where a sign read:

MELISSA TOAD, WITCH
LAUNDRY SERVICE:
CHECK YOUR PROBLEMS HERE BY NINE A.M.
PICK THEM UP, FRESH-CLEANED, AT DUSK

There was a smaller sign:

SPELLS, PHILTRES AGAINST DREAD CLIMATES, HOT OR COLD. POTIONS TO IN-SPIRE EMPLOYERS AND ASSURE PROMOTIONS. SALVES, UNGUENTS & MUMMY-DUSTS RENDERED DOWN FROM ANCIENT CORPORATION HEADS. REMEDIES FOR NOISE. EMOLLIENTS FOR GASEOUS OR POLLUTED AIRS. LOTIONS FOR PARANOID TRUCK DRIVERS. MEDICINES TO BE TAKEN BEFORE TRYING TO SWIM OFF THE NEW YORK DOCKS.

A few bottles were strewn in the display window, labeled:

PERFECT MEMORY.
BREATH OF SWEET APRIL WIND.
SILENCE AND THE TREMOR OF FINE BIRDSONG.

He laughed and stopped.

For the wind blew cool and creaked a door. And again there was the memory of frost from the white Ice House grottoes of childhood, a world cut from winter dreams and saved on into August.

"Come in," a voice whispered.

The door glided back.

Inside, a cold funeral awaited him.

A six-foot-long block of clear dripping ice rested like a giant February remembrance upon three sawhorses.

"Yes," he murmured. In his hometown-hardware-store window, a ma-gician's wife, MISS I. SICKLE, had been stashed in an immense rectangle of ice melted to fit her calligraphy. There she slept the nights away, a

Princess of Snow. Midnights, he and other boys snuck out to see her smile in her cold crystal sleep. They stood half the summer nights staring, four or five fiery-furnace boys of some fourteen years, hoping their red-hot gaze might melt the ice. . . .

The ice had never melted.

"Wait," he whispered. "Look . . ."

He took one more step within this dark night shop.

Lord, yes. There, in *this* ice! Weren't those the outlines where, only moments ago, a woman of snow napped away in cool night dreams? Yes. The ice was hollow and curved and lovely. But . . . the woman was gone. Where?

"Here," whispered the voice.

Beyond the bright cold funeral, shadows moved in a far corner.

"Welcome. Shut the door."

He sensed that she stood not far away in shadows. Her flesh, if you could touch it, would be cool, still fresh from her time within the dripping tomb of snow. If he just reached out his hand—

"What are you doing here?" her voice asked, gently.

"Hot night. Walking. Riding. Looking for a cool wind. I think I need help."

"You've come to the right place."

"But this is *mad!* I don't believe in psychiatrists. My friends hate me because I say Tinkerbell *and* Freud died twenty years back, with the circus. I don't believe in astrologers, numerologists, or palmistry quacks—"

"I don't read palms. But . . . give me your hand."

He put his hand out into the soft darkness.

Her fingers tapped his. It felt like the hand of a small girl who had just rummaged an icebox. He said:

"Your sign reads MELISSA TOAD, WITCH. What would a Witch be doing in New York in the summer of 1974?"

"You ever know a city needed a Witch more than New York does this year?"

"Yes. We've gone mad. But, *you?*"

"A Witch is born out of the true hungers of her time," she said. "I was born out of New York. The things that are most wrong here summoned me. Now you come, not knowing, to find me. Give me your other hand."

Though her face was only a ghost of cool flesh in the shadows, he felt her eyes move over his trembling palm.

"Oh, why did you wait so *long?*" she mourned. "It's almost too late."

"Too late for what?"

"To be saved. To take the gift that I can give."

His heart pounded. "*What* can you give me?"

"Peace," she said. "Serenity. Quietness in the midst of bedlam. I am a child of the poisonous wind that copulated with the East River on an oil-slick, garbage-infested midnight. I turn about on my own parentage. I inoculate against those very biles that brought me to light. I am a serum born of venoms. I am the antibody of all Time. I am the Cure. You die of the City, do you not? Manhattan is your punisher. Let me be your shield."

"How?"

"You would be my pupil. My protection could encircle you, like an invisible pack of hounds. The subway train would never violate your ear. Smog would never blight your lung or nostril or fever your vision. I could teach your tongue, at lunch, to taste the rich fields of Eden in the merest cut-rate too-ripe frankfurter. Water, sipped from your office cooler, would be a rare wine of a fine family. Cops, when you called, would answer. Taxis, off-duty rushing nowhere, would stop if you so much as blinked one eye. Theater tickets would appear if you stepped to a theater window. Traffic signals would change, at high noon, mind you! if you dared to drive your car from fifty-eighth down to the Square, and not one light red. Green all the way, if you go with me.

"If you go with me, our apartment will be a shadowed jungle glade full of bird cries and love calls from the first hot sour day of June till the last hour after Labor Day when the living dead, heat-beat, go mad on stopped trains coming back from the sea. Our rooms will be filled with crystal chimes. Our kitchen an Eskimo hut in July where we might share out a provender of Popsicles made of Mumm's and Château Lafite Rothschild. Our larder?—fresh apricots in August or February. Fresh orange juice each morning, cold milk at breakfast, cool kisses at four in the afternoon, my mouth always the flavor of chilled peaches, my body the taste of rimed plums. The flavor begins at the elbow, as Edith Wharton said.

"Any time you want to come home from the office the middle of a dreadful day, I will call your boss and it will be so. Soon after, you will be the boss and come home, anyway, for cold chicken, fruit wine punch, and me. Summer in the Virgin Isles. Autumns so ripe with promise you will indeed go lunatic in the right way. Winters, of course, will be the reverse. I will be your hearth. Sweet dog, lie there. I will fall upon you like snowflakes.

"In sum, everything will be given you. I ask little in return. Only your soul."

He stiffened and almost let go of her hand.

"Well, isn't that what you *expected* me to demand?" She laughed.

"But souls can't be sold. They can only be lost and never found again. Shall I tell you what I really want from you?"

"Tell."

"Marry me," she said.

Sell me your soul, he thought, and did not say it.

But she read his eyes. "Oh, dear," she said. "Is that so much to ask? For all I give?"

"I've got to think it over!"

Without noticing, he had moved back one step.

Her voice was very sad. "If you have to think a thing over, it will never be. When you finish a book you know if you like it, yes? At the end of a play you are awake or asleep, yes? Well, a beautiful woman is a beautiful woman, isn't she, and a good life a good life?"

"Why won't you come out in the light? How do I know you're beautiful?"

"You can't know unless you step into the dark. Can't you tell by my voice? No? Poor man. If you don't trust me now, you can't have me, ever."

"I need time to think. I'll come back tomorrow night! What can twenty-four hours mean?"

"To someone your age, everything."

"I'm only forty!"

"I speak of your soul, and *that* is late."

"Give me one more night!"

"You'll take it, anyway, at your own risk."

"Oh, God, oh, God, oh, God, God," he said, shutting his eyes.

"I wish He could help you right now. You'd better go. You're an ancient child. Pity. Pity. Is your mother alive?"

"Dead ten years."

"No, alive," she said.

He backed off toward the door and stopped, trying to still his confused heart, trying to move his leaden tongue:

"How long have you been in this place?"

She laughed, with the faintest touch of bitterness.

"Three summers now. And, in those three years, only six men have come into my shop. Two ran immediately. Two stayed awhile but left. One came back a second time, and vanished. The sixth man finally had to admit, after three visits, he didn't Believe. You see, no one Believes a really all-encompassing and protective love when they see it clear. A farmboy might have stayed forever, in his simplicity, which is rain and wind and seed. A New Yorker? Suspects everything.

"Whoever, whatever, you are, O good sir, stay and milk the cow and put the fresh milk in the dim cooling shed under the shade of the oak tree which grows in my attic. Stay and pick the watercress to clean your

teeth. Stay in the North Pantry with the scent of persimmons and kum-
quats and grapes. Stay and stop my tongue so I can cease talking this
way. Stay and stop my mouth so I can't breathe. Stay, for I am weary
of speech and must need love. Stay. Stay.''

So ardent was her voice, so tremulous, so gentle, so sweet, that he
knew he was lost if he did not run.

"Tomorrow night!'' he cried.

His shoe struck something. There on the floor lay a sharp icicle fallen
from the long block of ice.

He bent, seized the icicle, and ran.

The door *slammed*. The lights blinked out. Rushing, he could not see
the sign: MELISSA TOAD, WITCH.

Ugly, he thought, running. A beast, he thought, she *must* be a beast
and ugly. Yes, that's it! Lies! All of it, lies! She—

He collided with someone.

In the midst of the street, they gripped, they held, they stared.

Ned Amminger! My God, it was Old Ned!

It was four in the morning, the air still white-hot. And here was Ned
Amminger sleepwalking after cool winds, his clothes scrolled on his hot
flesh in rosettes, his face dripping sweat, his eyes dead, his feet creaking
in their hot baked leather shoes.

They swayed in the moment of collision.

A spasm of malice shook Will Morgan. He seized Old Ned Amminger,
spun him about, and pointed him into the dark alley. Far off deep in
there, had that shop-window light blinked *on* again? Yes!

"Ned! *That way! Go there!*''

Heat-blinded, dead-weary Old Ned Amminger stumbled off down
the alley.

"Wait!'' cried Will Morgan, regretting his malice.

But Amminger was gone.

In the subway, Will Morgan tasted the icicle.

It was Love. It was Delight. It was Woman.

By the time his train roared in, his hands were empty, his body rusted
with perspiration. And the sweet taste in his mouth? Dust.

Seven A.M. and no sleep.

Somewhere a huge blast furnace opened its door and burned New
York to ruins.

Get up, thought Will Morgan. Quick! Run to the Village!

For he remembered that sign:

LAUNDRY SERVICE: CHECK YOUR PROBLEMS
HERE BY NINE A.M.
PICK THEM UP, FRESH-CLEANED, AT NIGHT.

He did not go to the Village. He rose, showered, and went off into the furnace to lose his job forever.

He knew this as he rode up in the raving-hot elevator with Mr. Binns, the sunburned and furious personnel manager. Binns's eyebrows were jumping, his mouth worked over his teeth with unspoken curses. Beneath his suit, you could feel porcupines of boiled hair needling to the surface. By the time they reached the fortieth floor, Binns was anthropoid.

Around them, employees wandered like an Italian army coming to attend a lost war.

"Where's Old Amminger?" asked Will Morgan, staring at an empty desk.

"Called in sick. Heat prostration. Be here at noon," someone said.

Long before noon the water cooler was empty, and the air-conditioning system?—committed suicide at 11:32. Two hundred people became raw beasts chained to desks by windows which had been invented not to open.

At one minute to twelve, Mr. Binns, over the intercom, told them to line up by their desks. They lined up. They waited, swaying. The temperature stood at ninety-seven. Slowly, Binns began to stalk down the long line. A white-hot sizzle of invisible flies hung about him.

"All right, ladies and gentlemen," he said. "You all know there is a recession, no matter how happily the President of the United States put it. I would rather knife you in the stomach than stab you in the back. Now, as I move down the line, I will nod and whisper, 'You.' To those of you who hear this single word, turn, clean out your desks, and be gone. Four weeks' severance pay awaits you on the way out. Hold on! Someone's missing!"

"Old Ned Amminger," said Will Morgan, and bit his tongue.

"*Old* Ned?" said Mr. Binns, glaring. "Old? *Old?*"

Mr. Binns and Ned Amminger were exactly the same age.

Mr. Binns waited, ticking.

"Ned," said Will Morgan, strangling on self-curses, "should be here—"

"Now," said a voice.

They all turned.

At the far end of the line, in the door, stood Old Ned or Ned Amminger. He looked at the assembly of lost souls, read destruction in Binn's face, flinched, but then slunk into line next to Will Morgan.

"All right," said Binns. "Here goes."

He began to move, whisper, move, whisper, move, whisper. Two people, four, then six turned to clean out their desks.

Will Morgan took a deep breath, held it, waited.

Binns came to a full stop in front of him.

Don't say it? thought Morgan. Don't!

"You," whispered Binns.

Morgan spun about and caught hold of his heaving desk. *You,* the word cracked in his head, *you!*

Binns stepped to confront Ned Amminger.

"Well, *old* Ned," he said.

Morgan, eyes shut, thought: Say it, say it to him, you're fired, Ned, *fired!*

"Old Ned," said Binns, lovingly.

Morgan shrank at the strange, the friendly, the sweet sound of Binns's voice.

An idle South Seas wind passed softly on the air. Morgan blinked and stood-up, sniffing. The sun-blasted room was filled with scent of surf and cool white sand.

"Ned, why dear old Ned," said Mr. Binns, gently.

Stunned, Will Morgan waited. I am mad, he thought.

"Ned," said Mr. Binns, gently. "Stay with us. Stay on."

Then, swiftly: "That's all, everyone. Lunch!"

And Binns was gone and the wounded and dying were leaving the field. And Will Morgan turned at last to look full at Old Ned Amminger, thinking, Why, God, *why?*

And got his answer . . .

Ned Amminger stood there, not old, not young, but somehow in-between. And he was not the Ned Amminger who had leaned crazily out a hot train window last midnight or shambled in Washington Square at four in the morning.

This Ned Amminger stood quietly, as if hearing far green country sounds, wind and leaves and an amiable time which wandered in a fresh lake breeze.

The perspiration had dried on his fresh pink face. His eyes were not bloodshot but steady, blue, and quiet. He was an island oasis in this dead and unmoving sea of desks and typewriters which might start up and scream like electric insects. He stood watching the walking-dead depart. And he cared not. He was kept in a splendid and beautiful isolation within his own calm cool beautiful skin.

"No!" cried Will Morgan, and fled.

He didn't know where he was going until he found himself in the men's room frantically digging in the wastebasket.

He found what he knew he would find, a small bottle with the label:

DRINK ENTIRE: AGAINST THE MADNESS OF CROWDS

Trembling, he uncorked it. There was the merest cold blue drop left inside. Swaying by the shut hot window, he tapped it to his tongue.

In the instant, his body felt as if he had leaped into a tidal wave of coolness. His breath gusted out in a fount of crushed and savored clover.

He gripped the bottle so hard it broke. He gasped, watching the blood.

The door opened. Ned Amminger stood there, looking in. He stayed only a moment, then turned and went out. The door shut.

A few moments later, Morgan, with the junk from his desk rattling in his briefcase, went down in the elevator.

Stepping out, he turned to thank the operator.

His breath must have touched the operator's face.

The operator smiled.

A wild, an incomprehensible, a loving, a *beautiful* smile!

The lights were out at midnight in the little alley, in the little shop. There was no sign in the window which said MELISSA TOAD, WITCH. There were no bottles.

He beat on the door for a full five minutes, to no answer. He kicked the door for another two minutes.

And at last, with a sigh, not wanting to, the door opened.

A very tired voice said: "Come in."

Inside he found the air only slightly cool. The huge ice slab, in which he had seen the phantom shape of a lovely woman, had dwindled, had lost a good half of its weight, and now was dripping steadily to ruin.

Somewhere in the darkness, the woman waited for him. But he sensed that she was clothed now, dressed and packed, ready to leave. He opened his mouth to cry out, to reach, but her voice stopped him:

"I warned you. You're too late."

"It's never too late!" he said.

"Last night it wouldn't have been. But in the last twenty hours, the last little thread snapped in you. I feel. I know. I tell. It's gone, gone, gone."

"What's gone, God damn it?"

"Why, your soul, of course. Gone. Eaten up. Digested. Vanished. You're empty. Nothing there."

He saw her hand reach out of darkness. It touched at his chest. Perhaps he imagined that her fingers passed through his ribs to probe about his lights, his lungs, his beating and pitiful heart.

"Oh, yes, gone," she mourned. "How sad. The city unwrapped you like a candy bar and ate you all up. You're nothing but a dusty milk bottle left on a tenement porch, a spider building a nest across the top. Traffic din pounded your marrow to dust. Subway sucked your breath like a cat sucks the soul of a babe. Vacuum cleaners got your brain. Alcohol dissolved the rest. Typewriters and computers took your final dregs in and out their tripes, printed you on paper, punched you in confettis, threw you down a sewer vent. TV scribbled you in nervous tics on old ghost screens. Your final bones will be carried off by a big angry bulldog crosstown bus holding you munched in its big rubber-lipped mouth door.''

"No!'' he cried. "I've changed my mind! Marry me! Marry—''

His voice cracked the ice tomb. It shattered on the floor behind him. The shape of the beautiful woman melted into the floor. Spinning about, he plunged into darkness.

He fell against the wall just as a panel slammed shut and locked.

It was no use screaming. He was alone.

At dusk in July, a year later, in the subway, he saw Ned Amminger for the first time in 365 days.

In all the grind and ricochet and pour of fiery lava as trains banged through, taking a billion souls to hell, Amminger stood as cool as mint leaves in green rain. Around him wax people melted. He waded in his own private trout stream.

"Ned!'' cried Will Morgan, running up to seize his hand and pump it. "Ned, Ned! The best friend I ever had!''

"Yes, that's true, isn't it?'' said young Ned, smiling.

And oh God, how true it was! Dear Ned, fine Ned, friend of a lifetime! Breathe upon me, Ned! Give me your life's breath!

"You're president of the company, Ned! I heard!''

"Yes. Come along home for a drink?''

In the raging heat, a vapor of iced lemonade rose from his creamy fresh suit as they looked for a cab. In all the curses, yells, horns, Ned raised his hand.

A cab pulled up. They drove in serenity.

At the apartment house, in the dusk, a man with a gun stepped from the shadows.

"Give me everything,'' he said.

"Later,'' said Ned, smiling, breathing a scent of fresh summer apples upon the man.

"Later.'' The man stepped back to let them pass. "Later.''

On the way up in the elevator, Ned said, "Did you know I'm married? Almost a year. Fine wife.''

"Is she,'' said Will Morgan, and stopped, ". . . beautiful?''

"Oh, yes. You'll love her. You'll love the apartment.''

Yes, thought Morgan; a green glade, crystal chimes, cool grass for a carpet. I know, I know.

They stepped out into an apartment that was indeed a tropic isle. Young Ned poured huge goblets of iced champagne.

"What shall we drink to?''

"To you, Ned. To your wife. To me. To midnight, tonight.''

"Why midnight?"

"When I go back down to that man who is waiting downstairs with his gun. That man you said 'later' to. And he agreed 'later.' I'll be there alone with him. Funny, ridiculous, funny. And *my* breath just ordinary breath, not smelling of melons or pears. And him waiting all those long hours with his sweaty gun, irritable with heat. What a grand joke. Well . . . a toast?"

"A toast!"

They drank.

At which moment, the wife entered. She heard each of them laughing in a different way, and joined in their laughter.

But her eyes, when she looked at Will Morgan, suddenly filled with tears.

And he knew whom she was weeping for.

CANTATA CELEBRATING THE
EIGHTH DAY OF CREATION
AND THE PROMISE OF THE NINTH.

A Voice spoke in the dark,
And there was Light.
And summoned up by Light upon the Earth
The creatures swam
And moved unto the land
And lived in garden wilderness;
All this, we know.
The Seven Days are written in our blood
With hand of Fire.
And now we children of the seven eternal days
Inheritors of this, the Eighth Day of God,
The long Eighth Day of Man,
Stand upright in a weather of Time
In downfell snow
And hear the birds of morning
And much want wings
And look upon the beckonings of stars,
And need their fire.
In this time of Christmas,
We celebrate the Eighth Day of Man,
The Eighth Day of God,

Two billion years unending
From the first sunrise on Earth
To the last sunrise at our Going Away.
And the Ninth Day of the History of God
And the flesh of God which names itself Man
Will be spent on wings of fire
Claimed from sun and far burnings of sun starlight.
And the Ninth Day's sunrise
Will show us forth in light and wild surmise
Upon an even further shore.

We seek new Gardens there to know ourselves.
We seek new Wilderness,
And send us forth in wandering search.
Apollo's missions move, and Christus seek,

And wonder as we look among the stars
Did He know these?

In some far universal Deep
Did He tread Space
And visit worlds beyond our blood-warm dreaming?
Did He come down on lonely shore by sea
Not unlike Galilee
And are there Mangers on far worlds that knew His light?
And Virgins?
Sweet Pronouncements?
Annunciations? Visitations from angelic hosts?
And, shivering vast light among ten billion lights,
Was there some Star much like the star at Bethlehem
That struck the sight with awe and revelation
Upon a cold and most strange morn?

On worlds gone wandering and lost from this
Did Wise Men gather in the dawn
In cloudy steams of Beast
Within a place of straw now quickened to a Shrine
To look upon a stranger Child than ours?

How many stars of Bethlehem burnt bright
Beyond Orion or Centauri's blinding arc?
How many miracles of birth all innocent
Have blessed those worlds?

Does Herod tremble there
In dread facsimile of our dark and murderous King?
Does that mad keeper of an unimaginable realm
Send stranger soldiers forth
To slaughter down the Innocents
Of lands beyond the Horsehead Nebula?

It must be so.
For in this time of Christmas
In the long Day totalling up to Eight,
We see the light, we know the dark;
And creatures lifted, born, thrust free of so much night
No matter what the world or time or circumstance
Must love the light,
So, children of all lost unnumbered suns
Must fear the dark
Which mingles in a shadowing-forth on air.
And swarms the blood.
No matter what the color, shape, or size
Of beings who keep souls like breathing coals
In long midnights,
They *must* need saving of themselves.

So on far worlds in snowfalls deep and clear
Imagine how the rounding out of some dark year
Might celebrate with birthing one miraculous child!

A child?
Born in Andromeda's out-swept mysteries?
Then count its hands, its fingers,
Eyes, and most incredible holy limbs!
The sum of each?
No matter. Cease.
Let Child be fire as blue as water under Moon.
Let Child sport free in tides with human-seeming fish.
Let ink of octopi inhabit blood
Let skin take acid rains of chemistry
All falling down in nightmare storms of cleansing burn.

Christ wanders in the Universe
A flesh of stars,
He takes on creature shapes
To suit the mildest elements,

He dresses him in flesh beyond our ken.
There He walks, glides, flies, shambling of strangeness.
Here He walks Men.

Among the ten trillion beams
A billion Bible scrolls are scored
In hieroglyphs among God's amplitudes of worlds;
In alphabet multitudinous
Tongues which are not quite tongues
Sigh, sibilate, wonder, cry:
As Christ comes manifest from a thunder-crimsoned sky.

He walks upon the molecules of seas
All boiling stews of beast
All maddened broth and brew and rising up of yeast.
There Christ by many names is known.
We call him thus.
They call him otherwise.
His name on any mouth would be a sweet surprise.
He comes with gifts for all,
Here: wine and bread.
There: nameless foods
At breakfasts where the morsels fall from stars
And Last Suppers are doled forth with stuff of dreams.
So sit they there in times before the Man is crucified.
Here He has long been dead.
There He has not yet died.

Yet, still unsure, and all being doubt,
Much frightened man on Earth does cast about
And clothe himself in steel
And borrow fire
And himself in the great glass of the careless Void admire.
Man builds him rockets
And on thunder strides
In humble goings-forth
And most understandable prides.
Fearing that all else slumbers,
That ten billion worlds lie still,
We, grateful for the Prize and benefit of life,
Go to offer bread and harvest wine;
The blood and flesh of Him we Will
To other stars and worlds about those stars.

We cargo holy flesh
On stranger visitations,
Send forth angelic hosts,
To farflung worlds
To tell our walking on the waters of deep Space,
Arrivals, swift departures
Of most miraculous man
Who, God fuse-locked in every cell
Beats holy blood
And treads the tidal flood
And ocean shore of Universe,

A miracle of fish
We father, gather, build and strew
In metals to the winds
That circle Earth and wander Night beyond all Nights.
We soar, all arch-angelic, fire-sustained
In vast cathedral, acry apse, in domeless vault
Of constellations all blind dazzlement.

Christ is not dead
Nor does God sleep
While waking Man
Goes striding on the Deep

To birth ourselves anew
And love rebirth
From fear of straying long
On outworn Earth.
One harvest in, we broadcast seed for further reaping.
Thus ending Death
And Night,
And Time's demise,
And senseless weeping.

We seek for mangers in the Pleides
Where man the god-fleshed wandering babe
May lay him down with such as these
Who once drew round and worshipped innocence.

New Mangers lie waiting!
New Wise men Descry

Our hosts of machineries
Which write immortal life
And sign it God!
Down, down Alien skies.

And flown and gone, arrived and bedded safe to sleep
Upon some winters morning deep
Ten billion years of light
From where we stand us now and sing,
There will be time to cry eternal gratitudes
Time to know and see and love the Gift of Life itself,
Always diminished,
Always restored,
Out of one hand and into the other
Of the Lord.
Then wake we in that far lost
Nightmare keep of Beast
And see our star recelebrated in an East
Beyond all Easts.
Beyond a snowdrift sifting down of stars.
In this time of Christmas
Think on that Morn ahead!
For this let all your fears, your cries,
Your tears, your blood and prayers be shed!
All numb and wild one day
You shall be reborn
And hear the Trump break forth from rocket-trembled air
All humbled, all shorn
Of pride, but free of despair.
Now listen! Now hear!
It is the Ninth Day's morn!

Christ is risen!
God survives!
Gather, Universe!
Look, ye stars!
In the exultant countries of Space
In a sudden simple pasture
Far beyond Andromeda!
O Glory, Glory, a New Christmas
Torn
From the very pitch and rim of Death,
Snatched from his universal grip,

His teeth, his most cold breath!
Under a most strange sun
O Christ, O God,
O man breathed out of most incredible stuffs,
You are the Savior's Savior,
God's pulse and heart companion,
You! The Host *He* lifts
On high to consecrate;
His dear need to know and touch and cry wonders
At Himself.

In this time of Christmas
Prepare
In this holy time
Know yourself most rare!

Beyond the vast Abyss
See those men grown Wise
Who gather with their gifts
Which are but Life!
And Life that knows no end.
Behold the rockets, more than chaff, on air,
All seed that save a holy seed
And cast it everywhere in mindless Dark.
In this time of Christmas
This holy time of Christmas,
Like Him, you are God's son!
One Son? Many?
All are gathered now to One
And will wake cradled in Beast-summer breath
That warms the sleeping child to life eternal.

You must go there.
In the long winter of Space
And lie you down in grateful innocence
At last to sleep.
O New Christmas,
O God, far-motioning.
O Christ-of-many-fleshed made one,
Leave Earth!
God Himself cries out.
He Goes to Prepare the Way
For your rebirth

In a new time of Christmas,
A holy time of Christmas,
This New Time of Christmas,
From all *this* stay?
No, Man. You must not linger, wonder.
No, Christ. You must not pause.
Now.
Now.
It is the Time of Going Away.
Arise, and go.
Be born. Be born.
Welcome the morning of the Ninth Day.
It is the Time of Going away.
Praise God for this Annunciation!
Give praise,
Rejoice!
For the time of Christmas
And the Ninth Day,
Which is Forever's Celebration!

Tom Victor

About the Author

RAY BRADBURY, the author of more than thirty books, is the recipient of the National Book Foundation's 2000 Medal for Distinguished Contribution to American Letters. Some of his best-known works are *Fahrenheit 451, The Martian Chronicles, The Illustrated Man, Dandelion Wine,* and *Something Wicked This Way Comes.* A writer for both theater and cinema, he has adapted sixty-five of his stories for television's *The Ray Bradbury Theater.* He won an Emmy for his teleplay of *The Halloween Tree* and was nominated for an Academy Award. He lives with his wife, Marguerite, in Los Angeles.

BOOKS BY RAY BRADBURY

THE MARTIAN CHRONICLES
ISBN 0-380-97383-9 (hardcover)

FAHRENHEIT 451
ISBN 0-694-52627-4 (unabridged CD)
ISBN 0-694-52626-6
(unabridged cassette)

DANDELION WINE
ISBN 0-380-97726-5 (hardcover)

SOMETHING WICKED THIS WAY COMES
ISBN 0-380-97727-3 (hardcover)

DEATH IS A LONELY BUSINESS
ISBN 0-380-78965-5 (trade paperback)

A GRAVEYARD FOR LUNATICS
Another Tale of Two Cities
ISBN 0-380-81200-2 (trade paperback)

GREEN SHADOWS, WHITE WHALE
A Novel of Ray Bradbury's Adventures
Making Moby Dick with John Huston
in Ireland
ISBN 0-380-78966-3 (trade paperback)

FROM THE DUST RETURNED
ISBN 0-380-78961-2
(mass market paperback)
ISBN 0-694-52628-2
(unabridged cassette)

LET'S ALL KILL CONSTANCE
ISBN 0-06-056178-5
(mass market paperback)

THE ILLUSTRATED MAN
ISBN 0-380-97384-7 (hardcover)

A SOUND OF THUNDER AND OTHER STORIES
ISBN 0-06-078569-1 (trade paperback)

A MEDICINE FOR MELANCHOLY AND OTHER STORIES
ISBN 0-380-73086-3 (trade paperback)

THE OCTOBER COUNTRY
ISBN 0-380-97387-1 (hardcover)

I SING THE BODY ELECTRIC!
And Other Stories
ISBN 0-380-78962-0 (trade paperback)

QUICKER THAN THE EYE
ISBN 0-380-78959-0
(mass market paperback)

DRIVING BLIND
ISBN 0-380-78960-4
(mass market paperback)

ONE MORE FOR THE ROAD
ISBN 0-06-103203-4
(mass market paperback)
ISBN 0-06-008117-1
(unabridged cassette)

THE CAT'S PAJAMAS
Stories
ISBN 0-06-077733-8 (trade paperback)

BRADBURY STORIES
100 of His Most Celebrated Tales
ISBN 0-06-054488-0 (trade paperback)

AHMED AND THE OBLIVION MACHINES
A Fable
ISBN 0-380-97704-4 (hardcover)

BRADBURY SPEAKS
Too Soon from the Cave, Too Far
from the Stars
ISBN 0-06-058569-2 (trade paperback)

HARPER PERENNIAL